Garth Nix

THE SEVENTH TOWER™

Volumes

1–3

www.theseventhtower.com

SCHOLASTIC INC.
New York Toronto London Auckland Sydney
Mexico City New Delhi Hong Kong Buenos Aires

ISBN 0-439-48587-8

12 11 10 9 8 7 6 5 4 3 2 1   2 3 4 5 6 7/0

Printed in the U.S.A.

First bind-up edition, November 2002

The Fall   1

Castle   197

Aenir   415

THE SEVENTH TOWER™
THE FALL

To my family and friends, with a particular thank you to David Levithan, a very important architect in the building of the Seventh Tower.

·CHAPTER·
ZERO⊙

Tal stretched out his hand and pulled himself up onto the next out-thrust spike of the Tower. He stopped there to get his breath, and looked down the Red Tower, down to the twinkling lights that outlined the main buildings of the Castle. They were far below, a height that made Tal dizzy. He quickly looked back up.

The wind was much stronger than Tal had expected. It howled around the Red Tower and then spun through the other six Towers before coming back at him even stronger than before. It was also getting colder, making the climb even more difficult. Tal's Sunstone kept the worst of the chill at bay.

It had taken Tal two hours to climb to his current resting place — a hard climb, up through the spikes, gargoyles, and encrustations that covered the Tower. Now he was only four stretches below the point where the Tower appeared to suddenly end, meeting the lid of total blackness that lay across the sky.

This was the Veil, the strange barrier that kept the whole world in darkness, turning back the light of the sun.

Not that it was completely dark around Tal. Like most of the Castle, the Red Tower was lit with small Sunstones fixed into the walls and ceilings. The light from those Sunstones spilled out the windows, so Tal could see where to climb. The other six Towers blazed with light, too, brilliant shafts crisscrossing the sky.

The light made many shadows flicker outside. Every gargoyle and decorative flange cast a shadow, dark against the ocher red of the Tower. There was Tal's own shadow, too. Like all the Chosen of the Castle, Tal's shadow did not echo the shape of his body. The shadow that moved with him flowed and changed. Sometimes it had the general shape of a thirteen-year-old boy, sometimes it looked like a cat, or a two-headed Corvile, or something so fluid it was indescribable.

For Tal's shadow was not the one he had been born with. It was a shadowguard, a magical being from the spirit realm of Aenir. It had been bound to Tal when he was born, replacing his natural shadow, and was commanded to guard and help him. This was just as well, Tal thought. It was bad enough seeing his gangly limbs and scraggly hair in the mirror; he was relieved not to have a shadow of them following him around.

The shadowguard didn't show that Tal was shorter than most of the other boys his age. Or his slightly crooked smile that he thought made him look a bit slow. No one else did, but it mattered to Tal. He'd practice smiling in the mirror for hours, trying to straighten that curl on the left-hand side.

He didn't mind that the shadowguard was only one of the weakest spirits from Aenir, a child's servant. When Tal turned thirteen and three-quarters in two months' time, he would enter Aenir himself, and bind a real Spiritshadow to serve him.

If he was able to enter Aenir. Tal clutched the small Sunstone on the silver chain around his neck, feeling its warmth enter his chilled hands. To enter Aenir, he needed a Primary Sunstone. Not just for himself, but also for his mother and for his younger brother and sister.

Since his mother was very sick and his father and their family's Sunstone had disappeared mysteriously, it had suddenly become Tal's responsibility to look after the family. He wasn't prepared for this — but he didn't have a choice. He had to push his fear deep inside himself and keep it there. He had to be strong, even if he didn't know where to find that strength.

He wanted his father back. He wanted his mother well. But both would be lost to him forever if he failed now.

In order to save his family, he had to get a new Sunstone. A powerful one, not the child's stone he wore at his throat. Tal drew a deep breath and slipped the stone back under his shirt. He had to climb farther. Past the Veil. Out into the full sunlight.

He'd seen sunlight before, of course. He'd seen it many times in Aenir, the spirit world. But it was softer there, less bright. Tal had only seen the true sun once. When he was ten, his class was taken up beyond the Veil and shown the Sunstones growing in silver nets that hung from the Towers. It had been overcast, but even then all the children had needed their shadow-guards to cloak their eyes. Sunstones might capture the light of the sun, but even the most powerful could not compare to its strength and brilliance.

Back then, they'd climbed up the stairs inside the Orange Tower. Tal had never thought that one day he would be climbing the outside of one of the Towers . . . to *steal* a Sunstone.

"To steal a Sunstone," he repeated to himself. It was the last resort, the only thing he could think of that would save him and his family. He'd tried everything else.

It was also the riskiest thing he could imagine. It was a hard climb just to get where he was, but that was nothing. On the other side of the Veil, there would be guards and traps — powerful Spiritshadows that could chew up his shadowguard in a second and capture Tal. There could even be other Chosen, members of the Red Order, who would be only too pleased to catch a boy of the rival Orange Order. It would be the Hall of Nightmares for him then, or worse, and disaster for the family. . . .

Tal shook his head and started to climb again. He reached a gargoyle just below the Veil, and almost against his will crouched down to delay reaching the darkness that brooded above his head. It was almost like being underwater and looking up, thought Tal, except into darkness rather than light. Finally, he stretched his hand up into the Veil and shivered as it disappeared. But he could still feel it. It was still there.

Tal stood up. Instantly, he was caught in total darkness. He started to breathe hard, his lungs seeming to shrivel. He couldn't get enough air! The darkness was sucking the air out of him.

He ducked back into the comfortable twilight and the bright beams from the Towers, his hand clutched around his now blazing Sunstone. Tal quickly focused upon it, and the light dimmed. He didn't want to attract attention. Only a moment after his Sunstone dimmed, a faint cry echoed up from below. For a second Tal thought he'd been discovered, and he shrank back against the Tower wall. Then he realized that it hadn't been the shout of a guard, or the high-pitched, inhuman scream of a Spiritshadow. It sounded more like a cry for help.

It came again, and Tal felt his stomach go hollow and strange. He knew that voice! Quickly, he looked down. There, a good two hundred stretches below, was the flicker of a white shirt, touched with orange. It was the same sort of shirt that Tal wore, a child's uniform of white, the collar and cuffs bearing the color of his Order. Someone had followed him.

It had to be his younger brother, Gref, a nine-year-old desperado who tried to do everything his older brother did. Tal recognized the voice and the small, feeble Sunstone.

"If you touch me, Tal will blast you into bits! Get away! Get —"

Gref's voice was suddenly cut off. For an instant, Tal thought his brother had fallen, and his own heart seemed to stop.

But Gref hadn't fallen. He had been picked up by a huge Spiritshadow, one with the flickering shape of a Borzog, a creature long extinct in the flesh. It was easily four stretches tall, and enormously broad-shouldered. Its arms trailed below its knees, and the two tusks in its lower jaw were the size of Tal's hands. In the light from the Tower, it rippled in shades of darkness, a thing of soft edges and blurred lines.

It had Gref under one arm and had pulled Gref's shadowguard over his face like a gag. There was no sign of the Chosen the Spiritshadow was bound to. But whoever it served, it was taking Gref back down the Tower, probably to the balcony far below, where Tal had started his climb.

Tal hesitated. He wanted to rescue Gref, but he knew he'd just get caught as well. That wouldn't help either of them, or the family. As before, his only chance lay upward, with the Sunstones.

Tal faced the Veil once more. He'd made a mistake going into it slowly before. This time the thing to do was to reach up, get a handhold, and climb through as quickly as possible.

He took several deep breaths and stood up fast, with his hands outstretched above his head. His knuckles grazed stone, and then he felt something he could hold on to. A moment later, his head entered the Veil.

Once again, there was total darkness. But now, Tal was prepared for it. He pulled himself up onto the next gargoyle and thrust his hand up for another handhold. He found one, climbed again, and then repeated the process.

He still hadn't come out of the Veil, and his breath was going. Hesitantly, he took a small breath. It worked, but his fear of not being able to breathe was soon replaced by another terror. What if he was lost in the Veil? Maybe it was impossible to climb through it, except inside one of the towers. Maybe he was trapped inside the Veil forever!

He climbed faster, not caring that his hands were scratched and his knees bruised. Several times he almost fell, but even that didn't scare him as much as staying inside the Veil. He had to get out.

Suddenly, he broke out into the exact opposite of darkness. Tal screamed as the searing light of the sun hit his eyes. Again, he almost fell, but his shadow-guard was already weaving itself across his head, shading his eyes with its strange substance that could be as light as air, as flowing as water, or as solid as human flesh.

Tal hung on, half in the Veil, half out, as the burning slowly disappeared from his eyes. He could feel his shadowguard on his forehead, and the unfamiliar heat of the sun on his cheeks.

Slowly, Tal opened his eyes and looked around. There was a patch of blue sky directly above him, strange and unfriendly compared to the soft darkness of the sky under the Veil. Around this patch of blue there were puffy gray clouds, some already drifting down through the Veil, bringing a promise of snow. Right in the center of the blue was the sun, so bright he could not look directly at it. It felt dangerous, giving off so much light and heat that Tal felt as if he might suddenly burst into flame.

The Red Tower, like all the others, continued to soar up into the sky. But now, instead of gargoyles and spikes and carvings, the Tower walls were covered in long, protruding bronze rods as thick around as Tal's middle. Most of the rods had nets of silver mesh hanging from them.

And in those nets, there were Sunstones. Tal knew that Sunstones grew from small jewels brought back from Aenir, the spirit realm, but he had not yet been taught how they were prepared.

Tal didn't want to know either. Not now. All he wanted to do was climb up farther, because the most powerful stones would be higher up.

Slowly, he eased himself out of the Veil and crouched on the stone ledge, staying as close to the wall as possible. He couldn't see any Spiritshadows, or other Chosen. There was a half balcony farther up, though, and someone could easily be standing there, or on the walkway that went right around the top of the Tower, a hundred stretches above him.

"Shadowguard, shadowguard, weave me a cloak as red as the Tower," Tal whispered. At the same time, he concentrated on his Sunstone so it shone with the same red color as the Tower walls. He felt the shadowguard moving, and saw a long, thin finger of darkness stretch across and touch the stone. Instantly, the color of the stone bled into the shadow, until it was red as well. Then Tal felt the shadowguard spreading itself across his back and down to his ankles.

In a few seconds, Tal was covered in a hooded cloak exactly the same red as the Tower walls. As long as he climbed up slowly and didn't make too much noise, he would be almost invisible.

Carefully, he started to climb. The bronze rods were slippery, not as easy to grasp as the stone outcrops below, but they were closer together. Tal could use them like steps, moving around the Tower as he climbed.

He was almost to the balcony, when he looked up and saw a hideous head staring over the railing, directly at him. It was a Spiritshadow head, grotesque and scary, with multiple eyes and a mouth that stretched the full width of its face, lined with multiple rows of small but very sharp teeth. It was one of the largest Spiritshadows Tal had ever seen. This meant it was one of the most powerful. Far too powerful to be in the service of one of the Red, for they were the weakest of the Orders.

Tal froze, hoping it hadn't seen him.

He stayed frozen for what seemed like minutes. Clouds crossed the sun overhead, and suddenly it was much darker, making the Spiritshadow harder to see. Tal kept absolutely still, hardly breathing. His heart sounded loud, so loud he was sure the Spiritshadow could hear it.

Then it started to snow. Snowflakes began to drift down, only to be caught by the wind around the Towers and whipped sideways in sudden flurries.

Tal knew what snow was. He'd seen it many times through the triple-glazed windows of the Outer Walk. But he'd never been outside the Castle before. He'd never felt snow.

A snowflake landed on Tal's nose, cold and then suddenly wet.

He sneezed.

The Spiritshadow up above hissed and leaned over the rail. Tal held his breath, but it was too late. It had seen him. It leaned over still farther, revealing a body like a snake's, all long, smooth, and twisting. For a second Tal thought it was going to fall over, but the Spiritshadow slowly uncoiled down toward him. Its eyes, black points darker than the rest of its Shadowflesh, were firmly fixed on him.

Tal fought the feeling that it would capture him and he would be taken before the Lumenor of the Red, and then to the Hall of Nightmares. He would never gain a Primary Sunstone and would all too soon be cast down to join the ranks of the Underfolk. From there, he would be unable to help his mother, or Gref, or Kusi.

The Spiritshadow didn't try to grab him, though. It suddenly shot forward, and its toothy maw opened large enough to take Tal's head off in a single bite.

Tal's shadowguard pushed him over as the Spiritshadow struck. Despite his shock, Tal instinctively grabbed a rod and locked his legs around it.

Upside down, Tal stared up as the creature pulled itself back for another strike. His own shadowguard was letting out a shrill whistle, its warning sign, as it turned itself into a boy-sized shadow and pushed Tal away.

Tal pulled himself out along the bronze rod toward the Sunstone nets. He couldn't believe what was happening. Spiritshadows couldn't hurt one of the Chosen!

The Spiritshadow laughed, a horrible, high-pitched cackle that cut through Tal's shock and made him swing himself upright and move farther along the rod. Then the Spiritshadow spoke, scaring Tal even more. Spiritshadows could speak, un-like the shadowguards, but they never did so in public. They only spoke to their Masters, in private.

"Seek not the treasures of the sun," said the Spir-itshadow, its voice like fingernails dragged down stone. "I am the Keeper, and none may pass here, save those who know the Words."

"Words?" muttered Tal as he frantically tried to get farther away. He didn't know any Words, not ones that might work here. He'd never heard of the Keeper. Surely its Master would look over the bal-cony soon and stop it!

The Spiritshadow coiled itself completely around the other end of the bronze rod that Tal was sliding on. Tal's shadowguard balanced behind him, in the shape of a four-legged creature with claws and lots of teeth. It would try to guard him, but Tal knew it was too small and weak to slow the Spiritshadow for more than a few seconds.

Tal looked back at it and felt the panic rise in him again.

The snake Spiritshadow shrieked and slowly wound itself forward another stretch. It seemed in no hurry to get to Tal, though its mouth was working backward and forward, almost as if it were chewing.

"Help!" screamed Tal, his open mouth collecting a few snowflakes. He didn't care who came now, or how long he might be sentenced to spend in the Hall of Nightmares, or if he would be instantly demoted to the Underfolk. Anything would be better than facing the creature that was inching toward him.

"Help!"

"The Towers are silent, save for thee and me," said the Spiritshadow. It arched its long body forward in a sudden movement that sent Tal leaping forward into one of the nets. Frantically, he tried to stand up, but all he could do was roll around.

One of his feet broke through the mesh and caught fast, sending a small shower of Sunstones falling through the hole. Tal bent forward and tried to free his foot, ignoring the Sunstones that were everywhere around him.

He'd just gotten it free when the Spiritshadow struck. Tal flinched and gasped, but he was not the target. His shadowguard squealed as the thing's mouth closed on it. Instantly it lost its cat shape and began to change shape so quickly that Tal couldn't keep track. It was a Morlyx, a boy, a toppet, a bird-headed monster, all sorts of shapes and sizes. No matter what it changed into it couldn't get free of those terrible teeth and the grinding jaws. Finally, the Spiritshadow tossed it aside, and it hung off the net, a formless lump of shadow.

Tal bit back a sob. His shadowguard had always been with him, always at his heels. It had saved him from troubles both large and small. Now it had been destroyed in a few seconds.

He couldn't believe this was happening. Spirit-shadows didn't damage shadowguards. They couldn't hurt the Chosen. Unless, he thought suddenly, all the rules were different beyond the Veil. . . .

"I shall eat both shadow and flesh," said the Spir-itshadow as it reared back and lifted its head high above Tal. Snow whirled behind it like a cloak of white. Tal could see inside its huge mouth, see all the rows of teeth. There were strips of cloth and other things stuck in the teeth, accompanied by an awful, rotting smell.

In that moment, Tal realized that this thing had killed before. It was going to kill him, too. It did not matter that he was one of the Chosen of the Castle, a Lightbringer of the Orange Order, a potential Shadowmaster.

As the thing struck, Tal threw himself aside and out of the net.

Falling, he hit a net on the next level below. For the briefest second, Tal thought he was safe. Then he bounced out in a shower of Sunstones, out into the air, too far out to be caught in the nets below.

Tal saw the Tower spinning above him as he hurtled down, along with the snow clouds and the whirl of snow and the Sunstones that fell with him. The wind picked everything up, boy and snow and Sunstones, and blew them farther away and farther out, beyond any chance of being caught in the lower nets.

When he hit the Veil, everything went black. His mind, overloaded with fear, went black, too. He had only an instant before he became unconscious, time enough to break through the Veil and see the twinkling lights of the Castle so far below.

And time to think a single thought.

Why did I ever try to steal a Sunstone?

PART ONE:

BEFORE

·CHAPTER·
⊙ПЕ

Tal's search for a new Sunstone began the day his father disappeared. Eight days later, this search would lead him to the Red Tower, the nets, and the terrible Spiritshadow.

His whole life as a Chosen had been transformed one otherwise ordinary day, when he'd been called out of the Lectorium during a lesson and told by Lector Roum himself the fateful words.

"Your father is missing, believed to be dead."

Tal had initially fought back the tears, but they came freely as he ran through the bright corridors and down the Orange Stair to his family's residence. He tried to wipe them away as he ran, ignoring the stares of other Chosen of the Orange Order and the sideways glances of the Underfolk. It could not be true.

Tal wouldn't believe his father was dead. He was missing, but that wasn't the same thing. Lector Roum hadn't been able to give Tal any details. All that was known was that Rerem hadn't returned from a mission for the Empress, down in the deep caves beneath the castle.

He could be lost down there, Tal thought, imagining his solid, powerful father stranded in the darkness. But he would find his way back. He loved Tal, his brother and sister, and their mother too much to leave them. He was too strong to be killed.

Outside the door marked with his family sigil, an orange Sthil-beast leaping over a seven-pointed star, Tal stopped and dried his eyes properly. He had to lead the family. He must not show them a crying boy, but a young Chosen who was strong enough to help. That's what his father had said before he left.

"Tal, you must look after your mother, Gref, and Kusi while I'm gone. I'm depending on you."

How could he have known how long he'd be gone? How could he have known how much those words would mean to Tal?

Tal took several deep breaths, then entered his family's quarters. In the outer room, an Underfolk servant took his school tunic and helped Tal put on the flowing, orange-trimmed white robe he wore at home. Tal hardly noticed that it was a new servant, and a fairly clumsy one at that.

Underfolk were assigned to families by the Deputy Lumenor of the Orange Order. For some reason, since Tal's father had first gone away on his unexplained mission, their Underfolk servants were constantly being removed and replaced by others who weren't as capable.

Tal's mother, Graile, was where she had been for several months — confined to her bed, struck with some sort of wasting sickness that was beyond the healing powers of the Chosens' magic or medicine.

The only things that helped her were light and warmth, so her bed had been moved into the family's sunchamber, a room where every inch of the walls and ceiling was covered in tiny Sunstones. It was always bright there, and very warm. In addition to the Sunstones, the room had its own steam vent, filling it with hot, moist air from the Castle's central heating pools far below.

Tal went to his mother at once, striding through the antechamber so quickly that the three people there didn't have time to stand up and offer greetings, or get cross because Tal had failed to bow to his seniors and offer them light from his Sunstone.

Tal knew that they would complain later. Two of the three were Lallek and Korrek, his mother's female cousins, and complaining about Tal was one of their favorite activities. He didn't know the third person, a man with broad orange stripes on his robe and a collar of mirrors and Sunstones, signifying high rank in the Order.

The Spiritshadows of all three were quicker than their masters. They loomed up from the floor as Tal approached. His cousins' Spiritshadows both had the shape of a Dretch, quite a common inhabitant of Aenir. They each looked rather like a seven-foot-tall, grotesquely thin cross between a stick insect and a spider, complete with eight legs and bulbous eyes. Tal thought they were slightly more appealing than Lallek and Korrek themselves.

Tal didn't recognize the man's Spiritshadow. It seemed very short and broad, until it reared up. In the few seconds that it took to reach the door on the other side of the room, Tal caught a glimpse of something that had to bend under the nine-foot ceiling and was roughly egg-shaped in the middle, with a rather lizardlike head, four legs, and a tail.

Tal forgot about it as he went into the sunchamber. As expected, his mother was there. She had both Kusi, Tal's three-year-old sister, and Gref, his nine-year-old brother, in bed with her, holding them tight. They had all been crying. Tal wished he could crawl in, too, just for a moment's comfort.

Graile's Spiritshadow was under the bed, only its round, strangely blurred head visible. It had faded as Graile grew weak. Once it had been strong, taking the shape of a huge owl, with great tufted eyebrows, and had been one of the few Spiritshadows in the Castle that could fly a long way from its Master. Now, it looked like a melted wax model of an owl, its Shadowflesh light and almost transparent, even in the sunchamber.

Graile was obviously very sick. Her skin was gray and sweating, and she had lost so much weight in her face that she almost looked like someone else.

Tal felt like crying again as he looked at her. He couldn't believe his father wasn't coming back, and his mother looked so close to death. Even the Sunstone around her neck was going dark. It didn't flash as Tal raised his own and made his formal greeting.

"I greet you, Mother," he said, and his Sunstone brightened, giving her light as was her due.

Graile smiled a little, but could not take an arm away from her other two children to raise her Sunstone.

"Tal," she said, her voice so soft that he had to

come closer and crouch by the bed to hear her at all. "Tal."

"They said . . . they said Father isn't coming back," Tal said, his voice almost breaking. Gref and Kusi looked at him and started crying again.

"Shush, children," Graile comforted them. "It is true your father has not returned, but that doesn't mean he is lost forever. I think he will come back, in time. But until he does, we must all be brave. Can you be brave, for me, and for your father?"

"Yes," said Tal, though he had to swallow as he said it. Gref and Kusi nodded, both unable to speak.

"I need to talk to Tal alone," said Graile. "Gref, take Kusi out to Hudren. She will give you orange-cake and sweetwater."

Tal helped Kusi down from the bed, her shadow-guard slipping down first so it would be ready to catch her if Tal slipped. The little girl seemed almost happy to be going to Hudren and orangecake. Hudren was the one Underfolk servant they'd managed to keep assigned to them for any length of time. She had been Gref's nurse, and was now Kusi's.

"I want to stay," said Gref. "I'm almost as old as Tal."

"No you're not!" exclaimed Tal. He was almost five years older. "Can't you count?"

"Gref, go with your sister," Graile said gently as her Spiritshadow gestured with one taloned leg, reinforcing her command. Gref scowled at Tal, but went.

"Sit by me," Graile said. "Tal, I do believe your father will come back to us. But we must decide what to do if he has not returned by the Day of Ascension."

Tal paused. He had been so concerned about the news, and about his mother, that he hadn't thought about himself. He would be thirteen and three-quarters in two months, and shortly after that, on the Day of Ascension, all the Chosen would enter Aenir. Since he would have come of age, his shadowguard would be free, and he would have to find a creature of Aenir to bind as a Spiritshadow.

Tal had been preparing for that day for what seemed like forever. It would be his chance to bind a powerful Spiritshadow, to show his strength and mastery of light. Deep in his bones, he knew that his father had trained him well, and he had a natural gift. He would come back with a great and terrible Spiritshadow. With its help, he would one day rise beyond the Orange, to the Yellow or even the Blue. Tal's parents had lifted the family two levels within Orange. Tal would make sure that his own children would start from higher still.

But Tal couldn't enter Aenir without the help of a Primary Sunstone. He'd never had to think about that in the past, because his father had one, and had used it to help the whole family enter Aenir. Now, with Rerem gone, so was the Primary Sunstone. Unless his mother had one. . . .

"Haven't you got a Primary Sunstone?" Tal asked, desperately hoping that they'd only used his father's Sunstone for convenience. Most adult Chosens' Sunstones were Primaries, strong enough to enter Aenir.

Graile raised one very thin hand to her chest and touched the Sunstone on the silver chain around her neck. It barely sparked as her finger touched.

"Once, this was," she whispered. "But now I shall need help, too, and so will Gref and Kusi. You know what will happen if we cannot enter Aenir."

Tal nodded. If he was unable to enter Aenir and bind a Spiritshadow to himself, he would be separated from his family. Demoted, not just to the next Order down, the Red, but right out of the ranks of the Chosen. He would become one of the Underfolk, a servant for the rest of his days.

Worse than that, his mother's last chance of a cure would be lost. The spirit realm of Aenir was a place of magic and marvels, of creatures and beings that had wisdom as well as power. There, Graile might be cured, her life saved — if she could last until the Day of Ascension. It was forbidden to enter Aenir before that day.

"I will have to get a new Primary Sunstone," said Tal, his voice wavering despite his obvious determination. "For the family."

Graile nodded and squeezed his hand, her touch as light as a faint breeze. Her eyes closed, and she seemed to slip away from Tal, her face slowly smoothing into sleep.

"I will get a Primary Sunstone," repeated Tal quietly. "Somehow."

·CHAPTER· TWO☉

Tal sat by his mother for a long time, thinking of how he could get a new, powerful Sunstone. He could think of only three ways, and all carried some risk.

The first would be to ask his mother's cousins, Lallek and Korrek. They were higher up in the Orange Order, rumored to be going Yellow soon. They both wore several Sunstones — in their silver circlets, in the rings that flashed upon their fingers, even set in the points of their mirror-bright shoes. Tal thought they must have won them gambling. He'd never seen Lallek or Korrek do anything else.

But Lallek and Korrek were not known for their generosity, and Tal thought that they particularly disliked him. He couldn't understand why, though when he was younger he had set up a bucket of ash to fall on them, dulling their brilliance just before a family dinner. It had only been a joke, but they seemed to hold a grudge. Of course, it hadn't just been ash.

Still, Tal thought, they were family. And they were just outside, in the reception room. Though that was probably only because everyone would expect them to come, now that the news was out about Rerem's presumed death.

Tal sighed. His shadowguard, catching his mood, changed shape from a two-headed Corvile to an almost normal shadow. It shivered and made a sort of throwing-up motion, before slipping back into the long, catlike shape of a Corvile, though with only one head. It made Tal smile. Even his shadowguard disliked Lallek and Korrek.

This time, Tal stopped at the door and made the proper bow to his elders. He raised his Sunstone and said, "I greet you, Korrek, Lallek, and . . ."

"Shadowmaster Sushin," said the unknown man, negligently raising his own Sunstone and rudely blasting a very bright white light into Tal's face. Korrek and Lallek did the same, so Tal had to raise his hand to shield his eyes.

The light grew brighter still, and Tal felt an unpleasant heat on his hand. His shadowguard let out a low whistle, so low only Tal could hear. Tal felt anger building inside him, as hot and bright as the light. His cousins and this unknown Shadowmaster — a title that meant he served the Empress directly, in addition to his rank in the Orange Order — would never have dared treat him like this if his mother or father were around.

The light disappeared, and Tal brought his hand down. None of the three had bothered to get up, but their Spiritshadows had moved forward and were standing over Tal, unpleasantly close. The Shadowmaster's, Tal realized, was a deepwater Shellbeast. It had a flat shell or carapace that covered its middle.

"The Shadowmaster was not impressed by your rudeness," said Lallek. "Even under the circumstances, one must not forget the proper way to do things."

"I beg the Shadowmaster's forgiveness," Tal said slowly, forcing the words out. "May my light diminish no further in his eyes."

The Shadowmaster grunted. He looked like a pig, Tal thought. He had a fat face, ready to grub at any trough, like the pigs the Underfolk herded in the farm caverns far below.

"Take three deluminents," said the Shadowmaster, picking four clear bracelets out of his sleeve pocket and throwing them to Tal.

They landed on the ground, since Tal was too shocked to catch them. He bent to pick them up, slowly slipping each one over his hand, onto his wrist. Deluminents were visible punishments, marking an offense against the Order or the Empress. They could only be removed by someone higher than the person who'd given them in the first place. If Tal picked up seven deluminents, he would be demoted to the Red Order. Seven more after that, and he would be joining the Underfolk, even before the Day of Ascension.

After putting on the third bracelet, Tal stopped and looked at the Shadowmaster. Three deluminents was a ridiculously harsh punishment for not greeting his superiors properly. But the Shadowmaster had thrown four!

"There are four deluminents, Shadowmaster," he said, feeling his face flush with the humiliation. He had never had more than a single deluminent in his life.

"Three, four, it doesn't matter," said the Shadowmaster. "Put it on, Tal. You must learn to pay proper respect."

Slowly, Tal picked up the fourth deluminent and slid it on to his wrist. The bracelets were made of crystal, and jangled as they touched.

"How can I serve my distinguished visitors?" Tal asked, following the proper ritual, even though he wanted to pick up a jug of frosted sweetwater and throw it in their faces.

"I am the Shadowmaster Sushin, Brightstar of the Orange Order and Spectral Adept," announced the fat man. "I have come to offer the Empress's sorrow at the death of your father."

"He's not dead," Tal wanted to say, but he did not dare speak aloud. This Shadowmaster seemed to want him to be disrespectful. He was even reaching into his sleeve pocket to jangle the deluminents there, while he watched Tal struggle with his feelings.

"We thank the Empress," said Tal. He didn't really understand what was going on. Why was this Shadowmaster so hostile to him? He expected his cousins to be nasty, but this man was a stranger, a servant of the Empress.

"That's it, really," said Sushin. He took a handful of dried shrimps out of his voluminous pocket and stuffed them into his mouth, still talking. "You may go back to the Lectorium now, Tal. Must keep up with your studies."

Tal felt sick, watching the huge wad of pink, munched-up shrimps churning about in Sushin's mouth. The man was a pig *and* a bully.

Shrimps were his mother's favorite, and hard to come by, since they were rarely trapped in the deep underground streams by the Underfolk. Tal had been trying to get her some for weeks, without success.

"I desire to ask a question of my mother's cousins, if I may," Tal said carefully. Despite the anger he felt at having to ask permission to speak in his own home, he had no choice.

"Ask away," replied Sushin. He took another handful of shrimps and washed them down with a glass of sweetwater, spilling it down the deep furrows where his bloated cheeks met his mouth.

"Light shine on you, Shadowmaster," said Tal, bowing again. He turned to his cousins, who were smiling, but not in a nice way. They seemed to be looking forward to something. Their Spiritshadows jiggled in front of Tal, almost dancing, so he had to talk between them.

"Mother is ill," he began. "And since Father is missing, we will need help to enter Aenir when the Day of Ascension comes. I ask your help, as close cousins to my mother. Grant us a Sunstone of sufficient power to be a Primary Sunstone."

Lallek and Korrek looked at each other, and their smiles grew wider. Then they looked at Sushin and everyone smiled. Except Tal.

"Oh no," said Lallek, fingering the two very large Sunstones that flashed on her thumb and forefinger rings. "We really haven't any to spare."

"What a shame," added Korrek, lightly touching the pendant she wore that held four Sunstones, all of them twice as large as Tal's own. "But I'm sure you'll manage somehow . . . even though your father is dead."

Tal stared at them, his fury growing. Dimly he was aware of his shadowguard gripping him around the knees so he couldn't charge forward. He gripped his own Sunstone, wishing that he could throw light-spears from it, or the rain of sparks, or any of the other combat magic that he had only just begun to learn in the Lectorium.

Sushin broke the tension by shoveling the last of the shrimps into his mouth and pushing himself up out of the chair. Lallek and Korrek hastily jumped up as well. By rights, all three should have bowed to Tal, as they were in his house. But they didn't. Sushin just walked out, followed by the two women. The Spiritshadows backed away slowly. They knew, even if their masters did not, that Tal was very close to some sort of crazy attack.

When the Underfolk servant closed the door behind them, the shadowguard let Tal go. His breathing started to work again, and he could think.

His first plan to get a Sunstone had failed miserably. He would have to move on to the next plan. And he would have to try to find out why Shadowmaster Sushin wanted him to fail.

"You'll see," Tal whispered to the door. He raised his arm and jangled the deluminents. "You'll see. I'll get my Sunstone!"

His shadowguard grew an arm and shook it, too, in silent protest. It kept on after Tal stopped and had to race to catch up with him as he went to see how Gref and Kusi were coping with the terrible news.

·CHAPTER·
THREE

Tal's second plan would have to wait for seven days, when he could enter the next Achievement of Luminosity. While he waited, he tried very hard to be a model student. Whenever an idea for a practical joke came into his head, or he got bored as the Assistant Lector droned on about recursive light or spectral shifting, the soft chink of the deluminents on his wrist would remind him to behave.

Even with his best efforts, it was a hard week for Tal. After every evening meal Kusi would forget and ask for her father to put her to bed. She cried when he didn't come, and was too young to understand that it wasn't because he didn't want to. Graile was too weak to get out of bed herself, so it had fallen to Tal to tuck the little girl in and tell her a story. He then had to make sure that Gref actually went to bed at all.

It was all a constant reminder of his father's absence. Tal would lie awake at night, hoping that he would hear his father's footsteps outside his room and his familiar voice asking him if all was well.

Unfortunately, Tal was much more likely to hear Gref's voice saying something like, "Tal, why don't I sneak over to Lallek's rooms and steal a Sunstone?"

Or, "Tal, I bet I could drop a blanket on Korrek and get her bracelet off and she wouldn't know who did it."

Or Gref's most constant question, "Tal, why can't I help you get a new Sunstone?"

Kusi was not much better, in her own way. Besides having to read her a story, most nights he had to help her get back to sleep. She'd lie in bed looking up at him with her huge blue eyes and say, "I don't want Tal. I want Mummy."

To make matters worse, Shadowmaster Sushin seemed to have spread the word that Tal was to be picked on. Older Chosen he had never seen before tried to get in his way and blame him for the collision. Strange Spiritshadows followed him so often he stopped using the smaller stairways. He even avoided the best shortcut in the Castle: the Under-folk's laundry chute — a slippery slide that spiraled from the highest chambers of the Violet down to the Red, and then beneath to the Underfolk's work caverns.

Tal didn't want to meet a Spiritshadow in the laundry slide. Being in the slide was the closest you could get to real darkness in the Castle. There were no Sunstones inside. The only light came spilling in around the hatches on each of the forty-nine Order levels. These faint lines of light were also the only way for chute riders to know where they were, so they could push their feet out and bring themselves to a stop, usually with some damage to the soles of their shoes.

So Tal kept to the main stairs and the Colorless Corridors, the wide passageways that were not part of the realm of any particular Order.

In the Lectorium they were taught that all light served the Empress, that all the Orders were like a family.

Tal knew this was a load of shadowspit. The Chosen in the lower Orders were resentful of the higher ones, and the Chosen of the higher Orders liked putting everyone in their place. The children were the worst. If they caught Tal creeping about, they'd gang up to blind him with their Sunstones, a blindness that sometimes took days to fully wear off.

Tal just tried to avoid trouble. It was even more difficult because he had to look after Gref as well. His brother was in a different Lectorium, and he hadn't complained to Tal about any problems. Still, Tal tried to keep an eye on him.

Gref had a genius for trouble. He was very good at making it, and at avoiding responsibility for it. But even getting away with things eight times out of ten meant getting caught twice.

Gref's genius did not serve him well when it came to being picked on. Tal wasn't so much worried about what might happen to Gref, but what his younger brother might do to take revenge.

The case of the boy who had drawn a picture of Gref as a two-headed toppet was never far from Tal's mind. Gref had saved his allowance for seven months, then paid a much older student to create a light-puppet of himself as a truly vicious toppet, which he'd managed to get into the other boy's room at night. The boy had woken up with a scream they could hear in all seven Towers; he still couldn't see a light-puppet show without shaking nervously.

Gref's glory hadn't lasted long. It was clear to

the authorities where the light-puppet had come from, with Gref's face on it.

What worried Tal the most was that even after being punished, Gref said it was worth it — and he'd do it again. (Luckily he wasn't old enough to be given deluminants.)

All of this trouble was a constant worry for Tal, but it was nothing compared to the continuing absence of his father. If he came back, everything would be all right. With every day that passed without him, Tal's secret fear that his father might really be dead grew stronger.

He had to think harder about getting a Primary Sunstone. If only the horrible Lallek and Korrek had just given him a Sunstone, he wouldn't have to try to win an Achievement of Luminosity.

The Achievements of Luminosity were held every quarter month, and were technically open to everyone who wished to demonstrate their skill and artistic abilities. It was rare for someone who only had a shadowguard, like Tal, to participate.

The Achievements were divided into several categories, each held in different parts of the Castle. While all Achievements tested the participant's skill with a Sunstone and sense of light, each category tested other specific talents and abilities as well.

Tal had put his name down for the Achievement of Body. This Achievement was essentially an obstacle course, where fitness and dexterity were as important as light control. It was held in the Hall of Mirrors, which added an extra level of difficulty. Light had to be tightly controlled there, because the slightest slip would mean thousands of embarrassing reflections.

Over the week, Tal practiced on the course every afternoon after he finished at the Lectorium. There were seven obstacles, each of which had to be jumped, climbed, swung across, or crawled under. The ancient obstacles were made of solid light, a magic that was now lost to the Chosen, though some thought the Empress might know the secret ways.

Participants could make the obstacle change into something else by directing a beam of light from their Sunstone at exactly the right spot, in exactly the right color.

The secret to doing well at the Achievement of Body was to turn all the obstacles in front of yourself into something easy, like a Gasping Hole, which could be jumped across. At the same time you had to turn your competitors' obstacles into more difficult things, like a Surprising Wall.

Sometimes obstacles flickered through multiple

combinations right up until the last second, as light beams shot everywhere. It was not unknown for a Gasping Hole to become a Surprising Wall in the same instant that a competitor jumped, resulting in an unpleasant collision.

Tal wasn't worried so much about that. Getting knocked out by smacking his head into a Surprising Wall or tripping over a sudden Deep Tunnel wasn't a problem. The audience would just laugh. But any disregard of the rules of light could lead to more deluminents, and Tal couldn't afford that.

"That won't happen," he muttered after another exhausting practice. The winner of the Achievement was usually advanced several levels within his or her Order, or was permitted to ask for a Sunstone or some other reward instead.

Tal intended to be the winner. He'd always been good at the trial Achievements, which all the children competed in. The practices were going well. What could go wrong?

On the morning of the Achievements of Luminosity, Tal found out exactly what could go wrong. Nervous, he went to the Hall of Mirrors a good hour early — and discovered that his name was not on the list for that day's Achievement of Body. It wasn't on the list for next time, either, or the one after that.

"But I wrote it down," Tal insisted. "In the Registry. A week ago!"

The Half-Bright who had the list for the Achievement of Body shrugged. He was a low-ranking Chosen of the Red Order, better than a Dimmer but not much above an Underfolk, which was why he had an actual job. Most Chosen didn't do anything so menial, devoting themselves to their hobbies or interests, or in advancing themselves through Achievements or the politics of the Empress's court.

"You're not here," he said, holding up the huge leather-bound book. "Maybe you accidentally signed up for some other Achievement."

"I can't have," said Tal. His shadowguard shook its head, too.

"You'll have to go to the Registry and check," said the Half-Bright. His Spiritshadow was as lackluster as he was, a six-legged animal of some kind that slept around his ankles.

Tal nodded and sped away. Behind him, he heard the man snort something like "Orange idiot," but Tal didn't look back. He remembered exactly what he'd signed up for. He couldn't have made a mistake. . . .

Unless he'd signed up for the wrong Achievement. What if he'd signed up for the Achievement of Combat, or the Achievement of Healing? He wasn't properly trained for either of those. He'd get the White Ray of Disgust from the audience for sure, and have his arms loaded with deluminents. He'd become an Underfolk, his mother would die, and Gref and Kusi would follow him down into the dark servant halls below the Castle.

"I must not panic," Tal told himself. He stopped running and carefully bowed and gave light to a Brilliance of the Violet who passed by. He still had half an hour left.

"I must not panic," Tal repeated to himself. Taking deliberate, slow breaths, he walked quickly toward the Registry.

·CHAPTER·
FOUR

It was the Achievement of Music. Tal stared down at the Registry, unable to believe that his name was there. But it was, complete with his family sigil, etched in light.

He couldn't possibly have made this mistake . . . but obviously he had.

The Achievement of Music! After Combat and Healing, that was probably the worst. Tal didn't even have a composition to use. He couldn't withdraw, either. That wasn't allowed, unless he was sick or injured.

For a moment Tal thought of throwing himself down one of the steeper stairways. A broken arm or leg would let him off. For now. But then he would have no chance in any of the Achievements.

Tal glanced at his Sunstone, looking at the bands of color to work out the time. He had less than twenty minutes before he would have to perform an original composition of light and music.

It was impossible. Like all the Chosen, Tal was a trained musician. But he had never displayed any great talent, and he certainly didn't have time to write an entirely new piece of music. His only chance would be to use an old one. It would have to be something that had never been performed before, or so old no one recognized it.

"Old," Tal said to himself, and an idea suddenly came into his head. His shadowguard caught his thought and changed from a very ugly sort of lungfish into a thin, stooped man much taller than Tal, with a very pronounced nose. It was a caricature — one that Tal recognized. His great-uncle Ebbitt!

Ebbitt would help! Tal was off again, racing through the corridors. He had to forget about being careful, and took every shortcut he knew.

Two minutes later, Tal was throwing himself feet first into the laundry chute. A huge bag of clothes hurtled just ahead of him, then Tal was sliding down himself, counting the levels.

"Orange Three, Two, One, Red Six, Five, Four, Three," he said aloud, the sound of his own voice making him feel better. At "Red Two" he stuck his feet into the sides of the chute and felt the sudden heat through the soles of his shoes as friction slowed him down.

Ebbitt lived in Red One, the very lowest level of the Chosen. Below that lay the work caverns of the Underfolk. Tal had never been there. He knew there were few Sunstones in the Underfolk caverns, just enough to create a dim twilight so the servants could work. It was said to be perpetually steamy as well, from the hot pools that supplied the Castle's warmth. Below the pools, tunnels of lava flowed. The lava collection pools were the creation of the Castle's builders, the Chosen of long ago, who wielded many powers the current generations had long lost.

Tal felt a chill go through him as he climbed out of the chute. Soon he might be forced to join the Underfolk, and might never return to the bright levels of the Chosen. Even today, if he completely failed in the Achievement of Music and was given more deluminents . . .

He checked his Sunstone again. He only had fifteen minutes left until the Achievement. If Ebbitt wasn't home, Tal didn't know what he would do. He set off at a run, hoping that he didn't meet any Red Half-Brights or Dimmers who would be delighted to

47

politely delay an Orange boy. They wouldn't do any serious harm, but they would waste his precious time.

Ebbitt had once been a Shadowlord himself, a Brightblinder of the Indigo Order, the second highest in the Castle. Ebbitt had been the shining hope of the family and had seemed certain of climbing Violet. But something had gone terribly wrong for him when Tal was a baby. He had been forced all the way down to Red, and the lowest level. He was a Dimmer now, a single step above the Underfolk. Somehow he managed to stay there, despite his strange ways and outspoken tongue.

He chose to live in twilight, at the end of a rough tunnel, without a door. His weird collection of constantly rearranged furniture occupied a good hundred yards of corridor, and Ebbitt himself could be found anywhere around it. Tal had no idea how he stopped people coming in, or stealing his things. But he had never seen anyone there except family, or invited guests.

Today, a large wardrobe of white stone marked the beginning of Ebbitt's realm. It completely blocked the corridor, and Tal was momentarily stumped by it. Then he opened the door and saw that the wardrobe had no back. He went through, shutting the door behind him.

After carefully making his way around several chairs and desks, a huge birdcage, and a bronze orrery, Tal found Ebbitt sleeping on an old gilded throne. It had obviously once been studded with Sunstones, because it was covered in holes and scratch marks from when they had been removed.

Ebbitt himself was wearing a plain gray robe without any of the proper markings of his Order or position. He wore a single small Sunstone in a silver ring on his index finger. It flashed as Tal approached, and Ebbitt's Spiritshadow stepped out of the darkness behind the throne.

It was a huge cat, with a great mane around its head and a ridge along its back. Completely black even in the dim light — the mark of a powerful Spiritshadow — it yawned as Tal approached, showing lighter shadows inside its enormous mouth.

Tal's shadowguard turned itself into a smaller version of the maned cat, in tribute. Tal took a few steps forward, but not too many. He'd always been a bit afraid of Ebbitt's Spiritshadow, even though he knew it wouldn't hurt him.

"Great-uncle," he said. As Ebbitt still didn't move, he said it again, a bit louder. "Great-uncle!"

Ebbitt still didn't move. Tal took another step forward and almost shouted, "Uncle Ebbitt!"

The old man on the throne reacted to that. He jumped up and shouted, "Kill!"

The huge cat Spiritshadow leaped forward. Tal jumped back and fell over a small three-legged stool, hurtling toward the hard stone floor.

·CHAPTER·
FIVE

At the last moment, Tal's shadowguard shot underneath him, cushioning his head so he didn't knock himself out.

Ebbitt laughed as Tal slowly got up, and the maned cat slunk back to sit beside the throne, at the old man's right hand.

"That fooled you, boy," wheezed Ebbitt. "Thought I was asleep, didn't you?"

Tal got up angrily, but managed not to show it. There was no point in getting angry with Ebbitt. He just laughed and wheezed.

"I need your help, Uncle," Tal said quickly. Ebbitt might be a pain when it came to surprises and practical jokes, but he was a lot more use than Korrek and Lallek when it came to helping out.

"Help?" asked Ebbitt. His laugh was gone, and he

didn't look an old fool anymore. Obviously Tal's face and tone had told him that whatever the boy was concerned about, it was serious. "Tell me."

"You know about Father," said Tal, speaking so quickly his words ran into each other. "I don't know whether you knew . . . he had our Primary Sunstone. We have to get a new one. I asked Lallek and Korrek, but they wouldn't help, I think because Shadowmaster Sushin told them not to. So I put my name in for the Achievement of Body. Today. Only somehow . . . I must have made a mistake . . . I'm in for the Achievement of Music. But I don't have a composition. The Achievement is in . . . oh! Ten minutes!"

"Shadowmaster Sushin," muttered Ebbitt. "There are shadows here, and no mistake! But first you need some music."

He leaped out of his throne and clambered over a long table, then jumped across to a chest, his Spirit-shadow at his heels. From there he crawled under a hammock suspended in a frame. Tal lost sight of him behind a giant silver gong. He reappeared a moment later, holding a long scroll.

" 'March of the Muldren on Drashamore Hood'!" he exclaimed, weaving and jumping his way back to Tal.

"What?" asked Tal, taking the scroll. It was music, he saw, written in the traditional way, down the scroll. Music on the left side, light on the right.

"Name of the piece," replied Ebbitt. "Never performed. The Muldren were — are warriors in Aenir, beyond the parts where we Chosen normally go. The Drashamore Hood was a monster, I suppose."

"What happened?" Tal asked, staring down at the scroll.

"Tell you later," Ebbitt said. "You need to get to the Crystal Wood. Within nine minutes."

"Nine," Tal groaned, looking at his Sunstone. "I can't make it."

"We'll have to go by steam. Come on."

Ebbitt took Tal by the arm and led him through the furniture so quickly that Tal knocked several pieces over and banged both knees.

"Steam?" asked Tal. "What do you mean, steam? Where —"

He stopped suddenly as they came to a stairway leading down. A dark stairway. Ebbitt tugged at his arm, but Tal wouldn't move.

"That's going down!" he protested. "I have to go up!"

The maned Spiritshadow nudged him behind his legs, and Tal fell forward, held up only by Ebbitt's surprising strength.

"Have to go down to go up," said Ebbitt, laughing. Tal almost sobbed. His great-uncle had clearly gone completely crazy. He'd given Tal the music, but that was no help. He'd never get to the Crystal Wood now.

They ran through the dark to the bottom of the stairs. They were somewhere in the Underfolk caverns. Tal fumbled at his Sunstone, desperately trying to get some light. He couldn't bear this darkness!

Before Tal could do anything, Ebbitt raised his hand, and the Sunstone on his finger blazed into a bright, indigo light — a color forbidden to Ebbitt since his demotion to the Red.

Tal almost choked as he saw it, and forgot to breathe as Ebbitt moved his hand through a series of gestures, the light following in an almost solid band. Quickly, Ebbitt wove a shining cylinder around himself and Tal.

"Stay very close to me," Ebbitt cautioned. He didn't sound mad anymore, and Tal knew that the indigo cylinder of light around them was very powerful magic, certainly forbidden to Red Dimmers or Orange boys.

Tal stayed closed to Ebbitt as they shuffled forward. They came to a large metal door, locked by a wheel. Ebbitt turned it, but didn't open it. He gestured at his Spiritshadow instead. It moved forward under the cylinder of light, and thinned itself, becoming almost invisible. Then it slowly eased itself under the solid metal of the door.

It came back a moment later and nodded. Ebbitt opened the door. A rush of steam came out. Tal flinched, but the steam didn't pass through the blue light. It washed around it, and he felt no heat.

Ahead of them, he saw a shaft. Billowing steam obscured how deep it was, and how high up it went.

"Come on," Ebbitt said before stepping forward, seemingly into empty space. Tal hung back, but his great-uncle's grip was too strong.

Tal closed his eyes and followed. Obviously they were going to fall together, down into the boiling pools of the central heating system.

But they didn't fall. Tal opened his eyes and looked down. Indigo light shimmered under his feet, light solid enough to hold him up and to keep the heat of the steam at bay.

"Stand by for a surge of steam," Ebbitt warned as he closed the door behind him. The light moved out to cover his hands, as if it were cloth. Tal pushed at it experimentally, but it wouldn't budge for him. His shadowguard sat at his feet, in the shape of a dattu, a small, furry rodent that lived in hillsides in Aenir.

It was a harmless shape, one the shadowguard took when it didn't like what was happening but couldn't do anything about it.

"Steam!" shouted Ebbitt and pointed down. Tal looked and saw a solid-looking mass of white surging up the shaft. A moment later, it hit. They were suddenly propelled upward, so quickly that Tal fell over and even Ebbitt had to kneel and clutch at his Spiritshadow.

Faster and faster they shot up. Tal tried to get up, but some strange force kept him pressed to the floor of indigo light. He felt like several people were lying on him, trying to crush him flat.

Then he noticed that Ebbitt was counting, very quickly. At twenty-five, he suddenly pulled at the indigo light in front of him, tugging it away from the wall. Steam instantly rushed through the gap, and their rate of ascent slowed.

But they were still going up even faster than Tal had come down the slide. Too fast, it seemed, for Ebbitt. He looked at his Spiritshadow, and it lunged through the light to set its claws in the stone of the shaft.

Instantly, they slowed almost to a stop, accompanied by a hideous screeching sound from the Spiritshadow's claws. Tal started in recognition. He'd heard that sound before, coming from behind the walls. It was always explained as "the heating," but it must have been Ebbitt — or someone — using this strange method of transportation.

"We're there," said Ebbitt. "Or just past it. Three minutes to go. Hang on."

The Spiritshadow let go, and they suddenly fell about ten stretches. Steam still swirled around them, but not as much. Tal saw that there was another metal door in front of them. Ebbitt reached out, the indigo light still encasing his hands, and opened it. White light poured in, and Tal recognized one of the minor corridors.

From the neutral color of the Sunstones, he knew he was close to one of the Colorless Corridors, and on the level of the Crystal Wood.

"Out," said Ebbitt. Without warning, his Sunstone flashed, and he pushed Tal into the corridor, through the protective barrier of light. The door clanged shut behind the boy. In a second, Great-uncle Ebbitt and his strange steam-driven capsule of light were gone.

Tal got up, checked to make sure he had the scroll, and strode out into the larger corridor. At least now he had a chance — a very slim one, since he didn't know the music and was totally unpracticed with the composition.

But it was a chance, Tal told himself. Perhaps his only one. . . .

·CHAPTER· SIX

The Crystal Wood was another of the ancient artifacts of the Castle. It was made up of forty-nine trees of clear crystal, each ten stretches tall and with many branches. The trees stood at the center of a huge hall, surrounded by tiered benches for the audience.

The magic and marvel of the Crystal Wood lay in the fact that every branch of every tree could produce a single, clear note when it was correctly struck with a beam of light. The duration and intensity of the note depended on the color of the light beam and how long it touched the branch.

The Wood was played from a central stone, as tall as a man, with a silver spike set in it that held the scroll.

Tal climbed the stone in a state of eerie calm. He

was the first to perform that day, and there wasn't much of an audience. He saw a scattering of Chosen from all Orders, save the Violet, who were presumably too important to waste time listening and watching an unproven boy from the Orange.

Tal tried not to look at them as he fastened his scroll to the spike and let it roll down. Fortunately, Ebbitt scribed with a clear, large hand, and the symbols were easy to follow. It didn't look too hard a piece to perform.

Tal looked across to where the judges sat. There were three, and they would lead the audience reaction. In theory, everyone was allowed to show the light they wanted, whether it was the Red Ray of Disapproval, the Violet Ray of Attainment, or the dreaded White Ray of Disgust. In practice, they would follow the judges, who sat on their own high bench, with clear space to either side, obviously separate from the crowd.

Tal noted that something was going on at the judge's bench. One judge, a woman of the Green, was smiling and stepping down, making way for someone else. But Tal noted that despite her smile, her Spiritshadow was between her and her replacement, as if there was some danger there.

Tal started to look away, to study the scroll once

more, when something about the replacement judge caught his eye. His head whipped back, and a terrible feeling surged up in his chest. The replacement judge was Shadowmaster Sushin!

Sushin sat and looked across at Tal. Their eyes met, and Tal finally realized that what he saw in the older man's eyes was not merely a look of superiority. It was a look of hatred. Sushin really hated him. But Tal didn't know why. He hadn't done anything!

Shaking, he looked away. He had to concentrate on the Achievement of Music. It didn't matter that Sushin was a judge. If Tal did well enough, he would be rewarded. That was how things worked in the Castle.

All three judges settled at the bench. They looked at one another, then raised their Sunstones to send beams of light rippling at random through the Wood. Light met crystal, and music shimmered out through the hall. The audience settled, and Tal took a deep breath.

The judges' light beams rippled across again, and then withdrew. Tal raised his own Sunstone and said in a voice that was not quite a shout, "I am Tal Graile-Rerem. I will perform a composition of my great-uncle Ebbitt Nune-Taril, never before seen or heard. It is called 'March of the Muldren on Drashamore Hood.'"

As he finished speaking, Tal directed a beam of red light at the outermost branches of the central tree. Maintaining this, he cast out other beams to other trees and branches. Music came from the crystal, and light refracted into the air. Both music and light drew a picture. Bold warriors armed themselves on one side of the Wood, while a dark creature heaved itself out of the primordial bog on the other.

Slowly, the two parts of the light and music moved together, building up and up. The warriors circled the monster, the monster made sudden dashes at them. Then, in a crash of light and music that made the audience jump, battle was joined. Colors flashed everywhere as the music leaped and fought, louder and louder, rising to a crescendo.

Then, silence. All color lost. Four, five seconds passed as the audience held their breath. Who had won? Suddenly there was a tiny flash of red, the beginning of a tune. Then more red, as the surviving warriors gathered, and their song grew louder. Then the joyous sound of triumph. The monster was vanquished, the warriors could return to their homes. They began to march and a column of light swept through the Wood, right to the ends of the branches, and then leaped off seemingly into the audience on a final, long-sustained note.

Tal dropped his Sunstone back into his shirt and bowed. He felt exhausted, but proud. He had made no mistakes. He had performed better than he ever had before and much better than the artists in most of the ordinary Achievements of Music he had seen. Surely he had won his Sunstone!

Then the first Yellow Ray of Failed Ambition hit his face. He looked up and saw that it came from Shadowmaster Sushin. The other judges were looking at him, and Tal saw the beginnings of a Violet Ray of Attainment fade. Then they, too, were directing the same light at him. The Ray that was shone for those who tried too hard, who failed to achieve their object. It was not a bad result, as such, for it merely meant that he had tackled something too difficult. He would not be punished, or be given deluminents. But he would gain no awards, unless the audience refused to follow the judges.

Tal looked up, hoping his anxiety would not show. There were a few Violet rays coming through, a few Blue Rays of Commendation, an Indigo Ray of Extreme Approval. But not enough. Most of the audience, however reluctantly, was following the judges' lead.

The light in front of Tal grew more and more yellow, till the decision was absolutely clear. Failed Ambition it was. Tal bowed and held up his Sunstone, flashing the Orange of his Order to show his understanding and acceptance.

He climbed down the stone and walked out of the Crystal Wood, alone, except for his thoughts. The same thoughts that had been with him for every waking second of the last week.

He had to get a Primary Sunstone. Obviously he could not hope to win one through an Achievement. There was only one way left to him. Or only one way he could think of.

Tal considered going back to Ebbitt, but that would mean discussing his failed Achievement, and he wasn't ready for that now. It always took a lot of energy to talk to Ebbitt, to keep him even partly in the same conversation. Tal didn't have that energy. He couldn't face his mother, either. Or Gref and Kusi. They all depended on him, and so far, he was failing.

No. He would go on to his next plan immediately. He would go up to the highest level of the Violet and seek an audience with the Empress.

·CHAPTER·
SEVEN

Tal had never been into the Violet, the highest and most private levels of the Castle, save the Towers.

He was surprised to find that it was really no different than any of the other levels. There seemed to be fewer people around, and not all of them were members of the Violet Order. Tal carefully bowed and gave them light anyway, just to be safe. He almost bowed to an Underfolk servant and caught himself just in time.

The only problem was, now that Tal was on the seventh level of the Violet Order, he didn't know where to find the Empress. After wandering around the most obvious corridors, he finally plucked up the courage to ask a Brilliance of the Indigo, who didn't seem in too much of a hurry, and whose Spiritshadow was not too frightening. Tal didn't know what it was, but it had four legs, a tail, and a head, and wasn't showing lots of teeth. This was a big improvement over some of the horrendous Spiritshadows he'd seen.

"The Empress?" replied the Brilliance. He seemed more amused than annoyed that an Orange boy should ask him such a question. "You seek an audience, I suppose?"

"Yes," said Tal. His shadowguard nodded, too.

The Brilliance laughed. Tal wasn't entirely sure why. Then he gave Tal directions to the Outer Antechamber and to the Imperial Guard. They would decide whether or not to let Tal in.

Tal thanked the Brilliance properly, bowing deeply and giving light. The Brilliance was equally courteous, but he laughed again as Tal walked away.

Without the directions, Tal would never have found the Outer Antechamber. He had to go through several empty rooms and up some more stairs, leading him even higher than the Seventh Violet. Finally, he came to a much larger room, where several people were lounging about on chairs, drinking and talking.

All their talk stopped as Tal came into the room. Their Spiritshadows leaped up at once, and so did two of the Chosen. They were all of the Violet Order, Tal saw, but he didn't recognize the insignia they wore. They each had violet bands on their white robes, and wore gold bracers with blazing suns on them, chains of gold filigree, and many Sunstones.

Strangely, their Spiritshadows were all the same, which was unusual except in the case of twins or very close siblings. The Spiritshadows were tall, vaguely manlike creatures, but very broad-shouldered and with impossibly thin waists almost like spinning tops. They had no necks, and their broad heads seemed to be largely made up of enormous mouths. They also had four arms.

It wasn't until Tal saw that all the Chosen were wearing swords that he realized this must be the Imperial Guard that the Brilliance had told him about. Or some of them, anyway.

Tal bowed and offered light. His shadowguard sat at his feet, once again assuming the shape of an inoffensive Dattu.

"I am Ethar, Guardian of Her Majesty, Shadowlord of the Violet," said one of the guards, a tall woman who looked about the same age as Tal's mother. "What are you doing here?"

Tal straightened up from his bow, but still kept his eyes down at the floor. Suddenly he had a feeling that this was not his brightest idea. There was no one else here, apart from the guards. Maybe he should have gone somewhere else. Maybe the Indigo Brilliance had played a trick upon him.

"I . . . I wanted to see the Empress," Tal stuttered. The deluminents on his wrist jangled as he spoke, reminding him how close he already was to demotion to the Red, or worse. Perhaps he had just earned more deluminents by coming here.

"You want to see the Empress?" Ethar repeated grimly. She strode over to Tal, so she was looking down at him, her Spiritshadow close by, its four arms already stretching out as if it might grab Tal at any moment.

"Yes," said Tal. "I wanted to ask her for a new Sunstone for my family. We've lost our Primary Sunstone you see, because my father is missing —"

"What is your name?" Ethar interrupted.

"Tal Graile-Rerem," said Tal. "My father, Rerem, is a Shiner of the Fourth Circle. He . . . he was lost recently on a mission for the Empress."

Out of the corner of his eye, Tal saw that Ethar recognized his father's name, at least, because she looked back at the other guards for a second.

"So, Tal, why should we let you past to see the Empress?"

"Um, why?" repeated Tal. "Because I need your help?"

All the guards laughed at that, and Ethar took a step back, no longer so threatening. Her Spirit-shadow slid back, too, decreasing in size until it lay at her feet.

Tal let out a small sigh of relief. Whatever he'd said, they seemed friendlier now.

"It's not as easy as that," Ethar explained. "If you want to see the Empress, you must first ask the Seniors of your own Order, and gain passes from them. I don't suppose you've done that?"

"No," said Tal glumly. He thought of Shadow-master Sushin, Brightstar of the Orange Order. He would make sure Tal never got a pass. "I don't think they'd give me one."

The guards laughed again at that. Tal felt suddenly more angry than scared. Why was it so funny that his family was in trouble, and he was doing his best to help them?

"Well, since you're already here," Ethar said, a smile slowly spreading across her face. "I suppose we could play a game. If you win, we'll let you past. If you lose, you can . . . let me see . . . give me your Sunstone."

"What game?" whispered Tal. This was a chance,

it seemed. But if he lost his Sunstone, he would lose his shadowguard. He would no longer be a Chosen. He would have to join the Underfolk.

Ethar pointed to a side table, between two guards. Tal recognized the tabletop at once, for it was designed to be a game board. There was a row of seven rectangles cut into it around one half of the rim, a round circle of white marble in the middle, and another row of rectangles on the other side. A deck of large, pasteboard cards was on the circle of white marble.

"Beastmaker," said Ethar. "Do you accept the challenge?"

Tal knew how to play Beastmaker, though the sets were rare, since no one knew how to make either the cards or the battlecircle anymore. But Greatuncle Ebbitt had a set, and Tal had played quite often. Much more often than anyone would suspect of an Orange boy.

"Yes," said Tal, knowing that with one word he had sealed his fate. He would go on to see the Empress, or he would go down to join the Underfolk.

Everything depended on a single game of Beastmaker.

·CHAPTER·
EIGHT

Tal sat down at the game table, and Ethar sat opposite. Tal felt strangely calm now that he had accepted the challenge. He looked down at the seven rectangular depressions in the tabletop in front of him. He knew what they were, but he thought he'd pretend to know less about the game. That way Ethar might underestimate him.

"What order are these in again?" he asked, pointing to the rectangles.

"Head, Heart, Temper, Skin, Speed, Strength, and Special," said Ethar quickly.

Each rectangle would ultimately hold one card, and that card would specify the characteristics of the beast. The Strength card would determine the beast's strength, the Speed card would determine its quickness, and so on. When all the cards were in place and finalized, two five-inch-high beasts of solid light would be produced from the combined characteristics, to battle it out in the marble circle in the middle of the table. Whoever played their cards right and produced the victorious beast would win the game.

Each card could be changed twice by using light. So even when a card was in place, and your opponent could see it, it might still change. The trick of the game was to make the other player think you were making a certain sort of beast and then change it at the last moment by altering the cards that governed its seven characteristics.

There was also luck, of course. There were a hundred cards, but each player was only dealt seven, all of which had three possible variations.

Tal hoped that he would be lucky.

Another guard dealt the cards one at a time, as was the usual practice. Tal took his first card and felt the warmth. Beastmaker cards were somehow made with pinhead-sized Sunstones bonded to heavy pasteboard. The Sunstones made them warm, and also created very lifelike pictures of the beasts on the cards. Nearly all of the cards showed creatures from Aenir, plus a few other beasts that didn't seem to exist either in Aenir or the Castle.

Tal's first card was a Phalarope, a marine animal that floated around in the water and had thousands of poisonous tendrils. Its only real use was in the Special category, because then the made beast would have poisonous tendrils. Tal knew that this card would change to a Kurshken if he applied green light from his Sunstone. Kurshken were small but very smart and quick lizards, so would be good in either Speed or Head.

Unfortunately, Tal didn't know what the third variation of the card was. He had a faint memory that it might turn into a Hugthing under red light, but couldn't be sure. Hugthings were particularly nasty. They looked like a carpet of comfortable green moss, but could spring up and wrap themselves around you in an instant. For the game, a Hugthing card would be good in Skin or Strength.

"I will play first, if you like," said Ethar. This would give Tal a slight advantage, so he quickly nodded to say yes.

"Heart of a Borzog," announced Ethar, laying the card down on the second rectangle in front of her. Tal looked at the card, which showed a fearsome, semihuman, and very hairy creature roughly the size of three people across the shoulders. This was a good initial play. Borzogs would fight to the death, and beyond. Once they got a grip, they never let go, even when they were killed. Strong-hearted indeed.

"Um, err, Head of a . . . whatever this is . . ." announced Tal, playing the Phalarope into the Head rectangle. He was going to change it into a Kurshken later on, but he hoped Ethar would think he didn't know what he was doing.

"A Phalarope," said Ethar. She looked at the bulbous thing with its many tentacles and added, "It does look something like a giant brain."

"That's what I thought," said Tal, pretending he was relieved. "A giant brain. Perfect for the Head."

The other guard dealt them both another card. Tal picked his up slowly. At first, all he could see was a pair of red eyes in the card. Then he slowly became aware of an outline around them. The card was showing him something hidden in a cave or a hole, with only the eyes visible.

Then Tal remembered, and barely suppressed a shiver of horror. This card was of a Cavernmouth. They were horrible creatures in Aenir, who dug holes for themselves in the side of a mountain and then backed in and opened their enormous jaws. What he thought were glowing eyes were actually something like tonsils at the back of the thing's throat.

Whenever anything came close enough, the Cavernmouth's extendable jaws would snap out, grab its prey, and drag it inside to be slowly digested.

In the game of Beastmaker, the Cavernmouth card was unusual. It could be played in Speed, because its jaws were incredibly fast at snapping out. Or it could be played in Special, to give the created beast extendable jaws.

The variations were not so useful, or at least not as far as Tal knew. Orange light would turn the card into a Jorbit, which was a fairly fast, dim-witted nocturnal grass-eater. Violet light would change it to a Rorarch, one of the strange stone creatures of Aenir. This would seem useful in Skin, but actually the Rorarch was very brittle stone and could be broken into little pieces by a single, sharp blow. Tal didn't want the beast he made to shatter at the first hit, and he wasn't sure where else the Rorarch could be played.

"Speed of a Gorblag," said Ethar, playing a card that looked like a large, glowing blue toad that was too fat to do anything. But one of the variations of the Gorblag card was the incredibly zappy Fleamite, an insect that could move faster than a human eye could track it. Tal knew Ethar would change that card later on.

"Speed of a Cavernmouth," Tal countered, playing his card. He wouldn't be changing that. Even if Ethar did change her Speed card to the Fleamite, it wouldn't be much faster than a Cavernmouth.

"You have played before," remarked Ethar. "Few people remember the Cavernmouth can be played for Speed."

"I saw my great-uncle use it that way once," Tal said, still trying to give the impression he was an absolute beginner at Beastmaker.

The game moved more swiftly then. Within a few minutes, both Tal and Ethar had six of their seven rectangles filled with cards. If they filled the seventh, their beast would be made, without a chance to change any of the existing cards. Ethar had left her Strength rectangle empty, and Tal, the Temper.

As Tal had expected, Ethar started to change her cards instead of playing her seventh. With each change, Tal became more concerned. He was changing his, too, but he wasn't sure he was going to end up with the better beast.

"You hid your skill well," said Ethar as she changed the mild-mannered Klatha workbeast in her Temper rectangle to the insanely vicious Vengenarl, a creature that attacked even its own kind if they trespassed over its scent-marked boundaries.

Tal nodded, but he wasn't paying attention to what Ethar said. Everything depended on him getting the best beast. Now that Ethar had changed the Temper of her beast, Tal thought he knew what to play there. But once he put that card down, his beast would be complete. Did he need to make any changes?

Quickly, he scanned the seven rectangles. Head of a Kurshken. Skin of a Samheal Semidragon. Temper . . . that was to come. Heart of a Hrugen, which was a gamble, since that was actually a kind of weed that never gave up, it grew everywhere in Aenir and seemingly could not be eradicated. Speed of a Cavernmouth. Strength of a Jarghoul, a cannibalistic strangling snake of the jungles of Aenir that primarily ate others of its own kind after weeks-long battles to crush one another to death; Special, the ability of the Gossamer Bug to fly.

Tal ran over all the variations in his head, while Ethar arched her fingers into a steeple and waited for his move.

"To see the Empress, or lose your Sunstone," she said, "what is it to be?"

"Temper of an Icefang," said Tal, playing his final card, locking all the others in. This was his greatest gamble. He didn't know enough about this card or its properties. But he remembered Great-uncle Ebbitt saying that the Icefangs of Aenir were among the most dangerous of creatures in the spirit world. They never got angry, or demoralized, or had any emotions at all, it seemed. They just coldly fought to the very best of their ability, never distracted by danger, wounds, or anything else.

"And Strength of a ... Jarghoul," said Ethar, playing exactly the same card as Tal. "Let the battle begin!"

·CHAPTER·
ПІПЄ

Both Tal and Ethar stepped back from the table as the final cards were played. Although no one knew how to make Beastmaker boards anymore, everyone had heard about the one that exploded years before, every Sunstone in it suddenly igniting.

But this Beastmaker board seemed to work perfectly. The cards in their rectangles began to slowly glow brighter and brighter, and a luminous mist formed on each side of the table. Then the two clouds of mist drifted across to the battlecircle in the middle of the table and began to form into shapes.

Tal held his breath, wondering what his beast would look like. Inside his head, he urged the formless lump of bright mist on, willing it to be the best beast ever made, a champion that would win his entry to see the Empress. Soon, all his troubles could be over!

Then his cloud of bright mist solidified into a brightly colored beast. It was tall and slender and had the general shape of a lizard, except it stood up on its hind legs and had wings. Its skin was scaly and iridescent, sparkling in many different colors. Its huge, delicate-looking wings were also multi-colored and almost translucent.

It was pretty. It was even beautiful. But didn't look at all tough or dangerous.

Tal let out his breath in disappointment and shut his eyes. He didn't want to look at the opposing beast, which had also solidified out of the glowing ball of mist on the other side of the circle.

"Interesting," said Ethar in a puzzled tone. Tal opened one eye a fraction. Ethar's beast was really ugly. It resembled a blubbery, rust-colored ball that had three arm-legs coming out the top and three out the bottom. It had four pairs of eyes spaced around its middle, and a separate, many-toothed mouth under each pair of eyes.

As Tal watched, it flipped over onto its top legs and then flipped back again, very quickly. Then it deliberately fell back and actually bounced high into the air, without using its arm-legs at all.

Tal's beast just watched the bouncy ball thing and stood there, its wings flickering like a hummingbird's. It was only when Tal looked closely that he realized it wasn't standing — it was hovering an inch above the white marble of the battlecircle.

The battlecircle began to change color from white marble to red, the sign that the combat would commence. Tal took a step closer, as did Ethar and all the guards, who crowded around.

Quickly, Tal looked over at Ethar's cards, hoping he would see some flaw that his beast would exploit.

Ethar had played the Head of a Dofyn, which was fairly standard play, since the Dofyns were the enormously clever sea dwellers of Aenir. Then the Heart of a Niphrain Ape. The Temper of a Vengenarl. The Skin of a Blorem, which as far as Tal could remember would give the beast a skin of very resilient, thick blubber. The Speed of a Fleamite. The Strength of a Jarghoul. And finally, the Special of a Urglegurgle. Tal had no idea what that was, but now that he'd seen the made beast, he figured it had to be bouncing.

The battlecircle flashed red three times. On the third flash, Tal's lizard suddenly shot forward, just as Ethar's blubber-tub bounced. They met in a whirring of wings, teeth, and clawed arms — or legs — and parted just as quickly.

"By the Light!! A hit!" cried Ethar, pointing to the drops of bright emerald green blood that were welling out of the lizard-beast's forearms.

"Mine, too," said Tal, pointing at some ugly gashes in the blubber of the bouncing beast. But his heart sank, for the blubber was very thick and the gashes did not look deep.

Before Tal had finished speaking, the blubber-tub attacked again, acting on its Vengenarl temper. This time, the lizard-beast didn't meet it, but flew to one side, zipping and darting around in the air as the blubber-tub bounced and lunged, reaching out its multiple arm-legs to grab and rend.

The lizard-beast was too quick to be caught, but the blubber-tub was also too quick for it to easily strike. They bounced and flew, feinting attacks and withdrawals, moving so swiftly it was almost impossible to follow.

Then the lizard-thing suddenly swooped in and bit out the blubber-tub's eye. It shrieked in rage, the first sound either beast had made, and one of its three-fingered limbs gripped the very edge of the lizard-beast's wing.

There was a tearing sound, and part of the wing came off. The lizard-beast leaped back, but clearly it could no longer fly.

"No!" Tal groaned.

The lizard-beast made a yipping sound to taunt the blubber-tub on, as if it didn't care about its torn wing. The blubber-tub, its eye socket bleeding, threw itself back and then bounced forward to crush its opponent.

But even without wings, the lizard-beast was very fast. It zipped sideways, and a claw struck in to take out another of the blubber-tub's eyes. Furious, the great ball of blubber changed direction to hurl itself at the rainbow-colored lizard.

Once again, the lizard-beast got out of the way, just in time. Then it suddenly moved back, as the blubber-tub was changing direction, and bit the bulbous creature on the foot.

"Yes!" shouted Tal, punching the air. The lizard had bitten clean through the blubber-tub's leg, severing the foot.

It still had two on that side, though, and one of the other legs swung across, smacking the lizard in the head. The brightly colored beast was thrown halfway across the circle by the blow and seemed to be stunned. It lay there, unmoving, while the blubber-tub did a flip to get back on the three good legs on its other side.

"Get up! Go, lizard!" yelled Tal.

"Kill it!" shouted Ethar. The other guards

shouted, too, some encouraging Tal's beast, some encouraging Ethar's.

Slowly and murderously, the blubber-tub advanced on the motionless lizard. Then it started to bounce. A small bounce, then a slightly harder one, until it was bounding up a quarter stretch or more. With each bounce, it got closer and closer to the defenseless lizard. It clearly intended to crush Tal's beast to death.

Tal looked on, horrified. Even though the creatures were only created things of magical light, he couldn't bear to see his lizard killed. He stopped thinking about everything that depended on this little beast of many colors. He just wanted it to survive.

As the blubber-tub shot up for what had to be its final bounce, Tal shut his eyes. He felt sick. Everything was over now.

Suddenly the guards roared, but it was a shout of surprise, not triumph, from Ethar. Tal's eyes flashed open and saw the lizard-beast flying around a stunned blubber-tub, darting in to pluck out its eyes one by one.

"What happened?" he asked one of the guards who had been betting on his lizard.

"It tricked the blubber-thing," said the guard happily. "That lizard's got four or five layers of wing. It could still fly, and it wasn't knocked out. Smart beast, kid."

But despite losing more of its eyes, the battle was not yet over for the blubber-tub. It had the Heart of a Niphrain Ape, so it could not give up. Bleeding from a dozen wounds, it lurched after the lizard, chasing it around and around the battlecircle.

"Only a matter of time now, boy," said the friendly guard. "Well —"

Whatever the guard was going to say stopped in his throat, as the far door suddenly swung open with the screech of disused hinges. Like everyone else, Tal looked over.

Something huge and very, very dark was coming through the door. A Spiritshadow, Tal realized, but one bigger than he'd ever seen. Its head was all spikes and flanges, as wide and tall as the door, so it struggled to get through. A sinuous neck followed, but whatever body lay behind was too big, unless the Spiritshadow chose to shrink it.

Suddenly Tal realized he was the only one still standing up. All the guards had fallen to their knees and were bowing in the Spiritshadow's direction.

Tal stood there gawping, till his shadowguard reached up and pulled him down by the front of his tunic.

Only then did he realize what . . . or who . . . this Spiritshadow was. It had to be Sharrakor the Mighty, the Empress's own Spiritshadow. The Shadow-dragon that alone among its kind had a name.

Sharrakor's vast head reared up on its serpentine neck, and its jaws opened. Tal saw teeth of shadow, and swirling patterns of darkness.

Then Sharrakor spat a great glob of shadow that fizzed through the air, straight at Tal!

·CHAPTER·
TEN

Tal ducked, but the shadowspit wasn't aimed at him anyway. It struck the Beastmaker table. There was a flash of light, a sudden sizzling noise, and the still battling lizard-beast and blubber-tub were gone.

Tal looked at the empty battlecircle, where small shadows ran like water over the side of the table and onto the floor. He cringed as several shadow patches flowed past him, back toward Sharrakor. Tal realized, shivering, that the Spiritshadow had spat some portion of itself. Now all those small shadows were rejoining the whole.

Tal cleared his throat, about to protest the Spirit-shadow's destruction of the game, but his shadow-guard leaped up and thrust itself into his mouth, an instant gag. Tal reached up to pull it free, but the friendly Imperial Guard gripped him as well so he couldn't move.

The last pieces of shadowspit rejoined Sharrakor. The Shadowdragon's head swung slowly from side to side, as if seeking another target. Then it slowly withdrew back the way it had come. When it had fully withdrawn, the door creaked shut behind it.

Tal's shadowguard dropped out of his mouth, and the Imperial Guards visibly relaxed.

"What —" Tal began to say, but he got no further. The friendly guard and Ethar picked him up and practically threw him out the other door.

"Go!" said the friendly guard. "Go!"

"But I won!" Tal protested. "At least my beast was winning!"

"We should not have played," said Ethar, frowning. "It was my mistake, so you shall not be punished further."

"But I —" said Tal.

"Sharrakor came because the Empress did not like an Orange boy in the Upper Violet," said Ethar roughly. She pushed Tal quite hard in the chest, sending him staggering back, his shadowguard trying to hold him up around the legs. "Go back down, boy!"

Tal stared at her for a moment, furious at being cheated. But what he saw in Ethar's eyes was not anger, or loathing, but fear. The friendly guard was afraid, too.

"I'll be back," muttered Tal. "I'll see the Empress! I'll get my Sunstone!"

Then his courage failed him, for whatever scared two Shining Ones of the Violet was more than enough to scare Tal. He turned around and ran, back down the stairs to the normal Violet levels, then in a rush to the laundry chute.

Tal rode the chute all the way down forty-eight levels, from Seventh Violet to First Red. The leather soles of his shoes were smoking when he finally stopped.

He had come so close to winning the game of Beastmaker, to being let through to see the Empress.

But, Tal thought miserably, he hadn't won. He hadn't gotten a new Sunstone. All his plans had come to nothing and he had no new ideas. He thought of his mother, sleeping the sleep of sickness in her sunchamber. Of Gref trying to escape the blinding lights of Lectorium bullies. Of Kusi, who was too young to understand, but still cried because she knew everyone else was upset. And of his father, lost somewhere in the dark, trusting that Tal was looking after the family.

Great-uncle Ebbitt was his last hope. Surely Ebbitt would think of something.

The wardrobe of white bone was gone, though it had been there only that morning. It seemed such a long time ago, because so much had happened. Not for the first time, Tal wondered how Ebbitt moved everything around so quickly.

Tal moved cautiously through the furniture. He wasn't in the mood for one of Ebbitt's practical jokes, particularly since they often involved some sort of mild injury.

But his great-uncle was clearly in sight when Tal rounded a marble statue of a Chosen, caught forever in the stance of a light-sculptor, Sunstone at the ready. That was a good sign. When Ebbitt hid, the practical jokes were always much worse.

Coincidentally, the old man was sitting by a Beastmaker table, idly shuffling the cards. He got up as Tal approached.

"How was the Achievement?" he asked. "I heard it was a superb performance."

"I got the Yellow Ray of Failed Ambition," said Tal sullenly.

"I didn't ask about your results," snapped Ebbitt. "You would never be properly rewarded with Sushin as one of the judges."

"But why?" Tal sat down in a convenient but too large chair, and rested his head in his hands. "Everything I do, there seems to be someone against me!"

"Probably because there is," Ebbitt observed. "Sushin for one. He's always hated your father for besting him in the Achievement of Combat. Eight times, I believe, over the years. But he wouldn't dare act alone. I'm afraid that someone higher up has taken a dislike to our family."

"Who?" asked Tal.

"I don't know," said Ebbitt. Without warning, he suddenly pursed his lips and whistled a complicated birdcall, then cocked his head as if expecting a reply. When none came, he continued. "But I'll find out. Now, where have you been? The Achievement finished hours ago."

"I went to see the Empress —"

"You what?!" exclaimed Ebbitt.

"But the guards wouldn't let me in," Tal continued. "Ethar said she would if I won a game of Beast-maker, and I was winning, but then Sharrakor —"

"Sharrakor!" exclaimed Ebbitt, gripping his white hair and doing a strange, frenzied dance across to Tal.

"Sharrakor came in and spat on the game and the

beasts disappeared," said Tal. "Then Ethar and another guard kicked me out."

"Thank the Sun and the Stars and all things of Light," said Ebbitt, sinking to his knees. "Don't you know anything, boy? You must never, ever go to the Empress without permission!"

"I just wanted to get a Sunstone," Tal said wearily. It seemed he couldn't do anything right. "I have to get a Sunstone somehow. I've asked the cousins, and tried to win an Achievement, and tried to see the Empress. I can't think of anything else."

"Why not?" said Ebbitt. "You are my grand-nephew, aren't you? You must have inherited some of my tremendous thinking power."

"I don't know," said Tal. He wasn't sure Ebbitt had all that great thinking power. He had lots of weird thought power, but that wasn't the same.

"Where can you find Sunstones?" asked Ebbitt. "Sunstones that no one owns yet. Lots and lots of lovely Sunstones, ripe for the taking."

"Nowhere," Tal replied glumly.

Ebbitt stretched out his hands toward the ceiling and capered around in a circle, singing, "Up in the Sun, the Glorious Sun, where Stone Fingers stretch and stretch, up through the darksome Veil!"

"You mean the Towers?" asked Tal, unable to believe what Ebbitt was suggesting.

"Yes," said Ebbitt. He stopped capering and knelt down next to Tal, suddenly serious. "It's dangerous, but I believe it is the only hope now. All the usual means of gaining a Sunstone will be blocked by Sushin or the Chosen he is in league with. You will have to climb one of the towers and steal a Sunstone. Steal several, while you're at it."

"Steal a Sunstone?" asked Tal. "But what about the guards, and the Spiritshadows, and the traps?"

"Try the Red Tower," said Ebbitt. "It will be the least protected. Your shadowguard looks pretty smart. It'll help you find the traps."

Tal looked at his shadowguard. It had taken a shape similar to Tal's natural shadow, but with the chest bravely puffed out. Obviously it thought stealing a Sunstone was a good idea.

"How would I start?" asked Tal. "I don't even know how to get outside."

"I know," said Ebbitt. "Underfolk ways, unseen by Chosen. I'll show you."

Tal stared at the old man, and then down at his puffed-up shadowguard. It sounded extremely risky, but he really couldn't think of anything else.

"All right," he said finally. "But first I want to go home and have a rest."

And, he thought, he could say good-bye to his mother, and Gref, and Kusi.

In case he didn't come back.

"Excellent!" exclaimed Ebbitt. "I'm sure you'll have lots of fun!"

PART TWO:

AFTER

·CHAPTER·
ELEVEΠ

"Lots of fun, lots of fun, lots of fun, lots of fun . . ."

Ebbitt's voice was echoing inside Tal's head, accompanied by a weird, really loud rushing noise. It was also incredibly cold and dark. For a few seconds, Tal thought that he was in the middle of an awful nightmare. Any moment now he would wake up, to the soft light of his sleeping chamber. . . .

But he was awake!

He had taken Ebbitt's advice. He had climbed the Red Tower. And he'd fallen off, right through the Veil. In just a few seconds he would hit the Castle roofs and that would —

Suddenly Tal realized that he wasn't falling down so much as sideways, like a feather blown on the wind. Something was also gripping him quite painfully around the chest and waist.

Tal craned his head around, but couldn't see. It was absolutely black, the darkest he had ever experienced. Dark so fearful that his hand automatically went to his Sunstone.

But it wasn't there. The chain was still around his neck, but the Sunstone itself seemed to have gone. Desperately, Tal pulled at the chain, hoping that his fingers would find the Sunstone.

But the chain was caught somehow. It wouldn't move. Tal tugged at it again, and light suddenly blossomed behind him. At the same time, there was a sound that Tal found unbelievably comforting — his shadowguard's warning hiss!

He craned his head back again and saw that his shadowguard was gripping him. It had made four arms to hold him tight, and a pair of very long, very thin wings. That was why he wasn't falling! He and the shadowguard were gliding on the wind.

Tal laughed, a crazy laugh of relief. He was speeding away from the Castle, carried by the wind, out into darkness. But he had his shadowguard, and he had his Sunstone — he hoped.

The laughter stopped as everything went black

again. Tal clutched at his chain. It was still there. He tugged on it, and the shadowguard hissed. Tal tugged again, and the shadowguard hissed louder.

Finally, Tal understood. The shadowguard must have formed around the Sunstone, drawing every little bit of the stone's light to make itself as big and strong as it could. All shadows needed light to exist. Without the Sunstone, the shadowguard would dissipate in this total darkness, under the Veil.

There was a lot of snow. Cold, wet lumps kept hitting Tal in the face. He had become totally soaked by them. He remembered blacking out, but not for how long. By the feel of his frozen hands and face, it had been for quite a long time.

He looked down. There was nothing to see but darkness, a dark so terrifying that Tal had to shut his eyes. It was better to pretend to be asleep than to look into a world without light.

In fact, Tal thought, maybe he was dead. This was what happened after life. There wasn't anything outside the Castle. He'd died and gone *somewhere else*. Perhaps he would fall forever. . . .

But he didn't feel like he was dead. He could feel his body, which was shivering with both cold and fear. He felt the shadowguard shift a little, try to flow around him to give him extra protection from the wind, but most of its shadowflesh was being used in the wings that kept them gliding.

On and on they flew. Tal lost track of time, and all feeling in his face and hands. He opened his eyes every now and then, blinking against the onrush of snow and ice, blinking away his own frozen tears. But there was still no sign of light.

Later, Tal was almost unconscious again and totally frozen. He thought he was going to die and that this horrible flight through darkness and snow would never end. Then he saw it. A bright glow somewhere ahead and below.

"The Castle!" Tal shouted, or tried to, but his lips were frozen together, and all that came out was a muffled cry.

The shadowguard tilted its wings, and they turned toward the distant light. Surely it was the Castle, Tal thought, not caring that the wind must have taken them away from his home. As far as he knew, there was nothing else in the whole Dark World. It had to be the Castle.

But as they flew closer, he became puzzled, his tired, frozen mind grappling with what he saw. The light was too small to be coming from the Castle, too feeble. There should be hundreds of lights, thousands of lights!

He was still wondering what it might be when the shadowguard suddenly hissed and flapped its wings in a frenzy, desperately trying to slow them down.

Three very long seconds later, Tal and his winged shadowguard plowed into the side of a hill, snow spraying out in all directions as they bored into a deep, wet drift.

·CHAPTER·
TWELVE

They went a long way into the drift. So far that Tal seriously thought he'd be smothered before he could claw his way back to the surface. At least the shadowguard had let go of his Sunstone, so he had some light and could tell which way was up.

Or so he thought. Being buried in the drift was a bit like being underwater. The cold, wet snow was all around him and kept getting in his mouth and nose every time he tried to breathe. The only way to move was to use a half-swimming, half-digging action.

Fortunately the Sunstone warmed him and lit his path. When Tal finally clambered out of the drift and staggered to a point where he was only up to his waist in snow, he held the Sunstone up and concentrated on it. It grew brighter, and waves of warm air flowed from it over Tal's hands and sopping wet clothes.

Tal groaned and grimaced as the warm air returned feeling to his frozen hands and face.

Tal stood there for what seemed like hours with the warm air flowing around him, as much as he could generate from the Sunstone. But he still couldn't get really warm. His shadowguard was draped across his shoulders like an extra cloak, but it didn't help.

Even worse than the cold was his sense of disorientation. There was nothing but snow around him, as far as his Sunstone's light fell. There were no other lights in the darkness.

It was a completely alien landscape, even stranger to Tal than the spirit world of Aenir. At least he had been there before and was trained to cope with it. He also knew how to leave Aenir. What if he was trapped in this cold wasteland forever?

The warmth of his Sunstone helped Tal think a little. It was familiar and comforting, even if did melt the snow around his legs and make them wetter as the rest of him got dry.

"I have to get back to the Castle," said Tal. Saying it aloud made it seem more likely that he would. On his shoulder, the shadowguard made itself a head and nodded in agreement.

Saying it was easier than doing it, Tal thought as he looked around. The Sunstone illuminated a small area around him, but even ten stretches away it was dark again. There was no sign of that other light he'd seen from above.

"Which way is the Castle?" he asked, hoping his shadowguard would know.

It shuffled on his shoulder and then extruded a thin, one-fingered arm that pointed off at a right angle.

"That way," said Tal. It looked the same as any other way. "How far?"

The shadowguard did not answer, but he felt it make a motion like a shrug. Tal thought about the question for a moment, then rephrased it. He was used to working at communication with the shadowguard. He often had to ask the same question several different ways.

"How far to the Castle in stretches?" asked Tal. Distances inside the Castle were measured in stretches. Tal knew his arm from shoulder to wrist was almost exactly one stretch. They didn't need a larger measure.

The shadowguard extended a hand and grew ten or twelve fingers, which it wiggled up and down too quickly to count.

"A long way," Tal translated. He knew it had to be, but he'd somehow hoped it wasn't. "Well, I guess I'd better start walking."

Following the direction the shadowguard had given, he started to push through the snow. It was hard work, harder than he expected. The snow was tightly packed, and though the envelope of warm air around him melted it a little, it was not enough to make walking easier.

After a few hundred stretches of this, Tal was exhausted. He'd started to sneeze, too, and could feel fluid spreading in his chest, making it harder to breathe. Back in the Castle, he would simply have gone to his parents, who could heal such simple ailments with their Sunstones. But Tal had not yet learned Healing and so could only suffer.

But he wouldn't give up. Far away, his mother lay ill in her bed. And what had happened to Gref? What if the Spiritshadow that had taken Gref was like the one that had attacked Tal above the Veil? Gref could be dead, or lying wounded somewhere. Tal had to get back as soon as he could.

After a while, the snow got shallower, and while

it was easier to walk through, Tal started to slip more often. He realized he was walking on ice, under a light dusting of snow.

"One, two, three . . ."

He started counting steps. Somewhere around a thousand, he lost track of what he was up to and had to start again. His shadowguard was also having to point out the right direction every few minutes, as Tal started to turn into a circle. Everything looked the same. Ice and more ice, with nothing to see.

He was up to one thousand and ninety-eight steps when he suddenly realized that while he was still counting aloud, his legs had stopped moving. In fact, he had fallen over in the snow, too weary to immediately realize what was going on.

The shadowguard was tugging at him, hissing, trying to lever him back up again. Tal laughed at its efforts, a hysterical laugh that surprised him, because what was happening was the exact opposite of funny. But he did get up, and staggered on a few steps, his laughter turning into a choking cough.

Then he saw the light. A strange, soft green light that was moving over the ice faster than he could run. For a moment he thought it was two enormous green eyes in the head of a huge monster, sprinting toward him.

Then, as it drew closer and slowed, he saw that the light was coming from a box that was being drawn across the ice, in harness, by six shaggy-haired, four-legged creatures with tall heads and spiky branches sticking out between what he presumed were ears.

The box was some sort of cart, Tal realized, like the ones the Underfolk used to move things around. But it had very long, thin sort of feet-things, Tal guessed, instead of wheels.

The soft green light came from the globes that were mounted on either side of the strange cart. They were made of tightly woven strips of bone, with the light coming through the gaps in the weave.

Then Tal noticed that there was someone in the contraption. For a second he felt incredible relief. It had to be some of the Underfolk. He'd never really understood where they got all the food and goods used by the Chosen. Obviously they came out here to get something. He would commandeer their strange transport and have them take him back to the Castle immediately.

"Thank the Light," he gasped, staggering forward, holding up his Sunstone, ready to show light and prove himself a Chosen.

The next thing he knew, he was facedown on the ice, with his shadowguard wrapped around his knees — just as a spear whistled through the air exactly where his head had been!

·CHAPTER· THIRTEEN

Tal's attacker made a horrible keening noise as Tal desperately rolled to the side. New energy came from pure fright, as he pushed himself up and tried to run away.

But the spear-thrower was in front of him. A short monster covered in furs, concealing everything of its form. Its face was totally white, as pale as bone, with hideous markings and deep-set yellow eyes. Its mouth was a round, dark hole.

It also had an ax, a great-bladed thing, not of metal, but some sort of carved bone or translucent stone.

Instinctively, Tal raised his Sunstone and directed a blast of white, hot light at the creature. It yowled like a cat, raised one arm to shield itself, and advanced on its hind legs, swinging the ax viciously from side to side.

Tal stumbled back, while trying to keep the light focused on the creature's eyes. But it had tucked its chin into its chest, avoiding the beam. Even like this, it still came on, howling and chopping with its ax, the blade cutting the air just in front of Tal as he retreated.

It would catch him soon. He was too tired to keep focusing on his Sunstone, and would slip. If he didn't do something else he would be chopped into bits.

The shadowguard realized that, too, and Tal felt it slip off his shoulders. It fell to the ground as a dark splotch, but was up again immediately, as a Corvile that dashed at Tal's attacker.

The creature, head down, didn't see it till it was too late. The shadowguard nipped at one knee, shadow-teeth ripping through fur and possibly the flesh underneath.

"Ow!" exclaimed the monster, sounding surprisingly human. "By the Crone, you'll pay for that!"

Tal almost stopped in surprise as he heard that voice. This wasn't a monster. It was a girl! The hideous face was a mask, with amber lenses in the eyeholes!

Girl or monster, she was still very dangerous. She saw Tal's surprise and lunged forward, the blunt end of her ax striking him in the stomach with a sickening thud. Winded, Tal crumpled to the ice, his light beam shooting off into the sky.

"No, no," he begged, holding up one hand as if he could ward off the ax blow that followed. "Don't kill me!"

"Die, thief!" she shouted in return. "This is Far-Raider's Ice!"

Everything seemed to happen in slow motion then. Tal saw the girl raise her ax high above her head, the blade glinting in the Sunstone's light. The shadowguard was wrapped around her leg, biting, but she paid it no attention.

Higher and higher the ax went, and Tal could hear the deep in-drawing of the girl's breath as she prepared for a blow that would cut him in half.

Then, even as the ax came swinging down, someone else shouted. The loud, commanding voice of a woman who was used to being obeyed.

"Milla! Stop!"

But the call came too late to stop the ax. Tal stared at it, mesmerized, the moment of its fall drawn out into what seemed like a whole lifetime of terror.

In the very last fragment of a second, Milla's wrists twitched, and the ax smashed into the ground by Tal's head, smashing chips of ice all over his face.

He lay there, stunned, as the girl slid back her mask to reveal a pale, oval-shaped face and striking green eyes. But there was a spark there of extreme anger, and her cheeks were flushed with emotion.

"Don't think you'll live, shadow-eater," she growled, bending down so her face was close to Tal's, so close he could feel the heat coming off her skin. "The Crone will deliver you to me. We will fight again."

Then she stalked off, out of Tal's sight. His shadowguard came slinking back, to wrap around his neck. It seemed to be quite pleased to get away from this mad girl, too.

Tal kept lying still. It seemed to be the best thing to do, to gather his strength. He still had his Sunstone, and could use that better now that he was not surprised. He could see that the girl had only a natural shadow. She wasn't a Chosen, which meant that he had been right in guessing the Underfolk came out here, or once did. This girl did not look anything like any Underfolk he had ever seen. Her face was pale but red-cheeked, her hair white-blond, and her eyes piercingly green. Tal had never seen hair that color, and he realized he had never seen an Underfolk's eyes. They always kept their faces lowered.

He was still lying there when whoever had called out came to look down at him. This was an older woman, her mask already off. She had different clothing though, softer-looking furs. Tal realized Milla had some sort of armor on as well, but this woman didn't. She didn't have an ax, either.

"Get up," said the woman. "Or I'll have Milla cut you into pieces and feed you to the Wreska."

Tal got up. As his shadowguard moved, the woman stepped back, sucking air between her teeth.

"What is that?" she asked.

Tal thought for a moment, unsure of how to respond. These people, with their natural shadows, had to be some sort of Underfolk. There was only one way to treat Underfolk, and that was to give them orders. Possibly they still hadn't realized he was a Chosen!

"My shadowguard," said Tal proudly. "I am Tal Graile-Rerem, of the Orange Order of the Chosen of the Castle. Who are you?"

This seemed to be the wrong thing to say. Milla,

who had been walking away, suddenly turned with a growl and hefted her ax. But the older woman raised her hand, and the warrior girl stopped.

"He does not know our ways," said the woman. "A strange thing to find upon the ice. There is much here that we should know."

She paused, thinking, then said, "I am the Crone of the Far-Raider Clan of the Icecarls. That is Milla, who wishes to be a Shield Maiden, and may yet be. You will come with us back to the ship, Tal Graile-Rerem."

She pronounced his name strangely, and Tal didn't like the way she spoke to him at all. She only had a native shadow, after all.

"You will take me to the Castle," he commanded. "At once."

His voice quavered, and it sounded weak even to him. The business about showing Underfolk who was the boss clearly didn't work here. These Underfolk were feral. They might do anything.

"Um, please," he added, his voice breaking completely.

The Crone looked at him, then turned toward Milla. Tal didn't see what she did, but Milla pulled something out from under her furs. A flat, curved bone that she held by one end.

Tal was still wondering what it was when it hit him in the head and knocked him unconscious.

As Tal fell, his shadowguard caught him and lowered him down. Before it could do anything else, the Crone sprang on it, holding open the mouth of a large bag. She scooped up lots of snow, but also scooped up the shadowguard.

The shadowguard started to ooze through the tough Selski skin of the bag, but again the Crone was ready. She tucked Tal's Sunstone into his shirt, hiding its light.

"Without light, the shadow that walks alone cannot prosper," she announced in the darkness. "This is known to the Crones, Milla. I shall follow your sleigh, not too close, for fear the light will awaken it."

"Do I have to take that?" asked Milla petulantly, pointing at Tal.

"Yes," said the Crone. "And be quick. He is only a boy, and he has the wet sickness in his lungs. We must get him to the ship before a death sets upon him."

"I shall set his death," whispered Milla. She grunted as she picked up his arms and started to drag him back to her sleigh. "If he'd been a normal raider I would be wearing my first winner-sign by sleeptime!"

"But he is not a raider of any kind, normal or not," said the Crone. Her eyes seemed to shine in the darkness, though the lights on the sleigh were too far away for any reflection. "Quickly, child! Do I have to tell you everything twice?!"

·CHAPTER·
FOURTEEN

Tal slowly regained consciousness. His hearing came back first, his ears filled with strange sounds. There was a faint humming all around, and a crunching sound, that welled up through his bones.

He opened his eyes and they swam into focus. It wasn't dark, for which he was very thankful. Good Sunstone light fell on his face, bright and warm. But there was other light, too, around the edges. Soft, green light.

Tal's head hurt. So did just about every other part of him. He was warm though, thanks to the furs that someone had put on him while he was unconscious. It felt strange to have so much weight on him, but given the temperature, it was welcome.

He sat up, coughed, and looked around.

He was on the deck of a vessel of some kind, a

very large one, with three masts, well over a hundred stretches long and twenty wide. This was obviously the ship the Crone had talked about. Tal knew about boats and ships from Aenir, but this ship was sailing across the ice. Tal had no idea how it managed to slide so easily.

The sails above him were full, moving the ship along faster than Tal would have been able to run. The humming came from the wind in the rigging. The crunching, cutting sound came from a vibration that he could feel right through the deck, something to do with the way the ship moved.

Tal guessed that it was like Milla's weird cart-thing drawn by the — what were they? — Wreska. This ship was driven by the wind, but it must be supported on similar long, thin rails that cut into the ice.

There were people moving around on the deck. More Underfolk, with normal shadows. They all wore furs and skins, and most had vicious-looking weapons. None of them seemed at all interested in Tal.

He stared at them. They were like Beastmaker cards come to life, or illustrations from a story. Tal was tempted to touch one to see if that really was hair all the way down to his waist. The lump on his head told him that would not be a good idea.

The familiar light came from what had to be a large Sunstone, somewhere up above. Tal squinted and saw that it was somehow attached to the very top of the tallest mast, the middle one. A powerful Sunstone indeed, or perhaps a cluster of stones, for it illuminated not only all the ship, but the ice for several hundred stretches around.

But for all its power, there was something wrong with the Sunstone, Tal saw. The light flickered, instead of being true and strong, and the color changed a little every time the ship rocked or hit a bump.

The green light came from more of the tightly woven globes that Tal had seen before. One was quite close, so he got up and looked at it. As he'd thought, it was made of thin strips of something like bone, woven so there were tiny holes in the weave. Something buzzed around inside and created the green light.

"Moths," said a voice behind him. "Luminous moths."

Tal turned around. It was the old woman, the one who'd called herself the Crone. She was holding a pottery urn. Tal's eyes were instantly drawn to it, and he felt a wave of dizziness. For a second, it felt like he was inside the urn, unable to get out. At the same moment, he realized that his shadowguard was nowhere to be seen. Both things made him feel like throwing up.

"Your shadow is trapped in here," said the Crone, noticing Tal's frantic glances all around him. "It shall be released, if we decide to let you live."

"You wouldn't dare kill me," exclaimed Tal hotly. "You're Underfolk! The Chosen and their Spirit-shadows will . . . will kill everyone on this ship if you do!"

The Crone didn't say anything, but she kept looking at him. Her eyes were luminous, Tal realized, bright with some internal light that was not reflected. He felt them boring into him, as if the Crone could read his mind.

After a minute, Tal looked away and said, "I suppose they wouldn't, actually. They don't even know where I am. None of us ever leave the Castle anyway."

"But *you* have," said the Crone. "Tell me of this Castle, and why you have come here, to the hunting grounds of the Far-Raiders."

Tal wiped his nose with his sleeve. He was still

having difficulty coping with the fact that these people — who he *hoped* were Underfolk — could decide whether he lived or died. But there didn't seem to be any choice.

"Here," said the Crone. She set the urn down, close to Tal, and pulled a small wooden bottle out of her furs. Tal took it suspiciously, but drank. As the liquid went down his throat, he felt it spread warmth.

Slowly, occasionally sipping from the bottle, Tal began to talk. The Crone interrupted him from time to time, asking questions, but mostly she just let him talk. Tal was surprised to find himself saying so much. He even told the Crone about his father's disappearance, and his mother being sick, and how worried he was about what might have happened to Gref, which was probably his fault, too.

By the time he finished, a whole crowd of Icecarls was listening. Most of them were pretending to be doing something else, like coiling rope or looking overboard. Some just stood, or sat, and listened. They did not seem hostile.

Except for Milla, who Tal realized had been above him, up the mast, all along. Listening and watching, ready to drop on him if he attacked the Crone.

"A fine story, there," said one of the Icecarls, a

huge man with a beard dyed blue and plaited into three strands. "Do you have any others, boy?"

Tal stared at him. Clearly the man thought he'd made it all up.

"It's true," he protested. "I am one of the Chosen. I come from the Castle."

The Icecarl chuckled and said, "You'd not be the first boy who lost his ship and went storytelling around the Clans. But if you're not a storyteller, you must be a thief on our hunting grounds."

A murmur went around the crowd of Icecarls at the word *thief*. Tal felt a new hostility directed at him. Whatever these people did to thieves, it couldn't be good.

"If he is a thief, Forkbeard," the Crone said, "you can give him to the ice, and the Merwin will take him."

"I'm not a thief!" exclaimed Tal. "And I am telling the truth. I'll prove it to you!"

He pointed up to the flickering Sunstone, past Milla's scowling face. She spat downwind, a clear indication of her opinion of Tal's truthfulness.

"Your Sunstone must once have given a clear, steady light," he said. "Now it flickers and changes color."

"Any fool knows that!" said Forkbeard. He looked

angry now and was stroking his ax. "Any fool who's seen a Sunstone, though there's few enough around the Clans. Give him to the ice, I say!"

"But I can fix it," stammered Tal. "It just needs tuning."

"Good," said the Crone. "I was hoping you would say that. If you can mend our Sunstone, we will spare your life."

"If he can't mend it, can I fight him?" asked Milla. She dropped down from the mast, landing lightly on her feet. Tal instinctively moved back, closer to the urn with his shadowguard in it.

"No," said the Crone, her voice stern. "If he fails, he goes to the ice — and the Merwin."

·CHAPTER·
FIFTEEN

Tal had expected the Icecarls to bring the Sunstone down to him. But the Crone explained that they only did that when the ship was anchored. They needed the Sunstone's light to see any dangers that might lie ahead.

When Tal refused to climb, Milla took special delight in describing exactly what a Merwin was, and Tal's chances of surviving a meeting with one.

"Most Merwin are about ten times as long as you are tall," she said. "They have a single, shining horn that sticks out the front between their eyes. See Kral over there? That sword of his is a baby Merwin's horn. They stop glowing once they're dead. Now, the Merwin slide over the ice faster than you'd be able to run, because their skin is so slick, and they've got four big flippers to push themselves along. Mostly they stick their horn through whatever they're after, and then they bash it up and down on the ice. You'd be better off fighting me. All you have to do is ask. If you ask to fight me, the Crone will let you."

Tal ignored her. He didn't understand why she was so keen to fight him, but he knew that the Crone would protect him . . . as long as he fixed the Sunstone.

"I'll need my shadowguard," he said. "I need it to help me climb and fix the Sunstone."

The Crone looked at him again with those creepy, glowing eyes. Then she said, "No you don't."

Tal sighed. He didn't really, absolutely need his shadowguard, but he felt very strange without it nearby, dizzy and sick to his stomach. Climbing the mast would be ten times as hard without the shadow-guard, even if it just followed him like a normal shadow.

"Milla will help you climb up," said the Crone.

"I will not!" exclaimed Milla. "He's a lying thief! You cannot believe his talk of hundreds of lights and this 'castle' thing —"

The Crone turned her gaze to the girl and said,

"You wish to be a Shield Maiden, Milla, but you won't follow orders?"

The threat was clear. Tal didn't know what a Shield Maiden was, but Milla obviously really wanted to be one, and the Crone had the power to stop her.

Milla turned to Tal with a murderous scowl on her face and said, "All right! Start climbing, thief!"

"My name is Tal Graile-Rerem," Tal said. "I shall permit you to call me Tal. And even if I was a thief, you don't have anything I'd want to steal!"

At least, he told himself, he wasn't a thief as far as the Icecarls were concerned.

"Tal, Smal, Bal, Wal — whatever you call yourself," Milla said. "I don't suppose you can climb a line, so we'll have to go up the mast itself."

She pointed at the spikes that were stuck into the mast every stretch or so. Tal went over and put his foot on one, testing its strength. Then he reached up and started to climb.

The mast appeared to be a single bone of some kind, though Tal couldn't imagine what kind of monster would have a backbone forty stretches long. And the handholds weren't spikes as he'd thought. They were smaller bones that had been sawn off. Once they would have been like the bones of a fish, curving out from the backbone.

"Hurry up," called Milla from below.

Tal ignored her. The mast was swaying, and the ship and the ice seemed a long way down. For some weird reason it was scarier than when he climbed the Red Tower, though that was hundreds of times as high. Perhaps it was because there was no shadowguard to save him.

Milla kept harassing him all the way to the top, calling out and trying to crowd him. Tal focused his mind on climbing and ignored her.

Finally, Tal came to the Sunstone. It was held to the top of the mast by what seemed like large, curved teeth that were somehow bonded to the bone. The stone was so bright Tal had difficulty looking at it without his shadowguard to automatically shield his eyes.

Milla fell silent as they approached the stone. She also stopped several stretches below, instead of crowding Tal as she'd done all the way up. Her head was bowed. Clearly she couldn't stand the brightness of the Sunstone, not this close.

This high up the mast, Tal had the strange illusion that he was still, and it was the ship and the ice below that swung from side to side like a pendulum. Each time the world swung by, Tal had to fight back the feeling that he was going to fly off into space.

To make it even worse, he had to let go one of his handholds to touch the Sunstone. It was a powerful stone, but Tal knew it was also very old. Sunstones did wear out eventually, and had to be taken up to a Tower to be revitalized above the Veil.

Making sure he had a good grip with his left hand, Tal reached out and touched the Sunstone. He could feel the currents of power within it. Just as he learned in the Lectorium, Tal closed his eyes and focused his thought upon the Sunstone.

As he'd thought, it badly needed tuning. What power it had left was working against itself, rather than together. The energy bands needed to be re-aligned, brought back into harmony.

Tal carefully let go of the big Sunstone and reached into his shirt to pull his own Sunstone out. It brightened as he focused upon it, to find the correct pattern of energies and project it at the Icecarls' Sunstone.

It was hard work with the wind all around, and the mast swaying, and his stomach suddenly deciding it didn't like the Crone's warming cordial after all. But

Tal did it. A beam of pure light shot out of his Sunstone and into the Icecarls' larger stone.

"I've done it!" exclaimed Tal triumphantly. The Icecarls' stone shone bright and true.

Then it went out, and so did Tal's own stone, leaving him in total darkness, save the faint green glow of the moth-lamps on the deck far below.

·CHAPTER·
SIXTEEN

The roar of anger that came up from the deck was almost animal in its intensity. Tal had never heard anything like it. He glanced down, but couldn't see anything, not even Milla. Still, he could hear what was happening.

Every Icecarl aboard was leaping onto the ropes and rigging, climbing up to kill the boy who had ruined their Sunstone, their greatest treasure.

Tal's only hope was to get it going again. Unfortunately, he didn't even know why it had gone out.

Desperately, he grabbed his own Sunstone, no longer caring if he fell off. He focused on it, feeling for its power. It felt like his whole body and mind was bent on this one thing, every particle of his power concentrated on one small stone.

The power was still there, Tal perceived. But it

had somehow retreated into the depths of the stone. He had to bring it out, open it up, before Milla threw him off the mast. As he thought that, Tal felt her hand grip his ankle. Her fingers tightened, ready to pull him away.

"Light begets light," Tal heard his father's voice say, echoing up from the depths of his memory. That was one of the first lessons learned by every Chosen. Tal had heard it on his father's knee, when he was no older than Kusi was now.

Light begets light.

But he had no light. Milla was prying his foot away from the mast. He had to create some light to restart the Sunstones. He had to do something!

One foot came free, and Milla gave a shout of triumph. Tal kicked at her, but that made his position even worse. He slipped down a rung, and the chain around his neck broke. He still held the Sunstone, but that left only one hand for the mast.

"Quick as a Sunstone spark," said another voice in his mind. Great-uncle Ebbitt's voice. "Quick as a Sunstone spark."

"Light!" screamed Tal. Balancing solely on one foot, he struck the two Sunstones together. A huge spark shot out as they met, and all of a sudden his Sunstone burst back into glorious light. A moment later, so did the Icecarls' stone. It was brighter than it had been before, and the color was even, without flickering.

Milla put the foot she held back onto a rung and silently began to climb back down.

Tal looked and saw Icecarls everywhere, dropping back down onto the deck. He swallowed and took several very slow breaths.

"Thank you, Father," he whispered to the wind. "Thank you, Great-uncle Ebbitt."

Then he slowly climbed down, too. It had been a narrow escape.

On the deck, the Crone was waiting. Forkbeard stood next to her, his ax in its sheath upon his back.

"You have done as you said," she said. "So we will do likewise. We will not give you to the ice."

Tal nodded. Then, without knowing why he bothered to tell her more, he said, "I've only mended it for a while. The Sunstone is old. It will fade in time, and there is nothing I can do to make it last longer."

"Yes," said the Crone. "It is known that Sunstones die, as do all things upon the ice. But you have helped us now."

"And you have shown that I accused you falsely!" said Forkbeard. He raised his voice and added, "I,

Grim Forkbeard, say it so all can hear. You spoke truly, Tal. To mend my wrong, I . . . I offer to adopt you as my son and take you into the Clan of the Far-Raiders, blood and bone."

Tal stared at him. Obviously these people weren't really Underfolk, so the offer wasn't a complete insult.

But I don't want to be adopted; I have to get back home!

He started to answer, then saw the Crone narrow her eyes at him, as if in unspoken warning.

That made him think, and pause. Among these savages, Grim Forkbeard seemed quite important. He was also extremely large and fierce-looking. It was best to be polite to him, even if he wasn't one of the Chosen.

"I thank you, Grim Forkbeard," he said, bowing and raising his Sunstone, though he only let it spark out a little light. "But I have my own family in the Castle, and I must return there as soon as I can."

Forkbeard nodded. He looked a bit relieved, as if he'd been forced to make his offer out of good manners. Tal was surprised, because he wouldn't have thought the Icecarls had anything like manners.

The Crone nodded, too.

"Wisely spoken, Tal," she said. "Let us go below. We will eat Selski meat, drink vitska, and talk of what your future holds. Milla, you will come, too."

The Crone picked up the urn with Tal's shadow-guard and led the way to an open hatch.

Tal was surprised to see that below decks was a large, open space. All the Icecarls lived together down here. Light was provided by tall tubes of some clear material, filled with water and floating clots of jelly that shone with a yellowish light. As Tal passed by one of these tubes, he tapped it. The clots of jelly rushed to his finger, and he saw that they were marine creatures.

"Glowjellies," said the Crone. "Hard to catch, under the ice."

She led the way between sleeping Icecarls who were just lying against the curved ribs of the ship, wrapped in their furs. Tal was careful not to step on any of them, for all lay with their weapons by their hands, and he saw that many opened one eye as he approached.

As Tal's eyes adjusted more to the dim light, he saw that while it was a large, open space, there were partitions here and there. But even these only had thick curtains instead of doors. Curtains of fur and shiny black hide.

The Crone led Tal to one of these curtains and pulled it back, revealing a small chamber. A low table was in the middle, surrounded by cushions of all shapes and sizes.

"Sit," said the Crone as she placed the urn down. Tal sat down next to it and touched the smooth side, as if he might feel his shadowguard through the fired clay.

Milla sat down, too, as far away as she could. The Crone went back out, leaving the two of them alone.

For a while Tal tried to meet Milla's stare, but after she went for several minutes without blinking he got tired of that and looked away. She laughed, a scornful laugh that made him mad. But there was nothing he could do. She wanted him to attack her with his Sunstone, Tal knew.

She wanted an excuse to fight him.

·CHAPTER·
SEVENTEEN

Before Milla or Tal cracked and started to fight, the Crone came back in, carrying a bowl of something that steamed and smelled rather disgusting. She put it on the table and gave Tal an object that he supposed was meant to be a fork, though it was made of bone and only had two tines.

"Selski meat," the Crone said. "The lifeblood of our people. Where the Selski go, we follow, taking their old, the ill, and the weak. Selski meat fills our stomachs, Selski skin gives us clothes and sails, Selski bone our tools and weapons, Selski gut the strings for our harps."

"It tastes better than it smells," she added, pushing the bowl toward Tal. She must have seen his nose wrinkle.

Reluctantly, Tal jabbed at a piece of the meat and

put it in his mouth. Suddenly, as he tasted it, he became ravenous. It did taste all right, but mostly he was just incredibly hungry.

The Crone left while he ate, but Milla sat there, staring. If she blinked, she did it while Tal wasn't looking. She didn't eat, either.

"Why don't you have some?" Tal asked when he had eaten his fill. He pushed the bowl toward her tentatively, almost like a peace offering.

"A Shield Maiden does not eat in front of a prisoner," Milla said stiffly. "A Shield Maiden does not sleep in front of a prisoner. A Shield Maiden —"

"Tal is not a prisoner," interrupted the Crone, who had come back in. She held the curtain back to let whoever was with her in.

It was a very old woman, Tal saw. A hunched over, wrinkled, and faded lady, who was not much bigger than Gref. She looked at Tal, and he saw that her eyes were milky, without pupils. She was clearly blind.

The effect she had on Milla was striking. The girl leaped to her feet and pushed her clenched fists together in salute.

"Mother Crone!" Milla exclaimed.

Tal got up, too, since it seemed to be the thing to do. From Milla's exclamation, he figured that this blind old lady was more important than the Crone.

"This is the Mother Crone, most ancient and wise," said the Crone, leading the old lady over to Tal. "She has come to see what your future holds and help us decide what must be done with you."

The old lady did not speak. She took Tal's hands in her own and turned the palms up. Then with one long, very yellow fingernail, she traced the lines from his wrist across the palm.

Tal let her do it, but only because Milla was there and he knew she would do something to him if he tore his hand away. It felt really weird having this ancient fingernail drag across his skin. He couldn't help staring at it, so long and yellow, more like the talon of an animal than a human fingernail.

Then the Mother Crone lifted his hand to her face and pressed his fingers against her milky eyes. Tal flinched, and his disgust must have shown on his face, for Milla took a step forward, anger in her eyes.

Anything might have happened then, but the Mother Crone spoke, and at the sound of her voice, everyone was still. It wasn't loud, but it seemed to echo inside Tal's head. Even when the voice got softer, Tal found that he could hear nothing else. All the background noises of ship, ice, and Icecarls faded away.

There was only the voice of the Mother Crone.

Far have you fallen

Yet not so far

Long must you travel

Yet not so long

Home is the Castle

Yet it is not home

Shadows befriend you

Yet are not friends

Shield Maiden stands by you

Yet not back to back

Light warms you

Yet shadows fall

Blood binds you

Yet binds you not

Evil hunts you

Yet hungers not

Darkness hides you

Yet blinds you not

Sunstones fall from you

Yet into others' hands.

The voice trailed away. Tal sat down suddenly, the echo still going on inside his head. He was hardly aware of saying good-bye to the Mother Crone as she was led past the curtain, into waiting hands.

"That seems clear," said the Crone. She smiled, for the first time that Tal had seen, showing very white teeth.

"What seems clear?" Tal muttered. He felt really woozy, like he'd just woken up from a really long sleep.

"We're going to help you get back to your Castle. And you are going to get us a new Sunstone."

That broke Tal out of his dreamy state. "What?!"

"The Mother Crone has prophesied," said the Crone. "We will send someone with you, to help you on the Ice. When you get back to the Castle, you will give her a Sunstone in return."

"Her?" asked Tal suspiciously.

"Milla," replied the Crone, smiling again. "It will be her Shield Maiden Quest to see you safely to the Mountain of Light and to your Castle that is built upon it."

·CHAPTER·
EIGHTEEN

"What!" screamed Milla. "How could you do this to me?"

"'A Shield Maiden faces her faults,'" recited the Crone, still smiling. "Besides, this is the greatest quest I have ever given — to go to the Mountain of Light, to bring back a Sunstone."

"So you knew where the Castle was all along?" interrupted Tal. "You knew I was telling the truth?"

"Yes," said the Crone. "The Crones know of it, for your Castle is the only permanently bright thing in the sky, there atop its mountain. But it is forbidden to us, for we know it houses great evil, where shadows rule."

"That's not true!" exclaimed Tal. "Shadowspirits serve us. The Chosen rule them. They are servants, like my shadowguard you keep locked up there. That's all."

"That is no more than a Selski sprat is to a Merwin," said the Crone. She wasn't smiling now. "We know of what these shadows are, and how our ancestors fought them, and raised the darkness that protects us."

"Your ancestors!" said Tal. "They had nothing to do with the Veil. The Chosen made it, because the sun is too strong."

"Don't speak to the Crone like that," said Milla, and she raised her fist.

"Enough!" said the Crone. "We must bind you to the Quest. Tal, give me your arm."

Slowly, Tal put out his arm. The Crone took it and slid the sleeve of his fur coat back, to show his bare wrist. Tal waited, thinking she was going to read the future in it or say something like the Mother Crone had said. He was totally unprepared when she suddenly produced a large tusk and sliced it across his skin.

"Ahhh!" he shouted, pulling his hand back. Blood was already welling out. Tal saw that the Crone had actually cut him three times, very swiftly, making a strange, triangular pattern in his skin.

"Weakling," commented Milla and she held out her wrist. It was already scarred in the triangular pattern. The Crone cut near the old scars, and Milla watched the blood appear without flinching.

"Clench your fist to keep the blood coming," instructed the Crone. "And follow me."

"Keep it flowing?" asked Tal. These Icecarls were even madder than he thought. But he did clench his fist, watching the beads of blood come out. The Crone hadn't cut deep at all. She must have had lots of practice. Tal shuddered, thinking what might have happened if she wasn't so good at it.

They went back onto the deck. The Sunstone on the mast was still shining brightly, which Tal was glad to see. But it was snowing again, heavily, and visibility was poor. He kept his head tucked in as the Crone led him to the mast.

There she took his wrist and wiped the blood against the mast and then the deck. From the different color of the bone there, Tal guessed this ceremony had been done many times before. Milla did the same.

"Repeat these words after me," said the Crone, once more looking into Tal's eyes with her strange, luminous gaze. He nodded, licked his lips, and ate a snowflake by accident.

"I give my blood to the bone, bone of the ship," said the Crone.

"I give my blood to the bone, bone of the ship," repeated Tal and Milla. The Crone took his wrist and wiped it on the mast and the deck again. Milla followed.

"I give my blood to the Clan, Clan of my blood," said the Crone.

"I give my blood to the Clan, Clan of my blood," repeated Tal. The Crone took his wrist and forced it against Milla's upturned wrist, so their blood mingled. Milla looked away.

"I give my blood to the wind, blood to the ice," said the Crone, taking Tal's hand and shaking it so a drop of blood was taken by the wind and carried overboard.

Milla shook hers at the same time, and by some freak of the wind, the drops of blood met. But only the Crone's eyes were sharp enough to see that happen.

"By bone of the ship and blood of the Clan, I will gain a Sunstone for the Clan of the Far-Raiders. May wind destroy me, and ice freeze me if I fail," said the Crone.

Both Tal and Milla repeated the words, with the Crone holding their wrists.

"Now you are bound together in this Quest," the Crone said with satisfaction. "And Tal, you are at least a little bit an Icecarl."

Milla muttered something that was lost in the wind. Tal looked at her and didn't see any sudden friendliness. They might be bound together for a quest, but he still didn't trust her and she obviously still hated him.

"Milla, show Tal where he can sleep and then prepare for your journey. The Castle lies beyond the Selski migration, and there is a gap ahead. You will have to cross it quickly."

"By sleigh?" asked Milla stiffly. "Surely the boy cannot skate or ski."

"You may have a sleigh and six Wreska," said the Crone. "Jorntil will ready them for you."

"Hold on," said Tal. "You mean it's just the two of us who are going? I thought the ship —"

"No," said the Crone. "We follow the Selski, who only know one path. That is our life, and we cannot break it except at direst need. Milla will safeguard you. She is an expert hunter, one of the best on the ice. Your greatest danger will be time, for the Selski teem in uncountable numbers. We call it the Living Sea and the gaps in their migration path are narrow. But I am sure you will get across."

She turned away before Tal could ask another question, leaving him standing there, next to Milla. She was looking at her wrist. Tal looked at his and saw that the blood had already dried. The pattern remained.

"Follow me," said Milla, and she crossed the snow-slippery deck and went back through the hatch. Tal followed more clumsily. The Crone had said to sleep, but he didn't know how he was going to do that.

At the hatch, he looked back up at the Sunstone, half-shrouded in the flurries of snow. He gripped his own Sunstone and thought about exactly how much trouble he was in.

He was incredibly far away from the Castle. In just two months, he had to have a new Primary Sunstone or else he could never be a proper Chosen, his whole future, the whole rest of his life lost. His mother — he choked a little as he thought of her lying ill on her bed — needed that Sunstone. So did Gref and Kusi. His father, if he was still alive, would be counting on him to look after everyone else.

He had just sworn some sort of oath that he didn't mean to keep, but couldn't help taking seriously. He'd mingled his blood with — he didn't know what anymore, because they weren't Underfolk — but a crazy girl with a natural shadow who wanted to kill him and was only stopped by tradition.

When he woke up in the morning, he would have to leave even the small comforts of the ship and head out across the ice with the crazy girl, to cross a living sea of animals.

It was all too much. Tal gulped and fought back the tears that were forming in his eyes. It's just the wind, he told himself, but he knew that wasn't true.

Then he saw the Crone again. She was standing near the mast. She looked at him and threw something. Tal ducked, but whatever it was hit the deck and then rolled toward him. Something dark, which he instinctively reached for.

His shadowguard flowed past his feet, taking on his form, just like a natural shadow, and spread down the steps behind him. Tal had to look over his shoulder to see it as he sighed with relief.

"I have spoken to it," said the Crone, her voice carrying across the deck. "No one should be without their shadow. But as long as you travel with Icecarls, it must only be a shadow. There is no place for uncertainty about such things on the ice."

Tal smiled and went below. His shadow preceded him, looking no different from any Icecarl's. Tal had no idea if the Crone had taken away its power to change shape and make itself more solid. He didn't care. He was too tired to think about it now. He was just glad to have it back.

"I will wake you at the turn of the glowjellies," said Milla as she showed him a pile of furs between two snoring boys about his own age. She hesitated, then said in quite a matter-of-fact tone, "I still wish to kill you, but I see that I cannot. Not now we are bound to the Quest. I will protect you on the ice, and we will reach your Castle and gain the Sunstone."

Two Sunstones, Tal thought tiredly. He burrowed down in his furs. Everything had begun because he'd just wanted one Sunstone. What was going to happen now that he needed two?

Beside him, his shadowguard suddenly turned into a tiny version of Sharrakor, the Shadowdragon. Milla saw it flicker out of the corner of her eye and whirled around.

But by then it had become a normal shadow again, and Tal was sound asleep.

·CHAPTER·
NINETEEN

Milla woke Tal up what seemed like only an hour or two later, though his Sunstone said seven hours had passed. She didn't say anything, but just dumped a pile of heavy furs on his stomach, which hurt.

Obviously the furs were meant for him to wear. His Sunstone could be used to keep him warm, but after it had gone dark the night before, Tal didn't want to draw any power from it unless he had to.

The furs came in three distinct sets. Tal had to experiment with them for a while before he worked out that the light, waist-length one with hanging ribbons went on first, then the leggings, which tied to the ribbons, then the knee-length coat that went over everything. Even after trying it a few different ways, Tal wasn't entirely sure that the outer coat wasn't on backward. Not that the Icecarls seemed to care very much about how their clothes were worn.

They were very scruffy compared to the Chosen, Tal thought. He was only wearing the furs because he didn't have a full-strength Sunstone.

Milla came back while Tal was struggling with the thick Selski-skin gauntlets. She sniffed and helped him tie them onto his sleeves, so they would be ready to wear and could not be dropped or lost.

"We must be prepared to leave as soon as the Afterguards report a break in the Living Sea," the Icecarl girl said coldly. "Come on."

Tal followed her, his shadowguard dutifully remaining behind him like a normal shadow. It had even expanded to match his increased size. He felt weird under all the fur. It was like suddenly becoming very fat, for he was at least half a stretch wider than he used to be.

Even so, the broad Selski-skin belt he wore seemed to have been made for someone twice that size again. It kept slipping down, though he'd drawn it through the bone buckle as tightly as he could. Obviously it was Milla's idea of a joke. She didn't want him to be comfortable.

The ship was strangely still when Tal climbed out into the bright light of the Sunstone high above on the mast. At first he couldn't work out why, as he narrowed his eyes against the light. Then he saw that the ship wasn't moving. The sails were furled, and huge anchor ropes led over the stern and off into the darkness of the ice.

The wind still howled through the rigging and cut at Tal's face. He pulled out the bone face mask Milla had given him and slipped it on. It didn't fit properly, with one eyehole too far to one side to see through clearly. Tal fiddled around with it for a while before giving up and slipping on his gauntlets. His fingernails were already turning blue.

Milla went to the side and easily climbed over, disappearing from view. Tal followed clumsily, hitching at his belt. He hoped she hadn't just jumped down to the ice, because the deck was at least eight stretches high. She might be able to jump down that far, but he knew he couldn't.

She hadn't jumped. There was a ladder, another backbone of some kind, this time made with quite long side-bones or ribs. Tal climbed down after her, much more slowly than he normally would.

There were quite a few Icecarls already on the ice. Eight were returning from a hunting expedition, dragging a huge cube of bloody meat behind them. It was enormous, and Tal couldn't imagine what it had been carved out of. A Selski, perhaps.

Another Icecarl was holding the reins of the lead Wreska in a string of six, harnessed to the cart-thing Tal now knew was called a sleigh. The Icecarl had to be Jorntil, who the Crone had said would prepare the animals for them. As they approached, he touched his clenched fist to the hand that held the reins, in a fairly casual salute.

Milla responded by clapping her clenched fists together hard enough to make Tal wince. He raised his Sunstone and let out a small light, and it was Jorntil's turn to wince and look away.

"Sorry," said Tal quickly. "I was trying to be —"

"Get in the sleigh!" hissed Milla. But Jorntil only blinked, laughed, and fed the lead Wreska something that looked like the Selski meat Tal had eaten aboard the ship. That made Tal realize he hadn't eaten breakfast, or whatever these strange people ate when they woke up.

Tal didn't want to ask Milla about it and give her another chance to show off that she was tougher than he was. Instead he climbed aboard the sleigh. It rocked as he pulled himself up, and Tal was surprised by how lightly constructed it was. Most of it was made of very thin bones woven together, and the whole contraption creaked as he shifted his weight. It didn't seem strong enough to carry him, let alone the two of them.

To make matters worse, the part Tal was standing in didn't seem all that well connected to the two long, bladelike skates underneath. It was like a baby's bouncing basket, Tal thought, peering down. The two skates were solidly joined at the front and rear. The woven bone box he was in was precariously balanced between these supports, held up by six or seven wide bands of Selski skin. These springs would absorb the shock of hitting small bumps and holes, at the cost of bouncing around.

There were two spears and a whip in a long scabbard on the outside of the sleigh. For a moment, Tal thought about grabbing one and throwing it at Milla, and had a daydream about making his escape. But he couldn't drive the Wreska, and even with the shadowguard to point the way, he knew nothing about crossing the Living Sea.

The triple cut on his wrist burned as he thought of this, but Tal hardly noticed. There were enough good reasons to put up with Milla for the moment. Later he would find a way to get rid of her.

Milla jumped in, and the whole thing bounced

even more. Tal, unprepared, fell against her, and she pushed him off.

"Hang on," she said scornfully. She pulled a long whip out of a scabbard on the outside of the sleigh and with a practiced flick cracked it out to one side, sending ice crystals flying. The Wreska stirred in their traces and blew out their noses, sending jets of powdery snow all around.

Milla cracked the whip to one side again and then, in a fluid movement, sent it out over the lead Wreska's head. As it cracked, the Wreska snorted even louder, and the sleigh gave a sudden lurch.

"Eeeyyy-aarrr-haaaah!" screamed Milla, nearly deafening Tal. The Wreska responded by lurching forward, their shaggy legs and sharp three-toed hooves driving against the ice. The sleigh rocked and picked up speed.

"This is fun!" said Tal, startled by how quickly the sleigh was moving. They were moving across the ice faster than he could run, almost as fast as he slid down the laundry slide back in the Castle.

"It is not *fun*," scowled Milla. "It is only a means of travel. We are on a serious quest. There is no time for fun."

Tal didn't answer. Despite what Milla said, riding in the sleigh *was* fun. But the most important thing was that he was heading back to the Castle. He had been diverted from his own quest, but it wasn't over. He would get a Sunstone, and become a full-fledged Chosen. He would do it for his father, mother, Gref, and Kusi.

·CHAPTER· TWENTY

All too soon, the sleigh left the circle of light cast by the Icecarl's great Sunstone. Once again Tal felt the fear of darkness, and his hand crept to the newly mended chain around his neck. But there were two of the pale green moth-lamps on the sleigh, and the Wreskas' antlers, as the spiky branches on their heads were called, also glowed with faint luminescence.

Milla noticed Tal reach for his Sunstone, and he saw her smile. Slowly, he forced himself to let go of the chain. He didn't want to let her know he was afraid.

They drove on in silence for an hour or more, and Tal soon found that Milla was at least partly right. He found the speed of the sleigh exciting at first, but after a while, standing up as it bounced and swayed over the lumpy ice made his knees sore, and his fingers were aching from holding onto the side.

Not being able to see properly where they were going also made him nervous, though Milla did not seem concerned. Either she could see a lot better than he could in the dim light of the lanterns, or the Wreska could, and she trusted them.

After another hour, Tal was nearly fainting from weariness. He had slumped down, no longer trying to match Milla's upright stance. His shadowguard was the only thing propping him up, though it didn't dare do too much, since it had been told to behave like a natural shadow in order to placate the Icecarls.

"Will we stop soon?" Tal asked finally, when his weariness overcame his pride.

"Yes," said Milla. "We have nearly come to the Living Sea, by my reckoning. We should see the Selski — yes, there is the glow."

She pointed, at the same time hauling back on the reins to slow the Wreska down. Tal looked where she indicated. At first he couldn't see anything, but as they drew closer, he saw that the ice slanted gently down in front of them. Off in the distance and a little below them, there was a dull glow that seemed to cover all the horizon ahead.

"What is that light?" he asked.

"Kalakoi," said Milla, making a circle with her thumb and forefinger. "They are small . . . things . . . about so big, that grow on the Selski. They glow and bring moths and the Slepenish that the Selski eat. But the Kalakoi also eat the Selski, when they grow old and do not scrape enough of them off."

"Um, what are the Slurpernesh?" It grated on Tal that as a Chosen he had to ask these questions of a natural, but it was important to know.

"Sleep-en-ish," corrected Milla. "They go in front of the Selski always. They swarm in uncountable numbers, more even than the Selski. The Slepenish come up through the ice, and if the Selski do not eat them, they go back through it into the water below. Some say that these survivors change into something else in the deep water and birth new Slepenish. I do not know if this is true."

"What do they look like?" asked Tal nervously. He didn't like the sound of things that bore through the ice in uncountable numbers.

"Like the string of a harp, but you never see just one," said Milla. She seemed to struggle with her desire to treat Tal like dirt and an equal desire to show off her knowledge. Showing off won.

"They roil together, more in a single paced square than snowflakes in a storm. They are not dangerous, but when they first come through the ice they weaken it. That is why we never cross between the different hordes of the Living Sea, but only in the temporary gaps. There is always open water where Selski and Slepenish first meet."

Tal was silent for a while, digesting this information. The sleigh continued more slowly, heading down the slope in the ice. The glow grew brighter. Tal watched it nervously, understanding more about what the Icecarls meant when they called the Selski migration path the Living Sea. Certainly the light of their passage seemed to fill all the world ahead.

Suddenly, Milla pulled hard on the reins and called out the names of the two leaders, "Tarah! Rall!"

The Wreska came to a sliding, ice-shard-scattering halt. Milla pulled a spear out of the scabbard, choosing the one with the largest head, a wickedly pointed piece of bone as wide and long as Tal's arm.

"What is it?" asked Tal as he pulled out his Sunstone and raised it. All he could see was the glow in the distance. But as the Wreska stopped snorting, he heard a dull rumble as well, a sound like many distant drums. Low, loud, and continuous.

"Rogue Selski," snapped Milla. She jumped down onto the ice and lifted her face mask to see better.

"Broken off from the horde. We have to push it back in."

Tal peered into the distance. There was something there, dark upon the ice. He'd taken it for a small hillock or mound of some kind. Now he realized it was moving. Heading toward them.

"That's a Selski?" he asked in amazement. It had to be a hundred stretches long and twenty high. It was almost as big as the Icecarl's ship, a great, hulking black mass covered in glowing spots that made a pattern like the star-filled night above the Veil.

It was lifting itself up on its huge forelegs — or foreflippers — and then leaping and sliding forward. It was close enough now for Tal to hear the ice crack and shatter every time it came down. The sleigh shivered under his feet.

"Can't we just leave it alone?"

"No," said Milla. "Rogues are a danger to the ship and other Clans. It must be turned back to the horde."

"You won't be able to do anything to it with that." Tal nodded at her spear. The girl was even madder than he thought. Nothing could possibly turn that huge monster!

"A full harpoon would be better," Milla agreed,

in the same sort of tone a Chosen performer might use to describe an Achievement that was not quite worthy of the Indigo Ray of Extreme Approval. She drew her knife — another sharpened, curved bone — and added, "I will have to climb up between leaps and blind it in the left eye. That will make it turn aside."

"No!" Tal exclaimed. He couldn't get back to the Castle without Milla. She might be a dangerous lunatic, but he couldn't afford to lose her, at least not yet. "What about our quest? That has to be more important, doesn't it?"

Milla hesitated. For the first time, Tal saw her as a girl his own age. She looked like his friends at the Lectorium when they were asked a question they couldn't answer. Then the familiar control came back, and her face settled into its stern pattern.

"You are . . . correct," said Milla with obvious reluctance. She returned knife and spear to their scabbards, lowered her face mask, and jumped back on the sleigh. "The Quest is of the first importance. The Foreguard will take care of the rogue."

Tal breathed a sigh of relief and slipped his Sunstone back under his furs. Milla whipped the Wreska up again, and the sleigh moved off, turning a little to pass behind the rogue Selski.

"You do not need to be afraid," Milla said as they came closer. She had seen Tal shiver as ice chips blew across them from the Selski's strange leaping progress. "The Selski never turn back. They will change direction to one side, but never back."

A bit like an Icecarl, Tal thought. He peered at Milla through the amber eyepieces of his mask. She was obviously very brave. Climbing that Selski would have meant her own death for certain, but Tal knew she would have done it if he hadn't given her a good reason not to. He was reluctant to admit it, but he couldn't think of many Chosen who would die for their Order. Of course, they lived in a much more civilized way. . . .

Milla was prepared to change direction when she had to, Tal thought. And the danger of the Selski was over.

Or was it? As the sleigh continued on, Tal noticed that the continuous drumming sound was getting louder — much, much louder. And the glow that filed the ice and sky was brighter and closer.

Tal could see more huge shapes, too, leaping and sliding. Lots and lots of them. He was just about to say something when Milla suddenly cracked her whip and shouted. The Wreska broke into an even faster gait.

The sleigh picked up speed. Tal stared at the ice in front of them, willing it to be clearer than it was. To his left he could see a solid wall of Selski traveling away from them. To his right, there was a enormous mass of Selski sliding and leaping toward them, an almost solid wall of strangely glowing flesh, preceded by a rolling wave of ice and snow.

The drumming sound was now a bass roar that drowned all other sounds.

They had begun to cross the Living Sea of the Selski, but it didn't look like the right place or the right time to Tal. The onrushing Selski were too close, and the gap between the two parts of the horde was closing.

"We must take shelter at the rock!" Milla screamed, her words fighting against the noise of the Selski. She pointed to a dark mass ahead that Tal had thought was another Selski. He hadn't noticed that it wasn't moving.

He didn't think they could make it.

·CHAPTER·
TWENTY-ONE

The rock that thrust up through the ice was only as tall as the Selski themselves and not much broader than three of them abreast. Known as the Seventy-second Splitter to the Icecarls, it was just big enough to make the Selski pass to either side rather than try to jump over it.

The sleigh pulled into the shelter of the rock just as the leading Selski crashed down behind them, closing the gap. Tal stared back in shock, barely able to believe that they'd made it. Ice chips from the Selski's landing showered over him and into his open mouth.

Tal kept looking as the ice melted on his tongue. Huge bodies leaped and crashed, but somehow missed one another. Beyond the light of the sleigh lamps, Tal could only see the luminous patterns of the Kalikoi on the huge animals, a weaving tapestry of light that jumped and moved.

The creatures did not make any noise themselves, or if they did, it was lost in the crash and roar of so many thousands of them rising and falling upon the ice.

"What do we do now?" Tal asked finally. He had to shout close to Milla's ear.

"Climb the Splitter and look out for another gap!" Milla shouted back. She jumped down from the sleigh and started to check the Wreska's legs and their three-toed hooves, looking for strains or damage.

Tal sat down in the sleigh, pulled his hood as tight as it would go, and with his fingers on the outside, pushed the fur into his ears. Not that it helped much. The noise of the Selski's strange leaping movement vibrated through the sleigh and every bone in his body.

After ten minutes of trying to rest, Tal realized that fur stuffed into his ears didn't work. So he did what any of the Chosen would do in such a situation. He looked down at his shadowguard and said, "Shadowguard, shadowguard, shield me from sound."

The shadowguard, which was pale in the lantern light, merely twitched its copy of Tal's head in a slight sideways motion. Tal thought it hadn't heard him because of the Selski noise, so he repeated his instruction more loudly. Still nothing happened.

He was just about to shout at it, when Milla jumped back into the sleigh. Seeing Tal crouched down looking at his shadowguard, she growled and reached for her knife.

"No shadow magic!" she shouted. "You were told!"

The shadowguard didn't move. It might as well have been a natural shadow. Tal straightened up and pulled out the bits of hood that were stuck in his ears. He didn't say anything, but Milla slowly relaxed, letting her hand drift away from her knife.

"There is a gap coming!" she shouted. "We must be ready."

Tal couldn't hear every word, but he heard "gap" and got the gist of it. He turned to face forward and gripped the rail of the sleigh. Milla moved up next to him, carefully avoiding his shadow. She drew the whip and flicked it out next to the Wreska.

Selski still leaped ahead of them, without any sign of their numbers lessening. The glow from all their Kalakoi was no less bright, and the noise had not diminished.

Tal waited. When there were no Selski in sight ahead, Milla would start the Wreska, he thought. And once again they would be on their way to the Castle.

Milla cracked the whip and yelled at the Wreska while there were still Selski right in front of them. The sleigh began to move off, apparently into their path. Tal gripped the rail even harder and shouted "No!" though he couldn't even hear himself.

Then they were out of the shelter of the Splitter, crossing the churned up, split ice a scant few stretches behind the glowing, Kalakoi-riddled tail of a Selski. Tal instantly looked to the right, expecting to see one of the huge monsters in midair about to come crashing down on them.

But there were no Selski, at least not close.

Milla had seen a gap from atop the Splitter and noted the Kalakoi pattern on the last Selski.

The gap was a narrow one. Once again the Ice-carl shouted at the Wreska and cracked her whip over their heads. One of the leaders stumbled, and for a terrible moment Tal thought it would go down and the sleigh would crash. But it recovered, and they sped onward across the ice.

This time, Tal felt sure that the Selski would catch them, flatten them. The sleigh would be smashed into the ice . . . and him with it. He drew his Sunstone, though it was too small to offer much hope. A blast of light might make one Selski turn aside, but there would be hundreds . . . maybe even *thousands* behind that one.

The sleigh hit more broken ice and rocked to one side. Tal had to let his Sunstone go in order to grab the rail with both hands and avoid being thrown out. Milla shouted something and grabbed him, her grip on his arm so strong that it was like needles of ice.

The sleigh tipped again, one runner in the air. Milla threw herself the other way, Tal going with her. For a second it looked like that would be enough, but there was another bump and the sleigh catapulted into the air and tipped on its side.

Somehow, Milla managed to keep Tal with her as the sleigh screeched and careened on its side, no longer going straight but sliding off in a crazy arc. Wreska screamed, ice spikes flew everywhere. Tal wasn't even sure which way was up for a moment. All he could think of was the Selski bearing down on them.

Eventually he realized the sleigh had stopped.

Milla dragged him out, her knife in her hand. Tal stumbled along with her as she slashed the reins that held the Wreska to the wreckage. As soon as the traces were cut, the antlered animals bounded away. They knew the danger of the Selski, too.

"Run!" Milla screamed, shocking Tal into action. He'd been dazed without realizing it. Now he came back to life. Milla was snatching the one unbroken lantern and a pack from the ruined sleigh. The Selski were so close, the ice shivering at their approach.

He started to run, but in the wrong direction. Milla pushed him toward the onrushing wave of Selski. Tal resisted, till he realized that Milla was leading the way not just toward the Selski, but to a point where their line ended.

The other side of the Living Sea. It was so close — but so were the Selski.

Milla was already ahead, not looking back. Tal sucked in cold air, feeling it burn to the bottom of his lungs, but he needed it to keep his legs going. He ran as hard as he ever had in his life.

Ahead of him, Milla stumbled and went sprawling on the ice. Without even thinking, Tal slowed and swooped down to pick her up. She was much heavier than he expected, but somehow they got up together and now they ran clutching onto each other for balance, arms windmilling to correct their slips and slides.

They could see the outermost Selski clearly now, the one they had to pass to safety. The Kalakoi had grown on it in a pattern that made it seem to have many eyes, glowing red and yellow and orange, all seemingly focused on the two tiny figures that dashed in front of the leviathan.

The Selski hit the ice, and the force of its impact sent shallow cracks racing in all directions. They shot under Tal's and Milla's feet, so their run became a crazy dance to avoid tripping over a crack, which would be certain death.

The leviathan's mighty flippers pressed down on the ice again, and its great bulk began to lift. Just as it shot up and forward, Tal and Milla used all their remaining strength in a last desperate sprint that took them right in front of the straining beast. They saw its small, dark eye focus on them with surprise, and its great mouth that was always open, latticed with tiny teeth for straining Slepenish and moths.

Higher and higher it raised above them, filling the whole sky. Both of them screamed, and then they tripped and fell, sliding on backs and bellies across the ice.

The Selski leaped again, and its tail came crashing down.

Tal saw it coming down and closed his eyes. Milla saw, too, but she kept her eyes open. Icecarls believed in facing death.

·CHAPTER·
TWENTY–TWO ·

The tail missed them by a stretch, but they were struck with so many chunks of snow and ice that for a second Tal thought he had been hit and killed. It took a while to sink in that he was still alive.

Milla helped him up and they staggered off, the Icecarl girl leading. Selski kept thundering past behind them, but none so close.

It took them half an hour to walk far enough away to be able to talk, and for Milla to consider them safe from Selski who might be on the edges of the horde. She took off her pack and sat on it. Tal also sat, trusting his thick furs to keep the chill of the ice off his backside for a while.

"We have crossed the Living Sea," said Milla proudly, almost to herself. She didn't seem at all concerned about the loss of the sleigh and the Wreska, who had long since disappeared into the eternal night.

Something in her voice made Tal ask her a question. "You haven't crossed it before?"

"No." Milla slid off her face mask and smiled, though not at Tal particularly. "We do not cross the Living Sea except in times of direst need. They will sing a story of our crossing when I return."

"Great," said Tal bitterly. "I thought you did it all the time. I would never have agreed —"

He stopped as he saw that Milla wasn't even listening. She was completely crazy, and so were all the Icecarls. The sooner he was back in the Castle the better. Even Great-uncle Ebbitt wasn't as mad as Milla.

He looked out into the darkness. The paltry light of the moths in the lantern was barely enough to see Milla's face, and his shadowguard was almost invisible. Beyond that was absolute blackness. Once again, Tal had to fight a desire to lift his Sunstone up and call all the light he could.

There could be anything out there, lurking in the dark.

"You can rest for a while, then we'll go on," Milla

said. "I will keep watch. It will take us longer without the sleigh."

"Obviously," grumbled Tal. He could already feel the chill of the ice coming through his furs. How was he supposed to rest?

But somehow he did fall asleep. When he awoke, feeling cold and very stiff, Milla was preparing food. She had placed a bone dish on the ice, filled with oil of some kind, and was striking sparks with two small pieces of a dull silver metal over it. After a few tries, the sparks lit the oil. Milla then took a three-legged stand of bone from her pack, set it above the burning oil, and put a small pot on the stand. From the smell, Tal knew she was cooking more Selski meat.

"How do you hunt the Selski?" he asked as he got up and stamped his feet and clapped his hands to revive his circulation. The air around his chest, neck, and face was surprisingly warm, and his Sunstone felt almost hot against his chest. He must have unconsciously drawn upon its power while he was asleep. "They seem too big and too dangerous."

"We take the old and the slow," replied Milla. "On the fringes of the Living Sea. The ones that the Kalakoi have begun to eat. Even so it is dangerous,

175

and it can take twenty or thirty hunters many, many stretches to bring one to a stop."

"What happens then?" asked Tal. It was all so strange and mysterious, this world outside the Castle. A world none of the Chosen knew anything about. Or at least, Tal didn't *think* they did. Surely he would have heard of the Icecarls, the Selski, and the Merwin.

"They die," Milla said, with a shrug. "If the Selski stop, they die. Here, you eat first."

"Are we going to eat with the same spoon?" Tal asked, disgusted. She was so crude!

"You can go hungry instead and die," Milla snarled. Tal saw some of the old hatred flare up in her eyes. But she quickly looked away and began to spoon up chunks of warmed Selski meat.

When she was about halfway through, hunger overcame Tal's objections. He made a tentative reach for the pot. Without speaking, Milla handed him the spoon.

That marked how they got on for the next seven days — or at least Tal *thought* it was seven days. He could tell the time in the Castle from his Sunstone, but that only gave him hours. Sometimes he lost track.

All the days were the same anyway. They walked

and walked and walked, sometimes up icy hills, sometimes down, sometimes on the flat. Milla rarely spoke, except to give Tal orders. Every few hours they stopped to eat, or take turns to rest, or go to the toilet.

Toilet stops were a dangerous activity in the cold and dark. With only the one lantern, Tal had to use his Sunstone when he wandered off a little to take care of his needs, and call extra warmth from it to keep essential parts of him unfrozen. He didn't know how Milla managed. Presumably Icecarls had their ways.

Tal was just returning from such an excursion when Milla came bounding toward him, her green moth-lamp shuttered so its light only shone in front of her.

"Hide your light!" Milla commanded. She pulled at Tal's arm to make him crouch down.

Tal quickly focused on his Sunstone, dimmed its light, and slipped the chain back under his coat.

"What is it?" he whispered.

"Merwin," Milla whispered back. "A big one. It was on our trail, but I have thrown Selski meat to lure it aside. We must move away from here as quietly as we can, with as little light as possible."

Tal remembered Milla telling him back on the ship about the Merwin. It seemed like years ago.

"Hold onto my belt," Milla murmured. Tal gripped it, and they started off slowly. Milla shuttered the lantern down still more, pulling the handle at its base that closed the weave. Tal could hardly see at all, but somehow it didn't bother him half as much as it would have even a few days before. He was getting used to the dark.

And, he had to admit, he'd kind of gotten used to Milla, since she obviously did take the blood ritual thing seriously and would do her best to get him safely to the Castle. That was a huge improvement to when she'd just wanted to kill him. Not that she was anything more than the descendant of an escaped Underfolk or something.

Milla suddenly stopped. Tal almost ran into her. They both stood there silently, in the dark. They could hear each other breathing, cold rasps coming through their masks, no matter how quiet they tried to be.

Tal could sense Milla staring out at something, but it was too dark for him to see which way she was looking. He moved his own gaze slowly, looking for anything that stood out in the darkness.

When he did see something, it took him a second to remember what it must be. A long, thin light of surprising brightness that seemed to be moving by itself, slowly meandering from side to side.

A Merwin's horn.

·CHAPTER·
TWENTY-THREE

The glowing horn, three times as long as Tal, slowly came closer and closer. Tal felt rather than saw Milla draw her knife. Her spears had been broken in the crash of the sleigh.

A short piece of sharpened bone did not seem like much of a weapon against a hunting beast with a horn that could ram through Tal and Milla and still have plenty left over.

Slowly, trying to make the movement as hidden as he could, Tal reached into his coat and began to pull out his Sunstone.

He had it half out when the Merwin finally worked out where they were. A terrible, whistling screech filled the air, and the luminous horn suddenly rocketed forward.

Milla shouted something and pushed Tal away. She ran, too, but forward, toward the Merwin. Tal could see it clearly now, illuminated by its own terrible horn.

The picture he saw then would be etched in his mind forever.

The Merwin was even bigger than Milla's description — at least twenty stretches long. It looked like a Kralsnake from the Beastmaker game, all thin and sinewy. Except it had four long, clawed flippers instead of legs, and shiny black hide instead of scales.

It had only one eye — a huge golden eye, long and slitted, with a lid that kept flicking open and shut several times a second. The other side of its narrow head showed an empty, scarred eye socket, clearly a wound from long ago.

The horn grew from a ridge of bone between the Merwin's eyes. Under it was the creature's mouth, big enough, with its many shining teeth, to eat Tal in a single gulp.

As Milla charged toward it, the terrible horn struck. It came straight at the Icecarl and for an instant Tal thought it would go right through her.

But she dodged and almost got past. The Merwin

flicked its head, and the ferociously sharp point of the horn sliced across her chest, the force of it throwing her to the ice. She did not get up.

The Merwin hesitated. It started to move toward the motionless body of Milla, its horn scraping the ice. Once again Milla's words went through Tal's brain.

"... *they stick their horn through whatever they're after, and then they bash it up and down on the ice ...*"

The Merwin reared back to strike at the defenseless girl.

"No!" Tal screamed. He rushed forward with his Sunstone raised in his hand.

Faster than Tal's eye could catch, the Merwin changed targets. It lunged forward, extending its body, the luminous horn coming straight at Tal. He threw himself to one side and would have fallen, but his shadowguard was there to prop him up. Somehow he also managed to keep his Sunstone trained on the creature's one golden eye.

Tal knew he would only have time for a single blast of light before the sharp horn struck again. He focused all his thought on the Sunstone, drawing upon every fragment of power it possessed — and unleashed it at the Merwin.

The flash was so bright that Tal was blinded. The

Merwin shrieked, an awful, high-pitched sound that seemed all too close, but Tal didn't know whether he'd just annoyed it or burned out its one remaining eye.

He cursed himself for being so stupid and not closing his own eyes. He could hear the Merwin thrashing around and could imagine that horn stabbing toward him. He started to run, then stopped, disoriented. Maybe he was running toward the Merwin!

"Shadowguard!" he called, and he held out his hand. Something tingling and soft touched his fingers and jerked him to one side. Tal fell and felt the swish of air as something passed him, followed immediately by the sound of the Merwin's horn striking the ice.

Either it could still see or its other senses were good enough to find him. Tal rolled aside, then crawled as his shadowguard pulled at his hand. His sight was slowly coming back, the darkness becoming a mixture of floating blobs and fuzzy light.

The Merwin struck again, its horn skittering off the ice near Tal's feet. He turned to face it, his vision coming clear again. It was blind, at least temporarily, its golden eye closed and weeping. But it could hear or smell, or sense, for its head was pointed straight at him, as was the horn.

It would eventually get him, unless Tal did something first. But his Sunstone was finished, completely used up, and his shadowguard could not fight something like this.

Even if he did somehow manage to get away, he would be lost in the dark, without a light of any kind. Without light his shadowguard would dissipate. Without the shadowguard, he had no way of finding the Castle.

Perhaps he could get Milla's lantern and knife. Tal started to edge around, back toward the faint green glow where Milla had fallen. He was surprised to see that his blind escape from the Merwin had taken him so far from her body.

He was even more surprised when Milla suddenly leaped out of the darkness, onto the Merwin's neck. She wrapped her legs around it, locked her ankles together, and plunged her dagger deep into its head.

The Merwin screeched and reared up, its bright horn pointing directly at the sky. Milla stabbed it again, and it flung its head back down, smashing her legs into the ice. But she hung on and stabbed it again and again, despite its writhings and desperate banging against the ice.

Finally, it stopped moving, and the light from its

horn began to dim. Milla let go and crawled a short distance away. Tal could see the blood on her fur, and trails of Merwin ichor upon the ice.

Tal gulped. He had stood mesmerized while Milla fought the creature. Now he ran forward.

Milla lay on her back. Her hood had fallen down, and her mask was nowhere to be seen. In the fading light of the Merwin's horn, Tal saw that her face was even whiter and her lips were turning blue. The whole front of her coat was ripped to shreds and her fur leggings were rent in many places. As Tal watched, blood began to pool beneath her. Dark red blood, not the blue ichor of the Merwin.

"I die," said Milla, her voice soft. Clumsily, she wiped her wrist across her chest and held it up, all bloody to Tal. "By this blood that we share, blood of the clan, bone of the ship, the Quest must . . ."

Her voice trailed off and she seemed to see something that confused her. Her forehead furrowed, then her eyes slowly closed.

For a moment Tal thought that she was dead. But as he knelt by her side, he saw that she still breathed, though shallowly.

Taking great care, Tal peeled back her torn furs. He had to force himself to take slow breaths as he saw the wound that stretched across her left side. Having seen it, he didn't know what to do. His Sunstone was dead, and even if it wasn't, he didn't know enough to use it for healing.

Then he felt a soft touch at his arm. His shadowguard was plucking at his wrist, the wrist marked with the three cuts of the Icecarls.

Tal stared at the shadow. It was trying to tell him something. It had taken a shape he didn't recognize. Something human.

Then it hit him. The shadowguard had assumed the shape of Milla's shadow. It was saying that since she had some of his blood, it could help her. All Tal had to do was tell it to.

"Shadowguard, shadowguard," he blurted out. "Staunch Milla's wounds —"

Before he could finish, the shadowguard flowed over Milla. Most of it stuck to her ribs, but dark tendrils rippled down to her legs and out along her left arm. Wherever it touched, the bleeding stopped.

Tal pulled Milla's furs together over both girl and shadowguard. He retrieved the pack and lantern. It took him a moment to work out how to open it up again, then he sat it down next to Milla. The shadowguard would need all the light it could get.

Even once the bleeding stopped, Tal wasn't sure if Milla would survive. Now that he had a chance to think, he wasn't even sure he wanted her to. She had probably saved his life, but now he had the pack and the lantern. He might be better off heading straight for the Castle. He certainly didn't want to be bothered with trying to get her a Sunstone as well.

It wasn't as if she was family or a friend or anything.

What would his parents say, Tal suddenly thought. What would his father do if he was out here? Or his mother, if she were well?

They wouldn't leave her. Only someone like Shadowmaster Sushin would, and Tal did not want to be like him.

He sighed and opened the pack. First he got out a sleeping fur, which he carefully tucked around the unconscious girl, tilting her up to get it between her back and the ice. Then he set up the oil burner and began to heat some Selski broth. He supposed Milla would need something hot when she came to.

"What's happening to me?" he asked the dead carcass of the Merwin as the broth bubbled. "I am Tal Graile-Rerem of the Chosen. I'm not supposed to be sitting in the middle of nowhere looking after a . . . a mad Icecarl girl. I should be back home, with a new Sunstone, getting ready for the Day of Ascension."

The dead Merwin did not answer. But someone else did.

·CHAPTER·
TWENTY-FOUR

"And where exactly is your home?" said a voice out in the darkness, beyond the diminishing glow of the Merwin's horn. A woman's voice that sounded rather like the Crone of the Far-Raiders.

Tal jumped and scrabbled madly for Milla's knife. By the time he found it and held it out, the speaker was already at his side. She had a spear at his throat.

She was not alone.

A ring of Icecarls stood around Tal, Milla, and the dead Merwin. There at least twelve of them and they all had spears leveled, as if Tal was as dangerous as the creature Milla had killed.

He had not heard them approach. They might as well have blown in on the wind or sprouted up from the ice.

They wore different-colored furs than the Far-

Raiders, and their masks were decorated with wavy lines that glowed like the Kalakoi on the Selski. Clearly they were from a different clan. He hoped killing the Merwin didn't count as thieving on their hunting lands. Then again, Milla had tried to kill him just for being there. . . .

"I am a Chosen of the Castle," he said slowly. "But I am on a quest with Milla there, of the Far-Raiders. I am bound to the Clan and to the ship. Look!"

He held up his wrist and peeled his gauntlet back to show the marks on his wrist.

"You have no shadow," said the woman who had spoken. "Where is it?"

"Helping Milla," Tal said anxiously. Now he knew what Icecarls were really like, he didn't want to give them an excuse to kill him. "The Merwin hurt her. My shadow has just stopped the bleeding, that's all."

The woman looked down at Milla and pulled the fur aside. She still kept her spear pointed at Tal.

"Tell me how you came here from your Castle, and how you met the Far-Raiders," the woman commanded.

Tal told her, the words practically falling out of his mouth. This lot of Icecarls was even scarier than

Milla. The ones standing around hadn't moved at all. They just stood there, with their sharp spears glinting.

As Tal told his story, he surreptitiously looked at the Icecarls. Not only were their furs and masks different from the Far-Raiders', he noticed they were all wearing exactly the same clothes, not at all like the Icecarls he'd met before. He had almost gotten up to the part about the Merwin when he suddenly realized who they must be. They had to be Shield Maidens, the sisterhood that Milla wanted to join. They were like completely grown-up Millas, which was a really frightening thought.

He finished the story. The first woman stood in silence, towering above him. She started to raise her spear and Tal gulped. Surely he couldn't have come this far only to be stabbed to death because a mad Shield Maiden didn't believe his story!

"Breg, Libbe, Umen — see to the girl," said the woman. "You. Tal. You will come with us."

"Where?" asked Tal. "And . . . is it all right for me to ask who you are?"

"I am Arla, Shield Mother," replied the woman. "We are Shield Maidens, currently serving the Mother Crone of the Mountain of Light."

"The Mountain of Light?" asked Tal eagerly.

That was what the Far-Raiders' Crone had called the mountain the Castle was built upon. "Are we near to it?"

"Three sleeps," replied Arla. "You will soon see it in the sky."

"I'm going home!" exclaimed Tal. He jumped up, but stopped as several Shield Maidens thrust their spears out at him.

"You are a prisoner. We will take you to our Crone for judgment," Arla explained. "It is forbidden to climb the Mountain of Light, and I am not sure you have told the truth. If you or your shadow try to escape, or do magic, you will be killed. Do you understand?"

"Yes," said Tal. He felt very tired all of a sudden. Every time it seemed he might get back to the Castle without further difficulties, something happened.

"We have a sleigh," said Arla. "You can ride on it with your Clan-bond, Milla."

Tal remembered very little of the journey to the Shield Maidens' headquarters in the foothills of the Mountain of Light. Their sleigh was much bigger than Milla's, drawn by twelve Wreska. But it was built for cargo, and so was slower and uncomfortable. Tal and Milla were wedged between Selski-skin sacks containing something that smelled absolutely putrid.

Milla had only brief moments of consciousness and said little that made any sense. Tal wasn't entirely sure he spent much of the journey conscious, either. He slept or half slept most of the way, his dreams and recent events merging. He was stalked by Sharrakor, who became a one-eyed Merwin. He climbed a mast and found his father and Ebbitt perched there, drinking sweetwater.

Again and again, he dreamed of his fall from the Red Tower and of Sunstones. Sunstones falling all around him, just out of reach.

One thing he did remember and was sure was not a dream. That was his first sight of what the Icecarls called the Mountain of Light.

Woken by a strange chanting, he had looked over the side of the sleigh to see all the Shield Maidens lined up facing one direction, chanting something softly together. He had followed their gaze and had seen it.

The Castle. Far, far off, and high up but like a flower of light in the sky, a flower of a thousand brilliant petals. It seemed to hang there, the mountain invisible in the darkness beneath.

Home, thought Tal. *Home*.

Now he could see it, he knew he would return. The Shield Mother's Crone would see that he spoke the truth, like the one on the ship. She would let him continue his quest. She had to.

He looked down at Milla, who was lying still amid the sacks. His shadowguard had been replaced by bandages and poultices made with herbs and creams Tal didn't know.

Her hand was lying outside the furs, the three cuts on her wrist clearly visible. Tal looked at his own wrist, the healing scars quite bright in the green light of the moth-lamps.

Then he looked at her shadow. Somehow it didn't seem quite the same as the Underfolk's natural shadows. The Icecarls were different, Tal had decided. They weren't Chosen, but they certainly weren't servants.

"I will bring you to the Castle," Tal said. He bent down and touched his wrist to Milla's. "And we will *both* get Sunstones."

The next thing Tal knew, Milla's hand was at his throat, and she was staring at him wild-eyed and feverish. Despite her weakness, he only just managed to wrench her hand free and stagger to the other side of the sleigh.

"Why won't it die?" she asked. She shook her head from side to side, then collapsed back onto the furs.

"We're on our way to the Castle," croaked Tal, massaging his neck. He wished he hadn't said anything, because he already wanted to change his mind about taking Milla.

He could not believe how far he'd come, and how far he had to go. Despite battle-crazy Icecarls, hostile Spiritshadows, gigantic Merwin, and the freezing cold, he had somehow made it through these unknown lands. Could he possibly be the same boy who'd lived all his days in the Castle — all his days not knowing what existed outside?

195

No, he was not the same. He would never be the same again.

Of course, after he convinced the Crone to let them go, they would still have to climb the mountain. Then there was the question of how to get into the Castle itself. Having never left it — at least not on the ground — Tal had no idea how it was done.

All he knew was that somehow he would do it.

Tal was going home.

THE SEVENTH TOWER™

CASTLE

*To my family and friends, with a special thank you to
everyone at Lucasfilm who has helped build
and support The Seventh Tower, most particularly
Sarah Hines Stephens, Jane Mason, and
Lucy Autrey Wilson.*

·CHAPTER·
☉ΠΕ

The Ruin Ship had rested in the foothills for many centuries. A vast hulk of bright metal that never rusted, it was the model that all the iceships of the Icecarls were patterned on, though theirs were made of Selski bone and hide.

Over time, luminous mosses and lichens had grown on the ship, so that its deck and sides glowed with soft light in many colors, rare in the eternal night of the Dark World. Even with its masts broken and its sails long gone, the Ruin Ship was enormous. It was easily five times the size of a typical clan ship, and *they* held a hundred Icecarls or more, with all their gear and cargo.

Tal, who until two weeks ago had thought there was nothing outside his home but ice, could not believe the strangely glowing shape ahead of him was a ship. He felt sure it was some freak of nature.

For all but fourteen days of his thirteen and three-quarter years, Tal had lived within the physical and social boundaries of the Castle. He had been raised to take his place among the Chosen, the masters of Light and Shadow. Like all Chosen, he had always been sure there was nothing beyond the light-filled halls and towers of the Castle. He had been taught that apart from the Chosen, there were only Underfolk, born to be servants.

No part of his life in the Castle had prepared him for the reality of the Ice, and the Icecarls who lived upon it. But the experience of surviving each day had chipped away his previously rock-solid beliefs. Tal was still a Chosen, as the shadowguard that stood at his side proclaimed. But his absolute belief in his natural superiority had been severely rattled.

He had even begun to accept that Icecarls were not Underfolk, even though they only had natural shadows. But he still held fast to the belief that the Chosen alone could make things of beauty and power. The Ruin Ship, which was both strangely beautiful and powerful, had to be some sort of natural phenomenon.

As the sleigh crawled higher up the icy slope, the

six Wreska that pulled it had to work harder, their hot breath forming a constant cloud above their antlered heads, while their sharp X-toed hooves sprayed ice chips everywhere behind them.

"That's got to be a freak of . . ." Tal muttered as the sleigh grew closer and the Ruin Ship loomed higher. His voice trailed off as his mind registered that this was not just a giant lump of wind-carved stone.

"What?" asked Milla, the Icecarl girl he'd been forced to travel across the ice with. She was sitting back and could barely see over the side of the sleigh.

"Nothing," replied Tal, shaking his head. A row of small stalactites broke off his face mask and flew toward Milla. But before they could hit, her hand moved in a blur of motion, batting them away.

"Don't shake your head," Milla instructed. "It's rude to shower ice on your companions."

Tal started to shrug, and even more ice fell off his shoulders, more than Milla could bat away. She sighed and pulled her face mask down, an obvious snub.

Tal didn't care. The Icecarls made a big thing about showing or hiding their faces, but he really wasn't interested in mask etiquette. The wind was so cold that it seemed to go straight through his flesh, chilling his bones. Tal knew from bitter experience that without the mask, his teeth and cheekbones would quickly pick up a deep, internal ache that would last for hours.

Ignoring Milla, Tal looked ahead again. He had to accept that the Ruin Ship was constructed by humans. Even so, he stubbornly resisted the idea that the Icecarls had built it.

At the top of the ridge, the Icecarl who had been leading the Wreska halted for a few moments and turned the leaders toward a winding trail that was marked by luminous rocks, following the contour line down into darkness.

The ship was in a valley, the top of its broken masts level with the foothills of the Mountain of Light, the mountain on which the Castle was built. As the sleigh jerked into motion again, Tal looked away from the ship and into the dark sky. Disoriented by the glow of the ship, he had to look up much higher than he expected before he saw the distant lights of the Castle.

The Castle was far bigger than the Ruin Ship, and its lights were the only brightness in the sky. Its seven towers even pierced the Veil, which shrouded the whole world from the sun.

Tal was comforted by the sight of his distant home. All his life he had been taught that only the Chosen mattered, that only the Chosen ever did anything or created anything worthwhile. The Castle was still the greatest structure in existence, and this Ruin Ship of the Icecarls paled in comparison.

"Beautiful, isn't it?" Milla asked.

Tal looked back down. He'd never heard Milla say anything in such an awe-filled tone. For a moment he thought she'd finally accepted the importance of the Castle. Then he recognized that she had struggled up to look at the Ruin Ship.

"Shouldn't you be lying down?" he asked. Milla had been badly wounded fighting a one-eyed Merwin, a vicious creature that from horn to tail had been longer than the sleigh and all six Wreska in front of it. Tal had managed to blind it with his Sunstone, but it was Milla who had killed the monster. Tal tried to remember that when she was being particularly obnoxious.

"It is the birthplace of our people," said Milla. "There are many tales of the ship. Many of our greatest sagas begin and end here."

She paused and took a breath that must have pained her, but she gave no sign of it before she declaimed:

Green the ice glow, high on mast-head
Black the blood, caked and ash-cold
Red the ribbon, bound through beard
White the Wreska, hauling him home
Returns does Ragnar, dead many days.

Tal didn't say anything. All of the Icecarls' poetry — or whatever it was — seemed to be about people who got themselves killed heroically on the Ice.

"The Ruin Ship is the chief place of the Shield Maidens," added Milla.

Now Tal understood why Milla had clawed herself up the side of the sleigh. The Shield Maidens roamed the Ice and settled disputes among the different clans, hunted down outlaws, and killed dangerous creatures. As far as Tal could tell, the only people allowed to join were very scary women warriors with absolutely no sense of humor.

Milla kept staring at the Ruin Ship, ignoring the pain in her side. She had devoted her life to preparing herself to be a Shield Maiden. Icecarls measured their age in circlings, the time it took an iceship to complete one full circumnavigation of the world, following the continuous migration of the Selski.

From her fourth circling, as a small but ferocious

child, Milla had worked unceasingly to be the best skater, to excel in the use of all weapons, to dare the most dangerous hunts.

Now, though she had only seen fourteen circlings, Milla was an exceptional fighter, even by the standards of her warrior race. She had proved it in her battle with the one-eyed Merwin.

There were few Icecarls who could have defeated the creature, even considering that Tal had blinded it with his Sunstone. This particular Merwin had been renowned for its viciousness, and a full Hand of twelve Shield Maidens had been tracking it for many sleeps. They had come too late to fight the Merwin, but just in time to rescue Tal and the grievously wounded Milla.

Reluctantly, Milla looked down at the shadow that lay at Tal's feet. It looked normal enough now — but only because Tal had been warned that he would be killed if it behaved other than as an ordinary shadow. But she had seen it move by itself, and take different shapes. Tal called it his shadowguard. Because Milla had shared Tal's blood in an oath-taking ritual, it had been able to take her shape and staunch her wounds until the Shield Maidens came.

She almost wished that it hadn't, for free-willed

shadows were things of evil in Icecarl legend. Milla only hoped she would not be considered tainted by the shadow's touch, and so unfit to join the Shield Maidens.

As Milla was thinking of the Shield Maidens, Arla, the Shield Mother of the Hand, suddenly appeared out of the darkness. Without stopping to take off the thin, flat lengths of bone that she used to glide across the ice, she jumped onto the sleigh.

Tal flinched as she appeared. Arla was a stretch taller than him and the way she moved hinted at imminent violence. Her eyes were blue and as cold as the ice, and she never blinked when Tal was looking at her. She had horrific scars on her right arm that Milla said were from reaching into the gullet of an armor-skinned Krall to cut its throat from the inside.

Apart from the cold eyes, Arla was very beautiful behind her mask, with short golden hair that framed her oval face. Tal found the combination very disturbing.

"Only Shield Maidens may see the entrance to the Ruin Ship," Arla announced, pulling two long strips of soft Wreska skin out of one of the many pockets of her outer coat. "Tie these around your eyes as tight as you can. If you try to remove them, the punishment is death."

"Must I wear one, Shield Mother?" asked Milla. She had already taken the first step to being a novice Shield Maiden. In fact, the Quest that would make her a full Shield Maiden was to help Tal get back to the Castle — and find a new Sunstone for her clan ship.

"You are not yet a Shield Maiden," Arla observed. "Here we deal with what *is*, not with what *might* be."

Milla frowned, but didn't say anything. She took the blindfold and put it on. Tal put his on, too. For a moment, he thought of slipping it up a bit so he could see. After all, he was a Chosen of the Castle and should not have to obey anyone here. But something about the way Arla had said "the punishment is death" encouraged him not to peek.

It was strange traveling on without being able to see anything, but Tal didn't mind being blindfolded as long as he knew there would be light when he took it off.

Even in the worst moments he'd spent outside the Castle, there had always been some light around Tal. Like his own Sunstone — now just a dead piece of rock since he'd used all its power to blind the Merwin. Milla's huge extended family, the clan of the Far Raiders, had had a Sunstone on its iceship, though it was fading. He'd even become used to the pallid green light of the Icecarls' moth-lanterns, like the ones on the sleigh.

Despite the fact that he was a prisoner of the Shield Maidens, Tal felt surprisingly secure. At least they would protect him from Merwin and rogue Selski and whatever other awful Ice creatures they might come across. Then, once he made it to the Ruin Ship, he was fairly sure that the Mother Crone of the Mountain of Light would believe his story and let him go home.

He felt a familiar anxiety as he thought of home. Anything could have happened to his family while he was gone. His father, Rerem, had disappeared. His mother, Graile, was very ill. His younger brother, Gref, had been captured by a Spiritshadow while following Tal as he climbed the outside of the Red Tower. And to make everything even more troubling, there were powerful Chosen in the Castle who were definitely Tal's enemies, though the boy didn't know why.

He had tried to tell himself that they weren't really enemies, just Chosen indulging bad temper or boredom. But deep down, he knew that wasn't so. He couldn't stop thinking about it, even though it made him feel slightly sick. He kept trying to think of reasons why someone would want him to dim down to the Red or make him an Underfolk. He deliberately avoided taking the consequences of that thought further.

After all, it was simply impossible that any Chosen would want his father never to return and his mother to die.

"I have to get back," he whispered to himself. Milla rustled at his side, and he knew that she must have heard him. Tal bit his lip, wishing he hadn't spoken. Milla would just think he was being weak.

"Quiet," snapped Arla. Tal flinched. He hadn't realized the Shield Mother was still in the sleigh with them. She was so quiet. All of them were.

They traveled in silence for some time, the sleigh going down into the valley. Finally, it stopped. Tal could hear the Wreska being unharnessed and led away, their sharp X-toed hooves distinctive on the ice.

"Take my hand," instructed Arla, pushing her hand around Tal's. "Milla, you will be carried."

"I can walk!" Milla protested, though Tal knew she could barely sit up. The Merwin horn had cut her whole side open, and though the Shield Maidens had healed the actual wound very rapidly — with a treatment of foul-smelling ointment and weird, rhythmic chanting — Milla had still lost an awful lot of blood and was very weak.

Tal closed his hand, clumsy in its thick fur glove, around Arla's and let her lead him out of the sleigh. At first they walked on ice, with Tal slipping and sliding, and Arla completely balanced.

Then Arla said, "Ware steps!" and Tal's bone-nailed boots were no longer crunching on ice, but on something else. His footsteps let out a deep hollow clang, as if he trod on a metal plate. Tal was surprised — he hadn't seen the Icecarls use metal like this before. Everything they had was made of stone or bone, skin, gut, teeth, and other bits and pieces of animals.

Still, the sound continued. The wind that had blown around them suddenly cut off, too — they must have entered some sort of shelter. Perhaps they were already inside the ship. . . .

Tal put out his free hand and touched an entirely smooth surface, too smooth to be anything but highly worked stone or wood . . . or metal. He tapped it, and heard another dull ringing sound. He would have done the same on the other side, but Arla still held his hand in a grip he could not evade.

The noise changed again, and the ground felt softer under Tal's feet. Almost like the grass that grew in the garden caverns of the Chosen. But surely it was too cold for anything to grow here, even out of the wind?

They kept walking, with sudden changes of direction that totally confused Tal. Every now and then he was spun around several times, and made to climb up and down steps.

Tal desperately wanted to see, but he made no move toward his blindfold. It wasn't worth the risk.

Finally, they stopped. Arla let go of his hand, and then Tal felt fingers at the back of his head, undoing the blindfold. Light streamed in, and he blinked.

He was in a large, perfectly rectangular room. The walls and ceiling were a deep golden metal, polished enough so that he could see his own reflection. The floor was covered in a thick carpet of stitched-together squares of fur.

There was a Merwin horn in each corner of the room. Each horn had a Sunstone set on its tip, filling the room with bright, even light. In such light, there could be no shadows — save for Tal's shadowguard, which was doing its best to be small and stay close to its master's heels.

A long table of yellow bone stood in the middle of the room, loaded with knives, pots, a pile of wet and rubbery vegetable roots, and a large chunk of pale pink meat. A very old woman was cutting the meat into paper-thin slices with a sharp knife made of the same golden metal as the walls. It was the first metal knife Tal had seen since leaving the Castle.

It wasn't until he looked up from the hypnotic rise and fall of the knife that Tal noticed the old woman had the same milky eyes as the Mother Crone on the Far Raiders' ship. She had to be blind, though she didn't wield the knife as if she were. It chopped up and down with the rhythm of Tal's own heart, cutting perfect slices of almost see-through meat without endangering her fingers.

There was only one other person in the room. A younger Crone, sitting on a stool in the corner. She looked at Tal, and he saw the liquid silver flash of her eyes. All the Crones were very creepy. If they didn't have milky eyes, they had these unnaturally bright ones, which seemed to look right inside him.

As well as cutting the meat without difficulty, the milky-eyed Crone also seemed to know who was there. Without stopping her cutting, she looked across and said, "Arla. You have brought our visitors. Welcome to the Ruin Ship, Milla and Tal."

She raised her blade, and the metal flashed in the light.

"I've been expecting you," added the Crone, bringing the knife slashing back down.

·CHAPTER·
TWO☉

"We greet you, Mother Crone," said Milla, clapping her clenched fists together. Tal reached for his Sunstone to give light as a sign of respect, then re-membered that it was dead. He quickly bowed his head instead.

The Mother Crone stopped cutting the meat and wrapped several slices with strands of a black veg-etable. She put the resulting parcels on plates of translucent bone.

"Come, eat," she said. "We will talk."

There were no chairs, so Tal and Milla ap-proached the table. Arla and the other Crone on the stool didn't move. Obviously the invitation didn't apply to them.

Tal looked down at his plate and wished the invi-tation didn't apply to him, either. Not only was the meat raw, the black stuff wasn't a vegetable he recognized. It was wet, for a start, and looked sticky. He closed his eyes and swallowed the lump all in one mouthful. It went down so quickly he hardly tasted it.

"A rare treat," the Mother Crone said with a smile that made the wrinkles around her clouded eyes stand out even more. "Kerusk fish and seaweed, from under the Ice."

"Under the Ice?" Tal blurted out. How could you get under the Ice? He could understand catching fish by cutting a hole where the ice was thin and using a hook and line, but how would you harvest this seaweed?

"We have our ways," said the Mother Crone. "Now I wish to see your shadow, Tal."

"It's there," said Tal nervously, pointing down to where his shadowguard lay next to Milla's feet. It seemed a bit silly pointing out his shadow to a blind woman.

"No," said the Mother Crone. "I wish to see it walk without you."

She sounded quite stern now. Tal looked at her, wondering how her milky eyes could possibly see anything. Or perhaps the Mother Crone had another means of perceiving things?

"Shadowguard, shadowguard," he whispered, after a glance at Arla and Milla. "Make me a shape, as meek as you can."

As he spoke, the shadowguard lost its boy shape and slowly shifted into something else. A Dattu, Tal was relieved to see. A large, innocuous rodent that lived in the grassy hills of Aenir, the spirit world of the Chosen.

"Beware the shadow that walks alone," muttered Arla. She had seen the shadowguard help Milla stay alive after the Merwin attack. But after that, the Shield Mother had warned Tal that he would die if his shadow left him for an instant.

If the threat hadn't been so serious, Tal would have laughed. The Icecarls might be a cut above the Underfolk in some ways, but not by much. If they knew how to use Sunstones properly they wouldn't worry about a shadowguard like Tal's. He doubted they *could* learn how to use Sunstones properly, since that required concentrated thought. As far as Tal could see, Icecarls weren't deep thinkers. They acted on instinct, usually with violence.

"This is not one of those shadows," said the Mother Crone. "It is a lesser thing, still in its infancy. The ones we should fear cannot change their shape."

"Spiritshadows?" asked Tal, unable to suppress a superior smile. Even though he'd had some bad experiences with Spiritshadows, they were still only the tools of the Chosen who had mastered them. "They're only servants, like the Underfolk. Each is bound to obey its Master. No Chosen would set a Spiritshadow against you. What would be the point? There is nothing out here that would interest a real Chosen. I mean, no one has ever bothered to see if there was anything out here before, and even when they do find out, I don't think they will be interested. . . ."

His voice trailed off. It was hard to explain without being totally rude.

"Perhaps," said the Mother Crone. "Yet we have long known about your Castle and its seven Towers. And both Chosen and Shadows have come down from the mountain before."

Tal was silent. He didn't know what to say to that. The Mother Crone was probably trying to impress him and he doubted she really knew anything about the Castle and the Chosen. Nothing important, anyway.

"All I want is to get home," he muttered when the Mother Crone didn't say any more. "I have to get back and get a Sunstone!"

"Two Sunstones," he added, a split second after Milla looked at him, her eyes as sharp as knives. "One for the Far Raiders as well."

"Yes," said the Mother Crone. She took the knife and plunged it deep into the slab of meat in front of her, making Tal jump back. Milla didn't even flinch. "But in all the time that the Ruin Ship has been here, and the Shield Maidens have patrolled these hills, we have never let anyone climb the Mountain of Light, the source of Shadow. Why should we let *you* pass?"

Tal looked down at the floor as he struggled to think of a reason that would seem important to these Icecarls. But nothing came. No brilliant words. No clever answers. Just one truth.

"It's my home," Tal said miserably. "It's where I belong."

"Yes," said the Mother Crone. "To the ship comes the Icecarl, home from the Ice, while the Chosen goes home to the Castle."

She walked around the table and stood close to Tal. She seemed taller, closer up, a good head taller than Tal. She only wore light furs, and her arms were bare, showing many scars. Closer up, the milkiness in her eyes seemed more like the luminous glow of the moth-lamps than the result of age or illness.

From the scars, Tal guessed that the Mother Crone had once been a fierce Shield Maiden. She still had a forbidding menace when she wanted to.

"How can we return you without opening a way back to us, a way that Shadows may seek to use?"

"I don't know," said Tal. "But the Mother Crone of the Far Raiders said I would go back. Didn't she?"

He directed that question at Milla, who had heard the other Mother Crone's strange prophesy. But it was *this* Mother Crone who answered.

"*Home is the Castle, Yet it is not home*," she recited, repeating two lines of the prophecy. "Even among Crones, the truth of what we see is not always clear. Tell me, Shield Mother, what do you think we should do with Tal?"

"Give him to the Ice," said Arla, without expression.

"What?!" exclaimed Tal. That was the same as killing him.

"And you, Milla?" asked the Mother Crone. "What should we do with this boy who is bound to your Quest?"

"Mother Crone, the Far Raiders do need a Sunstone," said Milla. Tal looked at her gratefully, but she didn't meet his eyes.

"As do the Selski Runners and the Sharp Spears and the South Corner, among many others," replied the Mother Crone. "Many others. Too many. So we shall not be giving you to the Ice, Tal. Not while you can be useful."

"How?" asked Tal, though he could guess.

"Sunstones," said the Mother Crone. "The old ones fail, and though some are found, they do not last as long. Why do the Sunstones that fall to us fade so quickly? We do not know. That, and other things, trouble us. The clans need Sunstones. The Crones need knowledge. So we have decided that perhaps we will let you return to your Castle. Come."

She turned away and went over to a wall, pulling down a curtain of patchwork furs to reveal an open doorway. "You, too, Milla. Shield Mother, you may leave us."

Perhaps, Tal thought, was often only a way of saying *no*. But this time, he thought it meant *yes*. Only, knowing the Icecarls, there was bound to be some sort of catch. He'd already been forced into swearing he'd get a Sunstone for the Far Raiders. Maybe the Mother Crone would want one, too.

But then Tal would swear to anything, anything at all, in order to get home. He'd worry about the consequences later.

·CHAPTER·
THREE

The Crone Mother led Milla and Tal along a short corridor, into a huge chamber that Tal realized must once have been the main hold of the ship.

A vast area, it was not well-lit, and what light there was seemed to come from a mixture of Sunstones, moth-lamps, and glowjellies — an odd combination of color and illumination. To make it even stranger, Tal couldn't work out exactly where all the light was coming from.

Most of the room was filled with what looked like a very strange playing board. As Tal paced along behind the Crone, he estimated the board had to be eighty stretches long and forty wide, since one of his paces was roughly equivalent to a stretch.

The board — or whatever it was — occupied the entire middle section of the hold. Peering at it in the dim light, Tal saw that it was made up of many thousands of square tiles. There were twenty or thirty slipper-wearing Icecarls moving around on it, shifting small models of iceships or, not quite so frequently, rearranging the tiles with different ones they brought to the board.

The Icecarls were all girls around Milla's age, which Tal guessed was close to his own — a bit under fourteen.

They all wore indoor furs of the same white color, with similar patterns of black bars. Tal didn't know what sort of animal the furs came from. It wasn't the black, shiny Selski hide used in Milla's armor or the soft brown Wreska skin that lined his own gloves, and he hadn't seen the black-and-white pattern on any other Icecarls. Arla's Shield Maidens wore black Selski-hide breastplates, bracers, and greaves over white furs striped with silver.

The girls were under the direction of seven women, who sat in high-backed chairs of woven bone located at even intervals around the enormous playing board.

The women were Crones, Tal guessed. At least they all had the same telltale glow in their eyes, like the Crone of the Far Raiders, or the woman who had sat in the background when they met the Crone

Mother. Tal wondered how their eyes got so bright, and what happened to them when they became Mother Crones to make their eyes change again.

The seven Crones seemed to be looking out into space, but every now and then one would crook her finger, and a girl would lightly cross the board and go to her. There would be a whispered conversation, then the girl would go back to the board and move a ship, or perhaps exchange one of the tiles, taking a replacement from one of a number of cabinets that lined the far wall.

As they walked closer, the girls stopped whatever they were doing to acknowledge the Mother Crone by clapping their fists. When she stopped at the edge of the board, Tal went over to get a closer look. He saw that every tile was etched with faintly luminous symbols. Doing a quick estimation, Tal calculated that there were around fourteen hundred tiles and four or five hundred ship models.

He also saw that at the very center of the board there was one model that was not a ship. It was a mountain, with a building on top of it. A building with seven towers that glowed with tiny Sunstone chips. Clearly it was the Castle and the Mountain of Light. Below it was a model of the Ruin Ship, covered in the same luminous lichens that grew on the real thing.

"It's a map," Tal said suddenly. Each tile represented a certain area — he had no idea how big — and the symbols on it indicated the terrain, or perhaps the state of the Ice. Each model was also unique, representing a different Icecarl clan and ship.

Tal looked at Milla. She was staring at the girls with obvious longing. They had to be Shield Maiden cadets who had fulfilled their Quest and begun their training. They were what Milla wanted to be, with all her heart.

"We call it the Reckoner. It is a map of sorts," said the Mother Crone. "Look closely at the ships, Tal."

He peered at some of the closer ones. They were carved out of translucent bone, or maybe stone. The light actually came from inside the vessels. Some were filled with luminous moths, some with glowjellies, and some with a tiny Sunstone fragment. Tal wasn't sure what this meant, but fewer than forty in a hundred ships were lit by Sunstones.

"Once, nearly every clan had a Sunstone," said the Mother Crone. "Now it is as you see."

"How do you know?" asked Tal. Then he looked at the girls, moving ships from one tile to the next. "You mean this . . . Reckoner actually shows where all the ships are right *now*, and whether they've got a Sunstone?"

"*And* the conditions of the Ice," Milla added, staring at the table with rapt attention. "Among other things."

"But how?" Tal asked, alarmed. If there really were that many ships, there were far more Icecarls than he'd suspected. And they must have powerful magic to know where every ship was!

"What one Crone sees, all may see, waking or sleeping," said the Mother Crone. "And all clans have at least one Crone. We Icecarls are not without power, Tal. Remember that when you return to the Castle."

"I'll remember," said Tal quickly. But he wasn't really concerned with Icecarl magic. He'd just heard words that were much more magical to him than Crones who could see through one another's eyes. *When you return to the Castle.*

"But when can I go? And how do I get there?"

"This ship is not the only ruin that can be found on the Mountain of Light," the Mother Crone answered. "There was once a road that went from base to crown. Most of it has long since crumbled, and it no longer goes anywhere near the top. But even ruined, it will make your way easier, until you can enter the Castle by other ways."

"Other ways?"

Tal didn't like the sound of that. It made getting back to the Castle sound difficult, but even worse was the thought that the Icecarls might know secret ways into his home. To cover up how disturbed he was, he scratched under his eye, covering his expression with his hand.

"I am not sure exactly what or where these ways are, but I know they exist," said the Mother Crone. She walked away from the Reckoner and went to one of the cabinets, her fingers gently touching items on several shelves. Tal and Milla followed her, Milla still half watching the girls who moved the ships and tiles.

"Ah, this is it," said the old woman, taking a small and very dusty bag of Selski hide off the shelf and handing it to Tal. "Open it."

Tal opened the bag, sneezing as dust billowed from inside. There were two objects in there: a thin rectangle of bone no larger than his hand, and a magnifying glass with a gold rim.

"Long ago," the Mother Crone began, "when I was a little older than one of these young Shield Maidens, a man was found near the Ruin Ship — a man without a shadow. He had lost it, he said, and perhaps he had, though we noticed that he was afraid of *all* shadows, as if his own might return. He called himself a Chosen, from the Castle of Seven Towers, though he would say no more. We did not ask him to explain, for he was not the first stranger to come down the Mountain of Light. The memory of the Crones is long.

"He stayed with us for many sleeps, carving away at that bone, using this glass to keep his work smaller and more secret. He never said exactly what it was, but I think it is a map, showing a way into your Castle."

Tal looked at the tablet of bone with more interest, and raised the magnifying glass to his eye. It was a strong one, so even in the bad light he could make out tiny drawings etched into the surface. There were characters there, too, writing so fine that it must have been carved with the sharpest of needles. Tal needed better light to see what it said, though the alphabet was the one commonly used in the Castle, not the more complex runes used in the spirit world of Aenir.

"Did he tell you his name?" asked Tal. "What happened to him?"

"We called him Longface, for when he first came his eyebrows and much of his hair had been burned off, so that his forehead was tall and as smooth as his chin. After he finished that carving he grew weak, and could not be healed. We gave him to the Ice."

Tal shuddered. The Icecarls were too keen to put anyone weak or useless out onto the Ice. Tal had seen no old Icecarls, except for the Crones.

"You may have Longface's map," said the Mother Crone, "and any other supplies you need. Milla will have to rest for several days before you can go on, but after that, you are free to leave. If Milla returns with her Sunstone, we will know that the time has come for Icecarls and Chosen to meet. If not, we shall look for other ways to find our knowledge . . . and our Sunstones."

There was no menace in her voice, but Tal felt that this was a veiled threat. At first, he wasn't worried about it. The Icecarls were fierce and the Crones obviously had powers he did not understand, but they could never stand up to the Light magic of the Chosen and the strength of their Spiritshadows.

But as he thought about it, Tal looked out at the Reckoner again, and all the ships. There were an awful lot of them, perhaps close to five hundred. Spread all over the world, fortunately . . . but they greatly outnumbered the Chosen. If they could get into the Castle . . .

"Milla doesn't have to come," he said. "I could bring a Sunstone back."

"You would return here?" asked the Mother

Crone, with a faint hint of a smile. "I think it best if Milla does go with you and finds a Sunstone herself."

"Sure," said Tal unhappily. He'd gotten used to traveling with Milla when she was wounded — and quiet. He wasn't sure about traveling with her once she was healthy. He never knew what she was going to do, and he suspected that she would still like to kill him. In her mind, he had never been more than a trespasser who'd come up with a good excuse to save himself.

Still, she had sworn an oath. He could probably trust her — at least until they got to the Castle. Then Tal would have a whole new set of troubles. . . .

·CHAPTER·
FOUR

For the next four days and five sleeps, Tal tried to roam around the Ruin Ship. But whenever he went to open a hanging curtain or go through a doorway, one of the Shield Maiden cadets would pop up from behind, or in front, or from around the corner and politely lead him back to somewhere he'd already been.

Eventually he worked out that he was only allowed to be in the small sleeping chamber he'd been assigned, the Hall of the Reckoner, the Cadets' Feasting Hall where he had his meals (though he never saw anything he'd call a feast), and some of the time, the room where Milla had been ordered to stay in bed.

The only combat skill Milla could practice in bed was her bad temper. Since Tal was the only person she could practice on and get away with it, he found that visiting her was not much fun. But there was simply nothing else to do, except watch the ships and tiles get moved around on the Reckoner, and that was about as boring as the lecture on the basics of light that retired Lector Jannem gave every year.

On the positive side, though she was cross at being ordered to bed, Milla was bored, too, and sometimes she would actually answer Tal's questions. The Shield Maiden cadets wouldn't speak to him at all, unless it was to stop him from going somewhere or doing something he wasn't allowed to do.

"How come there are no men here?" Tal asked Milla on the second day, after he'd ducked a pillow she'd thrown at him. He handed it back to her, noting that her face had lost its sickly gray tinge and was returning to its normal, surprisingly delicate paleness. All the Icecarls were very pale, much more so than the Chosen.

Most Icecarls had the same color hair, too, like sunshine mixed with white ash. Tal's hair was the color of dirt, settling just above his shoulders. He felt that cutting his hair short would be an admission that he was no longer a proper Chosen.

"No men where?" snarled Milla.

"Here, the Ruin Ship."

"I told you," snapped Milla, "it is the chief place of the Shield Maidens. It is not like a normal clan ship. There are no families, no children, no hunters, no Selski. The only men who come here would be either lost hunters, messengers . . . or a Sword Thane."

"A Sword Thane?" asked Tal, suddenly interested.

"Women who wish to serve all the clans become Shield Maidens," explained Milla. "But men do not work so well together, so those who wish to be law-givers and protectors become Sword Thanes."

"What do you mean?" asked Tal.

"Everyone knows this." Milla frowned. "Some clans prefer a Sword Thane, though they can be un-reliable and hard to find. It makes a better saga, I sup-pose."

"Prefer a Sword Thane for what?"

"Trouble!" spat Milla. "When you have trouble, you send for the Shield Maidens, but sometimes a Sword Thane finds you and the trouble first."

"But aren't Shield Maidens heroes?" Tal inquired. "I mean, you killed the Merwin. Doesn't that make you a hero — which makes you a Sword Thane?"

"I wish to be a Shield Maiden, so I must try to be a hero," Milla repeated. "But only a man can be a Sword Thane. All Sword Thanes are heroes but not all heroes are Sword Thanes."

"What?" asked Tal. He was getting confused. "So what do you call a man who's a hero but not a Sword Thane? What if he uses an ax or a spear?"

Milla didn't answer. She picked up the Merwin horn sword that never left her side and readied it to throw like a spear. Tal didn't stay to be a target, or for further explanation about Shield Maidens and Sword Thanes. He disappeared around the corner, and did not visit Milla again till she was up and final preparations were being made for their departure.

They left the Ruin Ship after a stay of a full five sleeps, the same way they had entered, stumbling along blindfolded, guided by Arla. This time, at least, they were much better equipped. The Shield Maidens had been generous in providing new furs, climbing teeth, ropes of braided Selski hide, and other things they considered essential to climb the ruined road to the Mountain of Light.

Tal had used part of the time in the ship to study Longface's map. He had come to the conclusion that the bone had not actually been carved with a sharp tool, but cut by Sunstone light. That meant the Chosen who had done it had been extremely skilled, and that he still had his Sunstone when he had staggered down to the Ruin Ship. But not his Spiritshadow.

The tablet gave no clue to its maker's mystery. There was writing on it, in addition to regular marks that were obviously a map. But all the writing said was:

Half road down pyramid Imrir fallen 100 stretch entry heatway tunnel Underfolk 7.

Tal had puzzled over this for some time, but all he could guess was that it meant there was an entrance to the heating system of the Castle — which he knew went through the mountain, right down into the deep earth. *Underfolk 7* was almost certainly a reference to the lowest of the Underfolk levels, which Tal supposed was where the heatway tunnel came out. Presumably the entrance outside would be about halfway up the mountain, near a fallen pyramid.

Tal had a dim recollection that Imrir had been the Emperor long ago. The current Empress didn't have a name — Tal had never wondered about that before. Of course, she had been the Empress for much longer than most, fending off old age with her mastery of Sunstone magic. Maybe Emperors' or Empresses' names were only known after they died.

All thoughts of the Empress were gone by the time the blindfold came off. Arla left them, without a word. Tal watched with relief as she silently slid away. He felt like a caveroach about to be stepped on when Arla was around. Milla, of course, had a completely different reaction. Arla was everything Milla wanted to be twenty circlings from now.

Tal stood alone with Milla and the freezing wind. Far below, they could see the luminous outline of the Ruin Ship.

Both of them had moth-lanterns, but the dull green light only showed snow and patches of bare rock. If there was a road — even a ruined one — Tal couldn't see it.

"Come on," ordered Milla. She shouldered her pack and headed off. Tal fumbled on his own pack, groaning at the sudden weight. It was full of sleeping furs and climbing gear and food and what felt like at least his own weight in other things the Icecarls considered essential. Tal would have rather had a Sunstone, so he could properly warm himself. Even with inner and outer coats of thick fur, a cloth-lined bone face mask, and a short, hooded cape lined with the soft tails of something he couldn't pronounce, Tal was still cold.

Though he couldn't see a road through the amber lenses of his mask, he followed obediently. Either Milla could see something, or Arla had told her a secret sign to look for.

It was hard going, but not *too* hard. At times they had to clamber over great blocks of ice that had slid down from higher up, but it was clear they were on a path made by humans.

Once again, Tal regretted the absence of a Sunstone. He wanted to light up the whole mountainside, to see the sheer cliffs stretching up and up, and admire the way the rock had been carved away in precise lines to create the road, switchbacking its way up what would otherwise be impassable terrain.

But all he could see now was the occasional evidence of construction, particularly when there was a well-preserved stretch of road and mountainside forming a perfect right angle.

At other times, he had no idea how Milla found the road again after it had fallen away.

He asked her.

"The road smells of ghalt, the melting stone," Milla said. As usual, her voice bore a reluctance to talk to Tal, tempered with a desire to show off how superior Icecarls were. She bent down, swept away a light layer of snow and, with effort, pulled out a piece of black rock that shone in the moth-light.

"There are hot pools of ghalt in the far southern mountains," she said, holding the piece under Tal's nose. "When it is hot it pours like water and smells very sour. Even very old, cold ghalt smells. I do not know how the ancients brought it here for the road."

Tal raised his mask to sniff at it, but he couldn't smell anything. His face just got cold.

As the hours of walking wore on, Tal was no longer interested in how Milla found the road. He was just glad that she did. He was also hoping that she would stop soon so he could rest. She had to be tired, too, he reasoned, since she was still recovering from her wound. But she showed no signs of weariness.

When she did stop, it wasn't for a rest. She suddenly backed up, almost hitting Tal. While he gawped at her, she threw her arm around him and wrestled him into the nearest snowdrift, piled up against the mountainside.

As they plunged into the snow, Tal felt a great rush of air go past. He caught a momentary glimpse of enormous translucent eyes, each as large as his own head, followed by spread wings of great size.

"What was that?"

Milla clapped her hand over his mouth, her fur glove almost smothering Tal. He started to struggle, then stopped as she held a knife against his throat and ordered him in a whisper, "Stay still!"

They lay together in the snow, not moving. Finally, they heard a terrible screech some distance off, and Milla relaxed. The knife vanished from her hand, and she let Tal sit up.

"Perawl," she said. "They can't see you if you stay completely still. They're a bit deaf, as well."

"What was the ... the noise?" asked Tal. The unseen hunters in the air made this place even worse than being on the Ice. At least with the Selski you could hear them coming, and you could see a Merwin's luminous horn.

Milla didn't answer, so Tal repeated the question.

"It could be any one of a number of things," replied Milla evasively. "The Perawl's meal, I suppose."

"So the great Milla doesn't know everything," remarked Tal. Milla ignored him, her attention still focused downhill.

"Perhaps ... perhaps it was the other way

around," Tal added. The screech hadn't sounded like something being caught. It had sounded triumphant. "Maybe the Perawl was something else's meal."

They looked at each other, expressions unseen behind their face masks. But Milla started off again at a faster pace and Tal followed without complaint.

Without his Sunstone, Tal had no idea how much later it was when they finally stopped to rest and eat. As on the Ice, the meal was Selski meat heated over a Selski oil stove.

"We will have three watches. I will take the first and third," declared Milla when they had finished eating. "You need only stay awake for the middle watch."

"I can stand two watches," said Tal. "Let's have four watches."

"Do you know how to count every breath without thinking, even while asleep?" asked Milla.

"Uh, no," answered Tal. "What does —"

"That is how we count the passing time when there is no other means," explained Milla, as if she were speaking to a very small child. "So I will tell you when to begin and finish your watch."

Tal couldn't argue with that. Surreptitiously, he tried to count each individual breath, but he couldn't keep track. He half suspected that Milla couldn't, either, and she was just trying to be superior again.

It was a cold camp, and a dangerous one, with a long drop beside the road. They put their backs against the slope, and Tal silently told himself thirty times, *I must not walk in my sleep.*

Sleep did not come easily. The wind howled down the mountain and seemed to want to pick Tal and Milla up and take them with it all the way to the Ruin Ship far below. Because they were higher up, it was even colder than on the Ice, and Tal found himself huddling closer and closer to Milla to stay warm.

Milla seemed to take this as normal behavior, but Tal found even her fur-muffled closeness unnerving. He had never been so close to a girl before, let alone one who might kill him if he accidentally threw his arm around her while he was dreaming.

That thought didn't help him sleep. Neither did the noises he heard, or thought he heard, in the night. Even when Milla was supposed to be sleeping, she sat up every now and then to listen. Sometimes Tal wondered if she ever really slept. He wouldn't have been surprised to find that if she did sleep, it was with one eye open.

The middle watch seemed to go on and on forever. Tal decided to test if Milla was asleep. He leaned away from her, but she didn't stir. So he edged away a little more. She sank back into her furs, and Tal smiled. She really was asleep.

He reached across to lightly tickle under her chin, where a tiny square of skin showed clear of the mask and her laced-up collar. Tal had often done this to Gref, trailing his fingernail like an insect across him to see how long it took for his brother to wake up.

His gloved hand was just about to touch Milla's chin when her hand snaked out from under the sleeping fur, her knife held at roughly the same point under Tal's chin. For a frozen moment they faced each other, then Tal slowly withdrew his hand and Milla her knife.

"Two hundred and seventy-five breaths," said Milla. "I will know when it is my turn."

Tal was very wakeful for the rest of his watch, but sleep claimed him quickly when Milla took over.

Despite this, he felt like he'd had no sleep at all when Milla shook him awake, and they started off again. This time, the climbing became harder, as more of the road had been destroyed by avalanches. In some places the mountain had simply slipped away. They had to climb up very steep slopes of ice and stone, using ropes, Wreska jawbones full of sharp teeth strapped onto the sides of their boots, and bone spikes — called pitons — hammered in with a rounded stone as big as Tal's fist.

Milla was an experienced climber. Tal was not. Luckily he had his shadowguard to help, though he tried not to call on it too much. He didn't want Milla to think he was beholden to his shadow.

Tal's greatest difficulty was not being able to see. When climbing, the moth-lanterns had to be strapped to their backpacks, so most of the light fell behind them rather than in front.

It was even worse when it snowed. The first two "days" (by Milla's reckoning) stayed clear and cold. But halfway through their second sleep, the snow came down heavily, so much that they would have been buried under it if they'd been on level ground.

The snow kept up through their third day, then just as Tal was falling asleep turned into particularly wet and unpleasant sleet that came in sudden bursts, blowing horizontally in wet sheets that soaked the travelers' outer coats in an instant. Fortunately, the inner furs stayed dry, evidence of the Icecarls' long practice of living in the wild.

By this stage, Tal was so tired that as soon as Milla

told him he could sleep, he slept, no matter what the weather was doing.

On the fourth day, the sleet finally faltered and then stopped altogether. The wind died down, too, and the air became still. They made faster progress, and within a few hours they came to something that had to be the fallen pyramid mentioned on the bone tablet.

They first saw it when it reflected their lights, and for a heart-stopping instant, both thought themselves face-to-face with the eyes of some huge creature. But as the reflection multiplied, it became clear that what lay ahead was not a living thing.

Trudging wearily up the road, they saw that it was a pyramid. A pyramid of blue crystal, three times as tall as Milla. It must have slid down the mountain long ago, because it no longer stood upright. The point now angled back into the mountain, rather than up at the dark sky.

"The entry to the heatway tunnel must be close," said Tal. "Within a hundred stretches, the tablet says."

"Does it mention *that*?" asked Milla, raising her lantern. The green light spilled forward, and reflections from the pyramid swam back.

Right in front of the pyramid the road simply

wasn't there anymore. It had fallen away, leaving a frightening gap.

"Oh," said Tal. "No, it doesn't."

Cautiously, Tal and Milla crept to the edge. They could not see any bottom.

"Can we climb up and over?" asked Tal, looking at the mountainside.

Milla moved her lantern across, noting the loose rock and signs of recent slippage. Then she shook her head.

"The rock face is too loose," she announced. "We will have to jump the gap."

245
•

·CHAPTER·
FIVE

"Jump?" exclaimed Tal. "Impossible. It must be ten . . . even twelve stretches!"

Milla tilted her face mask back and looked at the chasm again.

"No, we can jump it," she said. "Even you."

"There has to be another way," Tal said desperately. He went over to the side of the road against the mountain and tested his weight against an outcropping of rock above his head.

The rock came free, with a lot more besides, nearly braining Tal. Milla was right. It was too loose.

Tal looked down at the gap again. It would be suicide to try to jump over it. He couldn't even see the bottom. They were almost at a turn in the road, so it would be a straight drop to the road below. That had to be at least five hundred stretches!

He looked back. Milla was strapping the toothy jawbones they used as spikes onto her boots. She had also taken out something Tal hadn't seen before. Gloves of thin Selski hide, with long curved claws of reddish bone.

"You will have to help me with the claw-hands," Milla said as she finished strapping on her boot-teeth. She then tried to hammer a bone piton into the road, but it wouldn't go through the sections where there was metal, and the stone crumbled everywhere else.

Finally, Milla shrugged and put the piton back. She left her pack lying on the ground and strapped her Merwin-horn sword onto her back instead. She slipped on the clawed gloves. Tal saw that they had to be tied onto her wrists, so he helped her, patiently following her instructions on how to do the right knots.

"Move the lanterns to the edge," said Milla. She had not put her mask back on. Tal saw her eyes move calculatingly to the far edge.

"Shouldn't you be tied to a rope?" he asked. "I could hold it . . ."

"There is nothing to secure it to," said Milla. "You would only be dragged down."

She hesitated, then said, "If I fail, Tal, you will try to go on? You will fulfill the Quest and get a Sunstone for my clan? Then I may become a Shield Maiden, even after death."

Tal looked at the dark gap and was tempted to say that if Milla couldn't jump it, he would have no chance. But she had used his name, and hadn't looked at him with her usual scorn. "I will try," he said, with a gulp.

"I would not ask, normally," said Milla. "But I am still not at my full strength."

"Great," Tal muttered under his breath. He looked at the gap again, then reached out to touch Milla's claw-hands.

"All right, I'll jump first," he said.

"What?" Milla was suddenly angry again. "Do you doubt my courage?"

She took her hands away and stalked back twenty or so steps, out of the light of the lanterns.

"I'll show you a Shield Maiden's courage!" she shouted angrily.

"No, Milla!" shouted Tal. "Wait! I didn't mean . . . take your time —"

Before he could finish, Milla came sprinting out

of the darkness. She passed Tal in a blur, her arms and legs pumping. Two paces from the edge, she threw herself forward, arms outstretched.

"Yaaaahhhhhhhh!"

Tal rushed to the edge. There was a clatter of rocks. He couldn't see Milla on the other side. He raised one of the lanterns, a sick feeling in his stomach.

Nothing moved in the small pool of light.

"Milla!" Tal shouted, his voice echoing into the emptiness.

No answer came, but one small movement caught Tal's eye. A clawed hand, reaching up over the lip on the far side.

Another followed it, then Milla's head. With a choking grunt, she pulled herself up over the edge and crawled a few paces forward. Anyone normal would have collapsed gratefully then, but Milla staggered to her feet and looked back at Tal.

As their eyes met, Tal realized that now he had to jump. Without the claw-hands.

But at least there was no wind.

"Throw over a rope," Milla yelled. "I will secure it to the pyramid."

Tal rummaged out a rope with relief. At least he would have a rope. If he did fall, it would only be . . . well, far enough to be seriously hurt instead of killed. If he was lucky.

When he turned to throw the rope over to Milla, she was bent over, her hands on her knees, obviously in pain. As soon as he moved, she shot back upright, as if she had never felt the slightest twinge.

Tal didn't say anything. He just threw over the coiled rope. He really didn't understand these Ice-carls.

Milla cut through the laces on her claw-hands, removed them, made a loop with the rope, and easily flipped it over the top of the pyramid. It seemed secure enough, though she inspected the edges to make sure the crystal would not cut the rope. Once the edges might have been sharp, but long exposure to wind, snow, and rain had rounded them off.

Tal caught the end she threw back.

"Tie a pack on," Milla instructed. "And one of the other ropes, so we can lower it down and then back up."

Tal quickly did as he was told. Passing the second rope behind his back, he lowered the pack down till Milla's rope was taut, so she could swing it across and pull it up. They then repeated the process with Tal's pack and one of the lanterns. The other lantern had a rope tied to it, but it would be left till last, so Tal could see where to jump.

Tal was glad that all this delayed his own crossing. He was still trying to work out another way to get across, though there didn't seem to be any alternative. Once again he walked to the edge and looked down. A momentary dizziness hit him, and he stepped back suddenly. So suddenly he almost fell.

There had to be another way! Ignoring Milla, he backtracked down the road, holding the lantern up to look at the sheer face of the mountainside. If he could find solid rock, he could climb higher and then across, to get past the gap.

He thought he could see a ledge, and for a moment he was filled with hope. Then he realized it was only an illusion, caused by a band of darker stone.

There was no other way across. No other way if he wanted to get back to the Castle.

Milla threw the rope over again. Tal tied it around himself and then the free end to the specially made loop on his new, wider belt.

"If I don't make it . . ." he said, then faltered. Even if he asked her to, Milla would never be able to find his father, save his mother, or rescue Gref. And the Chosen did not have posthumous promotions. If he fell here, he would never fulfill his dreams of rising Violet. Brilliance Tal Graile-Rerem, Shadow-lord of the Violet Order, would never be . . .

"What?" shouted Milla.

Tal shook his head slowly, clearing his head of dreams.

This time, Milla looped the rope twice more around the pyramid and left only enough slack so that Tal could lay it out to one side of his run, where he wouldn't trip over it.

When everything was ready, Tal backed up into the darkness. He stood there for some time, trying to get his heart to slow down enough so that he could actually tell individual heartbeats apart.

His shadowguard stood next to him, barely visible against the dark stone. It was too weak to be of much use, with only the moth-lanterns for light. Even so, it leaned forward like a racer about to start and Tal knew it was trying to encourage him.

It had gotten much colder, but Tal wasn't sure how much of that was just from standing still and how much was from fear.

Milla seemed to be a long way away, at the end of a tunnel. A small figure, lit in green, with the pyramid's reflections sparkling around her.

"It's just like the Achievement of the Body," Tal whispered to himself. "Someone has put a Gasping Hole in my way. I win if I jump it. Violet Ray of Attainment. Jump. Win. Jump."

Taking a very deep breath, he started to run. The teeth on his boots shrieked on the stone of the road. Rope whisked up next to him as green light and the darkness of the gap rushed at him, faster and faster.

"Yaaaaaaaahhhhh!" screamed Tal, as he hurled himself forward . . . into thin air.

·CHAPTER·
SIX

The other side of the gap hurtled toward him. He stretched out his arms and pulled up his feet, willing himself farther and farther on. He knew he wasn't going to make it. In an instant, he would be falling, not jumping, the rope whistling away above his head, his shadowguard weakly scrabbling at handholds —

He hit, fingers reaching for a hold, feet kicking to get the boot-teeth into a foothold. Then he realized he wasn't sliding down a vertical cliff. He was lying flat on the ground, desperately trying to prevent a fall that wasn't going to happen.

He'd made it — and he'd jumped farther than Milla!

He lay there, panting, while Milla undid the rope from his belt and the pyramid and coiled it up. She didn't say anything then, or as she stepped over him to bring in the other rope and the lantern.

Eventually Tal got up and picked up his pack. His shadowguard moved into its accustomed place at his feet. Maybe the Icecarls didn't congratulate one another on escaping death. They just got on with it.

Or perhaps not.

"Good jump," Milla said finally, as Tal shrugged his pack into a comfortable position.

"Thanks," Tal replied. But Milla had already pulled her face mask into place and turned away. Walking around the pyramid, she disappeared from sight.

"Look out for the tunnel entrance," Tal said as he hurriedly followed her. "It will be close."

The road continued past the pyramid, and was in better shape. Much more of the original metal remained, and the mountain had not collapsed onto it. Tal counted out a hundred stretches as he walked, holding his lantern high so he could see anything that might be a tunnel entrance.

But neither of them saw anything. After a hundred and twenty stretches, Milla stopped. She raised her mask and said, "Perhaps the entrance is on the other side."

"What?" asked Tal. He lifted his own mask and looked at Milla. "You mean the other side of the gap! It . . . it can't be! We would have seen it."

"We *should* have seen it." Milla nodded, her face expressionless. "We will have to jump back."

"No!" exclaimed Tal. "No. It *has* to be on this side."

Milla kept nodding. It took Tal a second to realize that she was trying not to laugh. Then she couldn't hold it in anymore and the laughter burst out. Tal couldn't remember even seeing her smile before.

"It is an Icecarl joke!" she spluttered, clapping her fists together. "We always joke about revisiting danger. Like Talgrim One-Arm, who thought he had to go back to kill the Blue Selski when Vilske had already finished it."

"I don't get it," said Tal, shaking his head.

Milla laughed again, and pointed.

"Look, we're standing next to the entrance!"

She pointed up above her head. There were square-cut stones laid around a circular hole that led into the mountainside. A tunnel.

Tal stared up at the tunnel in disbelief and felt his crooked smile starting to curve up one side of his face. He could put up with any number of stupid

Icecarl jokes to see the way home. Soon, he would be back in the Castle. Deliberately, he tried not to think of the troubles that awaited him there.

For now, all they had to do was get in that tunnel and follow the map. How hard could that be?

·CHAPTER·
SEVEN

It was unbearably hot inside the tunnel. Even with a wet cloth over his mouth and nose, Tal could hardly breathe. He was able to take only shallow breaths, and the lack of air made him very weak.

Once again he set down his Icecarl moth-lantern to look at the small rectangle of bone he held in his left hand, holding a magnifying glass close to his eyes so he could make out the tiny drawings scratched into the surface.

They had turned left at the last intersection of the narrow, crawl-size tunnels, so at the next intersection they should turn right.

A cough behind him — and then a tap at his heels — reminded him that Milla must find these overheated tunnels even more unbearable than he did. She was an Icecarl, born to travel the frozen wastelands. Tal had at least experienced real heat before, though this tunnel was even hotter than the Orchard Gardens or his sick mother's sunchamber.

He started crawling forward again. His shadow-guard flowed ahead of him, avoiding Milla. It was stronger in the confined space of the tunnels, where the light reflected from the walls, and so more noticeable.

At the next intersection, Tal looked at the miniature map once more. According to the carving they should turn right. But the boy hesitated. The light from the moth-lantern was green, and illuminated only a small area. Up ahead, in the right-hand tunnel, there was a faint red glow.

Tal was afraid he knew what that meant. He and Milla were in a network of tunnels that had probably once been used by the builders of the Castle's heating system. Below them — he hoped *far* below — there were much larger tunnels that channeled lava from the depths of the mountain. These tunnels heated vast reservoirs of water, the steam from which was then piped up to heat the Castle's many levels and rooms.

The red glow ahead suggested that one of the lava tunnels had broken open, and its deadly contents had bubbled their way up. The bone map in

Tal's hand was very old, and any number of changes could have taken place since it was made.

To make matters worse, the map didn't show any other way of getting into the Castle. In fact, apart from showing the key intersections, it had no detail at all. So Tal *couldn't* work out another way to go.

He took another shallow breath and started forward again. He could hear Milla following him, shuffling along in a half crouch, half crawl. She was coughing a lot but hadn't said anything. She probably wouldn't, even if she was about to pass out. From what Tal had seen, a Shield Maiden would probably keep on crawling even if she *had* passed out. . . .

The red light grew stronger, and became tinged with an even brighter yellow. It got hotter, too, the stone of the tunnel almost too warm to touch with bare skin. For the first time, Tal regretted dumping their heavy outer coats back near the beginning of the tunnels, though Milla still wore her Selski-hide armor. She probably never took it off, Tal thought, like the Merwin-horn sword glowing at her side.

At the next intersection, Tal had to wipe the sweat off his forehead and out of his eyes before he could focus on the bone map. Another right turn, and this time the red light came from all directions. There had to be a lot of lava ahead.

The air smelled even worse than it had before. Tal lay on his side to rewet his breathing rag from the water bottle the Shield Maidens had given him, a hollowed-out Wreska bone with a hide stopper. Milla did the same, then put her bone mask back on over the top. Tal had long since removed his, but Milla treated the mask like armor, to be worn at all times. Tal caught a brief glimpse of her pale face, set in determination, before the mask and its amber lenses hid her expression.

"Not much farther," croaked Tal.

Milla shrugged and answered, "I know you can't help crawling slowly."

"That's not . . . oh, never mind!" snapped Tal. Why had he bothered to waste his breath?

It took a long time to reach the next intersection. Not because it was a long way, but because they were both so sapped of energy by the heat and the lack of air.

Tal was so busy concentrating on keeping the lantern up and keeping himself moving forward that he forgot to look ahead. He actually ran into the skeleton before he realized what was going on.

When Tal *did* look to see what he'd bumped into, he backed up so quickly that he smacked into Milla. She cried out angrily and for a moment there was a tangle of his legs and her arms before Tal calmed down and Milla moved back.

"What . . . is . . . it?" she said, speaking with effort, taking a breath between each word.

"A skeleton," puffed Tal. He twisted the knob on the lamp to open the weave, letting more light from the luminous moths shine out. Tal's shadowguard slid back under his feet as he did so, to fall behind like a real shadow. Milla shuffled back still farther, so the shadowguard couldn't touch her.

The skeleton had obviously been there a long time, or else it had been scoured clean by scavengers. There were no scraps of clothing, or anything that might be a clue to who it was. Probably not an Icecarl, Tal thought, because there were no signs of any weapon. He'd never seen an unarmed Icecarl.

They would have to climb over the skeleton to get past. Steeling himself, Tal closed his eyes and reached out, but as his fingers touched bone he pulled them back. He couldn't help imagining that it was still someone's arm, and the skeleton would sit up and shout.

"Let me do it!" ordered Milla, but Tal wouldn't get out of her way.

He reached out and tugged at one arm, to pull the whole skeleton flat so they could crawl over it. But as he tugged, the arm came off, and then every individual bone fell apart. Tal gasped and dropped the arm. Something else fell, too, and clinked on the stone.

Tal saw it fall between his feet and roll behind him. A finger bone, with a ring stuck on it. A ring with a large jewel.

A Sunstone!

·CHAPTER·
EIGHT

Tal pushed his back against the tunnel wall, ignoring the heat of the rock, and looked behind. Milla was picking up the finger bone and sliding off the ring. As she touched it, the jewel suddenly blossomed into light, swinging wildly through every color in the spectrum. It was so bright that Tal had to close his eyes.

When he opened them again, Milla had closed her hand around the Sunstone ring. Light leaked out between her fingers and made her hand translucent.

"Give . . . it . . . to . . . me," said Tal. It was what he needed, what he had climbed the Red Tower to get — a new, powerful Sunstone, which he could use to become a full Chosen, to enter the spirit world of Aenir and save his family.

"No." Milla started to turn around.

"Wait!" Tal croaked. He twisted around, but Milla was quicker. She had already gone several stretches along the tunnel. "You don't know how to use it! And you'll . . . get . . . lost!"

Milla kept going. She probably remembered the turns, Tal thought. But he had to have the Sunstone. He could always get her another one later. He looked down at his shadowguard. Milla would never forgive him if he used it . . . but if he didn't . . .

"Shadowguard, shadowguard," coughed Tal. "Grab that girl, as quick as you can."

The shadowguard shot out from under him, growing long and thin, like the shadow of a slender giant. One arm grew even longer, and the hand on the end spread wide. It snatched at Milla's ankle and gripped tight.

Instantly, she rolled on her back, flexed forward, and struck at the shadow with a bone knife that sprung out of her sleeve. But that couldn't hurt the shadowguard and it held fast.

"Traitor!" hissed Milla. "You swore!"

Tal *had* sworn with his own blood and Milla's to get a Sunstone for the Far Raiders. He had the triple scar on his wrist to prove it. But he hadn't sworn to hand over the *first* Sunstone they came across.

265

"You swore, too," he said. "To help me reach the Castle. We aren't really there yet. Besides, that Sunstone isn't tuned."

Milla hesitated, but only for a second. She thought they were close enough to the Castle. Then she started crawling again, dragging the shadowguard with her.

"I saved your life!" Tal panted out desperately when Milla didn't stop. The shadowguard wasn't strong enough to hold Milla for long, and he didn't want to tell it to hurt her. "You owe me."

Milla stopped as if she had run into a wall. Tal *had* saved her life when his shadowguard had bound her wounds after the fight with the one-eyed Merwin. Arguably, she had saved his by killing the Merwin, but that was not so certain.

"I need that Sunstone," coughed Tal. "Come with me and I'll get you another one. If I can't within fourteen sleeps . . . I'll give it back. For the ship and . . . the clan."

Milla's knife disappeared up her sleeve. Then she opened her hand. Tal had to shield his eyes from the Sunstone's light as she threw the ring back to him.

"Fourteen sleeps!" Milla conceded angrily. "But I no longer owe you a life!"

"Agreed," said Tal. He picked up the ring and focused his mind on the Sunstone. It flared up again, then gradually dimmed as Tal took control. When it was no brighter than the moth-lantern, Tal tried the ring on his middle finger. It was too big, so he fastened it to the chain around his neck, next to the chunk of blackened rock that had been his old Sunstone.

The Sunstone in the ring was very old, but it had lost none of its power, lying unused here in the dark. The Chosen — for the skeleton must have been a Chosen — had made it go dormant before he or she died. That surprised Tal. He knew no Chosen of his time brave enough to die alone in the dark, just to save a Sunstone.

"Shadowguard, shadowguard," he muttered. "Come back to me."

The shadowguard let go of Milla and hastily retreated, flowing back into a regular shadow. One arm kept moving, waving backward and forward.

"What?" Tal asked. His mind felt a bit fuzzy.

The shadowguard waved again and Tal realized it was telling him to hurry. At the same time, he became aware that Milla had caught up to him again, and he hadn't even noticed. He must have blanked out for a few seconds.

"Air," Milla gasped. "Bad air."

She pushed at him. Tal turned and started crawling again.

They crawled for what seemed like hours but couldn't have been more than minutes. Then they were at yet another intersection. Slowly, Tal got out the bone map and tried to work out where they were. The red glow was bright, but not bright enough to read by, and for some reason the moth-lantern had dimmed. Tal shook it to liven up the moths, but that didn't work, and the spaces in the weave were as wide as they could go.

It was hard work to set the lamp down and get the new Sunstone out instead, since Tal's hands seemed to be weighed down and wouldn't go where he told them to. He finally managed it, and after a few bright flashes he did get the Sunstone to shine at a useful level.

In its light, he saw that all the luminous moths in the lantern were lying still on the bottom, their green abdomens fading. The moths were asleep . . . or dead. Sluggishly, Tal passed the lantern back to Milla. It was an Icecarl tool. She would know what to do with it.

He looked back at the map. It took some time to remember where they were. A right turn, and then a symbol that might represent a ladder, or perhaps a ramp. A way up, anyway.

Tal hoped.

Unless they were only at the intersection before that, in which case they should take a left and then a right. But they'd already done that, hadn't they?

Tal turned the map the other way up. Now that he looked at it, he wasn't sure that he hadn't had it upside down the whole time.

"On!" whispered Milla. "We must . . . go on!"

Tal couldn't remember which way they had turned, but after a while they came to an opening in the tunnel ceiling, and a ladder of the same crystal as the Crystal Wood in the Castle. Tal tried to direct a beam of light at it to make it sing, but for some reason he kept missing. Different-colored beams shot out everywhere from the Sunstone, but none hit.

It made Tal laugh. He couldn't help it — a choking giggle came out of him that sounded so strange, he looked around to see whom it might belong to.

Dimly he was aware of Milla pushing past him and starting to climb, then of his shadowguard pulling at him, placing his hands on the ladder and his foot on the lowest rung.

The ladder was strangely cool, here where everything was hot. The shock of it cleared Tal's head a little, and he realized with sudden panic that there was something poisonous in the air, fumes from the lava down below, that made his head strange and his limbs full of lead.

The shadowguard pulled at Tal's wrist, urging him to climb. Milla was only just ahead of him, climbing very slowly. She almost slipped a few times, but the shadowguard was watching her, too, and it zipped past to put her feet or hands back on the ladder.

Tal started seeing double. He reached for rungs that weren't there, and his fingers closed on air instead of crystal. His arms grew too tired to reach up. Slowly, ever so slowly, he put his legs through the ladder and sat, fumbling with his belt. He couldn't go on, but he could try and strap himself to the ladder so he wouldn't fall.

He managed to get his belt around the ladder. Then a final cautious thought made him slip the chain with the Sunstone over his head. For an instant it seemed certain he would drop it, before his shadowguard helped his trembling hand push it into the secret pocket inside his sleeve.

Then he passed out, only his broad Selski-hide

belt looped through the ladder preventing him from falling.

Milla lasted a little longer. She made it to a landing thirty stretches above, but that was all. Collapsing onto it, she only just managed to draw her knife — to face death armed — before she passed out as well.

The shadowguard made sure Tal's belt was secure, then tried to climb farther up the ladder. But as it passed the landing where Milla lay, it grew thinner and more transparent. A few stretches farther, it was no more than a dark outline, without substance. Reluctantly, it drew back, till it once again seemed like Tal's natural shadow.

Nothing could help Tal now.

CHAPTER NINE

"Kill them."

Tal heard the words as if they came from a long way off, carried on the wind. Somewhere, someone was talking about killing someone. Someone else was saying, "No. We don't know who they are."

"One looks like a Chosen. I say kill *him* at least."

"What's the point of dragging them up here, if we just kill them anyway? They haven't got Sunstones, they've both got normal shadows, and look at their clothes. They must be from somewhere else. Maybe they can help us."

The one who wanted to kill whoever it was laughed — a bitter, mocking laugh.

"Help us do what? Hide in these tunnels better? Live more miserably than we do now?"

Tal managed to get one eye open a fraction and saw that the people talking were standing quite close to him. There were three of them. Two boys who couldn't be much older than he was, and another taller one who looked a bit older. He hadn't spoken.

The two younger ones carried short, broad-bladed spears. They were all wearing dirty rags that Tal thought might once have been white Underfolk robes. The older one had a cap with a long black feather in it.

There was an oil lamp sitting on the floor behind the three boys. Its light cast long shadows from all three. Natural shadows.

They *were* Underfolk. Tal tried to order them to help him, but nothing came out. The effort needed to keep even one eyelid half open was immense.

"Kill them," said the first, blond boy.

"Talk to them," said the second boy.

Who were they talking about? Tal wanted to turn his head to see, but his neck wouldn't move, either. Maybe it was all a dream.

Both turned to the boy with the feather in his cap. Obviously he had to make the decision.

"Neither. We take them up to the top of the service levels and leave them there. They'll come round in an hour or so."

"Oh, Crow," complained the blond boy. "What'll that do?"

So the older boy with the feather was called Crow, thought Tal muzzily. The black feather had to be from a crow, then. But the only crows in the Castle were pets of very high Chosen. There was an old legend that when the last crow left the Castle, it would mean the end of the Chosen, and the seven Towers would fall.

"Unless I'm wrong, taking them up will deliver a problem to the Chosen," said Crow. "Gill, go and get Clovil and Ferek. We'll have to carry them."

Tal watched Gill, the second speaker, walk out of his field of vision. Gill was a girl's name, which was odd. Unless Gill *was* a girl. She might be, Tal thought, watching her disappear. His one half-open eye closed, and could not be reopened.

Things got even more dreamlike then. He felt himself floating up from the floor as weird noises echoed all around him. Possibly they were meant to be words, but Tal couldn't get a grip on them. They kept changing shape and slipping away. Words that some unconscious part of his brain knew were "up" and "heavy" and "you carry him, then" became "snurp" and "preefy" and "loll garly slimwen."

Nothing made sense. It was too hard. Tal fell back into total unconsciousness.

When he awoke the second time, he had a moment's perfect recall of his first waking. Then it was gone, replaced by a blinding headache that stabbed him right between the eyes.

He groaned and sat up, cradling his head in his hands. Then he remembered that he was tied to a ladder in the heating tunnels.

Tal snatched his hands away from his eyes and looked around.

He wasn't hanging off a ladder. He was lying on the floor of a hallway lit by a small Sunstone in the ceiling. There was another Sunstone about ten stretches on, and another ten stretches beyond that. They were plain, white Sunstones of very little power.

Something made a noise. Tal whipped around, and wished he hadn't as his headache struck even more savagely.

The noise was from Milla. She was sitting cross-legged behind him, slowly breathing in and out with great control. She had taken off her face mask and her skin had a nasty greenish tinge.

Tal pressed his thumbs into his temples and muttered, "What happened?"

Milla let out her breath very, very slowly.

"Bad air. Some people found us and carried us here. There was some talk of killing, but they didn't really want to. Lucky your shadow behaved itself. I think they would have killed you if it hadn't."

"Oh," said Tal, a vague memory coming back. "I thought that was a dream. Were you awake, then?"

Milla looked embarrassed. She started to take in a breath as if to ignore the question, then let it out suddenly and said, "I only recovered enough to hear. I couldn't move. You should take deep, slow breaths. It will clear the bad air out of your blood."

Tal nodded but didn't change his breathing. Those people had to be renegade Underfolk. And they'd talked about his Sunstone!

His hand flew to his neck. The chain with the old and the new Sunstone wasn't there! He had a moment of panic, before his shadowguard plucked at his sleeve, reminding him that the chain was in the secret pocket. He pulled it out and dropped it over his head with a sigh of relief.

"Thirteen sleeps, then it's mine," Milla said, watching him check the Sunstone. "We've just had one sleep."

Tal scowled at her. Slowly, he got up and walked a little way along the corridor. Every step sent stabs of pain through his head.

"Are we in your Castle now?" asked Milla. She pointed at the ceiling. "There are many Sunstones. Perhaps I should dig one out."

"They're too small," said Tal wearily. "They only last a few months before they have to be replaced. You can't do anything with them, either. They just give light."

Milla shrugged. "Light is a lot, in the dark."

Tal sighed. From the low level of light and the whitewashed walls of the corridor, they seemed to be on one of the Underfolk levels. There were lots of Underfolk levels, where the servants lived and worked and farmed. But Tal didn't think of these levels as part of the *real* Castle.

When they left these levels, they would be entering the Castle proper. Tal was suddenly struck by the realization that he had actually gotten back. He'd never thought beyond that, and now he didn't know what to do. What *could* he do?

He couldn't just go home, because his enemies would find him. He couldn't go to any public places dressed the way he was. There'd be a panic, or a lot of trouble at the least.

277

And that was just Tal. He hadn't properly thought about bringing Milla into the Castle at all. He knew she was an Icecarl and what that meant. No one else would. There was no knowing how the Chosen would react. As far as they were concerned no one lived outside the Castle. No one *could* live outside the Castle. They would think she was some kind of creature that had crossed from Aenir without becoming a shadow. A free spirit. An uncontrolled spirit.

That would be about the most frightening thing a Chosen could imagine. There would be white-hot rays of light and destruction, with Chosen blasting them on first sight. That's what Tal would have done if he'd encountered Milla in the Castle, he knew. If she wasn't a Chosen and wasn't an Underfolk, she had to be a monster. Why would any other Chosen think differently?

"Are we in your Castle now?" asked Milla again. She looked around at the bare, smooth walls. There were no trophies, no horned Merwin skulls or Selski flipper-toe bones, or the captured weapons of enemies. "It's not very impressive. Your guards should have found us by now, instead of those Outcasts."

"Those what?" asked Tal. He hadn't been listening. He was consumed by a new fear. What if he had done the absolutely wrong thing in bringing Milla to the Castle?

"Outcasts," said Milla. "That's what the people who brought us here were, weren't they? People without a clan, who follow the ship and live on scraps and scrapings?"

Tal stared at Milla. He'd never seen her so talkative before. Maybe it was something to do with the bad air. Or perhaps she was simply relieved they'd made it through the searing heat of the tunnels.

"I don't know who they were," he replied. "Underfolk. Servants. But I think ones who have escaped. They must live somewhere down here."

"Servants who cannot choose to leave?" asked Milla as she got up and flexed her arms. "You mean thralls. Some clans have them, though the Crones do not like it. The Far Raiders will not trade with thrall-takers."

"What's a thrall?" asked Tal. He hadn't heard the word before.

"Servants who cannot leave," said Milla. Seeing that Tal still didn't understand, she added, "People who can be bought and sold."

"Oh," said Tal. "Well, the Underfolk are different. Most of them are born to be servants . . . or they ended up as Underfolk for . . . good reasons. And they don't get bought and sold. Just reassigned."

"A thrall by any other name still stinks the ship," said Milla.

She emphasized this with a shrug and did two cartwheels along the corridor, to loosen up her muscles. Tal groaned and hit his head even more forcefully. Out of the corner of his eye he saw his shadowguard copy his action, until Milla noticed. Then it slid back to become a natural shadow once more.

Tal watched it go. It was only then he realized that he wasn't as pleased to be back as he should be. He should be kissing the floor and laughing with joy. After all, he'd survived a fall of thousands of stretches from the Red Tower. He'd lived through an encounter with Icecarls. He'd crossed the Living Sea. He'd helped kill a Merwin. He'd seen the Ruin Ship, climbed the Mountain of Light, and made it through the heatway tunnels.

But he didn't feel joyful. He felt tired, as if all this was only the beginning. He'd always thought that he'd go straight to his family's rooms when he returned, and see his mother. But that wasn't possible.

The trouble was, he didn't know what to do instead.

Milla cartwheeled back, reminding him that he'd brought the particular problem she represented on himself.

"What now?" asked Milla. "Do we go and meet your clan Crone?"

"Um," said Tal, brightening as an idea suddenly came to him. "Not exactly — but close to it!"

·CHAPTER·
TEn

"We're going to see a wise man," explained Tal, as they crept along the corridor that led to a stair up to the first Red level. "My great-uncle Ebbitt. He will help us work out what to do next."

And, Tal thought, he'll know what to do about Milla. Perhaps she could hide out while Tal found her a Sunstone.

Milla nodded, silent once again. Tal noted that her hand was on her sword, and her eyes constantly in movement, searching for enemies.

"He has a Spiritshadow," Tal added. "All the Chosen do. But they won't do anything unless they are ordered to."

"These Spiritshadows are like your little shadow, but bigger?" asked Milla.

"They're not always bigger," said Tal. "But stronger and more dangerous. They can't change shape like a shadowguard, but they can stretch and twist the shape they've got."

Milla thought about this for a while. A few steps farther on she asked, "What happens to a Spirit-shadow when its master is killed?"

Tal shook his head.

"The Spiritshadow fades with them —"

He broke off, reminded of his mother. She *had* to still be alive.

"Perhaps we will find out," said Milla.

Tal stopped and turned to look Milla in the eye.

"Milla, you can't fight in the Castle!" he warned her. "We have to be careful as it is. No one has ever come in from outside before. If you attack someone, it will just make everything worse."

"I only fight if I am attacked," said Milla. "But you are afraid of something. Why should you be afraid in your own ship . . . your own home?"

"I'm not afraid!" Tal snapped. "It's complicated. There are some Chosen who don't like my family, and there are some other things happening that I don't understand. I'm just being cautious."

"You know very little," said Milla. "I do not think

your Chosen teach their children well. We would not let anyone off the ship who was so ignorant of the Ice."

Tal started to reply, but he was too furious to get any words out. He took a long, slow breath, and finally managed to say, "It is *very* complicated, because it has to do with people, not animals or, or . . . the weather! *You* don't have the education to understand. So just follow me and be quiet!"

"I know how to be quiet," agreed Milla. "I can be much quieter than you."

"Good," snapped Tal. "Start now!"

They didn't meet anyone on the stairs or in the corridor that led to Ebbitt's rather strange quarters. This was not surprising, since Ebbitt had chosen to live in the least-used part of the lowest Red level. Apart from him, everyone here was a Dimmer — the lowest possible rank in Chosen society — and was desperate to rise.

As they left the stairs, Milla noticed the faint red tinge to the Sunstones in the corridor and the faded red stripes that adorned the ceiling, and asked about them. Tal found himself giving a garbled explanation about the different Orders and levels, which Milla reduced down to the rather simplistic "Many clans live in your Castle."

This whispered conversation lasted until they came to the beginning of the corridor that Ebbitt used as one big room. As usual, the entrance was blocked with a jumble of furniture and odds and ends. Strangely, there was no sign of the wardrobe that Tal had used before as a gate. In fact, there was no obvious way to get through the tangle of up-ended tables, stacked chairs, spiked hat stands, cabinets, carpets, marble sculptures, and wallhangings.

"Great-uncle Ebbitt is a bit . . ." Tal said, eyeing the pile that reached nearly to the ceiling. "Well, he's not exactly normal."

Milla nodded, then suddenly stepped back, her hand on the hilt of her Merwin-horn sword.

Tal couldn't see what Milla had reacted to, until she pointed to a large blue cushion at the base of the piled furniture. It was slowly moving outward, almost without a sound. Then it fell over, revealing a narrow triangular gap where two chairs had been leaning back-to-back. "Why couldn't you just have a door?" Tal asked, addressing the narrow tunnel through the furniture barrier. He got down on his knees and peered in. There was no sign of Ebbitt, but the falling cushion was clearly the old man's idea of a welcome.

"Come on," Tal said to Milla, stretching out so he

could slide through the gap. "It might look like it's going to fall down, but Ebbitt's an expert at this sort of thing."

"There is wisdom behind all this rubbish?" asked Milla, but she knelt down, ready to follow Tal.

The barrier of piled-up bits and pieces went much farther than Tal had expected. He had to wriggle through several turns before he finally emerged into a relatively clear area. Once again, everything had changed. There was no sign of Ebbitt's faded throne. But Ebbitt was there, dressed in an Underfolk robe of white and a jacket in the Indigo color forbidden to him since his decline to the Red.

He was lying on a long, heavily cushioned lounge, with a sleep blindfold wrapped around his eyes. His Spiritshadow, a great maned cat, was sitting at his feet, watching Tal emerge.

"Go away," said Ebbitt, waving a languid hand. "I have a headache."

"So do I," Tal replied. "I need your help, Uncle Ebbitt. It's very important."

"So important that you haven't been to see me in two weeks?" Ebbitt asked, without moving.

"I don't believe this!" Tal shouted. "I haven't been to see you because I FELL OFF THE RED TOWER!"

His shout made Ebbitt wince, but it had a more dramatic effect on Ebbitt's Spiritshadow. It leaped to its feet and stood poised to spring.

Then Tal realized it wasn't his shout the Spiritshadow was reacting to. Milla had just climbed out of the gap in the barrier.

"Don't do anything!" Tal ordered, though he wasn't sure whether he was talking to Milla or the Spiritshadow.

"What is going on?" Ebbitt asked testily. He tore off his blindfold and sat up, blinking. When he saw Milla, who had drawn her sword despite Tal's instruction, he raised his hand, the Sunstone ring on his finger swirling with sudden light.

"Don't!" Tal exclaimed again. "Don't anyone do anything."

"Who . . . or what . . . is that?" asked Ebbitt as he slowly got to his feet. He didn't lower his hand.

Tal saw that Milla had put her face mask back on and her hood up. The amber lenses shone horribly in the Sunstone light, and the mouth-hole was horribly dark. She *did* look like a monster.

"Please take off your mask, Milla," he sighed. "No one is going to attack you, right, Uncle?"

"If you say so," said Ebbitt, who seemed slightly relieved to hear the word *mask*, and even more so when Milla slowly removed it. "But again I ask, who are you? You have a natural shadow, but you do not look like any Underfolk I have ever seen."

"I am Milla of the Far Raiders. Daughter of Ylse, daughter of Emor, daughter of Rohen, daughter of Clyo, in the line of Danir since the Ruin of the Ship."

Ebbitt sat back down.

"She's from outside," said Tal. "They call themselves Icecarls."

Ebbitt didn't say anything. His Spiritshadow turned to look at him, then lumbered over to touch his face with one shadowy paw.

"Uncle Ebbitt?" Tal said, suddenly anxious.

The Spiritshadow pushed hard at Ebbitt's chest, and the old man let out a sudden, wheezing cough.

"Outside?" he gasped. "Outside the Castle?"

"Yes," Tal explained. "That's where I've been. I really did fall off the Red Tower. My shadowguard saved me."

Ebbitt took a deep breath, then reached under the lounge to pull out a long crystal bottle with a narrow neck. Tal saw that there was a glass next to it, but Ebbitt didn't bother with that. He took out the stopper and took several long drinks.

"Distilled cordial of Halo-flower," he said, setting it down. "From Aenir. Medicine for a mad old man. Come closer, Milla, daughter of Ylse and . . . all those others."

"You can put your sword away, too," Tal said, then added in an aside to Ebbitt, "It's made from a Merwin horn. That's why it glows."

Milla hesitated, then sheathed her sword and approached. A few feet away, she clapped her fists together, in the Icecarl salute.

"So there is some truth to the old legends," said Ebbitt, peering at Milla in fascination. "There is more out there than ice and snow."

"Much more," said Tal, with considerable feeling. "Most of it trying to kill me."

"Tell me everything," Ebbitt exclaimed, flapping his arms up and down in excitement. "This is the best thing that's happened in years."

"What about Mother?" asked Tal. "How is she? And Gref? And Kusi? What's happened while I've been gone?"

"Your mother is still not well," said Ebbitt evasively. He got up and went to a cupboard, fetching food and a bottle of sweetwater, obviously more suitable for his current guests than the distillation of Halo-flowers. "We will talk about them later. First, I must hear your story."

Tal frowned, but from long experience he knew he couldn't make Ebbitt do anything he didn't want to do. The quickest way to find out anything from his great-uncle would be to tell him what had happened.

"After I left you," he started, "I climbed the Red Tower. . . ."

·CHAPTER·
ELEVEN

Ebbitt paced up and down as Tal spoke. Occasionally he interrupted to ask questions, mostly of Tal but also of Milla. Sometimes he laughed, and sometimes he clapped his hands together and his laugh became a cackle. Milla moved back a bit when he did this, and her eyes flicked between the old man and the Spiritshadow.

She knew that Ebbitt must be as old as the Crone Mother of the Far Raiders, but he didn't look it. His hair was silver, not white, and grew long at the back while it receded at the front. His skin was lined, but his wrinkles could not compete with any Crone Mother's.

He was much taller than she'd expected, and moved more briskly. But his most dominant feature was his nose. In an Icecarl saga, Ebbitt would definitely be called Ebbitt Greatnose.

"Now," said Tal, as he finished with their strange rescue from the heating tunnels. "What about Gref? And Kusi? And Mother?"

"Your brother, Gref, is missing," Ebbitt said heavily. "I thought he might be with you, and that you were merely lying low to avoid the bloated Sushin. Kusi is with those tainted products of my niece's marriage, I'm afraid."

The bloated Sushin was Tal's enemy, Shadowmaster Sushin. It took Tal a second to realize that *the tainted products of my niece's marriage* meant his mother's cousins, Lallek and Korrek. They were just as bad as Sushin. Worse really, since they were supposed to be family. His small sister would not like being with them.

"But we wouldn't have tried to hide without telling Mother." Tal frowned. "You should've asked her! Anything could have happened to Gref!"

"I'm afraid I have not been able to speak to Graile," Ebbitt replied carefully. "She fell into a very deep sleep the day you disappeared — and has not awoken."

"What!" exclaimed Tal. His fingers twitched as he

paced the room. "She wasn't that bad when I left. I should have —"

"There is nothing you could have done," said Ebbitt. "She sleeps to save her strength. I think she can be awakened, but only as a last resort. It should not be done until she can be taken into Aenir on the Day of Ascension. There are several magics to be found there that will heal her spirit, and thus her flesh."

"I can take her into Aenir," exclaimed Tal, pulling out his new Sunstone. "I could do it today. I don't care about waiting for the Day."

Milla stirred, her hand once more falling to her sword. Tal looked at her, and slowly shook his head.

"No, I guess I can't," he said, letting the Sunstone fall back under his fur coat. "If you're sure Mother will just sleep till the Day of Ascension, then I should . . . well, Kusi will be miserable, but at least she's safe. So I need to find Gref, and get a Sunstone for Milla."

Ebbitt looked at the Icecarl girl.

"I don't think most of the Chosen are ready to hear about Icecarls and their ships and the Ice," he said. "You will have to disguise yourself as an Underfolk, Milla."

293

"Shield Maidens do not hide behind false banners," said Milla proudly. It sounded like she was reciting a rule.

"Mmmm," replied Ebbitt. "Perhaps we can discuss that later. As to finding Gref, I do have one small idea. One very small idea. So small that it could disappear if I don't snatch hold of it —"

"What idea, Uncle?" Tal interrupted. Ebbitt was starting to hop around in a circle, as if his idea were something he could physically pursue.

"Ssshhh," said Ebbitt. "I've almost got it!"

He made a sudden snatch and clapped his hands around seemingly thin air.

"Have you got it?" Tal asked. "The idea?"

Ebbitt opened his palms and inspected something.

"What?" he asked. "No, it's a piece of fluff. I wonder where that came from?"

Tal glanced at Milla. She was expressionless as usual, but a muscle under her eye twitched, just for a second. He hoped it was amusement.

"What about the idea?" he asked. "To find Gref."

Ebbitt blew the invisible piece of fluff off his palm.

"The Spiritshadow who took Gref away, outside the Red Tower," he said. He seemed to be addressing the air in front of him, rather than Tal. "You saw it clearly and remember what it looked like?"

"Yes," said Tal. He moved around so he was in front of Ebbitt, but the old man swiveled on one foot so he was looking at the wall. "It had the shape of a Borzog. I recognized it from your Beastmaker game."

"An unusual Spiritshadow," said Ebbitt. "Not one I have seen before. I know one thing, though."

"What?" asked Tal in exasperation, after Ebbitt didn't continue.

"Or two things actually," said Ebbitt, counting on his fingers. "One, two."

"What!"

"One. You must identify who that Spiritshadow's master is." Ebbitt folded back his finger so hard that he flinched. "Ow!"

"And the second thing?" Tal prompted.

"Second. The only reliable way to do this is to look that Spiritshadow up in the Codex."

"The Codex?"

"The Codex of All Things," Ebbitt whispered. "The Compendium of the Chosen. The record of our race, inscribed in light upon crystal. Speak and it shall answer. The greatest magic ever to come out of Aenir. The Codex that knows all names — all Chosen, all Spiritshadows, all shadowguards."

"Well, finding out who the Borzog Spiritshadow answers to will be a start," said Tal, though he was a little worried by the gleam in his great-uncle's eye. "Where can I find this Codex?"

"That's the catch," Ebbitt said dolefully. He collapsed back into his lounge. "It disappeared more than twenty years ago. Lost, to our great sorrow. Or stolen, which I am beginning to think might be the case. If that is true, then it is for reasons so horrible that I have forced myself to forget them."

Tal groaned and collapsed next to his great-uncle. His shadowguard crept to his feet and turned into a Dattu again, all floppy-eared and harmless. Ebbitt's Spiritshadow leaned across and licked it, a great shadow-tongue suddenly appearing from its dark mouth. Tal had never seen it do anything like that before, and was momentarily shocked.

"Why —" he began to say, when shadowguard, Spiritshadow, and Milla all suddenly stiffened to attention, heads turning to the furniture barrier and the entrance to the corridor.

Tal looked, too. To his horror, he saw dark shadows sliding under the mass of chairs and bric-a-brac. Long shadows, with a shape he recognized — almost manlike creatures, but with very broad shoulders and impossibly thin waists.

The Spiritshadows of the Imperial Guard! Once

Tal would not have been afraid of them, but now he knew some of the guard were in league with Sushin. How had they known he was back already?

"Out!" shouted Ebbitt. "This way!"

Ebbitt was up and over the back of the couch before Tal even realized what was happening. Ebbitt's great maned Spiritshadow was gone a moment later.

Tal hesitated. Should he run from the Imperial Guard? If they were true guards, they might take him before the Empress and he would get the chance to set everything straight. But if they were Sushin's cronies —

One of the Spiritshadows lunged forward, and a cold, shimmering hand clutched him around the ankle. Tal's own shadowguard jumped to his defense, but was instantly batted away.

The Spiritshadow pulled, and Tal went down. Too late, he tried to get his Sunstone out. He almost had it free when the Spiritshadow flowed across him, horribly swift, pinning him to the floor.

The hard landing on the floor and the cold, unpleasant touch of the Spiritshadow made up Tal's mind.

"Run, Milla!" he shouted. "Follow Ebbitt!"

Milla jumped to the top of a cupboard, but not to

get away. A Spiritshadow stretched itself up to attack her, but before it could, she stabbed it with her Merwin-horn sword.

Usually, physical objects could not hurt a Spiritshadow, so Tal was amazed to see the luminous sword actually tear through the Spiritshadow's head as if it were paper, ribbons of shadow flying out from the blade's passage.

The Spiritshadow shrieked, a noise Tal had never heard before. Then it hastily drew back, out of reach of the sword.

"Ha!" shouted Milla. "Death to shadows!"

She jumped across to another wardrobe, and slashed at the third Spiritshadow. It withdrew, too, stepping back as the sword left a trail of light through the air.

Light — that was why the sword worked on the Spiritshadows. They could only be harmed by light, and Milla's sword had the right color and intensity, even in its faded state.

Not that this helped Tal. The Spiritshadow on top of him did not let go, and Milla couldn't come down without exposing herself to a simultaneous attack from all three Spiritshadows.

"No!" shouted Tal. He was suddenly afraid, afraid

of the Spiritshadow that held him and of what the others would do to Milla, more afraid than he had ever been, even out on the Ice. It was like being attacked by the lectors who had taught him since childhood, a sudden craziness that he couldn't understand and couldn't predict. "Don't fight! Run!"

His shout was still echoing when Milla jumped down, struck at the back of the Spiritshadow that held him, snapped into a roll on the floor, and came out of the roll to spin on one foot. Her sword whistled in a complete circle around her — cutting right through the tiny waists of the other two Spiritshadows.

Tal crawled free as his Spiritshadow attacker let go. Somehow he got to his feet, and saw that two of the Spiritshadows had literally been cut in half. Unfortunately, each half still seemed to work, and they were now coming at Milla. The other Spiritshadow was still, its shadow-flesh slowly rippling back together where it had been cleaved apart.

Tal pulled out his Sunstone and started to concentrate on it.

He was about to unleash a bolt of pure light at the Spiritshadows when the whole furniture barrier exploded behind him in a burst of blinding fire.

·CHAPTER·
TWELVE

Most of the furniture disappeared in the flash, followed a moment later by a rolling cloud of smoke and hot ash. A rush of Chosen in the uniforms of the Imperial Guard stormed in — with even more Spiritshadows.

Tal had been knocked down by the blast, and was momentarily stunned. He couldn't believe they'd blasted the whole corridor. For all they knew there could have been lots of Chosen here, not just himself and Ebbitt.

Dazed by the shock, he staggered to his feet and was sweeping hot ashes off his cheek when he was knocked down a third time, by one of the guards. The guard immediately knelt on Tal's back and twisted his arms up so he couldn't get at his Sunstone or a weapon.

"Got him!" yelled the guard.

"You get down from there!" another guard shouted at Milla. He didn't sound too concerned, which puzzled Tal. Then he realized that they must have thought she was an Underfolk renegade, and that Tal was the one who had damaged the Spirit-shadows.

Underestimating Milla was not something anyone did more than once, Tal thought. But this time she needed to run, not fight. Desperately he willed her to run. His mouth seemed to be full of ash so he couldn't shout.

Milla didn't run. Tal heard a cry of surprised pain from the guard who'd ordered her down. He craned his head back to see, but all he caught was a pair of boots staggering back, many other boots charging forward, and lots of Spiritshadows moving around.

"It's not an Underfolk!"

"Some sort of creature, use Light!"

"Ware the sword!"

"Stand back!"

There was another flash of light and another explosion of ashes. But it hadn't hit Milla. A Spirit-shadow screeched, followed by cursing and shouting from the guards and the strange belling sound of steel meeting Merwin horn.

"Watch out! Left, go left!"

"Stay clear, stay — aarrghh!"

"Harl! Japen! That way. Ranil, drag that one back!"

Ranil let go of Tal's arms and started dragging him back by the ankles. From the shouting and running that was going on all around him, it was clear Milla was still free. But there were too many guards and Spiritshadows for her to resist for long.

"Milla!" Tal shouted again, spitting out ash. "Get away! They'll kill you!"

As he yelled, Tal writhed about, and momentarily broke free. Ranil cursed and tried to grab him again, while Tal kicked and wriggled and rolled around on the ground. He got under a table but there was nowhere to go from there.

In the few seconds he was hidden from view, Tal pulled the Sunstone ring off the chain and hid it in his mouth. He kept the chain in his hand, with the old burnt-out Sunstone still on it.

Ranil ripped the table away and sat on him again, but Tal was at an angle where he could see more of the corridor. He had a confused glimpse of Milla beating back three or four guardsmen, jumping between pieces of furniture. Then Ranil pushed his head into the floor and Tal couldn't see any-more.

Tal heard another exchange of blows, the sharp ring of metal and the strangely mellow note of steel striking the Merwin horn. One guard yelled and an-other yelped in pain. "Back!" commanded a guard and there was a rush of feet.

Tal made a superhuman effort, every muscle in his back straining, and twisted around. He saw ash swirling in circles, guards leaping back, Milla jump-ing from the top of a cupboard. Then a great blue electric spark shot from the hand of one of the guards, straight into Milla's chest. There was a crack like thunder, a brilliant flash, and the thud of Milla's body hitting the floor.

"That got it, whatever it was," said a guard, relief in his voice. There was a murmur of agreement.

Tal closed his eyes in total shock.

Milla was dead.

They had come so far and survived so much. He couldn't believe that it was all going to end here. Here in Ebbitt's dusty corridor.

Tal saw Milla's face, laughing as she told him they had to jump back across that dreadful chasm. Milla, who should have lived to become a Shield Maiden and have songs sung of her exploits. Now the Far Raiders would never even know what had become of their bravest daughter.

Rough hands rolled Tal over, and someone took the chain and his ruined Sunstone out of his hand. Tal opened his eyes as the guard searched him for weapons.

Everything had gone wrong in an instant. It was all over, not just for Milla, but for Tal, his family, everyone.

The guard's Spiritshadow knelt next to Tal's head, ready to grab him if he moved. The other claw held Tal's shadowguard up by the scruff of its neck. Once again it had taken the shape of a Dattu.

"You're Tal Graile-Rerem?" asked a voice, someone outside Tal's field of vision. He started to turn his head but stopped when the Spiritshadow's clawed hands closed around his neck.

"Yes," he muttered dully. He could hardly be bothered to hide the Sunstone in his cheek. Nothing mattered anymore. He had failed and Milla was dead.

"It's him," confirmed another voice. "I saw him play Beastmaker. Why does Sushin want him?"

Shadowmaster Sushin remained Tal's enemy,

though he didn't know why. Bleakly Tal wondered how Sushin — who was only a Brightstar of the Orange — had the power to send Imperial Guards after Tal. And why would he bother?

"Where did that other one come from, Tal?" asked the guard who'd questioned his identity. "From the Underfolk depths? Who made the sword for her?"

"She was my guest," mumbled Tal mechanically. His voice seemed to come from far away, as if it weren't really him speaking. "Milla. She is . . . she was an Icecarl. From outside."

Silence greeted this answer, as the guards stopped what they were doing. Then there was a nervous sort of half laugh and a cough before they all started moving again.

"Outside? What do you mean, *outside*?"

"Outside the Castle," said Tal. "From the Ice."

"You expect us to believe that?" asked the guard. She sounded angry now.

"No," replied Tal bitterly. "But it's true."

"Take them away," ordered the guard. "Tal to the Pit. The girl to the Hall of Nightmares. Let Fashnek get the truth out of her. And no one is to speak of this. Understood?"

There was a chorus of agreement and a sudden bustle of activity.

For a few seconds the full meaning of what the guard had said didn't sink in. The words slowly repeated over and over in his head.

The girl to the Hall of Nightmares.

He felt like a four-year-old struggling to read. Then it hit him, all at once.

Milla must be alive! They wouldn't take a corpse to answer questions in the Hall of Nightmares!

Tal found a tiny spark of hope light up the darkness inside him, but it did not lift it completely. Milla might be alive, but both of them were in terrible danger, Milla perhaps most of all.

The Hall of Nightmares was a place where Spiritshadows could enter your dreams and change them into nightmares. It was the place where Chosen who transgressed the Empress's laws were punished. For Milla, who had the Icecarls' loathing of free shadows, it would be absolutely terrifying.

Tal gasped as a Spiritshadow suddenly wound itself around him, securing his arms and legs, then extending a thin tentacle across his eyes. It felt something like his own shadowguard, but not entirely, like putting on a familiar shirt that was unexpectedly damp. It was also strong enough to completely bind him, and he could see nothing through its shadow-flesh blindfold.

Only then did he think about what was going to happen to him. Milla was going to the Hall of Nightmares, but he was being taken to the Pit.

Tal had never even heard of the Pit.

·CHAPTER·
THIRTEEN

Milla had been blinded and knocked out by the blast from the guard's Sunstone. Only her face mask and armor had saved her from being burned, and they were both charred, the amber lenses of the mask partly melted and the Selski hide black and peeling.

The guards had quickly stripped the armor and mask off and tied her wrists and ankles. Shrouding her in a tablecloth taken from Ebbitt's hoard, they rushed her away, taking the least-traveled corridors to the Hall of Nightmares.

Even so, people saw them, and many Chosen would later remark on the four disheveled, bruised, and bleeding guards and the body they carried between them. But all thought they were simply disposing of an Underfolk who had run amok, which was unusual, but not unheard of.

They did not see Milla's alien white-blond hair, or the strange clothing she wore. The Merwin sword was also wrapped, and could have been any makeshift weapon. One Chosen amused his friends by describing the stupid Underfolk who had gone mad with a table leg.

The guards were unlucky in one shortcut they chose. The Middle Garden was a large, open chamber of high-vaulted ceilings, restful tree ferns, reflective pools lined with small Sunstones, and crystal fountains that grew of their own accord and then collapsed to grow again.

It was unusual for more than four moody Chosen to be there. But that particular day, Brightstar Parl of the Blue was re-creating to forty-seven of his closest friends the Achievement of Poetry that had won him the Violet Ray of Attainment.

Parl was reciting his poem and writing all three hundred and eighty words of it in letters of acrobatic blue light when the guards came running through, completely putting him off. He faltered in midstanza, and the blue-light letters crashed into one another, producing a rather disgusting, lumpy cloud of greenish-brown that hung over the audience.

The onlookers took a moment to realize what had

happened. As they did, they turned their Sunstones on the guards, flashing Red Rays of Dissatisfaction, to show their displeasure at the insult to Parl's work of genius.

While the Chosen would do no more than this, their Spiritshadows reflected their masters' true feelings, looming up from the floor to make aggressive gestures at the guards.

The guards did not stop to offer Blue Rays of Respectful Apology. The audience was left to mutter and complain, while Parl collapsed sobbing, adding his tears to one of the Sunstone-filled pools.

Once clear of the Middle Garden, there were no more obstacles — only single Chosen who rapidly got out of their way. The Hall of Nightmares was located on the eastern side of the Castle, in an area of many empty rooms and chambers. Chosen did not go there, unless it was against their will. Most would only reluctantly admit that the Hall of Nightmares even existed.

Unlike most doors in the Castle, which were marked with the color of the Order and a family sign or official notice, the great gate to the Hall of Nightmares was completely white. It was securely shut, with a single Sunstone where the keyhole would normally be.

The guards lowered Milla's unconscious body to the floor, then one touched his Sunstone bracelet to the stone in the door. Violet light flashed, and the gate slowly groaned open. There was nothing but darkness beyond.

"One for you, Fashnek!" shouted a guard nervously. They made no attempt to pass through the gate.

Footsteps sounded in the hall beyond, and the guards moved back.

Slow footsteps, as if the walker found moving difficult or struggled with a great weight.

The guards shuffled even farther back as the yet-unseen Fashnek emerged into the light — and the reason for their fear became obvious.

Fashnek was a tall, very thin man with long black hair tied back behind his head. His most distinctive feature should have been his broad nose, with its widely flared nostrils, as if he smelled his way through life.

But when he stepped out into the light, all eyes were drawn to the left side of his body, because most of it was missing. Something had chewed on him from hip to shoulder, and his left arm was not human.

The missing flesh had been replaced by shadow.

Night-dark pincers flexed at the end of his new left arm. It, too, was made of shadow, and jointed in three places.

Even worse than the shadow filling in missing flesh, the rest of the Spiritshadow was joined to Fashnek like a bonded twin. It had filled Fashnek's missing body where it could, but was unable to significantly alter its own shape.

It had an insectoid form, with six multijointed limbs, a bulbous body, and a head with a long mouth like the neck of a bottle. The end of this hideous mouth was completely ringed with tiny curved teeth, disturbingly like a grossly enlarged leech. To keep Fashnek's appearance as human as it could, the Spiritshadow clung to his side and back, hiding as much as possible behind him.

Kept alive in such an appalling way, Fashnek was repulsive to other Chosen. He could never be welcomed to any Attainment, entertainment, or event. He could never be seen at the Empress's court, or in the Assembly.

But he had found his place in the Hall of Nightmares.

And now the others feared him. Reaching down with human hand and shadow-flesh pincer, he gripped the tablecloth and slowly pulled Milla's unconscious body into the Hall.

As Milla's heels passed the gate, it slowly ground shut. The guards, who had watched in silence, didn't move until a loud click pronounced the doors locked once more.

·CHAPTER·
FOURTEEN

Milla regained consciousness, instantly appraising her situation as she had been trained to do. This was not easy, since she was in total darkness. But she could still hear and smell. So she lay where she was, reaching out with senses made sharper without sight, while she went over what had happened.

She remembered Tal shouting at her to run. Then she had wounded one of the enemy in the arm. She wasn't sure what happened after that.

Clearly she had been captured. But she was not tied up, as she would have been by an enemy Icecarl clan. The Chosen might have other ways to restrain her.

Moving slowly and surreptitiously, Milla touched the floor. It was some sort of smooth, cool material, not stone or bone. The only things she could compare it to were the crystal ladder in the heating tunnels or the pyramid of Imrir.

Milla extended her arms, feeling with her fingertips. The floor started to curve up not very far out. It took Milla only a few seconds to work out that she was contained inside a globe. A crystal globe.

It was large enough for her to sit up, but she couldn't stand. And despite the absence of holes, fresh air somehow got in.

The situation appeared even worse than the plight of the legendary Ulla Strong-Arm, who had been swallowed by an ancient, broken-jawed Selski and had to cut her way free from its stomach. She had supposedly never eaten Selski meat again after that.

Crouching, Milla sniffed the air once more. As she thought, there was the hint of fresh air and the faintest draft. The globe must have tiny holes. She could smell dust, too, and at least one person. Sweat hung rank in the air. "So you have woken, Underfolk," said a voice in the darkness.

Milla moved to face the voice, calmly and slowly, as befitted a Shield Maiden. She had already begun the Rovkir-breathing, the steady intake and exhalation of breath that helped keep her fear under control.

A Shield Maiden should fear, for fear is human, she recited mentally. *But a Shield Maiden must not show fear, nor let it rule her.*

"I am not an Underfolk," she said aloud. "I am an Icecarl. Free me from this cage, and I will fight you."

"An Icecarl?" asked the voice. "You have an imagination. That is rare in Underfolk."

Milla did not answer. She closed her fists instead, and pushed them together. Breath came and went, and she slowly tensed and relaxed every muscle in her body, starting from her toes. Breathing caused a surprising amount of pain due to the bruises, burns, and dull ache in her side where the Merwin had struck her.

"Is that what you dream of?" asked the voice. "You invent yourself another life, where you are not just an Underfolk of the Castle. Well, let us see."

A faint hissing sound came from near Milla's feet. Instantly she jumped up, pressing her hands and feet against the globe to lift herself off the floor. It was not some sort of shadow coming in, as she'd feared. A sickly sweet smell attacked her nostrils.

Bad air, thought Milla, and she held her breath. But not bad air like in the heating tunnels. This smelled of cooking and metal. Instinctively she knew people had made it.

Light was beginning to blossom around the globe. Sunstones were sparking into life. Different-colored stones shone focused rays into the globe rather than diffusing light all around.

In the light of seven different colors, Milla could see that the crystal of the globe contained thousands of thin silver wires. The rays from the Sunstones hit these wires and sent light shooting through them, making a complex pattern whirl around and around the globe.

She also saw a colored mist slowly rising from the base of the globe, so she kept holding her breath. The colored lights were doing something to her, though. She could feel them as well as see them, even with her eyes closed. It felt as if they touched nerves under her skin. Her teeth ached, and it felt as if thousands of sharp needles were pricking all over her legs and arms.

She saw the Spiritshadow, and the man it was connected to. They were approaching the globe, hobbling together. It was as if the worst of the Mother Crones' cautionary tales had come alive in front of her. A shadow had overcome a man and absorbed him.

Shocked, she took a sudden, short breath. Even as she realized her mistake, the sweet smoke was entering her lungs. Milla felt dizzy and very, very tired. She slid slowly down the globe until she was once more resting on the bottom.

Her eyes closed, and she drifted into sleep.

Fashnek touched the globe. His Spiritshadow arm slowly pushed through the crystal. The pincer opened and extended itself around Milla's head. But the pincer did not close.

Fashnek smiled. Using his human hand, he raised a Sunstone. He concentrated on it, and it flashed with light. The other Sunstones all around flashed, too, filling the globe with swirling colors.

Fashnek shut his eyes, and entered Milla's dreams.

·CHAPTER·
FIFTEEN

Tal's first reaction to the Pit was relief that it wasn't the Hall of Nightmares. As he'd been carried through the back corridors of the Castle, he'd had plenty of time to imagine what the Pit might be like. His mind had flooded with possibilities, like a pit filled with water, where he'd have to swim constantly to avoid drowning.

But that would probably have been called the Pool. So he started to think of things that might be kept in pits. A rogue Spiritshadow, perhaps? The Pit would have to be kept in total darkness or lined with mirrors to hold the Spiritshadow in there, but it was certainly possible.

It was only since he had met the Icecarls that Tal had even considered the concept of a rogue Spirit-shadow. The idea had lingered like a dark seed in his brain, and it was now in full flower. He could imagine something uncurling in a dark corner, slowly reaching out to grab him while he lay tied up and unable to move. It would speak to him constantly, in a voice that would be the voice of the Keeper from the Red Tower, high and horrible. . . .

By the time they actually got to the Pit, Tal was sick with fear. He could barely breathe, and he had cramps in his stomach. His hands were twitching uncontrollably, like a light-puppet performance gone wrong.

When the Spiritshadow unpeeled itself from his eyes, Tal had to call on all his courage to look at what was awaiting him. But the Pit was just a pit. A circular shaft about fifteen stretches in diameter and maybe thirty stretches deep. There was no sign of anything waiting in it.

But as the Spiritshadow stepped back from him, Tal had another awful second in which he imagined a previously unconsidered possibility: They were going to push him in, and he would break his legs and lie there in agony until he died. Instinctively he looked for his shadowguard. It was still in the grip of the Spiritshadow.

The guards took a step forward. Tal gulped out of

nervousness, stopping himself just in time to avoid swallowing the Sunstone.

But they didn't push him in. They stopped a few paces from him, with their Spiritshadows between them, and raised their Sunstones. Violet rays rushed out, forming one broad beam that wrapped itself around Tal. His own Sunstone answered, so he had to quickly turn his head away from the guards to hide the light shining through his cheek and leaking through his tightly closed lips.

The Violet beam slowly took on a shape, turning into an enormous hand of light. It closed its fingers around Tal, and suddenly he was lifted into the air, his head almost smacking into the ceiling.

The guards had created a Hand of Light. Tal knew it was possible, but he had never seen it in practice. It took several Chosen of great skill and powerful Sunstones acting together. Of course, the guards were all members of the Violet Order, and were therefore among the most proficient users of Light magic in the Castle.

"Time for a little dance?" asked one guard, and the others laughed. The Hand immediately shook Tal from side to side, and then up and down, until he felt sick.

Because he had the Sunstone in his mouth, Tal couldn't scream or beg for mercy. This made the game boring for the guards, who soon lost interest. The Hand stopped its wild movements, and quickly lowered Tal down to the bottom of the Pit.

It let him go there, hovered just above his head, and waved its luminous fingers in farewell, accompanied by more laughter from the guards. Then it shrank away into nothing, as the four Chosen ceased concentrating on their Sunstones.

As the Hand disappeared, so did the light. Tal was left in semidarkness. The room above the Pit was lit by Sunstones, but very little of their light came down the deep hole to Tal. He was tempted to use his own stone, but there was a chance the guards hadn't gone very far. They would take it from him if it was discovered.

He could still see enough to explore what little there was at the bottom of the Pit. He was glad to see a moldy but serviceable mattress against one wall, and even more pleased to find that there was a small pool of water, fed by a pipe. On the other side of the Pit, there was a primitive toilet, just a narrow sewer that went straight down. It was too narrow to escape through, even if he could stand it.

There was also a basket in the corner, with half of a very stale loaf of bread in it. Tal took this as sign that food would probably be provided.

He sat down on the mattress and spat the Sunstone into his hand. Then he slipped it into his sleeve pocket. He was still wearing his Icecarl furs, though his big outer coat had been left at the entrance to the heatway tunnels. Even the inner furs were too warm, quite smelly, and uncomfortable.

As his eyes adjusted to the dim light, Tal sat and thought about his situation. He was well aware that he had done things that were not the actions of a proper Chosen. But even though he had probably broken a dozen laws, he wasn't supposed to be punished like this.

According to what he'd learned in the Lectorium, a Chosen couldn't be taken to a place like the Hall of Nightmares until they'd had a trial, and even after that, they could appeal to the Assembly of the Chosen, or to the Empress.

He should have been brought before the Lumenor of the Orange Order first and then been tried in the Old Court. He should have a Speaker for the Accused, an older Chosen with an interest in law, to represent him.

What was going on?

Tal sighed and bent his head. There were too many problems confronting him. He still hadn't seen his mother, let alone helped her. Gref was lost. Kusi was in the clutches of the ghastly cousins.

And Milla was in the Hall of Nightmares. She wouldn't even know what was going to happen to her there. Unlike Tal, who had heard awful stories about the Hall of Nightmares all his life. It was the worst punishment he could imagine.

Spiritshadows would enter Milla's dreams. They would change them into nightmares, nightmares that she would be unable to escape. She wouldn't be able to wake up until they let her.

Tal had seen what the Hall of Nightmares did to rebellious Underfolk. For years the same man had worked in the main passage outside Tal's family chambers. He was a sweeper and cleaner. One day he started throwing soapy water at passing Chosen, then the actual buckets, and a Half-Bright was knocked unconscious. The Underfolk was taken away to the Hall of Nightmares. When he came back, he shook and shivered for weeks and no longer smiled as the Chosen children played their games with light and shadow in the hallways.

He was one of the lucky ones.

Some never came back at all.

Tal didn't want to see Milla like that. Which meant that he had to rescue her. Then find the Codex, so he could find Gref. Then get his mother to Aenir so she could be cured. *Then* clear his name so he could become a proper Chosen. And *then* find a Sunstone for the Far Raiders, as he'd promised.

"One step at a time," Tal whispered. His father had always said that, when Tal complained about everything he had to do.

He suddenly remembered his father and mother helping Kusi to walk for the first time. They had stood on either side of the smiling baby, holding her hands, with Gref and Tal walking backward in front of her. "One step at a time," they'd all chanted, and Kusi had taken her first step, and then another and another. . . .

Tal's first step had to be to get out of the Pit. He couldn't do anything from a hole in the ground. He looked at the triple scar on his wrist, where he had been marked by the Crone. Something of the Icecarls must have gotten into him. Like the Icecarls, and the Selski they followed, Tal knew that if he stopped, he would die.

Having made the decision to escape, Tal put on the Sunstone ring, turning the stone inward so he could shield it with his hand. Then he called forth a very faint light and used it to search around the sides of the Pit. He had learned to climb well on the Mountain of Light. If there were any cracks in the wall he might be able to climb up, using them as toe- and fingerholds.

But the walls were smooth and seamless. By the time Tal had been halfway around he knew it was useless. The Pit hadn't been dug with normal tools, but cut through solid rock with Light, probably by Chosen using Sunstones. The walls were as smooth as glass, the rock actually fused.

He was about to give up when he noticed a small rough patch, right at eye level. Nothing that would help him climb, but Tal rushed over for a closer look anyway.

The roughness was not an accident. Someone had scratched letters and numbers into the rock. Several different people, Tal thought, from the variations in handwriting. Some scratches were faded, and clearly very old. Some were obviously fresher. There were fragments of names, and tally-marks that probably counted meals, for there would be no other way of keeping time. Unlike the Icecarls, Chosen did not care to count every breath, unconsciously or other-wise.

There had been prisoners who'd spent months here, or even years.

Was there *any* way to escape?

·CHAPTER· SIXTEEN

There were at least twenty names scratched into the stone. Tal held his Sunstone close, puzzling them out. None of the names were familiar to him, until he came to one of the most recent, down at the bottom.

When he saw it, he felt his skin go cold and his breath stop. He bent even closer, unable to believe it. Then he touched the stone, hoping the scratched letters might disappear under his fingertips.

But they didn't, and no matter how Tal looked, they still spelled out the same name. And he recognized the distinctive curve of the letters.

Rerem.

Tal's father. He had been here. In the Pit. That meant that he *hadn't* disappeared on a secret mission for the Empress, as Sushin had said. He had been kept here, until he had escaped . . . or something else had happened to him.

Tal shivered. He didn't want to think about anything but escape. His father was smarter and stronger than he was. He would have escaped. That was why he hadn't been able to come home. The enemies who had imprisoned him here would have been looking for him. He must be hiding somewhere, waiting for an opportunity to get word to the Empress or his friends.

That would be difficult, since some of the Imperial Guard were clearly involved with Rerem's enemies. A terrible plot was under way, though Tal couldn't imagine what that plot involved. Rerem must have discovered something, and that was why they wanted Tal imprisoned, too.

Tal felt certain that Shadowmaster Sushin was behind it all. Tal remembered how he'd enjoyed telling Tal that his father was dead, and then giving him the deluminents. Tal looked at his wrist and laughed. The crystal bracelets marking him for demotion were long gone, lost in the fall from the Red Tower. He'd probably be given even more for losing the first lot. Perhaps even a full seven, and an instant demotion to the Red Order. Or even fourteen, and a welcome to the ranks of the Underfolk.

Tal didn't care about deluminents anymore. Whoever his enemy was, Sushin or someone else, they didn't care about following the rules and laws of the Chosen. So Tal wouldn't, either.

Defiantly, he scratched his own name under his father's, using the same worn metal spoon that the others must have used. There was hardly any of it left; certainly it was of no use as a weapon.

Tal had just finished when he heard movement up above. Not the solid crash of the guards' boots, but a more slithery sound. Hastily, Tal dimmed his Sunstone and put it back in his pocket. Then he lay down on the moldy mattress and pretended to be asleep.

Looking up at the pale opening of the Pit, Tal saw a Spiritshadow peering over the edge — a tall, horned creature that rested its clawed forelegs on the lip of the Pit as if it might jump down. Tal kept his eyes on it and very slowly reached into his pocket for the Sunstone, his heart racing. If it did jump, he would blast it.

Or try to.

But the Spiritshadow turned away. It was replaced by a Chosen, a glittering figure wreathed in light by the many Sunstones on his rings, chain, and staff. The staff was one that belonged to a Deputy Lumenor, with the orange glow that marked him as of the Orange Order — Tal's own Order.

For a moment, Tal thought that everything was going to be set right. The Deputy Lumenor had come to release him. The guards and the other plotters would already be in the Old Court, facing up to their crimes.

Tal then realized that the Chosen above was not Neril, the Deputy Lumenor he knew, who had held the post for many, many years. It was someone else, someone taller and broader, lit so brightly that Tal couldn't see his or her face.

Then the Deputy Lumenor spoke, and Tal's hopes were destroyed. He knew that voice.

It was Shadowmaster Sushin. Somehow he had been promoted to Deputy Lumenor of the Orange Order. And to Brightblinder, judging from the new, larger chain of Sunstones he wore around his neck.

But that wasn't possible, or at least it wasn't according to what Tal had been taught. Brightstar was the highest rank in the Orange Order. To go higher you had to be in the Green Order at least. However he did it, Sushin seemed expert at getting promotions and titles, since he was a Shadowmaster, too, which was a title given directly by the Empress and usually went with a particular office or job. Sushin had never mentioned what that was.

"Young Tal," said Sushin, in the tone of voice a lector might use if he found his students somewhere they weren't supposed to be.

"What happened to Neril?" asked Tal, unable to keep the anger from his voice. "The proper Deputy Lumenor?"

"No, no," said Sushin. "That is no way to begin. Surely you have not forgotten all your manners, wherever you might have been."

"I haven't forgotten," replied Tal, but he made no move to get up and bow. "And even if I had a Sunstone I wouldn't offer light to you."

"Really?" asked Sushin dryly. "You are a rude boy."

He held up a chain, and the light from his Sunstones dimmed. Even so, it took Tal's eyes a moment to adjust and see what it was. His own chain, and the blackened remnant of his old Sunstone.

"What happened to your Sunstone?" asked Sushin.

"None of your business," said Tal.

"But it *is* my business," Sushin explained. "You see, without a Sunstone, you are not a Chosen, Tal."

Not a Chosen. The words went through Tal like a Merwin horn. He was caught now. If he admitted he had a new Sunstone, it would probably be taken away. If he didn't, Sushin could treat him like an Underfolk.

"As Deputy Lumenor of the Orange Order," the Shadowmaster continued, "I have to discover whether your loss was an accident, in which case the stone should be replaced, or whether it was deliberate destruction. In the latter case, your demotion to Underfolk would be immediate, as would other . . . punishments."

Tal didn't reply. He knew Sushin was just playing with him. The Shadowmaster was his enemy.

"I can replace your Sunstone," said Sushin. He reached into his pocket and pulled out a bright new chain of gold, with a large Sunstone set as the pendant. "A Primary Sunstone, Tal. Strong enough to take you and your family into Aenir on the Day of Ascension. The day when you become a full Chosen . . . or not. I understand that getting to Aenir is particularly important for your mother at the moment. Or so my dear friends Lallek and Korrek tell me. They are so concerned about your family."

Tal looked at the Sunstone. It dangled loosely in

Sushin's puffy fingers, as if he might drop it down at any moment.

"What about Gref?" asked Tal. "What have you done to him?"

"He could be found," Sushin replied, not really answering the question.

"What . . . what would I have to do?" Tal asked, his voice cracking. If he got the Sunstone and was reinstated in the Orange Order, Gref would be brought home and together they could take care of their mother. Later he could try to help Milla, find out what was going on, and discover what had happened to his father.

But could he trust Sushin?

·CHAPTER·
SEVENTEEN

"You must answer my questions, to begin with," Sushin said. "You were climbing the outside of the Red Tower, and you fell. Yet here you are. How? Who helped you?"

"The Icecarls," Tal told him.

Sushin sighed, and his Spiritshadow loomed threateningly over the edge.

"I want the names of the Chosen," said the Shadowmaster. "Not stories, and not your senile great-uncle Ebbitt. Someone helped you escape the Red Tower, someone with real power. Someone hid you these last few weeks. Tell me their names."

"No one," replied Tal. "I was taken by the wind, far from the Castle. The Icecarls found —"

"I said *I do not want stories!*" shouted Sushin. He

raised his hand, and a bolt of concentrated light shot out, striking the corner of the mattress, setting it alight. Tal rolled away, covering his eyes with his forearm. His shadowguard scuttled after him, spreading itself wide to shield him from the attack.

As Tal rolled, he saw Sushin throw another bolt. His Spiritshadow was behind him, its claws striking at the air, its huge fanged mouth snapping as if it might already have Tal in its jaws.

Tal suddenly realized that Sushin's Spiritshadow shouldn't be a fanged claw-beast. Last time he'd seen Sushin, his Spiritshadow had a domed shell and a long flat head. Spiritshadows could stretch and spread, but they couldn't completely change shape!

So Sushin must have gotten a completely new Spiritshadow. He must have gone into Aenir before the Day of Ascension. That was totally forbidden.

For a very long minute, Sushin threw bolts of white-hot light down at Tal. The boy ducked and weaved, but in the narrow confines of the Pit he knew he would be hit soon. His shadowguard had already deflected one bolt, and now had a rip through its shadow-flesh that would take days to heal. Finally Sushin calmed down and the bolts stopped. Tal stopped running, though his body was still tensed to jump aside.

"Who is the girl who was captured with you?" Sushin demanded. "Where did she steal her weapon? Are there other Underfolk who helped you?"

"Her name is Milla," said Tal. He didn't know how to answer the other questions. Clearly Sushin thought that Tal had used Light magic to fly down the Red Tower and then had hidden with renegade Underfolk in the lower levels.

"She's an Icecarl!" he shouted, jumping away from the expected bolt of light.

But Sushin didn't raise his hand. He said, "The Pit is a good place to think, Tal. You should remember that the only way out is to give the right answers. To me."

He turned to leave. Tal sighed with relief and looked down. In that instant, Sushin turned back and fired a final bolt. It struck the ground at Tal's feet, sparks flying up to strafe his legs. He was knocked down, his shadowguard cushioning his fall.

On his back, with his shadowguard under him, Tal could only look up as Sushin pointed his Sunstone-ring hand at him. He lay there, waiting for the killing bolt, but Sushin only laughed and turned away. This time, he did not come back.

Tal lay there for a long time, until his shadow-guard crept out from under him and started tugging at his foot. Wearily, the boy sat up and looked at his legs. The bolt had burned all the fur off his leggings, revealing the hide underneath. Sparks had burned through to scorch his skin in a few spots. But it wasn't serious.

Tal laughed. A month ago he would have gone straight to bed for a week with these tiny burns. Now he had grown closer to Icecarl standards. The burns were annoying, nothing more.

Getting to his feet, he went over to the water basin, stripped off his furs, and washed himself as best he could. He kept the clothes close, in case he heard Sushin returning.

Tal was just slipping his leggings back on when he heard footsteps again. Quickly he threw on his coat and retreated to the far side.

But it wasn't Sushin. Or at least it didn't sound like him. Whoever it was didn't slide his or her feet. Again it didn't sound like a guard's heavy boots.

Tal tensed as a shadow slid over the rim of the Pit. Then he relaxed. It was a natural shadow, and the person who cast it was close behind, in the white robe of an Underfolk.

An old woman, Tal saw, though she didn't meet his eyes. She knelt at the edge of the Pit and carefully lowered a basket down on a very thin rope, sufficient to support the basket but not Tal if he tried to grab it. When the basket hit the bottom, she kept lowering, till the hook on the rope swung clear and she hauled it back up again very quickly.

Stale bread, Tal thought gloomily. The Underfolk woman pointed at it and said something very quietly, then she quickly walked away.

It wasn't until she'd gone that Tal managed to work out that she'd said, "Compliments of your great-uncle."

Even with those words, Tal waited until he could no longer hear footsteps. Then he went over to the basket and lifted its lid.

Delightful aromas escaped, and Tal's mouth was suddenly no longer dry. There was half a fresh-baked pie, spiced with menahas sprigs, and two seed cakes. A stone bottle contained cold sweetwater.

Even though he was suddenly hungry, it was not the food and drink that most attracted Tal's attention. In one corner of the basket, there was a clump of pages. Judging from the torn stitching and absence of binding, it had been ripped from the middle of a book. Tal picked it up and saw that he only held a few chapters. It started at page 173 and ended in midsentence on page 215.

The first line was, "On Making a Stairway of Light."

·CHAPTER·
EIGHTEEN

Milla woke on the deck of an iceship. For a moment she was disoriented, then she felt the familiar bone under her feet and the wind in her hair. She heard the screech of the ship's runners on the ice.

But something was not quite right. She looked down at herself, and saw that she was not dressed in the full furs she should be wearing on deck. And her Merwin-horn sword was gone, as was her knife and throwing crescent. How could she have been so careless as to come on deck unclothed and unarmed?

The color of the Sunstone on the mast was wrong. It had an unpleasant greenish tint that made the Ice look sickly. And there was no one else on deck. Which was impossible. There was always a watch on deck. . . .

Milla looked around. There was no obvious sign

of an enemy, but she felt an unwelcome presence. She slowly went to lower her mask. But it wasn't there, either. Puzzled, Milla ran her hands over her hair, which was strangely long. No mask, no weapons, no outer furs, long hair.

The wind was howling through the rigging. The sails were full, the ship speeding across the ice. But Milla did not feel cold.

Milla knew there could only be one explanation for this. She must be dreaming.

There was no point trying to wake up from inside a dream. When her time came, she would wake. She took a deep, slow breath and sat down, drawing her legs up underneath her. Then she bent forward and laid her forehead on the deck, between her spread palms. She began to breathe in the Fourth Rovkir Pattern, which would send her into an even deeper level of consciousness, deeper and further down than dreams.

She didn't hear the creatures that came swarming over the sides of the ship, or feel their jaws and claws upon her. She didn't notice them disappear, or see the ship hit a huge rock and go into a cartwheeling explosion. She didn't see the Spiritshadows that rushed at her, intent on ripping her dream-self apart.

Milla had already left that dream-body. She had gone further, so far that she had lost her identity. She was a tiny glowing spark in a great void of nothingness that would hide until she was found by someone with the power to return her to her dream-body and then to her physical form.

Two different people were alerted by what Milla had done. One was close to her physically, and was puzzled — perhaps a little afraid. The other one was physically far away, and merely curious.

The first was Fashnek, master of the Hall of Nightmares. He had gone into Milla's dream and seen the iceship. That had been Milla's dreaming. But when Fashnek began to change it, sending monsters to attack, Milla's dream-shape had not responded as an Underfolk or a Chosen would. She should have run screaming and crying, trying to wake up. But she had stayed completely still and uncaring, and the monsters could not touch her.

Fashnek had put a great rock in the ship's path, and destroyed the vessel in the crash. But still Milla's dream-shape had not been touched. The piece of deck she lay on had simply sailed through the air and landed perfectly on the Ice.

Fashnek had called on his own and other Spirit-shadows then, bringing them directly into her dream. Even they could not touch her. Their shadow-claws and teeth simply passed through the dream-girl. She did not respond in any way.

Fashnek became angry. He retreated back into his damaged flesh, to change the settings of the Sunstones, to focus more power on the prisoner in the crystal globe. He sent a message, too, advising his own master that he had found someone whose dreams resisted his power.

While he was out of Milla's dream, another person entered it. She came skating across the ice, though her boots had no skates, and with each sliding footstep she moved farther than any real skater could. She wore no furs, just a plain black robe. Her eyes shone like stars and her long hair was as white as the ice. Tal would have recognized her as the Crone of the Far Raiders. Here in Milla's dream she was younger and taller by half a stretch.

She looked at the wreckage and sniffed at the ice around Milla's bent-over dream-body. Whatever she smelled made her nose wrinkle. She did not touch Milla, but turned away and shouted out into the darkness. The shout shattered the ice in front of her and sent pieces of bone debris flying into the air.

The shout was answered almost immediately. More black-robed figures came skating in over the

Ice. More star-eyed Crones, arriving in twos and threes until forty of them clustered close. They did not speak, but gathered around Milla's dream-body, waiting for someone.

Eventually, that someone came. A Crone Mother, milky-eyed, seated in a high-backed chair of palest bone. The chair moved across the Ice of its own accord. It stopped next to Milla, and the Crone Mother bent down and touched the girl's head.

Milla came back from wherever she had been to find herself still in a dream. She knew it was a dream because of all the Crones around her and the Crone Mother in her chair of bone. They were the familiar figures of her childhood, the Crones who came to send the nightmares away. All Icecarl children learned how to cope with nightmares, how to move within their dreams, and when to call the Crones.

As always, the Crones did not speak. But they didn't throw Milla up into the air, either, which was how they normally woke her up. The Crone Mother smiled at her and did not remove her hand. All the other Crones stood in a circle around her, looking out, still waiting.

They did not have to wait long.

·CHAPTER·
ПIПETEEП

Fashnek reentered Milla's dream. As he usually did in his prisoners' dreams, he made himself look like he had once been, before the accident that left him only half-alive. It was only in others' dreams that Fashnek could bear to look at himself.

The Chosen was surprised to see all the weird women in black circled around Milla. The ancient globe and its associated devices — which he fondly called his Nightmare machines — were set to prevent the dreamer from changing the dream. Fashnek was the only one who could do that. But the machines were as old as the Castle, and soaked up Light magic like a sponge drank water. Sometimes a Sunstone would fail during an interrogation, and the dreamer would have a little bit of freedom to invent things.

Not that it mattered. Fashnek was sure that he could make this one respond now. He had replaced all the Sunstones. The crystal globe and the mind boosters were all functioning at full power.

First, he would change the place back to something she hadn't dreamed herself. A place where he had more control. Like the Hunting Arena, where Chosen chased and killed rock lizards. He would change this girl into a lizard as well.

Fashnek thought of the changes he wanted. Transmitted by his Spiritshadow to the Nightmare machines, the changes should have been immediate. But they weren't. The Ice flickered for a moment, and Fashnek briefly saw the bright green of the ferns and the red flash of a lizard's back. Then it was gone and the Ice returned.

Fashnek frowned. A whole lot of Sunstones must have failed. He concentrated on the change again, but nothing happened.

Then he noticed that the creepy old women were sliding toward him, sliding across the ice in a way that was not possible. They were dream elements. They shouldn't be able to do anything without his permission.

They were all staring at him, too. Staring with luminous eyes, eyes that were not merely reflecting the light from Fashnek's Sunstones, or the one in the wreckage of the ship.

"Back!" Fashnek ordered, speaking aloud to reinforce his mental command. But they still came on, closer and closer.

Fashnek started to retreat, fear building inside him. This was all wrong. Prisoners came to the Hall of Nightmares to be made afraid by Fashnek. He controlled their dreams, not the other way around.

The gliding women drew knives of bone. Fashnek shivered when he saw them. He tried desperately to order Spiritshadows to come to his aid. None came. He conjured up monsters he had used before, things from Beastmaker games. None came.

Soon he was surrounded. There was only one thing left to do. Fashnek ordered the Nightmare machine to switch off and made himself wake up.

He disappeared. The Crones tucked their knives away, and skated back to Milla. She had watched them chase the Chosen away. She knew who he was, even though he appeared whole, here in her dream. He was her jailer. In the waking world, she was trapped inside a crystal globe. But at least he could not interfere with her dreams.

The Crone Mother took her hand off Milla's head as the others returned. They circled around Milla, towering over her. She was puzzled for a moment, until she realized that their size had been set when she first learned to call them to her nightmares. She had seen only five circlings then, and stood only waist-high. The Crones had always been double her size. Now that she was grown, in her dream they had grown, too.

The Crones picked her up. They held her over their heads, supported on a forest of old arms. Then they bounced her up and down a few times, making her laugh.

On the third bounce, they threw her up into the dark sky with all the strength they could muster. Milla flew, tumbling over and over, laughing at the rush and giddiness. It was like falling up forever.

Then there was a flash of light.

Milla woke up. She was still trapped in the crystal globe. Multicolored beams of light were still focused on her, but now they were just light. They had lost their effect upon her. Fresh air breezed through the globe, unaccompanied by the sickly sweet scent.

There was no sign of Fashnek. He had hurried

off to report in person. He had to report that the boy Tal had not been lying. This girl truly was from outside the Castle, and she had powers and allies that made Fashnek sweat and tremble as he lay at the feet of his master.

·CHAPTER·
TWENTY

It took Tal four hours to read the section of the book he had been given, and then another few hours to read parts of it with greater attention, as he tried to figure out exactly what the author meant. To make it harder, there were pages missing and the section ended with a sentence that began, "The final act to complete the stairway is —"

Tal flipped that final page at least twenty times before he accepted that there were no more. He would have to work out how to finish the stairway on his own.

If he got that far. The stairway used all seven colors of the Spectrum, and Tal had only been taught Red, Orange, Yellow, and Green. But he had always had a natural flair for Light magic, and both his father and Ebbitt had taught him things he'd never have learned in the Lectorium.

His first small attempts were total failures. The Sunstone was much more powerful than his old one had been, and he kept losing control of it. Colors blurred and intensity wavered all over the place. The three stairways he managed to produce all fell over when they were only three or four steps high.

"I can't do it," Tal muttered finally, throwing down the pages. His eyes hurt and he had a headache. He lay down on the mattress and closed his eyes. Just for a few minutes he told himself. Then he would try again.

Before he knew it, Tal was asleep and dreaming. He was out on the Ice again, this time without Milla. But he had a Sunstone, a very bright Sunstone that lit up everything. His shadowguard was there, too, but for some reason in the dream he didn't want it. It kept following at his heels, and he kept running away from it, slipping and sliding on the Ice. The shadowguard grew bigger, and then became Sushin's Spirit-shadow. It got larger still, until it filled all the sky behind him, its mouth yawning to swallow him up in a single gulp —

Tal woke with a start, sweating. His shadowguard sat up, too, in the shape of a comforting, inoffensive

Dattu. Tal looked at his Sunstone. Only twenty minutes had passed.

He splashed his face with water, and started working on the Stairway of Light again. This time his focus was more intense.

At first he made a very small stair, just a few steps, carefully weaving different-colored strands of light together into two short rainbows, which he then joined end to end to make three distinct steps.

Even when they hung there in the air, opaque and solid, Tal didn't really believe it would work till he put his foot on the first rainbow step and it supported him.

Elated, he ran up and down the three steps over and over, forgetting that the stairs would only last a few minutes after he stopped concentrating on his Sunstone. They failed just as his right foot came down on the highest step, sending him sprawling. His shadowguard, still repairing itself after Sushin's attack, was too slow to catch him. It hissed in warning — or exasperation — as he picked himself up and limped to the mattress.

A Stairway of Light big enough to get him out of the Pit would take between two and three hours to build, Tal estimated. If he could manage it.

He consulted his Sunstone. It probably hadn't

been calibrated by the Timestone in the Assembly for years, but might still be accurate. According to the color band in its depths, it was close to two o'clock in the morning. It was unlikely that Sushin or anyone else would visit him before the Waking Hour, at seven.

So he had time to escape. But he still hadn't decided if Sushin was being sincere when he offered him a new Sunstone and a safe return to his normal life as a Chosen.

Rubbing his forehead, Tal thought about all this. Eventually he decided that he had to build the stair now and take his chances on escaping. Sushin might be his superior in the Orange Order, but Tal didn't trust him. He'd put Tal in this Pit, after all, so he didn't care about doing things the right way. He might have put Tal's father in this Pit, too.

No, Sushin's offer was almost certainly false. He would just get rid of Tal once he found out that he had no allies.

Having made his decision, Tal ignored his headache and started to build the Stairway of Light. There were two methods explained in the book. One was quick and a bit easier, but would use up most of the Sunstone's energy. The other was slower and more difficult, but would not drain the stone too much.

Tal had learned the value of a Sunstone. He chose the slower method, though he got an empty feeling in his stomach as he raised his Sunstone. He would only have one real chance at this. It was a feat of magic that would not usually be attempted by anyone less than a Brightstar of the Blue, and a confident Light Mage at that. Yet here he was, a boy, not even a full Chosen, trying to build a Stairway of Light thirty stretches high!

Step by rainbow step, the stair started to spiral up and around the Pit. Tal stood in the center, his Sunstone raised high, sweat beading on his forehead. All his attention was on the stone and the light that poured from it. He had to mentally take each strand and weave it into six others, then when he had the short arc of a rainbow, float it up and attach it to the top of the last one.

When the stair was only a few stretches short of the top, Tal took a few steps. He had to concentrate so hard on keeping the whole stairway together and on making the last few stairs, that he almost fell off a couple of times.

Finally, the stair was complete. A multicolored,

shimmering spiral of many small rainbows, each one a rounded step of solid light. Tal sighed with relief, and climbed up more quickly.

He was three quarters of the way up when he heard the clatter of metal on stone and a voice raised in anger or pain.

Tal was momentarily distracted by the sound, and he lost control of his Sunstone. It flared in his hand, and a wild beam of multicolored light shot out. The beam whipped around and under him, cutting the stair in half. All the steps below Tal fell apart in a sudden snowstorm of brilliant light. The ones above him changed color, and he felt the step he was on get soft, like melting wax.

Tal threw himself forward and up, jumping three steps at a time. He didn't even try to fix the stair. He instinctively knew that whatever had gone wrong was beyond his power to fix. He was also ready for whoever or whatever was waiting for him at the top.

This time, he had a Sunstone in his hand, and he would fight!

The last step felt like a sponge, but it held long enough for Tal to spring up and out of the Pit. He landed on the edge in a crouch, Sunstone ring held ready, his eyes looking wildly from side to side.

But there was nothing to see. The Pit lay at the

end of an otherwise normal Castle corridor. A colorless corridor, whitewashed and lit by regularly spaced Sunstones. There was a door about thirty stretches down the corridor, but that was all.

Except, Tal suddenly noticed, there was a small, square dark hole in the ceiling and a metal hatch cover lying on the ground. That was what had made the noise.

Cautiously, Tal crept down the corridor. His every sense was alert for the sudden opening of the door and the rush of guards, or for someone — or something — to drop out of the odd hatch in the ceiling.

As he got closer, Tal heard a weird scuffling sound — whatever was up there was moving around. Then he heard a muffled voice cursing.

It sounded a bit familiar.

"Ebbitt?" asked Tal warily. "Is that you?"

·CHAPTER·
TWENTY-ONE

Tal was answered by a sudden explosion of foul-smelling green water, liberally mixed with what looked and smelled like clumps of rotten spearleaf. This was followed by Ebbitt's head, though it took Tal a moment to recognize him, since his hair was totally sodden and his face was bright green.

"Hurry up!" he said. "I can only hold the water back for a few —"

Whatever he was going to say disappeared into a gurgle as more water suddenly cascaded through the hole. At the same time, Tal heard the door at the end of the corridor being unlocked, and someone shouting on the other side.

Despite the smell, he jumped up and got a grip on the edge of the hole. Ebbitt helped him get up onto his elbows, and then he was able to squirm up the rest of the way.

To Tal's surprise, they were in another corridor, rather than some small tunnel. He was even more surprised to see that apart from where they were standing, it was full of water with lots of green floaty things in it. Two walls of light, obviously made by Ebbitt, were keeping the water at bay.

Or most of it. Ebbitt was constantly using his Sunstone to seal off sudden leaks.

"Pow! Kapang! Take that!" he yelled, suppressing three different outbreaks. Then, while the water was momentarily under control, he made a lasso of Indigo light and used it to pull up the metal hatch from the floor. A few seconds later, it was firmly back in place, welded in a sudden flurry of sparks from Ebbitt's Sunstone.

Those few seconds were long enough for Ebbitt's walls to break down. The water came in with a rush, picking up both of them and dumping them down. Filled with sudden panic, Tal struggled to right himself. What if the corridor was entirely full of water and there was nowhere to breathe?

He bobbed to the surface, gasping. Ebbitt was treading water next to him and plucking the rotten plant material off his face. Without a word, he pointed a bony finger past Tal and started to swim in that direction.

Tal followed him with difficulty. He wasn't a great swimmer. Unlike some Chosen of his age, he didn't spend his free time in the Cavern Lakes or the Underfolks' fish pools.

"Thanks, Uncle," he gasped as they swam to wherever it was they were going. Tal couldn't see an end to the corridor. "By the way, where are we?"

"Surge tank, splurge tank, roly-poly nurge tank," said Ebbitt. He stopped swimming to tread water again and said, "When the superheated steam has passed through the heating system it reaches the condenser-menser-spencer, where it's turned back into water-aughter-daughter. The water then drains back down through the Castle's caterpillars. Caper-tillers. Copillanies. Capilleeries. Capillaries. Every now and then, there's a big tank like this one."

He stopped talking, but didn't start swimming again. After a while, Tal said, "Uh, Uncle Ebbitt? Are we going somewhere?"

"Of course we're going *somewhere*," replied Ebbitt. "There's not much point rescuing you if we don't go *somewhere*."

"Can we go soon?" asked Tal. "I'm not much of a swimmer."

"Really?" said Ebbitt, looking surprised. "Neither am I. Does it matter?"

He stopped moving his arms, but didn't sink. Tal looked down and saw that the old man was standing on his Spiritshadow, who was gently paddling beneath him.

Tal's shadowguard was trying to do the same thing. Experimentally, Tal stopped paddling, but quickly started again when his head instantly sank beneath the surface. In its weakened condition his shadowguard didn't have the strength to keep him up.

Ebbitt started swimming again. They swam for what seemed like ages to Tal, before Ebbitt's Sunstone lit up the end of the corridor. Tal had expected to see a door or another hatch or some other obvious way out, but the corridor ended in a large chamber that was also half full of water. The three sides of the chamber were riddled with different-sized tunnel entrances, many of them well above water level.

Ebbitt pointed at one and said, "That's it. That's the one we want. Capillary 17824567834567 — or thereabouts. Smear this on your face and hands."

He handed Tal a jar. It still had the top on, so the boy had to tread water and undo it at the same time, resulting in several momentary disappearances underwater. The third time Tal went under, Ebbitt snatched the jar back and easily unscrewed the lid.

"No enterprise," said Ebbitt gloomily, as he gave it back.

Tal spat out some water angrily, not caring if he hit his great-uncle. Then he looked in the jar. Whatever it was smelled horrible, and it was a sickly yellow. Knowing Ebbitt, it was also probably totally unnecessary.

"What is it?" asked Tal.

"Insect repellent," said Ebbitt.

Tal hesitated. Surely it wasn't that important to put on insect repellent. Not now, even if it did look sticky enough to stay on in water.

"The people who built the Castle thought of everything," Ebbitt said absently, as he pointed to each tunnel entrance and mumbled numbers. Tal continued to hesitate, till his great-uncle added, "They even made these quite fascinating water spiders, about so big, to put in the cooling system and eat up any bits of meat, bodies, and so on that might get accidentally caught up in here. Keep it free of contamination. Pity the spiders don't eat this revolting weed as well."

Tal stared at Ebbitt for a second, then slowly started to smear the yellow goo on his face and neck. He still wasn't sure if Ebbitt was playing a practical joke, but since the old man had spread his arms as wide as they would go when he'd said "about so big," Tal didn't want to take any chances.

When Tal had finished, Ebbitt also applied the repellent. Tal could see traces of a previous application, so perhaps it wasn't a joke. Then they both climbed up to the tunnel — or capillary — that Ebbitt had pointed to.

It was even narrower than the heating tunnels, only wide enough to crawl through. Tal was relieved to see that it was almost dry, with the merest trickle of water in the middle. At least, he was relieved until Ebbitt mumbled something about the water spiders being called that because they could swim and dive as well as run around on dry land.

"We'll play Colours to see who goes first," announced Ebbitt, who was once again supported by his Spiritshadow. Tal, who was delicately balanced with his feet in one tunnel and his elbows on the next, groaned.

"I'll go first, or last, or whatever," he said. "Where does this tunnel go, anyway?"

"Now, now, don't spoil my fun," said Ebbitt. "This capillary goes to an artery, a bigger tunnel. We'll go along that, and then through another capillary, and then down through a valve, and then we'll come out right inside the Hall of Nightmares."

"Inside the Hall of Nightmares!"

"Of course." Ebbitt frowned. "Outside wouldn't be much use if we want to rescue your friend Milla, would it? Now, let's play."

He held up his hand, and the Sunstone ring there quickly shifted through the colors of the Seven Orders.

Tal groaned again, and reached out his hand with its own Sunstone ring. His other hand clutched at the lip of the upper tunnel, while his shadowguard hung anxiously to his knees.

"Go," said Ebbitt. His ring flashed red as Tal's flashed violet. Colours was a children's game, and often ended in stalemate. The object was to flash a Sunstone in a higher color than your opponent. The catch was that you could use each color only once in the entire game, and in the next round you couldn't use the next-highest or next-lowest color to the one just played.

Tal won the first round, but could no longer use Violet at all, or Indigo in the next round. Predictably, Ebbitt flashed Blue next, as did Tal. So it was still one-nil. Then Ebbitt flashed Violet, while Tal flashed Red. One-all. Then Tal flashed Indigo and Ebbitt Orange. Two-one in favor of Tal. Ebbitt countered with Indigo, beating Tal's Green to make it two-all. Ebbitt finished with Green, and Tal was left with Orange, the final score three-two in Ebbitt's favor.

"I win," announced Ebbitt. "But you can go first."

"Thanks," said Tal nervously. He slid into the tunnel, trying not to listen as Ebbitt muttered something under his breath about water spiders.

·CHAPTER·
TWENTY-TWO

Milla was lying in the crystal globe, saving her strength and pretending to be asleep, when she heard the sudden clang of metal hitting stone. She didn't react obviously, but her head moved slightly toward the sound, and her eyes opened to narrow slits. Had her jailer returned and tripped over some of his own apparatus?

Whatever had happened, it was in one of the dark corners of the Hall. The globe was still brightly lit by beams of colored light that continued to run through the silver wires. Everywhere else was dark.

Or was it? Milla watched a small light blossom in the far corner — a surreptitious light that moved slowly toward her. Milla opened her eyes a little more, peering at it. She could see shapes around the light.

And she could hear whispering as well. It sounded like the old man, Tal's great-uncle, whatever that meant. Milla had uncles, but not great ones.

"Probably have to carry her," he was saying. "Mind turned to jelly. Chance of recovery, mind you."

Milla kept silent. This could be a trick. But when she heard another whisper, she almost called out. It was Tal.

"She looks all right. Where's . . . who did you say . . . Fashnek?"

"Asleep, if we're lucky."

They came up to the globe. Milla kept still, though she was surprised to see that both were sodden and covered in little bits of dark muck that looked like the seaweed the Mother Crone had served them in the Ruin Ship.

Ebbitt cautiously moved the metal stands and their Sunstones, pointing their beams up to the ceiling. Tal touched the globe, then tapped on it, near Milla's face.

She sprang up, and he jumped back.

"Milla!"

"Who else would I be?" asked Milla. But she smiled, clearly with some effort, for it only lasted an instant.

"You're all right!" exclaimed Tal. "What happened?"

"The man who is half shadow tried to change my dreams," Milla said. "But I called the Crones, and they came to my dream and scared him away."

"Really?" asked Ebbitt. "I'd like to meet one of these Crones. I never married, but anyone who could —"

"Not now, Uncle," said Tal firmly, noticing Milla's expression. "Where's Fashnek?"

"He left," replied Milla. "Can you release me? I have not found the trick of opening this prison."

"Sure," said Tal, but it proved easier said than done. The globe appeared to be solid crystal. Under bright light there were lots of tiny holes in the bottom of it, but they couldn't help get Milla out.

While Tal pored over the globe trying to find a switch, lever, or something to open it, Ebbitt wandered about, looking at the Sunstones on their metal stands. The stands stood in grooved tracks on the floor so they could be accurately placed.

Several books were laid out on a table, beyond the

ring of Sunstones. Ebbitt flipped through them with interest, while his Spiritshadow stood guard near the door.

Finally, Tal had to admit that he couldn't find a way to open the globe.

"I suppose we'll have to wait for Fashnek," he said. "I guess I can blind him, and then we'll tie him up and make him open the globe."

Milla shook her head.

"He has three shadows with him, as well as the one that grows from his flesh," she said. "You could not overcome them all."

"Three S-S-Spiritshadows!" stuttered Tal. "He can't!"

"He could," said Ebbitt. "No one ever sees Fashnek. Well, no one he doesn't want to see. I suppose he must see someone. Or someone must see him."

"Sushin," Tal declared. "He's the one behind everything. He's got a new Spiritshadow, too. I just don't understand what he wants."

"I never understand," said Ebbitt. "Plots and schemes, secret meetings. It's all too hard. What's the point of going Violet, anyway?"

Tal shook his head, ignoring the old man. Sometimes he *really* didn't understand his great-uncle. Besides, whatever Sushin was up to, it wasn't anything as normal as trying to climb to a higher Order. He could do that the regular way, without putting people in pits and kidnapping children.

"By the way," Ebbitt added, "that book over there is very interesting. Did you know this globe was originally invented to help people with their dreams? Not to give them nightmares at all. The Castle builders were really very clever —"

"Did it tell you how to open the globe?" asked Tal crossly, before Ebbitt could blather on about what the globe used to be for.

"Naturally," Ebbitt replied. He raised his ring and sent a quick combination of colored lights at the globe. As they hit, there was a ringing sound, like a tuning fork or a crystal glass being struck. The globe split in half like an oyster.

Milla jumped out and stretched. Then she clapped her fists together to Ebbitt, showing thanks and respect. Tal waited for her to do it to him as well, but she didn't. Instead she immediately started looking for her Merwin-horn sword and armor.

"Where do we go now?" asked Tal nervously. "We'll have to hide somewhere. I'll need to put together some sort of disguise so I can go looking for the Codex and Gref."

"Mmmm," replied Ebbitt. He was momentarily intent on cleaning out his ear, which had suffered from an intrusion of the green weed. "I've been thinking about that, and thinking about my thinking, and then thinking about me thinking about my thinking —"

"And?" Tal interrupted.

"The Codex is probably in Aenir."

"Why?"

"Because there is no power in the Castle that could restrain the Codex, if it wanted to be consulted," said Ebbitt. "But there is in Aenir. The Codex is almost alive, my boy. It was made to be read. If it was in the Castle, it would have found a way for people to consult it. Therefore, it must be in Aenir. You'll have to bring it back."

"Right," said Tal slowly. "I can't believe this all started because I needed one Sunstone!"

"Is that when it started?" Ebbitt asked innocently. "I think you'll find that whatever it is, it started long ago. Sushin is not the only one with secret business and strange ways. Your father is not the only Chosen who is missing, nor is Gref the only child. I should have looked into matters long ago, but I missed my chance. I think it is long past time some-

371

one did what I didn't, and brought the Codex back and set all to rights. You seem to be just the right person for the job."

Tal looked at Ebbitt. For once, the old man seemed quite serious. He wasn't smiling dreamily, or cleaning his ear, or staring at something no one else could see.

"Well, there's one thing I can do right now," Tal said. "And that is to get Milla a Sunstone."

He reached out to grab the one closest to him, one that was set in a clawed hand atop a silver stand. But before his fingers closed on it, Ebbitt grabbed him and twisted his arm away.

"Not one of those!" said Ebbitt. "They're full of nightmares, full of evil dreams. No use to a charming young Icecarl."

Milla snorted, though Tal wasn't sure if this was because of the nightmare-filled Sunstone or because Ebbitt had called her charming. She'd found her charred armor and put it back on. She had also reclaimed her Merwin-horn sword.

"I have seen enough of your Castle and enough of its shadows," she announced. "Give me the Sunstone, Tal, so I may return to the clean Ice."

Tal looked at the ring. He could understand why Milla wanted to take it and go, but he still needed it.

"What about the thirteen sleeps?"

"Twelve now," said Milla sternly. "I will wait if I must. But I am asking you now as a friend of the clan, Tal. The clan whose blood you share."

Tal looked at the ring again, then at Milla. He did feel that he owed her something. It was his fault she'd gotten captured and been taken here, to the Hall of Nightmares. She was also clearly at risk in the Castle. Perhaps he should give her the Sunstone. It might even be easier for him to not have to worry about Milla. . . .

·CHAPTER·
TWENTY–THREE

"I can't give it to you," Tal finally said. "Not yet."

He met Milla's gaze, but saw no sign there of what she would do. Surely she wouldn't try to take the stone by force?

His shadowguard felt his tension and stood up beside him, stretching into the shape of a small Borzog. Ebbitt's Spiritshadow watched from the door, but rose up on all four legs and tensed to spring.

"What's all this fuss?" asked Ebbitt. "Give me that Sunstone, Tal."

"This is my business, Uncle," Tal snapped. It was the first time he had ever spoken in such a way to a full, adult Chosen. If he had done it in public, he would have earned deluminents from everyone around.

"Give it to me," Ebbitt repeated. He held out his bony hand. His Spiritshadow padded over and stood next to Tal, and tilted its head to look at him.

"Whose side are you on?" Tal asked. He took off the ring and angrily put it in Ebbitt's hand. Tears of rage were forming in his eyes, but there was nothing he could do. If Ebbitt wanted to take the Sunstone and give it to Milla, Tal would just have to put up with it. He could climb another Tower, the Orange one, and do a better job of stealing one. He would steal half a dozen Sunstones!

Ebbitt didn't hand the Sunstone to Milla. He held it up to his eye and flashed a rainbow of light at it from his own Sunstone. Then he threw it up in the air and a sharp white beam lanced out at it from the ring on his right hand. There was a spray of sparks and the old man caught the ring again.

Tal blinked, and then he saw that Ebbitt was holding two rings now. The old one had been perfectly sliced in half.

So had the Sunstone.

"One each," said Ebbitt, handing Tal and Milla smaller but still perfectly functioning Sunstones, judging from the glow in the depths of each stone.

"Is it strong enough to be a Primary?" asked Tal

as he slid the thinner ring on his finger. He'd had no idea that Sunstones could be split.

"Easily," said Ebbitt, sniffing. "That's a strong stone. One of the originals, I'd say. Not one of these modern imitations, with hardly ten years' sunlight in them. That's a three- or four-century stone. Besides, it was two stones to start with. Someone put them together long ago, when frogs still had legs."

"You can put Sunstones together?" asked Tal.

Why hadn't he been taught any of this Sunstone lore? He would be finished at the Lectorium in a month, and he knew there were no more classes on Sunstones. Perhaps the lectors didn't know themselves?

Ebbitt was an eccentric, but Tal had always known he was a very learned one. He hadn't suspected that this learning would include the secret ways of the Castle, or the nature of Sunstones, or anything like that.

"The Far Raiders thank you," said Milla. This time, she did knock her knuckles together for Tal as well as Ebbitt. "Now, how do I return to the heating tunnels?"

"Tricky," said Ebbitt. "They'll be looking for Tal now, and for you soon, Milla. What with Spiritshadows searching you out, it could be very hard to get back down."

"Searching us out?" asked Milla. "How? Like a Wrack Hound, by smell?"

"Wrack Hounds?" asked Ebbitt, brightening. "What might they be —"

"Spiritshadows, searching," interrupted Tal, to hasten the old man along. He glanced nervously at the door.

"Oh, yes," agreed Ebbitt. "Any of the Spiritshadows that have touched you will remember the feel of your essence. They can sense that from quite a long way away. Very clever. I've had mine do it, to track down friends. I wouldn't be surprised if they're already on their way."

"Well, let's not wait for them!" urged Tal.

Ebbitt let out a sigh and looked back at the apparatus and the books. Tal steered him back to the capillary tunnel. Tal and Milla bombarded him with questions as they helped the old man up into the ceiling.

"What do you mean, they sense us?"

"How far can they do this sensing?"

"Can anything stop them from sensing us?"

After Ebbitt was safely up in the capillary tunnel,

Tal suddenly stopped asking questions and said, "Ebbitt! The insect repellent! For Milla!"

Milla didn't ask what the yellow muck was. But she smeared it on immediately. She had just finished her face when the door to the Hall of Nightmares suddenly opened, letting in a rush of light.

Fashnek stood there, his Spiritshadow behind him, and two other Spiritshadows at his side. He gaped at the open globe, then saw Milla leaping up into what he thought was a solid ceiling.

"Seize her!" he roared. But he stepped back himself. He had been frightened by Milla and the Crones in her dream. Now she had escaped from the crystal globe, without a Sunstone! She was clearly an even more dangerous and powerful an enemy than he'd thought.

Ebbitt sealed the hatch behind them, then put his Sunstone down the front of his shirt. It was followed by his Spiritshadow, which shrank down and curled around it. Tal and his shadowguard did the same thing. Milla's stone still shone from her pocket, until Tal dimmed it for her. In total darkness they would be safe from the pursuing Spiritshadows, who needed light to be able to do anything.

"Hold my leg," whispered Ebbitt. "Milla, hold Tal's."

Clutching on to one another, they began to crawl. Tal had to fight the urge to get his Sunstone out. It was just like the Veil, when he'd passed through it. The darkness seemed to press on him physically, and he found it hard to breathe. It got worse and worse, until he was panting very quickly and clutching Ebbitt's foot so hard that the old man yelped in pain.

Tal was even more afraid because he wasn't sure that Ebbitt knew where he was going. They could be crawling anywhere — to the lair of the water spiders — thousands of them, boiling over, a great pit of water spiders, which would find that square of skin that Tal had missed putting repellent on, and their fangs would —

There was something on Tal's leg. It had to be a water spider. It had to be! Or maybe it was Milla, holding on. He wanted to kick at it and roll over, but maybe it was Milla and he couldn't breathe and —

Ebbitt stopped.

"We should be far enough away," he whispered. "I'm going to try a little light."

Tal almost sobbed with relief, but he couldn't help himself craning his head back to be ready when the light came. Though he had no idea what he'd do if he looked back and found himself staring into the multifaceted eyes and piercing fangs of a water spider . . .

The light came. There was only Milla, holding on to Tal's leg. There were no water spiders.

Tal's expression must have given him away, because Milla quickly ran her fingers across Tal's knee, like a spider. He flinched, and Milla laughed. It was only the second time Tal had heard Milla laugh.

"There was a spider," said Milla. "It had eyes like ice crystals, but with a light inside, not a reflection. It waved its legs at me but did not move."

"Where?" croaked Tal, his throat suddenly very, very dry.

"Back in the cross-tunnel," said Milla, pointing at an intersection that was far too close for Tal's liking. "But there was nothing to fear. I would have slain it if it approached."

"They are hard to kill," warned Ebbitt. "We had best get on before the repellent wears off."

"Where?" asked Milla.

Tal looked back at Ebbitt. The old man shrugged and smiled. The dreamy smile.

"If the Spiritshadows can sense us," Tal said, "it's going to be hard to hide anywhere and almost impossible to get you down to the Underfolk levels.

Even if we could make it there, I don't know where Crow and his friends found us."

"I'd find it," said Milla. "But I believe you. If we cannot go there yet, where can we go?"

"We have to let the Empress know that Sushin is doing things illegally in her name, and with her guards," said Tal. "Once she knows, she'll put everything right."

He hesitated, then added, "But I probably wouldn't be able to get to the Empress, either. Unless these capillaries go up to Violet?"

"They do," replied Ebbitt. "But they get ever so narrow and ever so small, almost like they're not there at all."

"But Milla might be able to use them to get down farther, down to the Underfolk levels," said Tal.

"No, no, no." Ebbitt shook his head. "The water spiders spin their webs below Red Seven. All part of the plan, you see, to catch what shouldn't get past. We were once so very clever."

"Can't go up, can't go down, can't see my mother, can't go anywhere normal," said Tal as he counted each possibility on his fingers. Then he made a fist and struck it into the palm of his other hand. "There must be *somewhere* we can go!"

"Aenir," said Ebbitt. "I told you. It's almost time

for you to get a Spiritshadow anyway, and you, we, *everyone* needs the Codex. The Spiritshadows won't be able to sniff you out here if you're there."

Tal thought about this for a good minute.

"It's forbidden to go to Aenir before the Day of Ascension," he pointed out.

"That's only because it's safer when all the Chosen are there together," said Ebbitt. "And it wasn't always forbidden. I've been over by myself. Several times."

Tal thought about that a bit longer. He didn't seem to have a lot of choice.

"If we go, what will happen to our bodies?" he asked finally. "We couldn't leave them here. We might be gone for weeks."

"What is Aenir?" asked Milla suddenly. "Why would we leave our bodies?"

"Aenir is the spirit world," Tal explained shortly. "It is another land, which the Chosen can enter. We leave our bodies here, and our spirits go there."

"Ah, like a dream," said Milla.

"No," said Tal. "It is real, but different. If you have the strength and a powerful Sunstone, you can take things there — and bring them back. It is a place of magic. The seeds that Sunstones grow from come from Aenir. So do Spiritshadows."

"The source of Shadow," Milla whispered. "Perhaps I should see this, to report to the Crones."

"We can't go unless our bodies are safe," said Tal. "So it's pointless thinking about it."

"The Mausoleum," said Ebbitt suddenly. "A good place for bodies. Dead or alive!"

·CHAPTER· TWENTY–FOUR

The Mausoleum was where Chosen were finally laid to rest. It was rare for a Chosen to die young because their lives could usually be prolonged by Sunstones, but there were always accidents, or those who had grown weary of life, or who made mistakes with the healing power of their stones.

The Mausoleum occupied the second-biggest chamber in the Castle, in the neutral levels on the southern side. It had a domed ceiling, cut from the rock and adorned with thousands of Sunstone chips to give the impression of stars. Unlike the rest of the Castle, it was not lit by anything brighter. The Mausoleum lay in perpetual twilight, under a night sky as it might be seen above the Veil.

Every single Chosen whose remains rested there occupied a lavishly decorated stone coffin, surmounted by a statue of their Spiritshadow. The vast hall was lined with row after row of fantastic statues, Spiritshadows carved in white-and-red marble, in greenstone, or in black, gold-shot granite. Many were adorned with gold and silver, or set with dull, ordinary gems like diamonds and rubies.

No capillaries of the cooling system entered the Mausoleum, so Ebbitt led them out nearby. They sneaked through the Preparing Room, which was fortunately empty of Chosen, dead or alive.

Instead of going through the huge metal gates that were covered with the names of the dead Chosen, Ebbitt pointed them through a nondescript door, into the Underfolk stonemasons' workshop.

An Underfolk sculptor working there looked at them, but Ebbitt made a sign with his hand, and the woman turned back to her steady chipping at a block of yellow-green stone. Underfolk did all the basic preparation of the statues, which were then finished by Chosen artists, who used Light rather than clumsy metal tools, not to mention their supposedly superior talents.

"Now all you have to do is find two very old coffins," whispered Ebbitt as they left the workshop and entered the Mausoleum proper, again through an unobtrusive door.

"What?" Tal whispered back. Somehow it didn't seem polite to speak normally in the Mausoleum, though there didn't appear to be anyone around to hear them. Milla kept scanning the rows, her eyes moving slowly from side to side, checking to see if anything moved.

"The north corner," suggested Ebbitt, leading the way down an aisle of coffins and statues. "The oldest. Nothing but dust inside. Not too icky. Scoop it out and settle in."

"You let bodies rot inside these stone boxes?" asked Milla with a shudder. It was the first time Tal had seen her show visible signs of disgust. "Aren't there any animals that could eat them?"

"It's just the way we do things here," said Tal. "It's different, that's all."

"Savages," Milla muttered under her breath. She longed to be out on the clean Ice again, with the cold wind blowing. It was too hot in the Castle, and too enclosed. There were always walls, even in the very big rooms like this one.

"I guess if we're going to do it, we'd better get on with it," said Tal as they came to coffins that were obviously older than the others they'd seen. The style of carved decorations was quite different from those to the south, and the stone was more worn.

Though the decorations were individual, the stone coffins all had the same basic design. The statue on top could be pushed and the lid would swivel to reveal an opening.

Tal and Milla had to try a couple before they found a statue that would move. It rumbled aside, and Tal hesitantly looked in while Milla stood by disapprovingly. There was nothing inside but what looked like a layer of old, old earth.

"Ebbitt, can you help Milla cross into Aenir before you go yourself?" asked Tal. "I think I can remember how . . . how Dad did it last Ascension."

"Hmmm?" Ebbitt had been staring at a particular statue, remembering the Spiritshadow and its master. They had been friends long ago, and his death was still an unexplained mystery. Ebbitt was only now realizing that this applied to many of his old, departed friends.

"Help Milla? Of course. But I'm not going with you."

"What? You have to!" Tal insisted. "I've only been to Aenir with everyone else! Without you —"

"I need to stay here," mumbled Ebbitt. "Someone will have to keep watch over your bodies. Even if they are hidden in the coffins."

"I'm not sure this is the best thing to do, then," said Tal, who was having serious second thoughts. "Maybe I should try to see the Empress first. Surely she would listen —"

Ebbitt shook his head. "The Empress sees no one she does not summon. Sushin and whoever he is in league with control the Imperial Guards, and that means they control access to Her Majesty. Find the Codex, and it will lead us to Gref, and perhaps more. The Codex knows much that is hidden. I think also that you must try to get the most powerful Spiritshadow you can, Tal. You will need its help in the days ahead."

Milla looked at Ebbitt and said bluntly, "Tal was wrong. You are not a crazy old man."

"I never said crazy," protested Tal. "I said *not exactly normal*."

"Crazy is more accurate," replied Ebbitt. "But there are different kinds of crazy."

"Can you try to see my mother?" asked Tal anxiously. "And make sure she is looked after until I can come back and get her? And Kusi, too?"

Ebbitt nodded, and his Spiritshadow bowed its great maned head.

"I will be back, with a Spiritshadow, and the Codex," Tal vowed. "And we'll find Gref, and my father, and heal Mother, and we'll see the Empress and get Sushin dimmed and . . ."

Tal's voice trailed off as he saw Ebbitt's expression. He had the look of someone who wanted to believe in something, but couldn't.

·CHAPTER·
TWENTY-FIVE

Tal climbed into the coffin and stretched out. It was cold and dark, but surprisingly comfortable. He took the Sunstone ring off his finger, and held it with the thumb and forefinger of both hands, resting it on his chest.

His shadowguard slipped over the side of the coffin and then slid in under him. Tal was surprised for a moment, then he realized that it wanted to go home to Aenir. He had turned thirteen and three-quarters, and it was time for Tal to release it, and bind a Spiritshadow instead.

He took a few deep breaths, closed his eyes, and began to mentally recite the Way to Aenir. As the words — which he had learned by rote without understanding their meaning — rolled through his mind, red light began to spill out of his Sunstone, flowing like water across his chest and down his stomach.

Tal could feel the light spreading but he continued his silent recitation. The red light flowed over his face, and over his feet. Then orange light welled out of the Sunstone and slowly covered him, swirling through the red.

More colors followed, till all seven had flowed out and mingled. Milla watched in fascination as Tal was covered in an iridescent rainbow cocoon that glowed and shimmered. His face could only be glimpsed through the shroud of many colors, but Milla noted that he didn't move at all. Even his chest had ceased the rise and fall of breath.

"He has gone to Aenir," said Ebbitt with satisfaction. He pushed at the statue, and the coffin lid slid back. In a second, it was just another Chosen tomb, with no sign of the hibernating boy inside.

"Now I go," said Milla. "But I do not know how."

They selected another coffin, one adorned with a Spiritshadow statue in a shape that vaguely reminded Milla of a Merwin. It had a single, long horn sprouting from its forehead, though otherwise it was more like a broad-shouldered, long-armed human. Its legs were a bit like a Wreska's, with toed hooves.

Milla settled into the coffin and held her Sunstone as Tal had done. She laid her sword under her elbow. She hoped it would go with her to this Spirit World. She hoped that the Crones would also be able to find her there, in case she dreamed. But that seemed unlikely. She had never heard them speak of Aenir.

"I will speak the Way to Aenir and you must repeat it silently inside your head," said Ebbitt. "You must also concentrate on each of the seven colors at the right time. I will throw a ray from my own Sunstone to show you. Do you understand?"

"Yes," said Milla. This was another adventure worthy of Ulla Strong-Arm. These Chosen — especially the ones conspiring against Tal — were very dangerous, and powerful. The more she learned of their secrets, the better. She would return to the Ruin Ship not only with a Sunstone, but knowledge for the good of all the clans.

Ebbitt began to speak, and Milla concentrated on his words.

Color spread across her, but she kept her eyes open, watching for Ebbitt's color changes. She could feel the colors change in the Sunstone, and each color produced a different sensation on her skin.

It wasn't at all like going to sleep and falling into

a dream, as she thought it might be. As each color passed her eyes, it changed the world a little. Ebbitt's face faded, and his Spiritshadow. They became patterns, and then blurs of light. Everything became a rainbow, so bright that Milla couldn't help blinking.

Then the colors started to separate again, and she saw other patterns. Her skin felt hot and cold at the same time, in different patches. Her toes tingled, and she felt as if she were falling, suddenly dizzy.

She could no longer hear Ebbitt's voice. For a moment she felt a stab of fear, as if without his words she might be lost between the two worlds.

Then the patches of color became sharper and sharper, solidifying into a bright blue band that filled the upper part of her vision. The light dimmed a little, but was still bright.

Milla closed her eyes. Sound suddenly hit her — a musical, happy sound, like a bone pipe played in trills.

Wind blew across her face. Milla opened her eyes. She stood upright on something soft and springy that looked a bit like long ice lichen. There were tall plants near her, larger than anything she had ever seen. Small colored animals with wings flew among the plants, making the whistling noises.

It was bright. There was a huge light in the sky, a hot, fierce light. Milla started to look up at it, but Tal was suddenly there, shielding her face with his hand.

"Don't look," he said. "That's the sun."

Milla looked at Tal instead. She recognized him, but he looked different. He was shorter and slighter, and his skin glowed with a soft luster. The Sunstone ring on his finger caught the light and surrounded his hand with tiny rainbows.

She looked at her own hands and saw that they glowed, too, and her fingers seemed longer.

"Am I me?" she asked in wonder.

"You are what you are here," said Tal. "Aenir is a realm of spirit and magic, and we are part of it now, less solid. Try to jump."

He jumped himself, and went soaring up to grab a branch, easily three or four times as high as Milla. Then he moved back down, falling slowly, like a feather.

Milla flexed her knees and saw her sword lying on the ground. She picked it up, stroking the soft, long lichen on the way.

"Grass," said Tal, seeing her puzzled look. "It's good to lie on in the sun."

Milla put the sword through her belt and took a

practice leap. That carried her almost into one of the big plants.

"Watch out for the trees!" laughed Tal.

"Trees," repeated Milla wonderingly. "We have a story about trees, before the Veil was made and the Ice came. I didn't think they were like this."

"This is a forest," said Tal. "Lots of trees together."

"It is good," said Milla, sniffing the wind. There was no scent of cold stone here. The only troubling thing was the light, but that was just habit. Her eyes must have changed with everything else, because she felt no need to squint.

"The only thing is," Tal said, "we should have come out at where we normally do, on the Chosen Plain. It's one of the few places that always stays the same, and we have houses and stores and so on there."

"We can walk there," said Milla, unconcerned.

"But I don't know where it is," Tal confessed. "I'm lost."

·CHAPTER· TWENTY-SIX

Instinctively, Tal looked for his shadowguard, to ask it where the Chosen Enclave was. Once he knew that, he would be able to work out where they should go.

But as Tal turned, his shadow moved with him. Just like a natural shadow. Too much like a natural shadow, in fact. The shadowguard had never been that good at mimicking an ordinary shadow.

Tal bent down to touch it, and felt grass rather than the cool touch of Shadowflesh.

"It's gone," he said numbly. "I've got my natural shadow back."

"Good," said Milla. She was looking around, nose wrinkling. Something had disturbed her, though she couldn't quite work out what it was.

"You don't understand," said Tal, shaking his

head in disbelief and sorrow. "It's been with me all my life. I knew it would go when it was time for me to get a Spiritshadow, but I thought it would wait till I was ready to let it go! It could have at least said good-bye. . . ."

Something hissed from behind one of the trees. The warning hiss of the shadowguard. Then a small, furry, but somehow recognizable animal sprang out, jumped up on Tal's chest, licked him across the face, and then jumped away again.

Milla had her knife in her hand, ready to throw, but she hesitated. Before she could change her mind, whatever it was disappeared at high speed through the trees.

"Was that it?" she asked hesitantly. "No longer shadow?"

"They're not shadows in Aenir, not until we bind them and take them back," replied Tal, wiping his face and his eyes with his sleeve. "I guess . . . I guess it always liked being a Dattu because it was one here."

He shook his head a few times, as if to clear it, then looked down at his natural shadow again. He felt very alone without his shadowguard. It had saved him countless times — from danger and embarrassment and difficulty. Now all he had was a useless shadow.

An *almost* useless shadow, he corrected himself, because he would use it as part of a trap to catch some creature of Aenir and turn it into a Spirit-shadow to take back to the Castle.

Milla was still poised in the clearing between the trees, a troubled look on her face.

"Something is happening," she said. "Listen!"

Tal stood still and listened. At first, all he could hear was the wind in the branches above him. Then he heard it, too. Distant thunder, which was slowly growing closer.

"Thunder," he said. "That means lightning, too."

"Lightning?" Milla asked. "What is that?"

"Um, hard to explain," said Tal. He'd only seen it in Aenir, for lightning did not pass through the Veil on the Dark World. But it did strike the towers, and he had often heard the thunder that accompanied lightning, even inside the Castle. The lectors had also given several lessons about lightning, and how it could be mimicked with Light magic.

The Icecarls would hear thunder, too, but they wouldn't know of its connection with lightning, because they would never see it. "Lightning is kind of concentrated light that comes down from the sky. You can work out how far away the lightning is by counting the time between the flash and the sound of the thunder."

"I can't see any flash," said Milla. "There are too many trees —"

She stopped in midsentence, because off in the distance a tree was slowly moving. Not just swaying from side to side, but actually walking.

Tal and Milla jumped at the same time, as a ripple spread through the grass under their feet. The closest tree shivered, and somehow stretched a little taller. One of its exposed roots flexed, and then pulled out of the ground with a popping sound.

"The trees, they walk?" asked Milla. She seemed more pleased at the notion than afraid.

"Not usually," replied Tal suspiciously, stepping back. "Though in Aenir, who knows?"

All the trees around them were uprooting themselves. They swayed and rolled, but somehow didn't fall. Tal and Milla backed away from the closest one, even though it made no threatening movements. When enough of its root system was clear, all the roots wriggled like thousands of tiny legs and the tree started slowly moving away from them.

All the trees were walking. They were heading off in every direction except toward the storm.

Walking away from the sound of thunder, which was getting closer with every passing moment.

"The trees are fleeing," said Milla. "From the thunder?"

"Maybe," said Tal. The forest had cleared out behind them, as trees shook and swayed, shedding leaves and branches in their haste to depart. "Sometimes things happen in Aenir for no reason."

Milla snorted, a sound that Tal knew meant she didn't think much of his local knowledge. He continued to look out at the sky, trying to remember everything he'd been taught about storms in Aenir. Dim memories of the Lectorium came into his head, mostly of Lector Norval droning on.

All he could remember was a story about Storm Shepherds, strange creatures that looked like human-shaped clouds, ten or twelve stretches tall, which were thought to be harmless if left alone. This didn't seem very useful.

Neither did Tal's memories of previous visits to Aenir with his family. They had always stayed close to the Chosen Enclave, though his father had traveled farther afield.

The trees continued to move away, and before long Tal and Milla could see a continuous line of dark clouds on the horizon. Flashes of lightning also became visible, forking down from the black sky. Tal looked at Milla, and saw her staring at the lightning, totally entranced. Then she shook her head and said, "It is not dishonorable to seek shelter from a storm. We should follow the trees."

"I'm not sure," replied Tal nervously. He looked at the rapidly retreating forest heading toward what he thought was probably south, then at the low line of barren, rocky hills to the east and west, and then at the clouds again. "Maybe we should go that way."

He pointed at the closer hills.

"Why?" asked Milla.

Tal gulped and said, "Because I think that storm is going to turn this whole place into a lake."

"A what?" asked Milla.

"Look at the darkness under the clouds!" Tal said urgently. "Look around! We're in a basin, and the clouds are dumping rain. This whole area's going to fill up. It's going to flood, turn into a lake. A small sea!"

Milla needed no further explanation. She took one calculating look at the encroaching clouds and then started to run to the closest hill. Tal was right behind her.

·CHAPTER·
TWENTY–SEVEN

They were barely halfway to the hill when Tal had to stop to regain his breath. Milla stopped, too. Even though she wasn't breathing hard, Tal noticed she held two fingers to her side, where she'd been wounded by the Merwin. It must be hurting.

Tal looked back at the storm front, and saw that not only was it much closer, it had already dumped so much rain that a small flood was running ahead of the clouds. Muddy water was rushing over the ground where the forest had stood, eddying into the tree root holes before flowing ever onward.

The thunder and lightning were fading, much to Tal's relief. Though it was probably only because the clouds were so full of rain. So the chance of being struck by lightning had decreased, but they were still in imminent danger of drowning.

"We'll make it," said Milla, as they started to run again. There was water under their feet now, and the first raindrops were falling around them. But the hill was close.

They made it with a few minutes to spare. Panting, they watched the front of the floodwater strike the high ground and be turned back in a flurry of ripples. The hill wasn't very large, only a hundred or so stretches tall, but Tal hoped the water would not rise that high.

"It is strange," said Milla, holding out her palm to catch several heavy raindrops that splashed off her fingers. "Like snow, but warmer and . . . more free."

"Not that much warmer," grumbled Tal. "We'd better find some shelter."

The hillside was rapidly turning into mud, but they managed to clamber up to the crest. Tal stopped to look back down, but Milla started down the other side.

Tal couldn't see very far because of the rain, but where the forest had been was now just a swirling mass of dirty water. If he hadn't seen the trees there before, he would never have believed it wasn't a muddy lake.

"Tal!"

Tal looked away and hurried down after Milla. She sounded like she'd found shelter.

She had. She was standing outside the mouth of a cave, with her Merwin-horn sword in her hand, holding it up so its light shone in the entrance.

Something reflected back, something red and shiny, deep inside. Tal saw it and instantly an image flashed into his head. A Beastmaker card, with two red eyes that were not eyes shining in a cave entrance.

The Cavernmouth card.

"Milla! Trap!" he screamed, thrusting out his hand with the Sunstone ring, thoughts focusing on its power.

Milla reacted instantly to his warning, throwing herself to one side. She felt the rush of air but didn't see the two enormous jaws that shot out from the cave — long jaws of dark bone and still darker teeth — hundreds and hundreds of teeth, crooked and shambling, like helter-skelter rows of thorns.

The jaws closed with a clash, exactly where Milla had been standing a split second before. As they opened again for another snatch, Tal sent a wide spray of white-hot sparks straight down the open gullet of the beast.

A hideous bellow echoed from inside the hill, and the jaws snapped back inside. Then the whole Cavernmouth retreated deeper into its burrow, dragging earth and stone down behind it as a last-ditch defense.

Tal lowered his hand, his whole arm shaking. The Sunstone on his finger still shone brightly, small sparks fizzing out to blacken his knuckles. Tal looked at the stone and brought it back under control.

Milla had crawled away, circling back up and around the crest, ready to counterattack. She came down the hill and looked at the pile of raw earth where the Cavernmouth's decoy hole had been.

"What was that?" she asked. Tal didn't notice that she had to moisten her mouth before she could speak.

"Cavernmouth," said Tal. "All jaws and stomach. I should have told you about them before."

Milla shrugged. "I did not tell you about everything that lives on the Ice. But I will be more careful. I must live to bring a Sunstone back to the Far Raiders."

"Well, we need to find the Codex before we can go back," Tal muttered. He raised his arm and watched the water run off it. "Though finding somewhere dry would do for now."

Milla gazed into the distance, then shook her head in disbelief. "You can see so far here! But the forest is already out of sight, and look! That hill is moving, too, like a dying Selski of earth and stone. I know it is not a dream, and yet I doubt my senses. It is too light. Soon it will be dark, like home. The sun is falling down."

She pointed at the red light that was spreading over the hills. Sure enough, the sun was beginning to set.

"It'll come up again," said Tal, as much to reassure himself as anything. "I guess we'll have to camp here, somehow."

It wasn't an attractive option. They only had their dirty, disheveled furs and Milla's stinking armor. No sleeping furs, or cooking stove, or anything. Just a muddy hillside and continuous, beating rain.

They sat down together and glumly looked down on the rising waters of the new lake. It was still filling up, or flowing elsewhere, because there was quite a strong current heading south, carrying all the debris left by the fleeing forest.

Tal looked at one particularly large leaf floating

past. It had curled up in the middle, and its stalk was like the prow of a proud ship. That started him thinking. If only they had a ship themselves, or at least a raft, they could let the current take them somewhere. Anywhere had to be better than this.

But they didn't have anything to make a raft with.

Except light, Tal suddenly thought. He could use the solid light spell, the one he'd learned in order to make the stairway leading out of the pit. If he could make a stairway, he could make a raft. With two of them to concentrate on it, it would be easier to maintain as well.

"We can make a boat!" he exclaimed, jumping up. "A boat of light."

Then he sighed and sat down again, even as Milla got up.

"I forgot you aren't a Chosen," he said. "I wouldn't be able to keep it going by myself, and you don't know how to use your Sunstone properly."

"Teach me," Milla said. It almost came out as an order, but there was a faint question there, too, a hopefulness that Tal wouldn't have noticed if he hadn't spent so much time with Milla.

Tal looked up at her. Could he teach her? The basics of concentration and reinforcement weren't that hard. He would make the boat, and Milla would only need to concentrate on color and intensity to reinforce his Sunstone with her own.

But *should* he teach her? She was an Icecarl. Maybe an enemy. He still thought she might try to kill him once she was free of the Crone's Quest. She might regret killing him, but she'd do it because she'd said she would.

If Tal taught her Light magic, he'd be handing her a weapon.

On the other hand, there were plenty more dangers in Aenir, and he might be the one who needed help next time.

"All right," he said finally. "I'll teach you about Sunstones. What you need to know, anyway."

"And I will teach you to fight," replied Milla.

She held out her hand and turned her wrist up, pushing back her wet and now even worse-smelling Selski-hide armor. Before Tal could groan, she'd reopened the triple cuts on her wrist.

The rain washed the blood away almost instantly, but Milla clenched her fist and waited till Tal hesitantly held out his wrist.

Milla cut as swiftly as the Crone, and just as accurately. Tal flinched as the barest point of her knife cut the skin, imagining as always something worse. He didn't understand why the Icecarls cut at the wrist. Why not just prick their fingers with a flame-sterilized pin?

"Blood of the clan and bone of the ship," chanted Milla, wiping her wrist across Tal's, then placing the flat of the bone knife against both of them. She looked fiercely at Tal, till he repeated the words.

"Master and Student under the Sunstone," she continued, then she reversed the bone knife, still holding it between their wrists. "Student and Master under the Sword. By blood of the clan and bone of the ship. This we swear, with blood to the wind —"

She flicked both their wrists out, sending blood flying, though there was very little wind to take it.

"And blood to the —"

She hesitated and looked around, for here she would normally have said "Ice."

"Rain," said Tal, turning his wrist up to the sky. "Blood to the rain."

"Blood to the rain," confirmed Milla, following his gesture.

Two perfect, tear-shaped raindrops fell then, splashing on their cuts, completely removing the last traces of blood. No more welled up, as if the raindrops had miraculously healed the skin.

Tal and Milla stared down at their wrists, then

looked up at the sky, blinking through further rain. Both jumped as thunder suddenly crashed above them, sending a shock through the air.

They continued to stare up in amazement as dark clouds shifted and roiled, and two clumps suddenly rolled down and out of the mass. Two vaguely man-shaped creatures of billowing black and gray formed out of the clumps. Their heads came first, then their arms grew out, and then their legs stretched down to the hilltop.

Small streaks of lightning played backward and forward in their eyes, which were the only patches of white on the cloud-creatures.

Milla and Tal backed away from the towering figures, which were easily three times their height.

One of the creatures loomed forward and roared.

"Who gives blood to the rain at sunfall on old Hrigga Hill?"

Then the second one bellowed:

"Who calls the Storm Shepherds?"

Then both shouted, the thunder of their voices knocking Tal and Milla to the ground.

"Who pays the blood price?"

Tal stared up at the huge figures, his mind racing. The blood price. In Aenir that meant a life. But he could trick them with his shadow, and use it to bind one of them to him as a Spiritshadow. A Storm Shepherd would be a great ally here and a very powerful Spiritshadow back in the Castle. But if he got any of the ritual wrong, his natural shadow would be lost and with it any chance of getting a Spiritshadow.

Should he take this chance, on the spur of the moment? Would there ever be a better opportunity? And what about Milla? There were two Storm Shepherds. The other one would demand her shadow as well, and Milla wouldn't give it up. He would have to make her. . . .

Tal darted a look at her. Their eyes met. He saw trust there. Milla expected him to fight at her side, not to try to sell her shadow.

Milla saw Tal's eyes flicker and his right hand rose with its Sunstone ring. Suddenly she knew that some betrayal lurked there. For all their blood pacts, he was not an Icecarl. She could not predict what he would do, or count on it being the best for clan and ship. An anger grew in her, and she felt the Merwin-horn sword rise in her hand. She could hit him with the flat of the blade, and then run —

Tal saw Milla's eyes grow hard, saw the sword rise.

He had to decide. Try and trick one Storm Shepherd with his shadow, and hope the other one would be able to take Milla's shadow, too?

The Storm Shepherds roared.

Chosen boy and Icecarl girl faced each other. Their gaze was locked. Both knew that their fragile alliance was on the verge of breaking forever. Whoever looked away, whoever moved first, everything that came from it would be their fault.

Seconds passed and still neither moved. The Storm Shepherds raged. Lightning flashed and thunder crashed around the hilltop.

A thousand moments flashed through Tal's mind. His first encounter with Milla in the snow. Climbing the mast of the iceship. Crossing the Living Sea of Selski. The feeling of relief as he saw Milla stabbing the Merwin through the eye. The jump across the chasm. The heatway tunnels. The crystal globe with Milla waiting patiently inside it, when a Chosen would be a gibbering wreck.

All this was clearer to him, easier to remember than his life in the Castle before he fell.

Memories rushed through Milla's mind, too. Tal helping her up in front of the Selski. Blinding the Merwin. His hand under her head when she lay dying, the Merwin horn shining behind him. The jump across the chasm. How he'd looked covered in green weed, when he'd dropped into the Hall of Nightmares.

He wasn't an Icecarl, but he had never failed her, not when it really mattered. If a saga was ever sung of Milla Merwin-Slayer, she realized, it would have a potential Sword Thane in it as well as a would-be Shield Maiden.

Milla lowered her sword. At exactly the same time Tal let his hand drop back to his side.

Milla tilted her head. Tal nodded.

Together, they turned to face the blustering Storm Shepherds.

"I am Milla of the Far Raiders!" called out Milla.

"I am Tal of the Chosen," announced Tal.

Together they shouted, "We shall pay no price!"

THE SEVENTH TOWER™

AENIR

To the total Seventh Tower team: All the people at Scholastic and Lucasfilm who have worked so hard on publishing the books and getting them to readers.

·CHAPTER·
⊙ΠΕ

The mountain appeared to be one gigantic mass of gray stone looming over the green river valley.

But it was not really a mountain.

It was a creature of stone. Old and cold and enormous, it liked to lie in one place for thousands of years, sleeping and dreaming of the time it was born from the fiery depths of the earth.

Since it had sat in one place for so long, most travelers thought that it was a fixed and permanent part of the terrain. Unlike the rest of Aenir, where forests walked and hills wrestled and rivers changed their courses whenever they felt like it.

On their maps the Chosen of the Castle called the great hulk of rock Cold Stone Mountain. Every year the Chosen came from another world to Aenir and spent many weeks trapping and enslaving the local creatures, to take back to their own place to serve as Spiritshadows.

But some of the Chosen knew that Cold Stone Mountain was not a mountain at all. One particular Chosen had even found out how to make the mountain move.

One day, he had made Cold Stone Mountain stretch and rumble and lift itself out of the bed of lesser rock that formed the valley floor.

While the mountain creature arched its back, two other Chosen — companions of the first — scuttled in, right under the massive belly of gold-flecked granite, and put something in one of the many holes and caverns that pockmarked Cold Stone Mountain's underside.

Unfortunately for those two Chosen, their master could not maintain the magic that made the mountain move. It settled back a little earlier than expected and the two men were crushed to death. The object they had put in the crevasse survived, locked away in darkness under six hundred stretches of solid rock.

The object was almost indestructible. A single crystal that had been grown into a rectangular shape, it was about as high as a tall Chosen, three times as wide, and only a hand-span thick. Even without light, its surface shone like water reflecting the moon, a mysterious silver luminosity.

Occasionally the light would ripple in a rainbow effect, and there would be pictures, absolutely lifelike pictures, that moved on its strange surface. Or there might be writing, in the elegant and complex script used by the Chosen, or the blocky runes of the Icecarls.

The strange, shining object was the Codex of the Chosen, and its rightful place was in the Castle, atop the Mountain of Light in the Dark World. It did not belong in Aenir and should never have been brought there.

The Codex had many powers, but none that would help it burrow through stone or make the mountain creature move. All of its power lay in knowledge — gathering knowledge and giving knowledge.

Down in the deep dark of its rocky prison, the Codex could only use one of its many powers. It could see and hear through the minds of animals, using them as its eyes and ears.

It started to seek out those minds as soon as the mountain that imprisoned it settled down.

In the first year, the Codex found eyeless, deaf worms.

In the second year, it found blind crickets that scuttled through the many cracks and fissures of the mountain.

In the third year the Codex found lumps of semi-intelligent mold, which had no senses at all that the magical artifact could understand.

For several years after that, the Codex continued to send out its questing mental tendrils, only to encounter useless creatures . . . or nothing at all.

It was not in the Codex's nature to give up. It would keep trying for a hundred years, or a thousand.

Fortunately it did not have to. A mere twenty-two years after it was stolen from the Castle and placed under the mountain, it found a Grugel. The Codex had not personally encountered a Grugel before, but it knew exactly what one was when it felt the mind of the small armor-plated rodent. The Grugel had come down from outside to eat the blind crickets, and now it was returning. It crossed the Codex's cave on its way to climb up a very narrow chimney, using the hooks on its legs and throwing its equally hooked tail ahead like a climbing rope.

The Codex entered the mind of the Grugel and went with it to the outside world. It could enter the minds of several thousand animal-level intelligences at once, or a single Aeniran creature of human intelligence, though this was very difficult. It could not enter the minds of actual humans. Its makers had prohibited that.

But the Codex had to be close to its first target, or be able to see out of one of its helper's eyes.

From the Grugel, it entered the minds of a roving pair of Lipits, and then a whole swarm of Frox. After that it kept adding eyes and ears from all sorts of creatures. Slowly, the Codex's perception ranged over almost the whole of Aenir.

It was not a constant presence, though. Sometimes creatures died or the Codex simply lost touch with them, as happened when they strayed too far from another one of the Codex's eyes and ears. The Codex had to constantly work at keeping the many thousands of minds in its unique spy network linked back to its dark prison.

Always the Codex hoped to see or hear someone ask the question it desperately wanted to answer: "Where is the Codex of the Chosen?" or "How can I find the Codex?"

Once the question was asked, the Codex could use one of the animals it controlled to guide the questioner, or communicate with them.

But it was the nature of the Codex that it could only answer questions. It could not act of its own accord.

So the Codex brooded in its prison, watching the life of Aenir through the eyes of its many agents and listening through their many ears.

It most closely watched the Chosen, for they were its people. On the Day of Ascension it would send hundreds of creatures running, jumping, flying, and burrowing toward the Chosen Enclave, waiting for the people of the Castle to appear from the Dark World, as they did every year.

The Codex knew that the Chosen were forbidden to come to Aenir before the Day of Ascension, but still some came. It watched these people with particular care. It had been brought to Aenir by Chosen who had crossed over before the Day.

The Codex didn't really feel human emotions — or so it told itself. But something very like excitement and wonder did ripple across its surface one rainy afternoon when one of its eyes, a flipper-footed, furry lozenge known as a Vabe, crawled out of a newly formed lake and up a hill.

Through the Vabe's eyes, the Codex saw something that it did not expect. It was still two weeks until the Day of Ascension, but there were two Dark Worlders on the hill. A boy and a girl.

Even stranger, the boy was a Chosen and the girl one of the Ship Folk, who now called themselves Icecarls.

Acting on instructions from the Codex, the Vabe crawled closer. It didn't want to, because there was a lot of thunder and lightning about. But the Codex drove it on.

Soon the Codex learned the boy's name was Tal. The girl was Milla.

It watched as they performed some ceremony that they obviously thought was important. Halfway through, as they offered drops of blood to the storm above them, the Codex realized what was going to happen.

Most places in Aenir were layered with magic and old traditions bound into the land. This was one of them. Blood given on Hrigga Hill would call the Storm Shepherds to a gathering, and they would perform a service for a price — a price that was always the same.

A life.

Sure enough, there in the black clouds above

were two Storm Shepherds. They would be forced to answer the call of blood, even if it was offered in ignorance.

It was too late to interfere. Besides, what could the Codex do with a single Vabe? It was only as big as the boy's foot, and couldn't even bite. Vabes chewed weeds. Very slowly.

The Storm Shepherds came down, giant human-like figures made of dark cloud and lightning. The Codex listened as they demanded the life that the Chosen and the Icecarl had unknowingly promised them. It would have liked to enter the mind of the larger Storm Shepherd, but its link with the Vabe was too tenuous, and the Codex knew it would not be able to make the connection. It would simply lose the Vabe.

All it could do was listen.

The Chosen and the Icecarl refused.

The Storm Shepherds raised their storm-cloud fists and lightning began to grow there, small sparks growing longer and longer. In a few seconds the Storm Shepherds would unleash the lightning bolts and blast the boy and girl off the hill.

A pang of hunger rippled through the Vabe. It hadn't eaten for an hour. The Codex tried to suppress the instinct to eat, to keep the animal focused on the Chosen boy and the Icecarl girl.

The Vabe's hunger grew stronger. The link wavered. The Codex's vision through the little animal blurred.

Then everything went black.

·CHAPTER· TWO ☉

Rain swept the hill, and lightning flickered all around it. Two small figures, a Chosen boy and an Icecarl girl, stood defiantly before the great cloud-creatures who towered over them.

"We demand a life!" roared the Storm Shepherds together, their voices as loud and blasting as a storm wind. "Who shall pay?"

"We won't give you anything!" Tal shouted as he raised his Sunstone ring. He focused his mind on it, and it shone brighter and brighter as he prepared to unleash a blast of concentrated light at the Storm Shepherds.

At his side, Milla raised her Merwin-horn sword. She had a Sunstone, too, but was not trained in its use. At least not yet. Tal hoped that her sword would be able to cut through the strange cloud-flesh of the Storm Shepherds as well as it cut through shadow, back in the Castle.

"You called us!" the larger of the two Storm Shepherds boomed. "Called by blood on old Hrigga Hill, we must take what is offered, and give you a gift in return."

Tal thought he heard an odd tone in the Storm Shepherd's voice. It sounded as if it didn't want to take a life, that it was being *forced* to claim one. He knew that many of the creatures of Aenir were bound by ancient spells, magic that the Chosen did not know. Perhaps these Storm Shepherds were subject to such a binding, which made them take a life if blood was spilled on this particular hill.

"We didn't mean to call you," he shouted back. It was hard to talk with the wind howling around the hilltop, and the constant spray of rain that came with it — not to mention the growling thunder of the Storm Shepherds and the crackle of the lightning in their hands.

"Yet call you did," roared the Storm Shepherd. It sounded almost sad.

As it spoke, it raised its hand higher still — and then suddenly threw a whole fistful of lightning at Tal and Milla!

"Ru — !" shouted Milla, but her warning was cut

off as the lightning exploded at their feet. Icecarl and Chosen were blinded and stunned, and then deafened as the thunderclap rolled around and around the hill.

Tal wasn't sure what happened next. He crawled around on all fours, fingers squelching in the mud. He tried to get up and face the attackers, to counterattack with blasts of light from his Sunstone. But he couldn't see or hear. He collided with Milla and they both fell onto their backs.

When Tal tried to get up, he felt an overpowering force pushing him down into the mud, pressing on his chest and shoulders so it was hard to breathe. He struggled, but it was no use.

"Milla!" he shouted. His own voice echoed inside his head, but he couldn't seem to hear it through his ears. He couldn't use his Sunstone, either, because he couldn't see it. He had to be able to see the light to focus and bend it to his will. Otherwise all he could do was make it glow.

If only he still had his shadowguard, he thought. It could have done something. But it was free now, free because he was old enough to bind his own Spiritshadow, to make one of the creatures of Aenir his servant, to cross back with him to the Castle and . . .

Old enough to bind a Spiritshadow . . .

Tal could try and bind the Storm Shepherd that was holding him down. He could make the creature serve him.

It might be the only way to save their lives. Even so, Tal hesitated, thoughts flickering through his mind like the Storm Shepherd's lightning. He could only bind an Aeniran to be his Spiritshadow once. It would be the most important thing he ever did. His Spiritshadow would influence his position in the Castle, would help him rise to Violet or fall to Red.

He had always thought he'd look over many different Aeniran creatures before he made his choice. He would weigh up their advantages and disadvantages. Talk with his parents about which creature would be best. Discuss it with his friends.

Tal didn't even know what a Storm Shepherd Spiritshadow would be like. He'd never seen one, either in Aenir or in the Castle. Maybe they made really rotten Spiritshadows.

Only, if Tal didn't bind the Storm Shepherd he would probably die. Then there would be no one to save Gref, or his mother, or Kusi, or to find his father.

What would Rerem do? Tal asked himself.

Tal could almost hear his father answer, feel his grip as they clasped forearms in farewell.

Look after your mother and the children, Tal. I'm depending upon you.

Tal felt the beginning of a sob rise in his throat. He had failed so far. His mother, Graile, was in a coma. His brother, Gref, was a prisoner, taken by a Spiritshadow that Tal hoped the Codex would identify. His youngest sister, Kusi, was being fostered by his cousins, friends of Shadowmaster Sushin, Tal's declared enemy. His father, Rerem, was lost, the only clue to his fate a scratched name in an illegal prison pit back in the Castle.

Tal's mouth set in determination. He would not fail anymore.

He would do whatever had to be done. His choice of Spiritshadow was nothing, though he couldn't help but feel a pang as he decided to give up a precious, long-cherished dream.

He would bind the Storm Shepherd.

But he had to be able to see.

Tal started to blink very quickly, hoping that would help. Surely he was only temporarily blinded? What if the Storm Shepherd killed him before he could see? But then, they only wanted one life . . .

The blinking did help. Slowly Tal's vision returned. Patches of fuzzy color joined together and became sharper.

The Storm Shepherd was holding him down with just one cloudy finger. The other Storm Shepherd needed two of its three fingers to hold Milla down. Tal's arms and hands were free. He could see his Sunstone again, despite the constant rain and the howling wind that whipped around the Storm Shepherds. Off the hill, it wasn't even raining.

Tal had practiced binding Aeniran creatures for many years. It was the culmination of all of a Chosen's child training, when they bound a creature and brought it back to the Castle and the Dark World to serve them as a Spiritshadow. He knew all the spells and rituals by heart.

First, he must Mark the Bounds. Then he had to Speak the Words. Finally, they had to Share the Shadow.

He had never thought he would do any of these things while lying on his back with an all-too-solid Storm Shepherd's finger pressing him into the mud.

"Which one of you shall die?" roared the Storm Shepherds, once again speaking in unison. This close, their voices were deafening.

Tal answered, but not in words. Instead he raised his Sunstone ring. A narrow beam of orange light sprang out of it, going straight through the nearest Storm Shepherd. It didn't seem to notice, but the beam wasn't meant to harm anyway. It was a marker.

Tal quickly used the beam to draw a circle that included the two Storm Shepherds and Milla, as well as himself. Where the beam of light struck the ground, the grass and mud took on an orange luminescence.

Constrained by the Storm Shepherd, the circle was a bit wonky. Certainly it wouldn't have got Tal a pass mark back in the Lectorium. But it was a closed circle of light, and so Tal had completed the first part of the Binding of a Spiritshadow. He had Marked the Bounds.

"What are you doing?" asked the Storm Shepherd. It didn't sound disturbed. Just curious. "You only need to decide which one of you is to die."

Now Tal spoke, but it was a spell that he chanted, not an answer. He did not know what the words meant, for he had been taught them by rote, and they were not of a language used by the Chosen. Because of this he had practiced Speaking the Words almost every day for years. Binding a Spiritshadow was the act that marked the beginning of his adult life, and the type and strength of the Spiritshadow he gained would greatly influence his ability to rise through the Orders of the Castle.

Tal suppressed a sudden image of himself trailing through the Red Corridors, while everyone laughed behind their hands, whispering, "Look at his Spiritshadow. He bound a Storm Shepherd, can you believe it?"

"Mestrel ol Tel, Asteyr, Mestrel ol Lameth, amsal gebborn yeo nebedi —"

"What are you doing!" Milla shrieked. She threw herself forward so violently that the Storm Shepherd holding her had to use its third and last finger to bring her under control. "You can't say that!"

"What!" exclaimed Tal, shocked by the sudden outburst. In that moment, he lost track of the spell. The words had to be said exactly, without pause. He had felt the power building in them and had *known* he would be able to bind the Storm Shepherd. Now, as the power of the words dissipated, the bounds faded, too.

Milla had spoiled his one chance to bind the Storm Shepherd. If he'd managed it, he could have set his new servant against the other Storm Shepherd. They wouldn't have to choose who had to die.

"You've ruined it!" Tal shouted. He tried to roll over to Milla, but the cloud finger held him fast.

"Ruined what?" asked Milla angrily. "How did you learn the Crones' Talk?"

"You have to decide," interrupted the smaller Storm Shepherd. "One of you has to die —"

"Shut up!" Tal yelled. Surprisingly, the Storm Shepherd did. "What do you mean Crones' Talk? I was Speaking the Words. I was trying to bind the Storm Shepherd and save your stupid life!"

"It was Crones' Talk, the Old Tongue," insisted Milla. "The Prayer to Asteyr, which can only be said by a Crone Mother. It is forbidden to everyone else."

"How do you know that's what I was saying?" asked Tal.

The two Storm Shepherds nodded, as if he'd asked a good question.

"I have heard it," said Milla, her voice low. "Five times. The last was only a half-circling ago, when Olof Snowswimmer slew Ifrim No-Nose in his sleep. Olof would not accept the judgment of the Crone Mother, and she had to say the prayer."

"What happened?" growled the smaller Storm Shepherd. All the lightning that it had held in its hand was gone now, and its eyes sparked more brightly.

"The Crone Mother called on Asteyr, and she

made Olof walk into the Living Sea," said Milla. "He was not crushed by the Selski, but caught on a fluke, and dragged for many stretches across the Ice before he died."

Tal was silent. *Asteyr* was one of the words in the binding spell, repeated several times. But how could the Chosen's binding spell be the same as the Ice-carl's Prayer to Asteyr?

"This is all very interesting," grumbled the larger Storm Shepherd. "But you still have to decide. Which of you is to die?"

·CHAPTER·
THREE

As the Storm Shepherd finished speaking, Milla suddenly struck at the one holding her down, plunging her bone knife into the creature's middle finger. The knife sank hilt-deep into the cloud-flesh and then bounced out again, the cloud reforming.

"Don't do that," said the Storm Shepherd. "It tickles."

Milla slid her knife back into her sleeve and took a deep breath.

"I will be the one to die," she announced. "But only if Tal promises to take my Sunstone to the Far Raiders, and tell the Crone Mother of the Ship everything I have seen."

"Hold on!" said Tal. He'd been thinking about the Storm Shepherds' curious reluctance to actually go ahead and kill one of them. "I don't think either of us has to die."

"Blood has been offered on Old Hrigga Hill!" roared the larger Storm Shepherd. "A life must be given, and a gift granted. The girl has offered her life, and we will take it!"

"No, take mine," said Tal quickly. "I'm offering as well. But only if Milla helps find the Codex and takes it back to Ebbitt so he can find Gref."

"Two lives . . ." muttered the larger Storm Shepherd. It sounded confused. "This is not the way of things. One life, one gift. That is the rule of the hill."

"What if we don't ask for a gift?" questioned Tal. "Say we gave *you* a gift instead of a life?"

437

"No," grumbled the Storm Shepherd, shaking its head. "Never before has this happened on Old Hrigga Hill. One life is taken, one gift given!"

"I would like a gift, Adras," said the other Storm Shepherd. "No one has ever given us a gift."

"There is no choice, Odris," said the larger Storm Shepherd. "We are bound to the hill, and must serve its wants."

"Adras and Odris," said Milla. "I am Milla of the Far Raiders, and that is Tal."

"Of the Chosen," added Tal. The pressure on his chest was lightening. The Storm Shepherds obviously found it harder to crush people they'd been introduced to.

Now that he knew their names, Tal could see differences between the two Storm Shepherds. Adras was taller by several stretches and wider, and had more lightning running along its puffy arms and hands. Odris was slighter and there were many more sparks in its eyes. From their shapes, Tal could tell Adras was male and Odris female.

"One must die," repeated Adras. He was stuck on that.

"But we have to decide, don't we?" asked Tal. "That's the nature of the binding, isn't it?"

Tal knew that the great majority of the creatures of Aenir were bound to particular places, or to follow certain paths, or to roam within severely limited boundaries. Within these bounds, they were also constrained to follow age-old spells and rituals.

If Tal could work out the exact nature of the binding, he might be able to save himself and Milla.

Adras didn't answer, but Tal saw Odris wink.

"Let us up so we can talk about it," said Tal. "After all, you can catch us if we try to run away."

The Storm Shepherds looked at each other. Then

they lifted their hands and billowed back. Tal and Milla stood up and wiped the mud off their bodies. Most of it was on their backs. After a moment's hesitation, they helped each other get the worst of it off.

"Now, let me get this straight," said Tal. "You two are bound to this hill. If blood is spilled here, then you must come and ask for a life and give a gift in return."

"So it has always been," rumbled Adras.

"Since the Forgetting," added Odris.

"The Forgetting?" asked Tal, curious. "What was that?"

"We do not know," replied Odris. "There is only the time before the Forgetting, which we do not know, and the time after, which we do."

"How is this going to help us?" whispered Milla to Tal. "Blind them with your Sunstone, and we will run. They have said they are bound here. Once off the hill we will be safe."

"Their lightning isn't bound," Tal whispered back. "If we run they'll probably roast us both."

"No whispering!" ordered Adras. He was getting impatient again. "Which one will die?"

"If you weren't bound to this hill, you wouldn't have to take a life, would you?" asked Tal.

His question surprised the Storm Shepherds. Thunder crackled around them, and they bowed their heads together. They obviously thought their whispers could not be heard, but even whispering, their voices were as loud as a human speaking normally.

"Freedom?"

"Can he free us?"

"What will Hrigga do?"

"I can free you," announced Tal. "Sort of, anyway."

He hesitated before he continued. What he said next would seal his future and could not be unsaid.

"How?" boomed Adras. "How?"

"You will have to volunteer to become our Spiritshadows," Tal blurted out. He felt sick, knowing that he was giving up the future he'd dreamed about, of a dragon Spiritshadow like the Empress's, or a majestic maned cat like Ebbitt's. That made him feel guilty, too. How could he even temporarily value that more than Gref's freedom, or his mother's life?

He'd also forgotten what it would mean to Milla.

"What!" exploded Milla. She looked at Tal as if he had suddenly turned into a Merwin. "I cannot have a Spiritshadow!"

"It's the only thing I can think of," explained Tal

wretchedly. "Great-uncle Ebbitt told me once about an Aeniran creature who *volunteered* to be a Spirit-shadow, instead of being forced. It bound itself freely to a Chosen, and so became free of the bonds that held it to a place. Of course, the Chosen who let it wasn't allowed to bring it back until it was re-bound to be an actual servant, not a companion . . . anyway, if they volunteer, we don't have to Mark the Bounds or Speak the Words. We just Share the Shadow, which means giving them our natural shadows —"

"My shadow?" asked Milla, her voice as cold as the ice she came from. Her hand was on the hilt of her Merwin-horn sword. "We have shared much, Tal of the Chosen. But do not think you have made me like you. I will not give up my shadow. I would rather die."

Tal shook as he held back angry words. He couldn't believe Milla was being so stubborn. Everything depended on this. Their own lives. His whole family.

Besides, he was honoring her, giving her the op-portunity to get a Spiritshadow, to become almost like a Chosen!

He turned back to the Storm Shepherds, but Odris forestalled his next question.

"Both of us must be freed from the hill. You must take both of us to be Spiritshadows."

Milla shook her head.

Tal stared at her. Their eyes met, but neither Chosen nor Icecarl blinked. It was a test of wills. Tal was sure that asking the Storm Shepherds to voluntarily join them as Spiritshadows was the only way to avoid either himself or Milla being sacrificed.

They were still staring when the ground beneath their feet suddenly shook, dropping at least a stretch. Tal and Milla both fell over again. Milla went over backward, and struck her head on a stone.

"Hrigga wakes!" roared Adras. "We accept your offer!"

He reached forward and placed his hand around Tal's shadow, as if he would pick it up. But he did not close his fingers. Odris did the same to Milla's shadow. Tal expected the Icecarl to protest or move away, but Milla had struck her head sharply. She groggily tried to sit up, but her shadow didn't move enough to evade Odris's grasp.

Both Storm Shepherds paused. The ground continued to quake under Tal's feet, and he saw thin cracks suddenly run through the mud. Then they grew wider and joined, till one huge crack ran under Tal and Milla.

"Light!" boomed Odris. "We cannot take your shadows without your light!"

Tal tore his attention away from the quickly widening crack under him. It was opening like a mouth, to swallow him up. He looked at Milla for an instant — and made his decision.

Look after your mother and the children, Tal. I'm depending upon you.

He raised his Sunstone above his head and called the light that was used in the final part of a Spiritshadow binding, the light that moved through all seven colors, the light that shared the shadow.

In that strange rainbow flicker, both his and Milla's shadows appeared more solid, more real. The Storm Shepherds picked them up and thrust them into the middle of their cloud-bodies, where their hearts would be if they had them.

Tal felt a wrench as his shadow disappeared, and a rush of cold air that seemed to pass through his head. Immediately he became more aware of the amount of moisture in the air, and of the wind and sky. Small sparks shot out of his fingers and around his Sunstone. On the ground, Milla was also briefly surrounded by crackling sparks.

Then the hill split completely in two, revealing a deep, dark abyss.

Tal teetered on the edge, flailing his arms as he tried to regain his balance. Milla, still half-unconscious, slid over the edge in a fountain of loose dirt, mud, and stone.

Both fell into the dark earth.

·CHAPTER·
FOUR

As Tal and Milla fell, the Storm Shepherds dived after them. Swooping down, they grabbed their new companions and shot back out of the crevasse. Just as they cleared the rim, the giant crack snapped shut, spraying earth, stones, and mud into the sky.

"Free!" boomed Adras as he rose up into the sky, Tal dangling from one puffy hand. "Free!"

"Free!" sang Odris. "Free at last, of the hateful hill!"

"Well, not exactly," shouted Tal. "You are Spirit-shadows after all. Or you will be when we get back to the Castle."

He wasn't sure what the procedure was now. If he'd bound Adras to him in the usual way, the

Storm Shepherd would be a servant and would have to do what he was told. But he was a free companion.

Somehow, Tal thought, every time he got himself out of trouble he created a whole lot more for himself as well. Nothing was ever simple.

Thinking of trouble made Tal look across at Milla. She was hanging limply in Odris's grip, clearly still dazed by the blow to her head.

"And you are my Chosen," answered Adras, which made Tal frown. "Where do we travel, Tal?"

"Down, for a start," said Tal, suppressing a shiver. They'd gone up a long way very quickly and it was cold. Old Hrigga Hill was far below them, with the new lake surrounding it. He could see the forest, the one where the trees had walked away. They had stopped on higher ground, quite a long way south.

The sun was almost down now. It had settled behind the line of hills to the west. The stars were quite clear above the hills, gleaming in the constellations of Aenir, many of them familiar to Tal from his early childhood. His family had always spent their first night in Aenir after the Day of Ascension looking at the stars. There was the many-starred cluster called the Jewel Box, and the triangular formation known as the Dragonhead, though Tal didn't think it really looked like one.

They reminded him of his family — so far away, beyond his grasp.

It was easy to keep staring at the stars, but that would not help his mission. Tal looked away. He had to think of what to do next. He had to forget about his lost Spiritshadow and focus on finding the Codex.

The Codex would help him find Gref. Gref was the first step toward reuniting his family.

One step at a time.

"Adras has not left the bounds since the Forgetting, and I have been bound all my life," said Odris, gliding closer and interrupting Tal's thoughts. "It is strange to do more than look upon distant lands. Where shall we alight?"

Tal peered down. There was the lake, the forest, and wide patches of bare grassland. He could see a ring of standing stones, but that was probably best avoided, for strong magic and stronger creatures made such places their home.

There were also some low hills, but Tal didn't like the look of them, after his experience with Old Hrigga. That was the trouble with Aenir, he thought. You could never tell when a hill was just a hill.

"How about there?" he asked, pointing to an area of burnt-out grassland. It looked like a fire had raced through within the last few days. Hopefully this meant that the earth was just earth, and anything else that might have lurked there would have fled the fire.

The Storm Shepherds began to drop down. Tal noticed that Adras got quite a lot colder as they fell, and that he kept looking across at Odris and adjusting his rate of fall to match her speed.

Tal sighed. It was already clear that Adras — who would be his Spiritshadow back in the Castle — was not the smartest of Storm Shepherds. Big and powerful, but a bit of a Dimmer when it came to brainpower. It was even worse than he feared. A smart Spiritshadow was of enormous help to an ambitious Chosen. A stupid one was quite the reverse.

"Milla? Are you all right?" Tal called out as Adras dropped him the last few stretches down on the blackened earth. The fire had been recent, because he could still smell it. The odor of burnt grass was very strong.

Odris hovered even lower than Adras and gently lay Milla down. The Icecarl didn't move.

Tal hurried over. Milla must have hit her head

448

harder than he'd thought. He knelt down beside her and mentally ran over the healing spells he could cast with his Sunstone. But if she had a really serious head injury there was nothing —

Suddenly he found himself on his back, with Milla's knee on his chest, and her bone knife at his throat. She leaned close, her eyes wild and her mouth set in an animal snarl.

"Traitor!" she shouted and dug the point of her knife into his neck, hard enough to draw a thin trickle of blood. "You sold my shadow!"

"But we had to —" Tal tried to say. Milla was really going to kill him this time, he suddenly knew. The knife hurt and she would need to slide it in only a little bit more.

"I *should* kill you," hissed Milla. "Shadow-stealer!"

She returned the knife to her sleeve. Tal sighed in relief. But his sigh was cut off as Milla suddenly pushed her thumbs against two nerves on his neck. She pushed quickly three times. On the third push, Tal's eyes closed and his head fell back.

Milla stood up. The two Storm Shepherds looked at her.

"I suppose I should defend my companion," said

449

Adras, looking down at Tal's unconscious form. "I felt that, too, you know."

"But then you would have to fight me, brother," said Odris.

Adras shrugged. "He seems to be unhurt."

"Give me back my shadow!" Milla screamed. She drew her Merwin-horn sword and cut at Odris, but the sword just went straight through the cloud-flesh. The bright Merwin horn could cut shadow, but here in Aenir, Odris was not a shadow.

"I can't," said Odris plaintively. "We are tied together now, until the end of our days. I will go with you to your —"

"No! No! No!" screamed Milla, hacking away at the Storm Shepherd. But her furious blows only exhausted her. Odris bore them without flinching. Adras merely watched Tal, crouching at his side like a huge statue carved from fog.

Finally Milla stood back and took several very slow breaths. She was using a Rovkir exercise, to prevent the onset of berserk fury.

"You'll get used to it," said Odris.

"No I won't," said Milla. "I will give myself to the Ice."

"There isn't much Ice on Aenir," said Odris.

"There might not be any. It's a hot place, on the whole —"

"I will return to the Dark World," Milla stated coldly. "I will find the Chosen Enclave and force one of them to show me how to cross back. *Then* I will give myself to the Ice."

"Why?" asked Odris.

Milla stood staring into space for a moment, then she whispered, "I cannot be an Icecarl without my shadow. I cannot be a Shield Maiden without my shadow. I am no one without my shadow."

"But I'll be your shadow when we —" Odris started to say. Before the Storm Shepherd could continue, Milla turned and ran out into the star-flecked darkness.

Odris sighed, a big sigh that swept up a cloud of charcoal dust that blew over Adras. He growled, and puffed himself up a few times to shake it off.

"I have to go after her," said Odris. She sounded a bit surprised. "It feels very odd to be bound to a person rather than to a place."

"It does, doesn't it?" agreed Adras. "I hope mine wakes up soon."

"I will try to bring mine back," said Odris. "Make sure you tell the wind where you are, Adras, so I can find you. And don't go across to the Dark World without me."

"I will — won't," replied Adras. "I mean, I will tell the wind and I won't cross."

The two Storm Shepherds slowly billowed their arms out to touch palms. Then Odris leapt up into the sky. She drew the wind around her and set off after Milla.

Adras sat back down and looked at Tal. Somehow he could feel that the boy was all right. He was only sleeping now.

It *was* odd being bound to a person, Adras thought, as his own breathing matched Tal's, and he felt his lightning-charged eyes begin to close. Storm Shepherds rarely slept, but he felt like it now.

As his eyes closed, his body lost its form, arms and legs spreading till they joined. The dark, threatening cloud in his middle smoothed into fluffy white.

Within minutes, Adras became a circular mass of low cloud, hovering above the sleeping Tal.

Out in the darkness, three creatures looked upon the sleeping boy and considered what he might be like to eat. Tongues flicked in and out, sampling the air. There was a bitter tang to it, something to do with the cloud. Something that hinted of danger.

The creatures hesitated. Perhaps the sleeping Chosen was not the easy prey they sought. They touched tongues, exchanging information. Together they would decide whether to attack . . . or not.

·CHAPTER·
FIVE

Milla fled through the darkness. But it was not the darkness she knew. There were tiny lights in the sky, stars, as Tal called them. There were unfamiliar scents in the air. Strange sounds, the calls of creatures that she did not know.

She didn't even know which direction she was running in. It was an unusual feeling for her. She had never been lost on the Ice, not for an instant. There was always a smell, a sound, the texture of the ice, the direction of the wind or the Selski migration.

There was always *something*. Now there was nothing to tell her where she was.

Milla was lost in a strange land. Another world.

She had lost her shadow, and with it, her future.

She had always wanted to be a Shield Maiden, dedicating her life to all the clans, and the protection of all Icecarls. Free-willed shadows were one of the things the Shield Maidens swore to protect their people from.

Back in the Dark World, Odris would be just such a shadow. Milla could never return to her people with Odris.

But perhaps, she thought, if she could get back to the Dark World and the Ruin Ship without Odris following, the Mother Crone would be able to get her normal shadow back.

Milla scowled. Here she was in a strange world, and she was distracting herself with dreams that could not be.

Her duty was clear. Return to the Dark World, deliver the Sunstone ring to her clan, report to the Mother Crone, and give herself to the Ice.

Something rustled ahead of her, and Milla froze. She had no idea what it could be. There didn't seem to be anything there, but she was sure she'd heard something. The starlight was bright enough to see a silhouette at least — unless whatever made the noise was lying on the ground.

Milla drew her sword and advanced slowly. The

glow of the Merwin horn was enough to light up the ground under her feet, but no farther. She halted every few steps to listen and look carefully ahead of her.

There was nothing to see. The burned grassland had stopped twenty or thirty stretches behind her. Now there was just short green and yellow grass ahead. Too short to hide a creature bigger than Milla's foot.

Milla took a few more steps forward. Something didn't feel quite right, but she wasn't sure what it was. There was a faint smell, something different than the burned patches or the usual smell of the grass.

She sniffed experimentally. The smell was close. It was the scent of slightly rotting meat, overlaid by the fresh scent of grass.

It was very close. Milla looked at the Sunstone ring on her hand. She didn't really know how to use it, but she thought she could probably raise some sort of light. Tal and Ebbitt had shown her how to concentrate on the stone.

The ground rippled slightly under her feet. Milla frowned. She still couldn't see anything in this starlight, and she didn't know what she was smelling.

It was time to risk a light.

She raised her hand so she could look directly at the Sunstone. It reflected the starlight, but there was also the faintest hint of yellow fire at its center. Milla stared at it, willing it to grow brighter.

It did start to grow brighter. Milla smiled. She could feel it in the middle of her forehead, and could think it brighter. So she did.

It grew brighter still, till she couldn't see her hand for the brightness. It was a harsh light, very different from the soft illumination of Icecarl moth-lamps.

Milla raised her hand above her head and looked around. She still couldn't see anything threatening. The only oddity was that she was standing on a large, irregular square of grass that was greener than all the rest. . . .

Even as she saw that, Milla realized this was more than odd.

She jumped forward, just as the Hugthing writhed up from the ground, wrapping its flat, mossy body around her legs and waist like a blanket.

Milla fell forward. If she hadn't jumped she would have been totally smothered by the Hugthing. But even with her arms and head free, the creature held her in a grip that was too strong to escape. Milla kicked and struck at it with her sword, but the moss simply absorbed the blows and tightened even more.

Desperately, Milla lunged forward and bit the Hugthing. Her teeth couldn't tear the moss.

The Hugthing squeezed tighter, and Milla felt her muscles being crushed as she tried to resist. It was climbing up her stomach, too, and would soon have a grip on her lungs.

She had to do something.

Fire was probably the only thing that could hurt it. Milla suddenly realized that someone had tried to burn this monstrosity back where Tal and the Storm Shepherds were. That was why there was a trail of burnt grassland.

Milla pushed her Sunstone against the moss and focused all her will on it, instinctively falling into the correct Rovkir-breathing pattern to shut off the pain of being crushed.

This time she wanted heat as well as light. She wanted the Sunstone to burn as hot as its namesake. Even if she lost her ring finger, she would escape this terrible living trap.

The Sunstone grew brighter and brighter, so

bright that Milla had to half close her eyes and turn away.

But the stone didn't get any hotter, and the Hugthing squeezed and squeezed and Milla felt her joints cracking and the air slowly being forced from her lungs. . . .

·CHAPTER· SIX

There was a sudden rush of cold air above Milla. A cloud blotted out the stars, and then a jagged bolt of lightning lit up the sky. It struck the green moss-back of the Hugthing and Milla felt a strange shock go through her body. The creature reared back, let out a high whistle, and immediately let go of Milla. More lightning struck and thunder boomed. Milla crawled rapidly away. Her legs and ribs hurt, but as far as she could tell nothing was broken. She was just bruised, and that was nothing to an Icecarl.

Above her head, Odris sent down a dozen more lightning bolts, driving the Hugthing farther away. But even though it rippled and undulated across the ground at a frightful speed, it didn't seem badly hurt. It was clearly afraid of the lightning, and each strike did leave a blackened mark on its green moss-back, but that was all.

Milla watched it flowing off and shuddered. Something that hard to slay was very dangerous indeed. At least she knew the smell of it now. Fresh-cut grass mixed with rotting meat.

She hoped she had a flaming torch and a bottle of Selski oil in her hand next time she saw one.

Odris sent one last bolt of lightning after the Hugthing, then circled back and settled down near Milla, growing two long legs to anchor herself in one place.

"I thank you," said Milla grudgingly.

"It was nothing," Odris replied modestly. "A Hugthing is no danger to me, of course. But they are vicious hunters of anything made of . . . meat."

"A Hugthing," said Milla, feeling along her legs to make certain they were only bruised. "It is well-named."

"Can I come with you now?" asked Odris. "I can help you."

"I can't stop you," said Milla bitterly. It had been a mistake coming to Aenir. She should have tried harder to leave the Castle and deliver the Sunstone to her clan. Now there was a chance she might not be able to get back at all, and the Far Raiders would soon have nothing but moth-lamps and glowjellies to light their way.

Her chances of returning would be better if she let Odris help her. She hadn't properly thought everything through before. She'd panicked — something she never thought she'd do.

Milla frowned, and forced herself to go back and think the problem through from the beginning.

Her quest was to deliver a Sunstone to the Far Raiders. She had forgotten that, letting herself imagine even greater triumphs, returning to the Ship with information even the Crone Mothers did not know. She had wanted to be a famous Shield Maiden, the one who had gone to another world and learned of new dangers to the clans.

That ambition had led her from her duty. Neglect of her true purpose had destroyed her dream of being a Shield Maiden. She had wagered her future and had lost her shadow, all for pride and ambition. She had demonstrated to the world — and to herself — that she was not fit to be a Shield Maiden.

She knew she had to get back as soon as possible, deliver the Sunstone and then . . . the Ice would judge her.

So she *should* let Odris help her, at least for now.

"Where is the Chosen Enclave?" Milla asked. "Do you know?"

"I have heard travelers speak of it, and Chosen have come to our hill to offer lives in exchange for gifts," said Odris. "I think it lies far to the north and east."

"How far?"

"Many days for me, even upon the wind," said Odris. "I can carry you for a while each day, but my strength is not great enough to do more."

"Which way is east?" asked Milla slowly. She hated not knowing directions.

"That way." Odris extended her arm to point. "You see the bright star, halfway up the sky, that is all alone? The one that shines a little blue? That is Norrin, sad star of the east, who weeps for company."

"What? How can it weep? Why is it blue?"

"It is only a story!" Odris laughed. "Stars are distant suns. I do not know why that one is blue. But Norrin always shows the way east."

"I do not understand stars," said Milla. "We do not have them."

"Ah, I have heard of the Veil," said Odris. "That must be strange, to live always in darkness."

Milla was silent. The Dark World was not strange

to her, but for the first time she wondered why it was so. The Veil was not a natural thing. It had been made, placed in the heavens to block out the light. Who had made it? And why?

"I will sleep now," said Milla. "Will you watch? I will count my breaths and wake when it is my turn."

"Sleep your fill!" encouraged Odris. "Storm Shepherds rarely sleep. We have long dozed above and around Old Hrigga Hill, so I am rested. Sleep!"

"The Hugthing has gone, hasn't it?" asked Milla. She made her Sunstone brighten and carefully examined the grass all around. It was satisfactorily brown and uneven, but she still felt a faint buzz of fear as she lay down. It was odd to sleep without heavy furs, but the night was warm.

Milla made sure her sword was under her hand, and then she began the process of telling herself to wake up after fourteen hundred breaths.

That done, she sank quickly into sleep.

Odris yawned, surprising herself. To keep awake, she launched herself into the air. She hadn't expected to feel sleepy, but it made sense. She could feel Milla's shadow inside her, and the connection from it to the sleeping Icecarl.

Odris could also sense some part of Milla's dreams. It was like seeing something out of the corner of her eyes. She kept getting fleeting glimpses of a great expanse of ice, and strange creatures, and men and women in furs, and a ship. . . .

Odris blinked again, shutting the images out. Then she shot around in a wide circle, exerting herself in order to keep awake. There was no sign of the Hugthing, but there were many creatures that roamed the night in Aenir. Odris kept some lightning crackling in her right hand, and her eyes on the ground.

She must not fall asleep. Her companion was counting on her.

·CHAPTER· SEVEN

Tal woke to find Adras floating above him, blocking out the sun. Judging from the heat and how high the sun was, it was late morning. Tal looked around at the grass blowing in the light breeze and sighed.

His neck hurt. There was no sign of Milla, or the other Storm Shepherd, Odris.

Perhaps there was something else he could have done, Tal thought as he massaged his neck. But he couldn't think of anything, even now. Besides, what was done was done.

The important thing was to move on. To find the Codex, which would lead him to Gref.

But he couldn't help thinking about Milla.

"I had to do it," he protested aloud, reassuring himself. "I had to do it."

The more he thought about it, the more convinced he was that he'd been absolutely right and Milla was merely a barbarian who didn't understand.

She had no right to try and strangle him. After all the things he'd done for her. She had a Sunstone. Now she would have a Spiritshadow as well. She was practically a Chosen, and she owed it all to Tal. Her silly Icecarl superstitions weren't worth bothering about.

He supposed she was an enemy now. If he saw her again he'd have to blast her before she could attack him.

He wished he hadn't thought of that. His anger melted away, and he felt depressed. And hungry.

Still rubbing his neck, Tal walked out into the sun. Its heat cheered him up a little. He reminded himself that what he had to do *now* was work out where to go and what to do.

He had to forget about Milla and get on with finding the Codex.

A large flying beetle, all blue and gold, buzzed up and Tal brushed it away from his face. As he did so, he saw part of the Storm Shepherd's shadow move. There was an area there that was darker, in the outline of a boy. Tal moved his hand again and that darker shadow moved, too.

Tal had not been taught about this in the Lectorium. He walked a few paces farther away, and moved his arms up and down. The darker boy-shadow in the middle of the Storm Shepherd's shadow moved its arms up and down.

Tal walked even farther away, but the boy-shadow stayed exactly in the middle of Adras's shadow. It mimicked his movements, but did not follow him as a real shadow would.

Tal shook his head. There was so much to try and understand. Only a few months ago he had thought he knew pretty much everything he needed to know. He had supposed he was well on the way to becoming a Shadowmaster.

Now he only knew how much he didn't know.

"Hey, Adras!" he shouted. "I want to talk to you."

The cloud shivered and then started to reform into man-shape again. It grew darker, and lightning began to flicker in the shape of eyes. It took a few minutes to completely regain its form, then the Storm Shepherd bobbed a few stretches away from Tal.

"Were you asleep?" asked Tal.

"No!" exclaimed Adras, but he spoiled his answer by stretching his arms above his head and yawning, a yawn that sent a blast of cold air across Tal. "I was keeping watch."

"Sure," said Tal. "What happened to Milla and Odris?"

"They left," said Adras.

"I can see that," said Tal. "Where did they go?"

Adras shrugged and yawned again.

"Brilliant," muttered Tal. "I don't suppose you know anything about the Codex of the Chosen?"

"The what?" Adras swatted at the beetle that had suddenly returned. His huge hand narrowly missed Tal, who was blown back a step by the sudden rush of air.

"Careful!" shouted Tal. He walked back a few stretches and started again.

"The Codex of the Chosen. It's some sort of book. It can answer all sorts of questions. Have you heard of it, or where it might be?"

Adras scratched his head, small lightnings flickering across his scalp. The beetle circled Tal's head, almost as if it was listening.

"No," Adras said finally. "Odris is the one to ask. She knows a lot."

"But we don't know where she's gone to," said Tal, keeping his temper in check. "Is there anyone else around who might be able to answer my questions? Is there anyone who can help me find the Codex?"

Adras raised one hand and rested his chin upon it, deep in thought. The beetle flew around Tal's head the other way and then made a series of strange up and down movements that Tal ignored.

"I suppose we could —" said Adras and stopped.

"Suppose what?" asked Tal.

"Follow Odris?" Adras suggested hopefully.

"But we don't know where she went." Tal was starting to feel very cross.

"I don't know where Odris went, but I can find her," said Adras eagerly. "She will whisper to the wind, and it will tell me."

"And you think Odris will know something about the Codex?" Tal was a little distracted by the blue and gold bug that had been flying so strangely. Now there were two bugs, and then a third flew in, followed by a fourth. They were flying into a pattern right in front of his face.

"She might," said Adras. "Odris always talked to visitors more than I did."

Tal was no longer really listening. More and more bugs had flown in, and now they were landing on the burnt ground at his feet and moving into a very deliberate pattern.

Tal looked down at it, perplexed. Fifty or sixty bugs had formed an arrow pointing southeast, and there were at least as many building up some sort of symbol next to the arrow.

The symbol was about three-quarters formed when Tal realized what it was. A letter of the alphabet the Chosen used for Light Magic. The letter C.

"C!" said Tal. "Is that C for Codex?"

"What?" asked Adras. He leaned forward to look at the bugs. Unfortunately his breath blew half of them away, just as they were forming another letter, obviously in answer to Tal's question. It looked like a Y, but the bugs were blown away before it could be finished.

Tal took a very deep breath.

"What?" asked Adras again, puzzled. The bugs weren't doing anything organized now. They were crawling around aimlessly, or taking wing to disappear in all directions.

"It was a message," said Tal. He pointed in the direction the temporary arrow of bugs had indicated. "We're going this way."

"But Odris is in that direction," said Adras, pointing more north than east.

Tal hesitated. He had no way of knowing who had sent the bugs, or how it was done. But finding

471

the Codex was everything. With it he could find out who held his brother, Gref, captive, and a lot more besides.

He looked down at the scars on his wrist, the marks of the oaths he had sworn with Milla. Then he deliberately pulled his sleeves down over them and started walking.

·CHAPTER·
EIGHT

Milla woke exactly as she had ordered herself, on the exhalation of her fourteen-hundredth breath.

Night was ending, and the sun was starting to rise. Milla stared at it in fascination. It really was like a gigantic Sunstone climbing above the hills.

"Thank the sky you're awake," said Odris. "I've been so sleepy."

Milla looked across at the Storm Shepherd. It was not so bad now, but every time she looked she imagined what the creature would be like as a shadow.

"You may rest," she said curtly. "I will watch."

"Oh, I'm not tired now," said Odris. "It's just that with the bond between us —"

"There is no bond!" said Milla angrily. "Or if there is, it is a false one."

Odris didn't answer. She simply flew off a short distance, to give Milla more space.

Milla did some stretches, ignoring the pain from her bruises. In the light of day she saw that her legs were mottled with dark patches and scratches. There would be swelling, too, in her joints. It would not be easy for her to walk.

But she didn't need to, now that she had decided to use the Storm Shepherd to help her.

"Odris!" she called. The Storm Shepherd drifted closer.

"Pick me up," Milla ordered, holding up her arms. "We will fly to the closest water. I need to drink and wash."

Odris reached down and gripped Milla's forearms with her puffy fingers. Then she rose up in a series of jerks, trailing Milla only a few stretches above the ground.

They headed east, but Odris could not lift Milla very high. Every now and then she actually dropped down far enough that Milla's feet touched, which hurt, since they were flying quite fast. Milla noticed that Odris seemed able to change the wind so it always blew behind her, driving in the direction the Storm Shepherd chose.

The grassland continued for a long time. Odris

started to dip more often and Milla's feet got quite sore, until finally they saw a small lake ahead. Bright blue, it glittered in the morning sun, an irregular patch of water about as big as a full-grown Selski and much the same shape.

"Set me down," Milla demanded.

Once again, Odris complied without speaking. She dropped Milla gently enough, right by the water's edge, then shot sharply up to rest fifty stretches or more above the Icecarl.

Milla looked at the water carefully. On her world, open water was rare and very dangerous. Apart from a few permanent areas near hot springs, it only occurred where the living sea of the Selski met the Slepenish that came up through the ice. The result of that encounter was always a vast swath of broken ice and choppy seas.

This water was very clear. Milla could see right down to its sandy bottom. She could see no sign of any fish, but there were small clumps of weeds.

Even so, Milla was cautious. She drew her Merwin-horn sword. Keeping it in her right hand, she knelt down to dip her left hand in the lake and take a drink of water.

As her fingers touched the surface, the water suddenly frothed and a current began to swirl violently around the edges. Milla snatched her hand back and retreated, sword at the ready.

The water continued to swirl. Then a huge shape suddenly rose out of the middle of the lake. For a moment Milla thought it was something like a Merwin emerging. Then she saw that it was actually more water, but water that had risen in a definite shape.

A second later, Milla realized that it was a nose. And there were two deep black holes that were eyes, and ridges of eyebrows made of darker, greener water.

The water from the lake had formed a giant face. The mouth was only a few stretches away from where Milla had knelt. It opened. Water pushed up to form lips, and drained away at the same time to create a throat.

The lips moved and a gurgling roar came out, accompanied by a fine spray that splashed over Milla. She winced and drew back. It took her a while to recognize that the gurgle was actually speech, and that she could understand it.

"Who is it comes to take my blood?"

Milla didn't answer. She started to back away. This was all too reminiscent of Hrigga Hill and the Storm Shepherd's Challenge.

As she backed away, her left hand suddenly thrust itself forward, without her control. Milla grimaced as the jolt ran through into her shoulder. It felt like her hand was held by an invisible rope, but all she could see were a few drops of water where she'd dipped it in the lake.

"Who comes, who comes to drink my blood?" said the face in the water. "Do you seek to leave so soon?"

Milla tugged on her hand, but it would not budge. There was magic at work here, magic that worked through the water her hand had touched.

For a moment, Milla considered cutting off her hand. But that would reduce her chances of surviving long enough to return to the Ruin Ship and deliver the Sunstone. It might have to be done, but she should try everything else first.

Milla looked up, but Odris had come no closer. Either the Storm Shepherd was biding her time before coming to help, or she was sulking over Milla's behavior toward her.

"I am Milla." She didn't bother announcing her parentage. It would mean nothing to this strange water spirit. "What do you want of me?"

"Ah, she speaks," said the Face, and the whole lake tilted up so it could look at her. "I want nothing, save a little conversation to pass the idle days. It is lonely here, and I am forbidden to slosh my way to more interesting parts."

"I do not like talk," said Milla. "Let me go."

The Face smiled, its watery lips curving back.

"No, no," it said. "It is not as simple as that. I am bound here, and must play my part. You have come here, and must play yours."

"What part?" asked Milla. "I am no singer, to imitate the voices of others."

"You wear a Sunstone," said the Face. "And I see you have a Storm Shepherd. It is destined to be your new Spiritshadow, I would guess, and you a Chosen who has recently bound it. Congratulations."

"I am not a Chosen," Milla said, but her words were smothered by a crash of thunder from overhead, as lightning flashed down into the water.

"You are aided by an angry Storm Shepherd," said the Face, smiling again. "But lightning can do nothing to a lake. Though it *could* do much to a Chosen." A trickle of water shot out from where the face's chin would be and circled around Milla's foot.

Milla tried to lift her foot, but the water was like glue. She could only get her heel a few fingerwidths off the ground before the water sucked it back down.

The Icecarl considered cutting at the water, but that was almost certain not to work and would only make her look foolish. Once again she regretted not knowing how to use her Sunstone. A proper blast from that could boil the lake like Selski blubber in a melting pot. She didn't think the Face would enjoy being turned into steam.

But she didn't know how to blast it. And she couldn't fight it. It was a very strange feeling. There was nothing on the Dark World she couldn't at least try to fight.

"What do you want?" she asked again.

·CHAPTER·
NINE

"A game," said the Face. "We will play a riddle game. If you can answer three riddles, I will let you go. I will even give you a gift. For each riddle you cannot answer, you will stay with me for a hundred days, and we will talk. As I said, it is lonely here. Too many travelers know of my fondness for conversation."

Riddling was popular among Icecarls, but Milla had never been good at it, or particularly interested. Riddling was Crone-work, really, or for singers and Sword-Thanes.

"Don't *I* get to ask *you* three riddles?" she asked. She could not possibly let herself be trapped here for even one day, let alone a hundred.

"No," replied the Face. It pouted its great watery lips. "It is my game, not yours."

"Can I ask Odris — the Storm Shepherd — to answer with me?" asked Milla.

"For one riddle," said the Face, after a moment's thought. "Are you ready?"

Milla nodded.

"Here is riddle the first," said the Face.

"A maiden's head so deathly still
Cold and quiet, yet not ill
Her long tresses hang toward the sky
Hair that burns when it is dry
Food to man and creature's lair
Name both her and her hair."

481

Milla listened without expression, committing the words to memory. Odris drifted down toward her.

"I know," the Storm Shepherd said eagerly. "It's —"

"Quiet," ordered Milla. She didn't want to waste the Storm Shepherd's help so early. If the Face asked her a riddle that depended on some knowledge of Aenir, she would have to rely on Odris, much as she hated to do so.

"But I know!" exclaimed Odris. "Why are you so difficult? I wish I'd picked the other one."

Milla ignored her. She was going over all the

riddles she knew, in case they inspired her. The answers to most of the Icecarls' riddles could be found in their everyday lives. That might be the case here. But what would the everyday life of this strange Face in the water be like? There was nothing here except the lake and whatever was in it. . . .

In it. That was the clue. Milla laughed as she looked into the water. It had been staring her in the face all the time.

"She is a rock," said the Icecarl. "Her hair is the seaweed that grows from the rock."

"Too easy, too easy," groaned the Face. "I must find something more difficult. A tricky riddle for a smart Chosen, yes?"

"No," said Milla. "I am not —"

Once again thunder smothered her words, but the lightning struck the earth on the far side of the lake. Whatever Odris was playing at, she was being careful. Milla frowned as she also recognized that she now knew much more about lightning than she ever had before. Like the fact that if a bolt hit water near her, its force could travel through the water and hurt her. No one had told Milla about this. She just knew it.

It had to be a result of her shadow being absorbed by the Storm Shepherd.

"I have it!" said the Face. "This is riddle the second."

"A traveler begins a journey. For the first week, he is carried south. For the second week, he carries others. In the third week, he flies up into the sky. In the fourth week, he falls back down. Who is the traveler?"

"That's it?" asked Odris incredulously. "That's the best you can do?"

"Quiet," ordered Milla again. She was annoyed that the Storm Shepherd seemed to know the answer already. Surely she could do better than a cloud-woman.

"This is a very hard riddle for a Chosen," chuckled the Face. "You'll never get this. We shall talk and talk and talk —"

"The traveler is an iceberg to begin with," interrupted Milla. "Then it is free-flowing water. Then it is water-cloud, as from a kettle or where the hot metal boils under the Ice. Then it is rain, or snow."

"That's not it!" groaned Odris.

"Yes it is," said the Face angrily. "You are no Chosen! No Chosen knows anything of icebergs. What are you?"

"I am an Icecarl," said Milla. "I am Milla of the

Far Raiders. Daughter of Ylse, daughter of Emor, daughter of Rohen, daughter of Clyo, in the line of Danir since the Ruin of the Ship."

"Danir?" said the Face, its mouth and forehead twisted in rage. "Danir? You are of Danir's get!"

The whole Face reared up out of the water. Long teeth grew where none had been before, and a great tongue came lashing out to grip Milla.

But before it could grab hold, the Face suddenly froze. Ice crystals formed in a great ring around it and started to spread inward in thousands of tiny branching lines.

The Face screamed and groaned, and settled back into the lake bed. The ice retreated, and was soon gone.

Milla stood, still trapped, her heart hammering. She had been helpless, certain that she would be eaten — or perhaps drowned — by the Face. Then the ice had come. But from where?

"The riddle game binds you as much as Milla and must be played out to the end," said Odris to the Face. "But tell me. Who was Danir that you hate her so?"

"I will ask my third riddle," said the Face sullenly, ignoring Odris's question.

"Danir is the ancestor of my line," Milla answered. "I, too, am curious why she should have an enemy from another world, from a time so long ago."

"This is riddle the third," muttered the Face, ignoring them.

"There was a being proud and free, who through no fault of its own was caught up in a war between the rulers of two worlds. The war had gone on for many, many years, and there was much hate between the two sides. Finally the war ended in a great working of magic. An arcane barrier was raised on one world, to keep light — and the enemy — without. On the other world, a spell caused most of the inhabitants to forget their powers and much of their past. Bereft of both memory and magic, these once-proud beings were easily bound, each to its own allotted cell. Only a descendant of the original binder could free them, either by moving their binding from the place to their person, or simply loosing their chains.

I am such a prisoner, and I was bound here by Danir, who you claim as your far ancestress. Will you free me?"

"That's not a riddle," said Odris indignantly. "That's a question. Or a statement. Or something."

Milla frowned. It wasn't a riddle, but the Face seemed to sincerely believe that Milla could free it.

"I don't understand," she said. "Danir is the far ancestor of my clan, but she was an Icecarl. Icecarls have never come to this world, to Aenir. We live on the Ice, in the Dark World."

"I don't care what your people call you now," said the Face. "And I can't remember what you called yourselves then. All I know is that soon after the creation of the Veil and the Forgetting, I was bound here by a sorceress called Danir."

Milla shook her head. This was a matter for Crones to ponder over, not for a warrior. She longed for the clean Ice and an enemy that she could fight and kill. Not these games of words and magic.

"Even if the Danir who bound you was the same as my far ancestor, I do not have the knowledge to free you," Milla said. "I do not count this answer as the third in the game. You must ask a proper riddle."

"No, no," sobbed the Face, tears of darker water streaming down its cheeks. "You must free me. So many Chosen have come over the centuries, but none could free me, for none were of Danir's line. I would serve as your Spiritshadow —"

"She's already got me!" interrupted Odris. "What would she need a great lump of wet for?"

"Please," begged the Face. "I have sat here too long. Set me free!"

"I do not know how," whispered Milla. She felt the Face's desire for freedom. The worst punishment an Icecarl could imagine would be to be penned up and unable to move. If the Icecarls could not follow the Selski migration, they would die.

"I do," said Odris. "Do you want me to tell you how?"

·CHAPTER·
TEΠ

After a few hours of steady walking, Tal had left the grasslands behind. Possibly they had been moving the other way as well, all the time. In Aenir it was hard to be sure.

The grass ended in a completely straight border that stretched as far as Tal could see to the north and south. On the western side it was grass, on the eastern, a strange desert of red sand and spiky blue crystals that grew up in columns, looking from a distance almost like trees.

The major difference was that the crystals were very sharp, and they seemed to be carnivorous. At least, there were scraps of flesh and skin hanging off many of the "plants," and all of them were surrounded by rings of broken bones.

Tal gave each crystal plant a wide berth. As far as

he could tell, they couldn't move, but he didn't trust them. They might be like the trees of the forest where he'd arrived and would move when it suited them.

As he walked farther into the desert, it got much hotter. The crystals shone more brightly, with a hypnotic glare. This was how they caught their prey, and Tal had to stop himself several times from walking into one of the plants. He wished for his old shadowguard. It would have shaded his head from the sun, and shielded his eyes. But the shadowguard was gone, back to living its life as a growing Dattu.

Then Tal remembered that he did have a companion that could shade him. He stopped and looked up. Adras had been trailing behind, quite high up. Now he was nowhere to be seen. But he wasn't too far away. Tal could feel his presence, a connection between them. He recognized it as being like the link he'd had with his shadowguard.

"Adras!" Tal shouted. His voice was hoarse. He'd drunk from a small stream that morning, but had been wanting another drink for some hours. This desert was much hotter than it had any right to be.

Adras did not answer his call.

Tal called again, and listened. There was a faint boom up ahead, a rather pathetic thunderclap.

Tal sighed and began to slog toward the sound, carefully winding his way between the crystal plants.

A few hundred stretches farther on, he came to an oasis in the blue crystal desert — a patch of more usual earth, with a small bubbling spring surrounded by a stand of tall, thin trees with greeny-purple fronds.

Adras was hovering above the spring, sucking up moisture. A thick column of vapor spun out of the spring and into his open mouth.

Tal hurried down to get a drink. There might be something to eat, too, for the trees had fruit between the fronds.

There was also fruit on the ground. Tal had a drink, then picked up a piece of fruit and examined it. It had a hard skin, but was soft and pulpy inside. He had seen such fruit before, though only in baskets brought to the Chosen Enclave. His mother had called it cakefruit, cut it into slices, and cooked it in the oven.

Tal couldn't do that here, but he did roast the fruit with a beam of hot white light from his Sunstone, until the pulp browned. Eating it brought back memories of better times, when his family was all together and the worst thing Tal had to worry about was going back to a new term at the Lectorium.

Tal spat out the last mouthful of cakefruit. He didn't want to remember any more. It was too dispiriting to think about his family and their troubles. He had to focus on the immediate objective.

"I have to find the Codex," he said aloud.

Above him, Adras nodded his head, but did not stop soaking up water vapor. The desert had been hard on the Storm Shepherd. He had shrunk to three quarters his normal size in the dry air. Now he was intent on taking in as much water as possible, to last him till the cooler night.

"It's better that Milla left," Tal added. He was looking at Adras, but he was really talking to himself. "It makes everything more . . . I don't know . . . straightforward. I mean, she didn't want to find the Codex, really. She just wanted to know about Aenir to tell that weird old woman."

Adras stopped taking in water vapor long enough to burp. Then he started sucking again, his powerful breath twisting the water into vapor and up into his mouth.

"Beautiful," said Tal. "You're a big help."

Despite the heat, now at its most intense, Tal didn't

want to wait. Every minute spent in the oasis was time lost. Anything could be happening while he sat around eating cakefruit. To Gref, or to his mother.

Anything.

"Come on," he said. But he had only gone a few stretches from the shade of the trees when the heat from the sand burnt through the soles of his shoes, sending him hopping and swearing back to the pool.

"Too hot to travel," said Adras, yawning. "We should wait till it cools off."

"I guess so," said Tal reluctantly. He inspected his boots. He hadn't noticed before, but the morning's trek through the strange desert had burned several holes through the hide. They were Icecarl boots, built for ice, not burning sands. "We'll have to make up the time tonight."

Adras nodded.

Tal put his back against one of the trees, looked up to make sure that no cakefruit was likely to fall on him, and closed his eyes. He wouldn't sleep, he vowed. He'd just think everything through. Finding the Codex was the first step, but there was a lot more to think about.

"How do I find the Codex?" he mumbled to himself. Did he just keep on walking east till he fell over it?

Tal knew it wouldn't be as easy as that. He would rest now and save his strength. Then he would walk all night. He'd make up the lost time. He had to.

But the sun was very hot, even in the shade of the cakefruit trees, and Tal's thoughts drifted off into dreams.

He slept, even when the breeze came up and cakefruit dropped with soft plopping noises all around him.

He slept on, even as something slithered down the trunk of the cakefruit tree above him. Something long and scaly, though very flat and thin. It had thousands of tiny hooked legs. They rippled under it, each hook digging out minute flecks of bark as it made its circular way down and around the trunk.

It had two heads at the end of its ribbonlike body. They were of unequal sizes. The smaller head had a bulbous cluster of eight multifaceted eyes, and two jointed tendrils that quested ahead. The other head was twice as big. It was all mouth, currently shut.

The thing seemed in no hurry. It moved steadily down, until it was right above Tal's sleeping head. The tendrils from its small head brushed his hair, and the eyes glittered as it measured up the Chosen boy.

Then its mouth began to open. At first it didn't seem possible that it could open wide enough to do Tal any harm. But the lower section of the thing's head continued to open wider and wider, the mouth spreading back well past the second head, into the creature's body.

It didn't have any teeth, but an ugly green spit began to drip from the back of its throat.

The thing shifted a little to line Tal up better, and then slowly began to lower its jaws down over his head, as the green drool spread across his scalp.

494
•

·CHAPTER·
ELEVEΠ

Tal awoke to the sound of strange rumbling, and a sun that was low in the sky. He sat up a little straighter and scratched his head. Something sticky came off on his hand and Tal jerked his fingers back down to look.

"Errrch!" he yelled, and stood up. Some disgusting tree sap or something had dropped on his head while he was asleep. He rushed over to the spring and washed his hand off, then stuck his head in and gave that a good wash as well.

The level of the spring had sunk a good hand's breadth, and it was easy to see where it had gone, and where the strange rumbling sound was coming from. Adras was floating just above Tal's head, snoring. He had taken in so much water he was a fat butterball of a cloud, all fluffy white, without a streak of the lean, mean darkness of a storm.

"Call yourself a Storm Shepherd!" said Tal, but he didn't say it too loud. He could hardly blame Adras for falling asleep. He was disgusted that he had himself, though they probably would not have been able to set out any earlier anyway.

Mind you, he thought, it was lucky nothing happened. Aenir was not a world where it paid to sleep unguarded.

He was just thinking that when he saw the hideous creature with two heads. It was on the ground only a few stretches away, wriggling toward him, a trail of the hideous green slime dribbling from its mouth.

Tal raised his hand and focused on the Sunstone. He would blast it with a Red Ray of Fiery Destruction.

The Sunstone flashed red and began to shine. But before the Red Ray was complete, Tal blinked and lowered his hand.

The grotesque two-headed worm or snake or whatever it was had left a trail of its own bright saliva in particular patterns. It had scribed a whole series of characters onto the ground under the trees.

Tal stared at the writing. At first he couldn't work

it out. Then he realized that he was looking at everything upside down. So he walked around, taking care to give plenty of space to the two-headed snake, which was still writing.

There was the letter C again, and an arrow pointing east. But there was also a picture of something. A key, Tal thought. And then several letters, which spelled out H-A-Z-R-O-R.

"Who are you?" asked Tal, talking to the snake. "How do you communicate through creatures?"

The snake twitched and began to drip another letter onto the ground. Tal walked a bit closer, keen to work out what the letter was going to be. It looked like the first part of a C.

He was only a stretch away when there was a titanic explosion of air. Tal was thrown backward and a great spray of dirt shot into the sky, accompanied by pieces of two-headed snake.

"I got it!" roared Adras, punching the air with one huge cloud-fist. "I've saved you!"

Tal picked himself up and counted to ten. Adras was worse than Gref. At least Gref *knew* he was annoying when he interfered with whatever Tal was doing.

"Why did you do that?" Tal asked slowly, when he could get the words out without screaming.

"It was a Two-Headed Gulper," said Adras, as if that was explanation enough. "Lucky I was keeping an eye open."

This was too much for Tal.

"You were sound asleep, you idiot!" he shouted. "And it was writing me a message. A message from the Codex!"

"It wasn't a Two-Headed Gulper?" asked Adras innocently.

"Yes, it was," agreed Tal. "But it wasn't . . . I don't know . . . being one right at that second."

"What have you done to your hair?" asked Adras, tilting his puffy head to one side as if he couldn't work it out.

"What?" asked Tal. "What?"

"Your hair," said Adras. "It's changed color."

Tal forgot about telling the Storm Shepherd exactly how stupid he was and rushed over to the spring. But it was bubbling too much to be a useful mirror.

"Green," added Adras. "In streaks."

Tal touched his hair again. It seemed all right, but when he pulled out a few hairs they were bright green.

As green as the saliva of the Two-Headed Gulper, he realized. It must have been dripping on his head, just before it was taken over — or what-ever the Codex did — and made to write the message.

He looked back at the tree where he'd been sleeping, and saw the pattern of the Gulper's clawed feet heading down, and a few patches of green on the bark just above where his head would have been.

"I feel sick," he said suddenly.

Adras watched in total puzzlement as the boy staggered over to another tree and threw up. It seemed rather an excessive reaction just because his hair had changed color. Storm Shepherds changed color all the time.

When Tal had stopped being sick, he turned back to Adras.

"Adras," said Tal. "I think it's time we set down some rules. First of all, you must not go to sleep when I am asleep. You must keep watch."

"But I feel sleepy when you're sleepy," answered Adras. "Because we share a bond."

"I am the Chosen," ordered Tal. "You are my Spiritshadow. Or you will be. You must obey."

"Why?" asked Adras. "Why shouldn't we work things out together?"

Tal stared up at the sky. This was *not* how he'd imagined dealing with his own Spiritshadow. If only Milla hadn't interrupted him back at the Hill, he would have bound this hulking great creature properly. Now Tal had given away his shadow, instead of using it to secure absolute obedience.

Adras mistook Tal's silence for some sort of sulk.

"Well, if that's the way you want it," he said, "I'll sleep when you're awake. I'll sleep now."

"No!" exclaimed Tal. "We need to keep moving. The sky is clear — I'll be able to see well enough to find a path through the crystals."

"But where?" asked Adras. "To find Odris?"

"No!" said Tal. "We've been over that. The Codex — at least I think it's the Codex — has sent me another message."

He frowned, thinking about the arrow, and the pictures of the key and the letters that spelled out "Hazror."

"We will head east, and there is somewhere called Hazror, where we will look for a key," Tal announced confidently. It was important to sound in charge in front of a wayward servant. He'd learned that as a child, instructing Underfolk.

He didn't feel confident, though. What if he'd got the message totally wrong?

"Hazror?" asked Adras. "Haze-roar?"

"Yes," said Tal. "Do you know anything about it?"

"I know something about a *creature* called Hazror," said Adras. His chest turned dark and stormy and lightning flashed at his fingertips. "Enough to know that we don't want to go anywhere *near* him."

·CHAPTER· TWELVE

"No," said Milla, after she considered what Odris had said, and the Face's plea for freedom. "If Danir did indeed bind you here, it is not for me to free you."

The Face snarled at this answer. Only the spell that bound it in place and the pact of the riddle game prevented it from attacking Milla.

"But I will report what you have told me to the Crones," Milla added. "I do not think Danir would want any living thing fixed in one place for so long."

"Tell the Crones!" spat the Face, a spray of cold water splashing over Milla. "What use is that to me?"

"It may be, one day," said Milla calmly. "Now you must release me. I have answered three riddles."

"The third was not a riddle," grumbled the Face. "I will ask another. Riddle the —"

It stopped, its tongue suddenly frosted, frozen in place. Its eyes rolled and its cheeks swelled as it tried to continue speaking, but the frost held it fast.

Milla looked down and saw that the thin trickle of water that held her foot was frozen. Experimentally, she tried to shift her leg. The ice cracked and broke.

She tried to move her hand. The water droplets there were now flecks of ice, and they fell off.

She was free!

She ran around the pool and away. Odris cruised above her, calling back toward the Face.

"Hah! That's what you get when you try and cheat on the riddle game!" the Storm Shepherd shouted.

Milla and Odris were a hundred stretches away when the Face's tongue unfroze. They heard its shout behind them, plaintive and sad.

"Remember! Speak to your Crones! Free me!"

They heard the Face calling for almost an hour after that, its voice fading as the distance between them slowly increased.

The grassland gave way to a sparse forest of gray, sick-looking trees. After examining them carefully to make sure they were not likely to move or attack her, Milla cut several branches and sharpened the ends into points to create makeshift spears. They did not throw well, but they were serviceable. She also picked up several smooth stones, again checking them carefully to make sure they were not eggs or something worse.

Odris watched from overhead without comment. Milla was tempted to ask the Storm Shepherd about the trees and the stones, but she chose not to. She must not become dependent on the creature, the Icecarl told herself.

Milla walked through the forest for several hours. After a while the ground started to rise. It was quite gradual, but even so it placed an extra strain on her bruised ankles and knees. So she told Odris to pick her up again, to fly for a while.

"I'm too tired," said Odris. "Besides, why should I carry you? You haven't been nice to me at all."

"I didn't ask you to eat my shadow," said Milla. "Give it back and I will go on alone."

"I didn't *eat* it. I'm sharing it. And I can't give it back."

"Tell me. What was the Face talking about back there? What war between two worlds?"

"Will you be nice to me if I tell you?"

"Shield Maidens do not barter favors." Milla started walking again.

"Oh, all right, I'll tell you anyway," said Odris. "The war was between the world you come from and Aenir. I don't know much about it, really, because I'm only two thousand years old and it happened just before I was created. Nearly every Aeniran who was alive back then suffered the Forgetting, so they couldn't tell me what happened either. I've just picked up pieces of the story here and there."

Two thousand years, thought Milla. A year was a circling, she knew, or close enough. She silently counted through the generations, back to Danir. It did add up. Danir would have been living roughly two thousand years ago. But she was an Icecarl ancestor, not one of the Chosen.

505

"The Face spoke of the Veil being made at the same time as the Forgetting," said Milla. She'd stopped walking, intent on the questions she was asking. "Who made the Veil? And who . . . how . . . was the Forgetting done?"

"I'm not really sure," replied Odris. Her lightning-eyes were very bright — she was clearly interested in this subject. "The people on your world — the ones that now call themselves the Chosen, though they had a different name then — made the Veil to keep Aeniran creatures out of your world. Because we have always become shadows in your world, blocking the sun was the ultimate defense. However, the Veil was only part of the plan, which was carried out by two different sorts of Chosen. The first kind created the Veil. The second kind cast the Forgetting and bound almost every Aeniran in place while we were weak and powerless from the Forgetting. These Chosen bound everyone, whether we'd been shadows in your world or not. Danir was one of this second sort of Chosen, I'm sure."

"But what happened to them?" asked Milla. "The ones who did the Forgetting and the Binding?"

"When the job was done, they left Aenir and went back to your world," said Odris. "For a long time after that everyone on Aenir was stuck within their bounds. You know, in a cave, or on a hill, or in a lake or whatever. It was very boring. Then the Chosen showed up again, and released lots of us to be Spiritshadows. They took young Aenirans to be shadowguards, and quite a few Aenirans got released by accident as well. Only no one wanted to bind Adras and me as Spiritshadows until you and your friend Tal came along —"

"He is not my friend!" Milla said. She started

walking again. There was much to think about. She had always known that there was a time before the Veil, but not that the barrier against the sun had been created to keep out Aenirans. Though it made sense. They became shadows on her world, and would be greatly weakened by darkness.

The Forgetting and the Binding of the Aenirans was also very interesting. It sounded like exactly the sort of thing that the Crones could do, which suggested that "the second sort of Chosen" were in fact Icecarls.

It all added up to the horrible realization that two thousand years ago, Chosen and Icecarls had joined together to fight against the threat from Aenir. Then they had gone about their separate ways. But now the Chosen seemed to be undoing everything that had been won. They were releasing Aenirans and taking them to the Dark World to become Spiritshadows. And their excessive use of Sunstones weakened the defense against Spiritshadows offered by the Veil.

Milla wondered if the Crones knew about all this. Did they know about Aenir, and the War, and their ancestors' part in it? Did they know what the Chosen were doing to Aenirans, and what it could mean to the Icecarls?

Something moved ahead of Milla, interrupting her thoughts. Whatever it was, it was coming straight toward her. Without thinking, she threw the stone in her hand. It whizzed between the trees and struck with a loud and fatal-sounding crack.

·CHAPTER·
THIRTEEN

Milla drew her sword and advanced cautiously.

A small fluffy creature lay on the ground, its head crushed by the stone. Milla prodded it cautiously with her sword. It had the same sort of strange, thin fur on light bones that she'd seen before on the singing animals in the trees. Birds, as Tal had called them. But this bird had no wings and it had been running along the ground. And it was blue all over, except for its pointy beak, which was bright red.

"What is this called?" Milla asked Odris.

"Nanuch," said Odris. "Stupid and single-minded. They come in —"

Before she could finish, several more birds came running straight at Milla. The leader leaped up at her face and struck savagely with its pointed beak.

Milla ducked, and struck back, but it had already run on, not looking back. She barely had time to turn as three more jumped up at her. Milla got the first one with a flung stone and then quickly stabbed the other two. But there were even more behind them, all running in a single, straight line straight toward her.

"Flocks," continued Odris. "They should ignore you if you get out of the way. There's something else about them, too, but I can't remember . . ."

Milla kicked the dead birds aside and got out of the way. She stood watching in disbelief for a long time after that, as a seemingly inexhaustible line of stupid bright blue birds ran past.

If she'd known they wanted right of way she'd have given it to them.

When the last bird had passed, Milla picked up the dead ones. They looked like they'd make good eating, if she could cook them.

She'd just thrust the last one's head through her belt and made sure it wouldn't fall out when Odris swooped down and held out her hands.

"Time to go up!"

Milla was about to ask why when she saw a much, much larger version of the same blue, red-beaked bird she'd just put in her belt come crashing through the trees.

A giant Nanuch.

It was followed by three more, but they weren't running stupidly in line. They were weaving their way carefully around the trees, and their fierce and intelligent eyes were looking everywhere about them.

The lead bird saw Milla and the carcasses arrayed around her belt.

It clacked its beak, a sharp, urgent sound that was louder than a shout. It was immediately echoed by all the other birds Milla could see — and even more of them somewhere behind.

Milla didn't wait to count them. These birds were as tall as she was, their beaks were as long as her sword, and she could hear them clacking all over the place.

She held up her arms in one swift motion. Odris gripped them.

"Unnnhh," grunted the Storm Shepherd as she took off straight up. Milla pulled up her legs as far as they could go, just as the lead bird leaped at her. Its sharp beak stabbed empty air a hairbreadth under her feet.

Odris grunted again and stopped rising.

"Up! Up!" shouted Milla. She wished she'd kept one hand free now, to fight back. But it was too late. Odris had her in a grip that could not be broken.

"I'm trying!" shouted Odris.

The bird jumped up at Milla again and this time its beak slashed across the sole of her boot. It didn't get through, but Milla felt it. Its beak was sharp.

"You're too heavy!" said Odris, though she did rise up a little.

"Let go of my left arm," ordered Milla quickly. There were three birds below her now, all jumping up to attack. A slightly smarter one was backing up the hill to take a running leap.

Odris let go of her arm, and Milla quickly pulled one of the dead birds out of her belt. She swung it around and around and then let it fly off into the distance.

As she'd hoped, two of the big birds chased after it, including the one who'd backed up the hill.

She repeated the process with all the dead birds, and all were chased. But there were so many more huge Nanuch arriving that it didn't make much difference.

It did lighten the load a bit, so Odris was able to go higher. She also started to glide away, with the birds following underneath. Their beak-clacking was so loud that it sounded like a hailstorm.

Milla would have preferred that. She knew how to survive a hailstorm.

"I'm not sure how long I can keep you up!" puffed Odris after they had traveled a few hundred stretches, with the birds still trailing along underneath.

"Keep going!" Milla encouraged the Storm Shepherd. She could see some of the big birds turning back, obviously to go after the single file of the lesser birds. Their children, she thought. Or maybe their parents. Who knew on this strange world?

"I really can't keep going," Odris panted. "I need water."

"Just a bit farther," urged Milla. The crowd of birds chasing them was thinning out. "Can't you hit a few with your lightning?"

"Not unless you want to get hit, too," panted Odris. She dropped a stretch and several birds leaped up, beaks flashing in the sun. They only missed Milla because she swung herself violently up, her feet striking Odris under her armpit.

"Whoa!" exclaimed the Storm Shepherd. She shot up several stretches, well out of the bird's reach.

Milla didn't reply, though she noted that Odris had

greater strength than she was admitting to. That was an enemy's trick, not one you expected from an ally.

"Ah, look there!" exclaimed Odris. She swung her arm forward to point, forgetting that Milla was attached, and they both went into a spin that took them dangerously close to the birds again.

For a moment all Milla saw were red beaks and blue feathers, then Odris managed to right herself and the Icecarl saw what the Storm Shepherd had been pointing at.

There was a building ahead. A strange building.

It was a tower that had been carved out of the stump of a truly mighty tree, a vast block of gray and green, with stunted branches cut clean close to the trunk. The stump was at least as tall as the mast of the Far Raiders' iceship, and forty stretches in diameter. It had many narrow windows, but there was no sign of a door or gate on the side Milla could see.

But better than that, it had a flat walkway around its crown. If Odris could get high enough, she could land Milla there.

"The top!" shouted Milla. "Take me to the top!"

"I can't!" shrieked Odris. "I'm falling!"

Below them, the Nanuch jumped, clacking their beaks even louder as it looked like their enemy might escape.

·CHAPTER·
FOURTEEN

It turned out that Adras didn't really know anything about Hazror, except that it wasn't the name of a place, but of a creature. A very bad and truly terrible creature.

Like the grassland before it, the desert of blue crystal trees ended suddenly. The border was once again an exact straight line. On the other side, there was soft yellow sand, piling up into dunes as far as Tal could see.

Tal walked over, and his feet sank in halfway to his ankles. The sand was still very hot, even though the sun was setting and it was long past the full heat of the day.

Wearily, Tal picked a dune that looked to be east from its opposition to the setting sun, and started to trudge.

He had gone up and down two dunes and was resting at the top of the third, wondering whether to try and camp there for the night, when he saw something flash farther along the ridge of sand.

It flashed again, and he realized that it was coming toward him.

"Adras!" Tal called. "Watch out!"

"I'm watching," rumbled Adras. He'd lost some of the extra water he'd taken on. It had evaporated while crossing the blue crystal desert and now the hot sands, but he was still fat and rather slow to move.

Tal raised his Sunstone. He wouldn't be caught napping this time.

516

As it drew closer, Tal recognized the creature. It was a thin animal, about the length of his forearm, with long, spindly legs and short forearms. It had a short tail and a long, thin snout. But its most distinctive characteristic was the silvery sheen of its skin. That skin was made up of many tiny, armored scales, but they were not like a reptile's. Under its armor, the creature was a mammal. The females even had pouches to carry their young.

It was a Samheal Semidragon.

Tal knew of it from the Beastmaker game. But he couldn't remember whether they were aggressive.

Samheal Semidragons were always played for Skin, not Temper or anything else.

He also wasn't sure if there was anything he could do to hurt it. That silver skin was protection against heat as well as weapons, though something sufficiently sharp wielded with enough strength would get through.

A two-handed ax in the hands of a Borzog might be enough. Unfortunately all Tal had was his Sunstone. And Adras.

He hoped that Samheal Semidragons were friendly.

This one stopped a few paces away, skidding to a halt on its back legs. It stood upright and waved its paws at Tal, making skittering noises.

"Tch-tch-tch," it said.

Tal shook his head.

"Adras. Do you know what it said?"

"Tch-tch-tch," repeated Adras. "Whatever that means."

"Thanks," said Tal. He should have known better than to ask.

The Semidragon hopped forward and swept the dune clean behind it with its tail. Then it turned around and with one silver claw began to trace a line in the sand.

"The Codex!" exclaimed Tal. "I wonder if this is another messenger?"

He felt fairly sure it was the Codex using these animals somehow, a confidence reinforced when the Semidragon looked back at him and traced out the letter C. After that it drew another arrow, pointing east across the sand. Then it drew a key again, but this time it also drew another picture next to it. Something that looked like a pipe or a tube, with several holes drilled into it.

"What's that?" asked Tal.

The Semidragon didn't answer. It stared around in fright, as if it had suddenly found itself aware of its surroundings. Its muscles tensed to jump away. Before it could, a shudder went through its small body. Its eyes clouded and it settled down. A moment later it drew another symbol.

Tal stared down at the rough mark. It was a musical note, written in the notation the Chosen used to perform in the Crystal Wood, back in the Castle. But what did it mean, a single note all by itself? It was a very high one, too high for Tal or any human to sing or hum. It could only be created by light of the correct color striking the right crystal in the Wood.

The Semidragon started to draw something else,

but it stopped in midmotion and shuddered again. This time it did jump away, leaving the last letter or picture unfinished.

It looked like an unfinished drawing of a human skull, Tal thought, but it was probably meant to be part of a letter. He wished that the Semidragon had been able to finish it. Obviously the Codex could only use such animals briefly. Still, it had given him some more information.

If only he knew what it meant.

He kept thinking about it all as he trudged on, but his thoughts were beginning to wander in the direction of food and shelter for the night. Neither looked likely to appear in this sandy desert.

Yet over the next sand dune, as the last light faded from the sky, Tal did see something that might offer shelter of some kind. A few ruined walls jutted out of the sand in the hollow below him. Just four corners, with nothing between them and no roof overhead. But it would be better than trying to sleep on top of a sand dune.

He started down. Adras followed above and behind, muttering something to himself. Tal didn't even try to listen.

Closer to the ruins, it became clear that the building had not been a normal house. There were too many stones lying around it, scattered through the sand. It must have been a fortification of some kind, Tal realized. Or else there were a lot of other foundations nearby buried under the sand.

There was also something painted on one of the walls. A sign of some kind. Two rough circles, one inside the other. In the twilight it was hard to see what they were painted with, but Tal had a nasty suspicion it was blood.

He had never seen the sign before and did not know what it meant.

But Adras did. The Storm Shepherd stopped abruptly and rumbled, "Beware! This is Hazror's place."

"What?" asked Tal. "This ruin?"

"Yes," said a voice that was soft and strangely childlike. It issued out of the ground, seemingly from several places at once.

The sand in front of Tal suddenly started to shift sideways, as if moved by a giant invisible hand. In a few seconds, it had cleared away to reveal stone steps going down. A long way down.

"Come in," said the voice. It sounded strangely familiar to Tal, though not in a reassuring way. Like the voice of someone he knew, but disturbingly altered.

He peered down at the newly revealed steps. The sand was being held back by walls of light, very similar to the ones that Ebbitt had used to hold back the water when he'd helped Tal escape from the Pit back in the Castle.

Tal looked at the light walls very carefully, noting the flecks of color. It was mostly Yellow but occasionally Blue. Whoever was making these walls appear had a powerful Sunstone and was very good at using it.

Better than Ebbitt, because there was no sand leaking through these walls.

Hazror must be a Chosen.

If the walls collapsed while Tal was down there, he would have no way out. Unless he could move the sand back himself.

Tal considered that prospect. He thought he could build himself a tunnel of light through the sand. If he had to.

He took a step forward, onto the steps.

"Don't go!" Adras pleaded. He wrung his hands together and a couple of buckets of rain fell down, narrowly missing Tal. "Hazror will eat you. Then I will be eaten, too."

"Don't be ridiculous," said Tal, though he said it with more confidence than he felt. He indicated the walls of light that lined the steps. "Hazror has to be a Chosen. We don't eat people. Besides, I don't have a choice. I *have* to find the Codex."

He started down the steps. Then he looked back and said, "Stay there until I come back."

He looked back again when he was halfway down, and saw the walls of light close in behind him. Sand poured back down.

On the surface, there was no sign of the stairs or of Tal. There were only sand, ruins, and a cloud that spun around in a circle crying, "I told you not to go!"

·CHAPTER·
FIFTEEN

Odris was falling. Or she was until Milla swung up and fluttered her hand across Odris's armpit.

"Ah!" screeched the Storm Shepherd. She suddenly climbed even higher than the stump tower ahead. "Stop! Eee! Ah! It tickles!"

Milla didn't stop tickling. Odris shivered and shook from side to side but she also kept climbing. The Nanuch were left far below, jumping and clacking their beaks in disappointment.

"Stop! Stop!" giggled Odris. "I can't stand it!"

"I'll stop when you put me down on top of the tower," said Milla grimly. She was disappointed in the Storm Shepherd. Odris clearly had plenty of strength left if a mere tickling could produce this surge of energy.

Giggling and shaking, Odris complied. She

dropped Milla on the walkway and then collapsed herself, a thick layer of fog draped around the spire.

Milla had half expected to see some guard or watchman on the walkway, hidden behind the central spire. But there was no one there. She walked around and saw an open door and a circular stairway, but the tower was quiet and there was no hint of anyone coming up.

Closer, it was hard to work out how the tower had been made. It *was* carved out of a gigantic stump. But there were no signs of tools upon the wood. No chisel marks or any other evidence that people had done the work.

Milla couldn't even begin to imagine how big the original tree must have been. Ten or twelve times the height of the Ruin Ship, at least. As tall as a small mountain.

Another oddity was the faint smell of burning, as if there had been a recent fire. But there was no sign of a fire upon the wood. All Milla could see was the natural grain and the thousands and thousands of growth rings spreading in circles under her feet.

"You shouldn't have tickled me," said Odris reproachfully.

"You shouldn't have lied about your strength," said Milla. "Come on. I'm going downstairs."

"I need a rest," said Odris. "I'll wait here."

"Do what you will," said Milla. She went through the door and disappeared.

After a moment, Odris sighed and wafted over to the door. She put her head in and then forced her shoulders through, her cloud-body ballooning up behind her. Gradually her body reshaped itself till she was longer and thinner, and the rest of her followed her head and arms down the stairway.

An hour later, Odris came squirming back the same way, followed by Milla. They had visited every level of the strange tower but had found nothing of interest. Every room was empty. Stranger still, there was a door at the bottom. An open door, which the Nanuch had made no attempt to enter. There were still twenty or thirty of them hanging around, but they simply watched Milla when she stood looking out through the doorway.

This disturbed the Icecarl. There had to be some reason that the giant birds were afraid to enter the tower. Perhaps it was the lair of some awful creature that would soon return. Or perhaps it was the smell of burnt wood. It was stronger on the lower levels, but there were still no signs of fire damage.

The rooftop was the safest place, Milla decided, which was why they had climbed back up. If some creature did return to the tower, they would hear it coming up the stairs. And it kept them out of reach of the waiting Nanuch. It looked like a dedicated score of the giant birds were determined to wait her out. She could see them clustered around the tower.

Even so, Milla was uneasy. The tower was too good a shelter to be so deserted. On her world, there would be all sorts of animals and insects living in it, taking cover from the elements.

But the tower was completely devoid of life. She hadn't even seen a caveroach or a spider.

"We'll stay here till dawn," she said to Odris finally. "Then we will see if the Nanuch still wait. You may have to carry me again."

"I'm not sure I can," said Odris. "I think I've lost too much water vapor. I need to build up. You must be thirsty, too."

Milla didn't answer. She *was* thirsty, and hungry. But she had practiced suppressing hunger pangs and water cravings almost all her life. It was a pity she had been forced to throw all the small Nanuch away. She could have eaten one raw, or tried once more to get heat from her Sunstone to cook it.

"I'll take the first watch," Milla announced. "You sleep."

Odris looked at the sun. It was still some way from setting.

"But I'm not sleepy," the Storm Shepherd said. "We don't usually sleep very much. It's only since I've been bound to you that I get sleepy."

"Then don't sleep," said Milla. "But be quiet."

Odris sniffed. She really did wish she'd picked the other one. It was typical of Adras. He wasn't smart, but he *was* lucky.

They sat in silence for a long time after that, listening to the sounds around them. The Nanuch settled down, too, except for the occasional bout of beak-clacking. There were other, more distant noises — the calls of strange creatures. Once something flew past, too quick to be seen.

The sun set, and the stars came out. Milla stretched and paced, her legs still sore from the Hugthing.

Hours passed, but when the time came for Odris to watch, Milla did not go to sleep. The more she paced upon the top of the tower, the more she felt like it was not a refuge but a trap.

Finally she decided they should try and sneak past the Nanuch, before the dawn. Immediately she felt better. Taking action was the Shield Maiden

527

way. She would never be one now, but at least she could act like one. And die like one, if that was how it ended.

Once again they went down the stairs. Milla trod as lightly as she could, and the only sound Odris made could be mistaken for the wind through the tower windows.

At the bottom, Milla drew her dagger. Her sword's natural luminescence would alert the Nanuch.

Unfortunately there was no dust or dirt she could smear her furs or Selski-hide breastplate with, but at least the armor was fairly dark. She didn't put on her face mask. It was white bone and would shine too brightly under the stars. It felt strange going out to fight without it.

Milla crouched by the door for quite a long time, letting her eyes adjust to the starlit forest outside. It was bright enough to make out the shapes of trees — and several Nanuch. They stood completely still, never moving. Milla hoped this meant they were asleep.

She slid out through the door.

At least that's what she thought she did. But somehow she ended up back inside the lower room, looking out.

Puzzled, she stepped forward again. For an instant she was in the doorway, with her foot about to land on the bare earth outside.

Then it came down on a wooden floor. She *had* stepped through the door, but it didn't lead outside. It took her back inside.

There was some magic at work. Dire magic, Milla thought. Worse than anything she'd expected.

Now she was sure it was a trap.

·CHAPTER·
SIXTEEN

Tal heard the slither of the sand pouring back behind him, but he didn't look around. The light walls on either side of him stayed steady and comforting. The stairs continued down in front.

They came to an end in front of a tall doorway. Obviously it had once been blocked by the enormous stone door that lay half across it, as if someone had ripped it open and let it fall.

That made Tal stop for a moment. But the Codex had told him to come here, he reasoned.

Finding the Codex meant finding Gref.

He who hesitates heads Redward, she who seizes opportunity soars to Violet.

Ebbitt used to repeat that back to front and laugh his head off, but Tal took the saying seriously.

He climbed over the fallen door and through the doorway.

The room beyond had walls of stone and light, both holding back sand, judging from the piles that had oozed through gaps where the magic barriers intersected with the stone.

In the middle of the room, a boy sat cross-legged, staring at Tal. A boy not much older than Tal, dressed in white trousers and a white shirt with blue cuffs. A Chosen boy.

Tal even knew who it was: Lenan of the Blue. He had disappeared last year. Every Day of Ascension all the Chosen children who had come of age would go forth to seek a Spiritshadow to bind. Not all of them came back.

But what was Lenan doing here? And where was Hazror?

"Greetings, Chosen," said Lenan. His voice sounded a little strange. Too high-pitched.

Tal had started to walk forward to greet Lenan properly, but when he heard the voice, he stopped.

The voice wasn't the only thing that was strange. Lenan was wearing several Sunstones around his neck. One was bright, obviously working to keep the walls in place. But the boy had two more, both sparkling, though not currently active.

There was something odd about the light in the room as well. The walls were shifting through several colors, which was reasonable, as it made them stronger. But now that Tal looked at them, he realized that the overall color in the room was a sickly gray. No normal Chosen ever used that color.

Tal raised his hand and bright white flashed out, flooding every corner of the room.

In its stark illumination, Tal saw that Lenan was not really Lenan. The Chosen boy was just a picture woven from light, masking something much larger. An only approximately human thing of rotting flesh and naked bone that rose up and cast its disguise away.

This was what Adras was afraid of.

Hazror.

The three Sunstones Lenan had worn were not an illusion. Hazror picked one up in a hand that was more claw than anything else. Light flickered in the stone, building in intensity.

Tal didn't wait for whatever Hazror was going to do. In the first flash of white light he'd seen what he'd come for. Hanging around Hazror's neck, next to the Sunstones, was a thin tube. A tube with three holes.

Tal recognized it instantly. A whistle made of the

same material as the trees in the Crystal Wood. It had to be what the Codex had told him to get.

He'd also seen the piles of bones around Hazror's feet and the broken skulls. They were human and most looked less than adult-sized. Lenan must have been only the most recent Chosen to meet his end here, in Hazror's lair. The Semidragon must have been drawing a skull, a warning from the Codex!

Tal changed the light in his Sunstone from white to red and sent a Red Ray of Destruction blasting out at Hazror's head.

Hazror countered with a Violet Shield of Discontinuity, and the Red Ray disappeared into some other, unknown reality. But the Shield only covered his head. Blasting off another ray at his enemy's knees, Tal dove to the ground.

That saved his life. Hazror instantly counterattacked and a great blast of Indigo light flashed over Tal's head. Tal didn't even know what the spell was, except that it was enormously destructive.

His Red Ray hit Hazror, but several hidden Sunstones flashed around his calves, absorbing the strike. Other stones glittered into life along his arms and thighs.

Tal gasped in shock as an aura of light sprang up all around the creature.

Hazror was literally covered in Sunstones. Hundreds and hundreds of them.

With so many defensive Sunstones, Tal's light attacks were useless.

Hazror was invulnerable.

Tal rolled away as another Indigo blast smoked the ground where he'd been a second ago. He kept on rolling, fear making his mind work faster than it ever had before.

He couldn't run. He'd need time to create walls to hold back the sand.

He couldn't fight Hazror with light.

Hazror laughed. His voice was still Lenan's, though much higher and more shrill.

"Another Chosen come to play, another Chosen come to pay!"

There was only one thing left to do, Tal thought. Something no Chosen would ever think of.

But Tal wasn't only a Chosen now. Whether he wanted to or not, he had learned something of being an Icecarl.

He snapped out of his roll, ducked another blast, and threw himself feetfirst at Hazror.

The creature's laugh was cut off as Tal's boots crashed into his stomach. He went flying over backward. A ray of Violet light sprang out of his Sunstone, melting a hole through a wall.

But it missed Tal. He grabbed Hazror's arm and twisted it behind his back. He'd half expected the creature to be enormously strong, but Hazror howled in pain and did not resist.

He did start screaming.

"Arval! Rowthr! Govror!"

At these words, one of the walls of light suddenly winked out, revealing more steps leading down. Bestial roars echoed through the doorway, coming from far below.

Obviously Hazror's servants or guards — or whatever they were — were on their way.

"You will suffer for this!" hissed Hazror as Tal dragged him across to the stairs. "You will suffer!"

Tal didn't answer. He reached around and ripped the chain that held the Sunstones and the whistle from Hazror's neck. The creature screamed and whimpered.

"My neck! You've hurt my neck!"

It was only then that Tal realized that Hazror had no shadow.

He was *not* an Aeniran creature.

He was just a very, very old man. An ancient

man. And he must have once been a Chosen. But he had left that behind when he came here. Judging from the bones and the Sunstones, he had lured tens if not hundreds of young Chosen to their deaths.

Tal felt the disgust rise in him. How could anyone do what this man had done? How could he betray his own people?

"You'll suffer," whimpered Hazror. "I'll show you how light can hurt —"

Tal didn't listen to him anymore.

He let go.

The old man, poised on the brink of the stairs, suddenly caught his breath and stopped his threats. He teetered there for a moment, arms flailing.

Tal saw glowing red eyes coming up from below. Ferocious eyes, as large as his hands. Vengenarl eyes.

Hazror swung forward, screaming.

Before he could swing back, Tal gave him a push.

·CHAPTER·
SEVENTEEN

Milla tried to pass through the door seven times and Odris eighteen. Each and every time they ended up exactly where they'd left.

Milla also tried hacking at the wood, but neither her bone knife nor Merwin-horn sword could even scratch it.

"We'll have to fly off the roof," Milla said finally.

But when they climbed back up, they could no more leave the roof than they could the door. Every time Odris launched herself off one side of the tower, they found themselves landing on the other side.

They could see out, but they couldn't get there.

"I wonder what happens next," said Milla. She instinctively knew it was a trap with a purpose. Something would happen soon.

Something lethal, she suspected. Something that had to do with the smell of burning, which was growing stronger as the night wore on.

She paced around the walkway several more times, thinking. Then she said, "Come on," to Odris and went back downstairs.

At the bottom, she stood in front of the door and raised her Sunstone. Concentrating on it, she called it into full light. Bright white light that filled the bottom level and spilled out into the night.

"I'm here!" yelled Milla to the waiting Nanuch. "Here!"

"What are you doing?" asked Odris anxiously.

"I'm trying to get one to come in," explained Milla. "I might be able to jump out as one jumps in."

"Oh," said Odris. "But what about me?"

"I'll throw one in for you," said Milla.

It was a good plan. But it didn't work because the Nanuch wouldn't come any closer.

Something else did, though. A small green lizard approached the door. It walked upright on its hind legs, wearing a harness made from woven grass, from which hung a sword no longer than Milla's forefinger. It bore a quiver of tiny arrows on its back, and carried a bow only slighter shorter than it was tall.

"A Kurshken," said Odris. "I wonder what *it* wants."

The Kurshken came up within a few stretches of the door and bowed. Then it spoke, in a surprisingly deep voice for one so small.

"Greetings, Milla and Odris. I am Quorr Quorr Quorr Ahhtorn Sezicka. You may call me Zicka."

"Greetings," said Milla, bowing in turn. "How do you know our names?"

"The Codex of the Chosen has spoken in my head," said Zicka. "It told me to come here. Soon it will speak through my mouth."

"Do you know how we can get out of here?" asked Milla. "Or does the Codex know?"

Zicka started to speak, then froze. His eyes grew cloudy. Rather like a Crone Mother's, Milla noticed. Then he spoke again, and his voice sounded different, the words coming less fluently.

"I am the Codex. I need your help. Tal alone cannot free me. You must meet him. Zicka will show you where."

"What if we don't want to help?" asked Milla. "I see no reason to help any Chosen, least of all Tal. He has betrayed —"

"I have little time to speak thus," interrupted the Codex. "Tal has done what he had to do. If you agree to help, Zicka will free you from the Dawn House. If not, you will die."

"The Dawn House?" asked Milla. "What is —"

Before she could finish the question, Zicka's eyes cleared.

"Well?" he said, his voice normal again. "What is it to be?"

"A Shield Maiden does not barter favors," Milla said angrily. "Free us from this prison. Then I will decide."

"That is not the instruction of the Codex," said Zicka. He looked up at the sky and added, "You had best think quickly. Dawn is not far away."

"What happens at dawn?" asked Odris. "By the way, I'm happy to help anyone who'll help me."

"With the rising of the sun, the Dawn House burns," said Zicka.

"Why?" asked Milla. She shook her head. Nothing in Aenir made sense to her.

"It was not always so," said Zicka. "It is a curse, I suppose. Something left over from the war. Perhaps something hid here, only to be burned out, and the spell continues. The fire only destroys whatever is *in* the Dawn House. The tower itself is never harmed."

Milla looked at the Sunstone on her finger. She

had to get that back to the clan. And there was much information, too.

But was it more important than the laws of the Shield Maidens?

A Shield Maiden does not barter favors. But that was only the seventh law. It was not the most important.

Besides, it might be in the interest of all Icecarls for Milla to help Tal return the Codex to the Castle.

Even if he was a traitor to her, and had ruined her future, she had to ignore that and think of what was most important to the clans.

The Codex's words also sat in her mind, squatting like unwelcome guests on the deck of an iceship. *Tal has done what he had to do....*

"The first red glow shows on the horizon," said Zicka calmly. "The house will soon begin to burn."

Milla paced across the room, wrestling with the decision. It felt like surrendering, and she could never surrender. But was it really?

Tiny tendrils of smoke started to rise up around her feet as she walked. Odris floated closer to the doorway, and cleared her throat several times. But she did not speak. The Storm Shepherd could feel the turmoil in Milla, the difficulty of the decision.

Besides, Odris thought she'd probably survive a

fire. It would hurt, and she would be spread through every room, but she could probably pull herself back together. Though she would need water immediately afterward. And that would be difficult if she was still trapped. . . .

"Milla!" Odris said anxiously. "We're on fire!"

Tiny flames were licking up the walls and the smoke tendrils were winding together into thicker plumes.

Milla ignored smoke, flame, and Odris. She went to the door.

"What is it to be?" asked Zicka quickly.

·CHAPTER·
EIGHTEEN

H azror fell down the stairs, screaming all the way. A third of the way down he catapulted straight into the path of his three Vengenarls. All four of them got tangled together and fell another thirty steps.

Tal didn't wait to look. He raced back to where he'd come in. A wall of light blocked the steps to the surface, drowned in sand. Tal had already thought of how to deal with that.

He would make a Hand of Light and use it to carry himself up to the surface.

There was only one slight flaw in this plan. Tal had only ever seen a Hand of Light made once, by three Guards who were all much more experienced light mages than he was. But he had found that making the Stairway of Light in the Pit had opened up his mind to all sorts of Light Magic that he couldn't previously do or hadn't ever known about. Tal was pretty certain he knew how to make a Hand.

Actually there were *two* flaws. The other one was that he had to make the Hand in the few minutes he had before Hazror and the Vengenarls stopped falling down the stairs and came ravening up them instead.

Tal put all those thoughts to the very back of his mind and concentrated on his Sunstone. He had two other stones now, taken from Hazror, but the one in his ring he knew best.

He knew Orange light best, too, so it was with that he decided to weave his hand. First of all he sent out a thin beam. He gradually widened that until it was like a band of cloth, which he wove backward and forward to build up his Hand.

Because time was short he actually made more of a Mitten than a Hand. It had a thumb, but no fingers. It hovered a stretch away from him, as tall as he was and four times as wide.

Tal concentrated on the Hand. Slowly it drifted toward him. For a moment he thought he'd made it too insubstantial, but when it touched him it felt solid.

The Hand closed with Tal inside it and backed away from the wall of light that covered the exit.

Then it rushed forward, knuckles out, Tal braced inside for the shock.

The Hand hit the wall of light and smashed straight through. Orange light flared and sand started geysering in through the V of the thumb, where there was a slight gap.

Up! thought Tal urgently, his head bent over his Sunstone in intense concentration. *Up!*

The Hand pushed its way through the sand. Tal's Sunstone shone so brightly he had to close his eyes as it pumped power into the Hand.

Behind him, sand poured like a tidal wave through the broken wall of light into Hazror's lair. Tal hadn't planned it like that, but the sand was covering his retreat. With his best Sunstones taken, Hazror would be hard put to stem the flow of sand. He would not be able to pursue immediately.

Tal kept urging the Hand up. Even when it burst out on the surface, flinging sand and slabs of stone in all directions, he kept it going.

He was almost two hundred stretches up in the air when Adras caught up with him and said, "Tal! What are you doing?"

Distracted, Tal lost concentration. The Hand rippled from Orange to Yellow and then through the entire spectrum.

"Dark take it!" cursed Tal.

He lost control completely. His Sunstone went dark. The Hand vanished and Tal started to fall.

He didn't start screaming until he was halfway down, because he'd thought Adras would catch him.

Unfortunately Adras didn't realize he was needed until it was almost too late. He came diving down and snatched at Tal's hands when the boy was certain he was about to die.

Tal kept screaming after Adras saved him, but this time it was because his arms had been almost pulled out of their sockets.

After a moment he recovered and stopped his panicked howling. They were still quite high up, and there was no sign of movement in the sand below.

"Fly east!" Tal croaked. He could stand the pain in his shoulders a bit longer. "Fly as far as you can."

"Sure," said Adras. He craned his head down to look at his companion. "I guess Hazror wasn't so bad after all. He gave you one . . . two . . . Sunstones. And what's that other thing?"

"I think it's a key," said Tal. He was shivering now, in delayed shock. "And Hazror didn't give it to me, or the Sunstones. That's why we have to fly as far as we can."

"Why?" asked Adras. Then, in a slightly different tone, he added, "Oh. I see. Hazror will want them back."

Then later still, the Storm Shepherd gingerly asked, "How bad and terrible is he, by the way?"

"Very. Both," said Tal. Worse than he'd imagined, because he was not an Aeniran creature.

How could a Chosen become like Hazror? Why did he live like he did, preying on innocent young Chosen?

Then a much nastier thought came to Tal's mind.

How did the young Chosen find Hazror? Why would they go there in the first place? It wasn't as if his lair was easy to locate, or in any well-known place for finding and binding Spiritshadows.

Had they all been sent by the Codex, like he was? Sacrificed to try and get the bone whistle that now hung around his own neck?

Or had someone else sent them to their deaths?

Lenan had been a very smart boy, Tal recalled. He'd graduated first from the Lectorium last year. Maybe he had discovered some of the things that Tal had been finding out.

Tal had a lot of questions. He hoped he'd find the Codex soon and that it could answer some of them.

Even if he was afraid of the answers.

547

·CHAPTER·
ПIПETEEП

"I will help Tal with the Codex," coughed Milla. The smoke had thickened so fast that she was already choking, and she couldn't see Odris at all. Even so, Milla tried to speak slowly and with pride. She was not begging to be saved from the fire.

"Excellent!" said Zicka. "Catch!"

He drew an arrow from his quiver, tied an almost invisible cord of spider silk to it, and with one elegant arch of his arm and back, fired it close to Milla's hand. She caught the arrow easily. Out in the Dark World, she had caught bigger arrows that were actually aimed at her. It was a rare skill and another mark of her prowess as a warrior.

"You are connected to the outside now," said Zicka. "Grab hold of Odris and walk slowly outside. Do not break the cord!"

He started stepping backward, uncoiling more spider silk as he did.

Milla reached behind her and grabbed something soft and squishy that she hoped was Odris. The Storm Shepherd didn't feel like she usually did, but Milla's eyes were streaming so much from the smoke she couldn't see.

Bending down low to find the clearest air, she stepped out.

Smoke billowed out with air but she kept on walking, to make sure Odris was completely out as well.

"Good!" cried Zicka. "Now we have to outrun the Nanuch before they wake up."

"Which way?" asked Milla. She could only see out of one tear-swimming eye.

"This way!" shouted Zicka, and he was off. Milla staggered after him, still dragging Odris. The Storm Shepherd was silent.

The amount of smoke that billowed out covered their escape, so that none of the Nanuch noticed they were gone. Even so, Zicka led them at a run through the gray wood for a long time. Milla was gasping from the exertion when the wood suddenly came to an end, the trees stopping all along a perfectly straight line.

Beyond the wood lay an ordered expanse of trimmed hedges and lawns, interspersed with flower beds alive with color.

Zicka stopped just past the trees.

"We'll rest here," said the Kurshken. "Then we can follow the edge of the forest north. It is best not to go into the Garden."

"Why?" asked Milla. It took an effort to find the breath to speak.

"I don't know," replied Zicka. "Only that anyone who goes past the first row of hedges does not return."

Milla stared out over the perfectly ordered garden. It stretched as far as she could see and looked entirely harmless. There were insects of some kind flying around the flowers, and she could see birds in the distance. Small ones that darted in and out of the hedges.

"Are you sure about this?" asked Odris. "I can see a pool not too far in, and I do need water."

"I only know that it is not safe. The Codex may know the secret of it," said Zicka. "Or the Hollow Oracle, or the Old Khamsoul. Since we cannot ask any of them, I suggest we simply avoid the place."

"But I really do need a drink," wailed Odris. "Can't I just fly over there a little bit?"

"No!" ordered Milla. Zicka had proved to be truthful about the dangers of the Dawn House. Milla had to presume the Kurshken was also right about the Garden. "I need a drink, too, but it isn't worth risking our lives."

"I bet it's just walking creatures that have to worry," said Odris petulantly. "Look at those birds. They're perfectly all right."

"They are bait," said Zicka, his voice ominous. The lizard started walking along the line of trees, not bothering to check if the others were following.

Milla followed immediately. Odris hesitated, taking one last look at the pool of water just beyond the first hedges. It did look rather too perfect, she realized with a shiver, and followed Milla.

They walked north for a long time. The sun was almost directly above them when they came to a broad river — more than two hundred stretches wide — that marked the northern border of the gray forest and the Garden. Beyond the river lay a stony wasteland of sinkholes and terraced hills of stone.

"It is safe to drink here," said Zicka. "I also have food aboard my ship. It is not much for someone your size, Milla —"

"Any food is welcome," interrupted Milla. "But where is your ship?"

Zicka pointed at the river's edge. For a moment Milla couldn't work out what the lizard was pointing at. Then she realized he must mean the partially submerged log that was lying in the shallows.

"That is a ship?" asked Odris. She didn't need to add that it looked like a piece of debris thrown up by the river.

"Come," said Zicka proudly. "I will show you. She is called 'Roquollollollahahinanahbek' in our own tongue, which is to say, 'The Fire of Many Suns on First Blue of Deep Water,' in the shared speech. She is an heirloom of our people, a gift from long ago."

"It's a log," whispered Odris to Milla. "A piece of a tree. The Kurshken's mad."

"Quiet!" ordered Milla.

The lizard jumped down to the log, and ran along its length. Milla stopped at the shore. One end of the log was buried under mud and earth. There was no chance that this log could be pushed out into the river to make even a raft.

Then Zicka bent down and put his head underwater. Bubbles came up and Milla heard a burbling noise.

The Kurshken was talking underwater.

For a moment Milla was in agreement with Odris. The lizard was mad.

The moment passed quickly. For as Zicka pulled his head out of the water, there was a disturbance in the middle of the river. Ripples suddenly spread where the water had been calm.

A mast shot up out of the water, a slender pole that was quickly followed by a carved bow and stern and then an entire ship. Water gushed off and out of it as it rose and the bow turned to the shore where Zicka was waiting.

Milla stared. The ship, apart from its lack of runners, was an exact replica of a small Icecarl iceship, of the kind called an Orskir. It was a three- or four-person vessel that a Sword-Thane might have, or a Shield Maiden messenger. It even had similar carvings on its bow and stern, whorls and curves that mimicked cloud and wind.

Its hull was not bone, or even wood, as might be expected on this world. It was metal, the same deep golden metal that the Ruin Ship was made from. But it was also set with many Sunstones, hundreds and hundreds of them that glittered in the sunlight.

Milla found herself kneeling on the log. She knew this ship from the tales told by the Crones when the whole clan was huddled in the hold, while the worst of the winter storms howled about the many-times-anchored vessel.

This was Asteyr's ship. Asteyr, the mother of Danir and Susir and Grettir, who in turn were the foremothers of all the clans. But in the stories the Orskir of Asteyr traveled on ice. What was it doing here in Aenir, on a river, in the possession of a lizard?

"Asteyr's ship," croaked Milla. "How . . . how did your people come by this?"

"Yes, yes," replied Zicka, his purple tongue flickering. "It was Asteyr's ship, in the faraway times. We did her a service, but the ship was given to us later, from the hands of her daughter Danir. That is why we agreed to the Codex's request — to help a daughter of Danir."

"What service?" asked Milla, still staring in awe at the ship. "What did you do?"

"I cannot say, even to a daughter of Danir," said Zicka. "It is a secret of our folk. I cannot speak of it without the permission of the Kurshken Allthing."

The fabled ship had drifted up to the log. Zicka leaped up and gripped the gunwale, then vaulted over. Milla climbed up reverently and stood upon the deck.

The ship was completely dry and there were no pools of water, nothing to show that it had been submerged. Milla stood near the bow, strangely afraid to go farther, to walk where Asteyr and Danir had once walked. She felt like she should clean her boots, or change her clothes, or something.

Odris drifted across above her, and settled around the mast, rather like a sail. There was no sail, nor boom, nor any of the rigging that Milla would have expected of an iceship. There was also no wheel or steering oar. Nevertheless, the ship swung out into the river and began to move.

"Where do we go?" asked Milla. But Zicka had moved to the stern and didn't hear her. Reluctantly, Milla tiptoed toward him, keeping close to the rail.

"Where do we go?" she repeated.

"Four Rivers Meet," said Zicka. "Close by Cold Stone Mountain. The Chosen Tal should be there, too, all being well."

·CHAPTER·
TWEПTY

Tal's shoulder sockets hurt so much he wanted to land long before Adras got tired of carrying him. By then they were already well beyond the sand dunes of Hazror's realm. The country below them was now a jungle, a canopy of green, broken here and there by taller trees thrusting out.

Under the starlight, the canopy looked black rather than green. It reminded Tal of the Veil and the Seven Towers, which was comforting. But it made it difficult to land. Tal kept thinking he could see a clearing, but it was always a trick of the light, just a dip in the canopy.

Tal thought his arms were actually going to fall off when he finally saw a large expanse that had to be a clearing.

Adras landed him gently, but Tal still fell over. All his muscles hurt, not just his shoulders. Even so, he forced himself up out of the wet leaf-litter. There was no time to rest. Now that he had the whistle he felt closer to the Codex somehow. But that only increased his anxiety. What if he found the Codex, and found out who was keeping Gref captive, but it was too late?

Tal got up and looked around, raising light from his Sunstone.

He was in a clearing, but the leaf-litter was still knee-deep. There were shrubs and ferns almost as tall as he was, but none of the enormous, vine-circled trees that filled the jungle proper.

"I like it here," boomed Adras suddenly, making Tal jump. "Lots of moisture in the air. Ahhh!"

Tal didn't like it so much. There were lots of things moving in the darkness. He could hear squelching and crackling and slithering, though whenever he shined the beam of light from his Sunstone there was nothing to be seen.

Even worse than that, he'd suddenly remembered the last game of Beastmaker he'd played, and one of the cards. The Jarghoul, the giant strangling snake of the Aeniran jungle.

This was the Aeniran jungle. This was exactly where you could expect to find a thirty-stretch-long Jarghoul that would be thicker than he was tall.

It could be a Jarghoul making those slithering noises over there!

Tal spun around, intensifying the light from his Sunstone.

Light reflected back from two enormous, pale yellow eyes. Eyes that bulged on stalks above slimy blue flesh that continued to glow even when Tal's shaking hand moved the light away.

"Jarghoul!" Tal screamed, and he turned to run.

He'd gone several steps when his panicked brain properly processed what he'd seen.

It wasn't a Jarghoul. They weren't blue and they didn't glow in the dark.

It was a Gorblag, a sort of slithering toad. Or at the worst, its close cousin, a Klorbag, which spat disgusting but harmless slimeballs.

"A what?" asked Adras. "Do you want me to smack it?"

"Ah, no," said Tal, after he took a deep breath. "It's . . . it's only a Gorblag. They're harmless."

The glowing blue toad hadn't moved. It just sat there, its long-finned tail slithering from side to side. Then it slowly inflated the fleshy bags under its stomach and became twice as large.

Tal got out of the direct line of fire in case it was a Klorbag preparing to spit.

It didn't. Its eyes clouded and its mouth pursed in a way that no Gorblag's mouth had ever pursed before. Then its airbags started to deflate, and a whistle came out of its mouth.

Tal had already realized it had been taken over by the Codex. Even so, he was surprised that the whistle was actually a reedy, high-pitched voice.

"What is it?" he asked. "What do you want me to do?"

"Tal. Aim one hand left of the blue star and fly. Milla at Four Rivers Meet by dawn. Follow Zicka to Cold Stone Mountain. Have a Storm Shepherd blow the Pipe. You and Milla fetch me from under the Mountain. No Aeniran can touch me. Go now!"

"What?" asked Tal. "But Milla will kill me!"

"No!" the Gorblag whistled. "Go! Four Rivers Meet. Zicka. Cold Stone Mountain. Blow Pipe. Fetch Codex from under Mountain."

"Milla *will* kill me," protested Tal. "And how am I going to get under the mountain?"

It was too late. The Codex had lost contact. The

Gorblag's eyes cleared. It stopped pursing its lips and opened its mouth wide. An instant later a huge gob of sticky, foul-smelling slime whizzed past Tal's face.

The Klorbag dived down into the leaf-litter and squirmed away before Tal or Adras could retaliate. Tal watched its dorsal fin snaking through the rotting vegetation, to make sure it wasn't going to turn for a parting shot.

Then he held up his hands.

"We've got to get going again," he said to Adras. "The Codex wants us to go to somewhere called Four Rivers Meet. And it has somehow got Milla to help."

"Milla?" asked Adras eagerly. "The other one? With Odris?"

"Yes," said Tal. "We have to aim a hand's width left of the blue star, so once we're up out of this jungle I guess I'll have to hang by one arm and try — "

He stopped talking, as it was obvious Adras wasn't listening. He had reared up and had his head cocked to one side, as if he were listening to something that Tal couldn't hear.

"Find Odris, find Milla," the Storm Shepherd announced. "That's right?"

"Yes." Tal sighed. "If you know where Odris is."

"I know." Adras bent down and gripped Tal's

forearms, not noticing the boy wince with pain. "The wind tells me."

"Good," said Tal faintly. His shoulder sockets felt like they'd had molten metal poured inside them, and the pain was spreading through to his neck and head. But the Codex had said to go on, and so he must.

As Adras rose up out of the jungle, Tal's thoughts turned to Milla. He hoped the Codex had told her she wasn't going to kill him.

He also felt the slight twinge of guilt he'd had previously grow stronger inside him.

Tal still thought he'd done the right thing. The only thing. But now he was wondering if Milla could ever see it his way. Maybe making her swap her shadow for a Spiritshadow was like a Chosen not having a Spiritshadow.

Maybe . . . maybe he'd turned her into a sort of Icecarl Underfolk.

He'd really destroyed her future, he realized, when all *he'd* given up was his *choice* of Spiritshadow.

She would want to kill him, Tal decided. But he couldn't let her, because right now saving Gref and his family was more important than anything else.

No matter what it cost.

·CHAPTER·
TWENTY-ONE

It took Tal and Adras all night to fly to Four Rivers Meet. They had to make frequent stops for Tal to massage his arms and rotate his shoulders. Eventually Adras had to actually carry Tal, the Storm Shepherd's arms wrapped completely around the Chosen boy. It was somewhat humiliating, but Tal had long since given up caring about that. He was merely glad that it didn't hurt.

They sighted Four Rivers Meet shortly after dawn. At least Tal presumed that's what it was. Certainly he could see four rivers flowing in from north, south, east, and west, to meet in a crazy four-way delta of black mud and thousands of channels that made no sense to Tal.

How could four rivers all flow *into* the same patchwork of channels? The four deltas should end in a lake, but they didn't. At least one of the rivers should be flowing the other way. But none did.

The rivers just kept on spreading and dividing, their many fingers stretching across a wide plain. A completely flat plain, Tal thought at first. But then as the sun rose higher he saw that there was something in the very middle of the delta.

A mountain, surrounded on all sides by narrow streams and reedy islets.

None of it made sense. The water from the four rivers had to go somewhere. But the mountain was sitting where a lake should be.

Tal looked away and blinked and then looked back. But everything was still there. A huge mass of gray stone in the middle of a vast channel system that couldn't possibly work.

That's Aenir, Tal told himself. *Aeniran Magic.*

"Odris!" Adras exclaimed. He started to point, but remembered that he was cradling Tal and stopped.

Tal looked down. There was a ship below them, moving quite quickly along one of the larger channels. It sparkled in the morning sun, and Tal's trained eye picked up the glint of Sunstones. Many Sunstones.

He could see a dot on the deck that he presumed

was Milla, and Odris was quite clearly the cloud that was twined about the mast. There was something else moving on deck, too, something small. Tal couldn't see what it was at that distance.

Adras started to descend. Tal closed his eyes and tried to think of what he was going to say to Milla. Would it help if he apologized? Did Icecarls apologize? Or would she just think less of him?

Should he try and stun her with a Blue Slap before she could do anything to him?

He wasn't afraid exactly. He just felt terrible. No matter how he tried, he simply couldn't think of Milla as someone whose life didn't matter.

Then he felt a bump as if they'd hit something solid, and he opened his eyes. They hadn't hit anything, but Adras was suddenly climbing, very quickly.

"Adras!" Tal shouted in sudden panic. "What are you doing? We're supposed to be going down!"

"Updraft!" Adras boomed. "A hot air current, too strong for me to fly against. I am only a cloud."

"What!" Tal screamed. Desperately he tried to think of something he could do. They were rising so rapidly that he was beginning to feel faint. They must already be thousands of stretches up, as high as the Seven Towers back on the Dark World. Far too high to build a Stairway of Light.

"How do we get down?" he shouted.

"When the air cools, we will fall," Adras roared. "Have patience!"

"But I can't breathe!" gasped Tal.

Adras was silent. Tal had already noticed that his Storm Shepherd companion had trouble when he had to think new thoughts or consider how other beings lived.

Cool air, he thought. Somehow he had to make the air cooler. But how? He could make it hotter with his Sunstone, but not cooler.

Then it came to him.

"Adras!" he shouted. The shout took most of his breath, and the next words came out as little more than a whisper. "Rain! Rain will make it cooler!"

"What?"

"Rain!"

"Ah! Rain!" bellowed Adras. He swung his arms forward, so quickly Tal thought he was about to be thrown off into space. But he was only shifting him out of the way. The rest of his cloud-body roiled and rippled, spreading out into a broad circular shape and becoming even puffier.

The cloud grew blacker. Tal rolled onto his side so he could see. He could already smell the fresh scent of rain, and the temperature dropped several degrees.

It got colder still and there was a hideous grinding noise inside the Storm Shepherd. Tal saw flecks of white appearing in the darkness of the cloud. Then large chunks of ice started to fall.

Very large chunks of ice. In fact, gigantic hailstones the size of Tal's head. Some were thrown out at a sharp angle, narrowly missing the boy as he twisted and turned in the Storm Shepherd's arms.

With the hailstones, the temperature dropped to freezing. Slowly at first, the Storm Shepherd began to fall.

"I said rain!" shouted Tal as they fell faster and faster. "Milla's down there somewhere, you idiot! She could get killed by a hailstone!"

Then the cold really took effect, and cloud and boy dropped as fast as the hailstones.

"Soooooooooorrrrrrrryyyyyyy!" boomed Adras.

"Slow down!" shrieked Tal. But his voice was lost in the rush of their descent. He was shivering uncontrollably now, the chill of the wind making the icy temperature even lower. He felt as cold as he ever had out on the Ice.

But now he had a Sunstone, Tal thought. Several in fact. He hadn't really had time to examine the ones he'd taken from Hazror and he wasn't going to start while he was dropping like a stone from the sky.

Tal held out his hand. His fingers were already blue and he could hardly feel them. But the Sunstone glinted there. He focused on it, willing it to warm the air around his body.

At first he thought he'd failed. It was one of the simplest spells that almost any Chosen child could perform with a Sunstone. But he was still freezing.

Then he realized that he just couldn't feel the heat, because the cold was so intense. He'd have to increase the amount of heat the Sunstone put out.

He concentrated again and felt a wave of heat come off the top of the Sunstone and blow back around him. Some went into Adras as well.

They were still falling almost straight down. Tal risked a look, but his eyes instantly filled with tears from the rushing wind. Even through teary eyes, he could see that the river was very close.

Tal told the Sunstone to put out even more heat, but there was a limit to the amount it could radiate outward without heating up the ring and burning his finger. Waves of hot air billowed off it, but it was not enough to counteract the cold.

"Haaaaannnngggg oooonnnnn!" yelled Adras, and the Storm Shepherd reared back. Their vertical descent turned into a long glide. They were still dropping but it now looked like there was a slight chance they would pull up before smacking into a channel or one of the muddy islands.

But they didn't.

Adras roared and Tal shouted as the water loomed closer and closer. Tal just had time to take a deep breath, a breath that was knocked out of him a second later as they hit the water.

Storm Shepherd and Chosen boy went under, a long way underwater and actually into the mud of the river floor.

Tal found himself trapped not only by Adras's arms but also by sticky mud that refused to let go. He couldn't breathe and he couldn't see. He flailed his arms and his legs as he tried to break free.

His whole mind was filled with panic. He just wanted to take a breath. He had to breathe. He had to suck something into his lungs.

Even if it was water.

·CHAPTER· TWENTY–TWO·

Milla and Odris saw Adras and Tal hit the water about two hundred stretches in front of them, sending up a plume of spray higher than the ship's mast.

Milla rushed to the bow and climbed up to look out. As the spray subsided she expected to see Tal's head bob up and a cloud emerge. But there were only the ripples of the impact.

Milla hesitated. She felt that she should dive in, but she was not a strong swimmer. Icecarls did not swim unless the Ice broke, in which case they had less than two minutes to get out of the water anyway.

"Odris!" she called. "Help them!"

"What for?" asked Odris. "Adras will work out what to do before too long. What an idiot! I couldn't believe it when I saw the hail. You'd never know he was the older of the pair of us, and that by two hundred years."

"Tal will drown!" shouted Milla. "Go and help!"

"He can't live underwater?" asked Odris, shocked. She suddenly launched off the mast and shot over Milla's head. A moment later there was another, smaller plume of spray as the second Storm Shepherd plunged into the water.

Milla watched anxiously. For all his faults, Tal didn't deserve to drown.

A few air bubbles burst on the surface of the river, then one very heavy-looking Storm Shepherd emerged, lurching up to hang only a few stretches above the water. Milla couldn't tell which one it was, till it reached down and dragged another one up, who held Tal in its dripping arms.

The Chosen boy was covered in mud but he was alive, judging by the coughing and spluttering Milla could hear.

Asteyr's boat moved up close to the bedraggled Storm Shepherds and their human cargo. Adras was about to put Tal on board when Milla cried out.

"Wait! He's too muddy! Rinse him off first!"

Adras immediately complied, dunking Tal back into the river. The Chosen boy only just had time to shout, "No!" before he was completely submerged yet again.

Tal was lifted out spitting, coughing, and furious. Dropped onto the deck, he tried to get up to shout at Milla, but he was taken by a fit of coughing. Too weak to rise, he tried to crawl away from Milla. But he had only gone half a stretch when she grabbed him.

For a second he thought she was going to throw him over the side. Then he realized she was helping him up so he could vomit up water over the gunwale.

And she wasn't screaming death threats at him. She was just telling him to be careful he wasn't sick on the boat.

Even when no more water seemed likely to come up, Tal kept hanging over the side. He felt as limp and washed out as an old Underfolk mop.

But at least he was alive. And Milla hadn't tried to kill him. Even if she was being extremely weird about messing up this riverboat.

"So," croaked Tal. "We meet again."

"Yes," said Milla coldly. "Traitor. I have not forgotten. However, I have agreed to help find your Codex and return it to the Dark World. I will return to my people, too, to tell them what I have learned of Aenir and the Chosen's folly. After that, I will give myself to the Ice."

"What?" asked Tal. "What's the Chosen's folly?"

"Do not pretend you do not know," said Milla scornfully. "I have learned that the Veil was made to keep Aenirans out of our world. It is you Chosen who have broken faith with our ancestors, bringing Spirit-shadows back to the Castle. You have let the Aenirans establish a foothold on our world once more."

"What are you talking about?" asked Tal. He felt dizzy and his head was clogged with water. "We have always had Spiritshadows; we have always come to Aenir for them. The Veil has nothing to do with it."

"That is not correct," said a voice Tal hadn't heard before. He lifted himself off the gunwale with effort and turned to see who it was. He hadn't expected it to be a Kurshken. He knew from the Beastmaker game that the lizards were very smart but he didn't know they could talk.

"I am Quorr Quorr Quorr Ahhtorn Sezicka. You may call me Zicka. As with so many of my kind, I am a historian. As such, I can inform you that you are quite incorrect. The Chosen first started coming to Aenir for the purposes of taking slaves — whom you term Spiritshadows — less than nine hundred years ago. Prior to that, there was a period of more than a thousand years when there was no communication between the Dark World and Aenir. This was due to the ban on traveling between the two worlds that was established by Asteyr and Ramellan after the creation of the Veil on your world and the execution of the Forgetting in ours."

"What?" Tal asked again. He felt like this was the only word he knew how to say. Then he got angry. What was he doing listening to a lizard and a savage? They knew nothing of the Chosen and the Castle and its history.

"I don't know where you heard these stories," Tal said. "But I know that we have always had Spiritshadows. We have always come to Aenir for them. That is what Aenirans are for!"

573

"Always?" questioned Zicka. "That is not a specific measurement of time. And you think this whole world exists purely for the purpose of providing Chosen with Spiritshadows?"

Tal was silent. He didn't know how to answer that question. He didn't feel strong enough to debate it. While he would never admit it to Milla or this Zicka lizard, he knew that his knowledge of Chosen, Castle, Dark World, and Aenir was severely limited.

"The Codex knows the true history," Tal said finally. "You'll see when we get the Codex."

Zicka smiled. At least Tal thought that was what it was doing with its mouth. Milla frowned. Before she could say anything, Tal spoke again.

"Zicka. The Codex mentioned you. You are to take us to Cold Stone Mountain. Then I have to get one of the Storm Shepherds to blow this whistle —"

Tal's hand went to his pocket to pull out the chain with the two Sunstones and the bone whistle he'd taken from Hazror. But when the chain came out, there was nothing on it.

"No!" exclaimed Tal. He dropped the chain and started frantically turning out his pockets. "I had the whistle . . . and two Sunstones . . . Gref . . ."

·CHAPTER·
TWENTY-THREE

Tal's hand closed on something wedged across the bottom of his pocket. He brought it out with a huge sigh of relief. It was the bone whistle. But there was no sign of the two Sunstones. They had been washed out and were now somewhere on the bottom of the river. Fortunately his own Sunstone ring was secure on his finger.

"I've lost two Sunstones," Tal said mournfully.

But at least he had the whistle. That was the key to gaining the Codex and saving Gref. That was all he could think about now. The rest about the Veil and Aenir was too much.

Use the whistle. Get the Codex. Return to the Dark World. Find and save Gref.

It was like a light chant that Tal said over and over in his mind.

"The whistle is essential," said Zicka, indicating the bone instrument. "It is the device that will make the mountain move. As long as it continues to sound, the mountain will arch its back. While it does, Tal, you and Milla must rush under its belly and bring the Codex out."

"A Storm Shepherd would be faster," said Milla. She was thinking as she would for a hunt or a battle. "And stronger. How heavy is the Codex?"

Zicka's tongue flicked out in a Kurshken negative. Realizing that this meant nothing to the others, he quickly said, "No. The Codex cannot be touched by any creature of Aenir. That is part of its protection. As to its size, I believe that it can shrink and grow at will, within certain limits. But its weight remains the same."

"Which is?" asked Milla.

"Fairly heavy," said the Kurshken. "I do not know your measurements of weight. But perhaps the same as Tal."

Tal shook his head. He didn't feel up to walking fifty stretches, let alone running under a lifting mountain to bring out something that weighed as much as he did.

"How far will we have to go?" asked Milla. "And

how long can Odris . . . or Adras . . . blow the whistle?"

"I believe about five ship lengths," said Zicka, indicating the distance from stern to bow with his arms. "And I do not know how long the whistle can be sounded."

Odris peered down at the bone whistle.

"Days, I should think," she said. "Unless it's magical."

"It *is* magical," Tal said wearily. "Otherwise it wouldn't move a mountain."

"Let me try it now," said Odris.

She took the whistle, and raised it to her mouth. But no sound came out when she blew. Her cheeks bulged out farther and farther until she looked rather like a Gorblag. But still no sound came from the whistle.

"It has been made for a single purpose and can only be used near the mountain," said Tal with confidence. Aenir was full of magical items that only worked in certain circumstances or particular places. "Though I hope you can blow it there. Maybe Adras should do it. He can probably hold his breath longer."

"No he can't!" said Odris.

"Yes I can!" growled Adras. "Let's have a competition."

Both started to suck in air, requiring Tal, Milla, and Zicka to move sternward to avoid being pulled over.

Tal started to sit down with his back to the mast, but Milla jerked him back up.

"Don't! You'll get the deck wet!"

Tal angrily shrugged her hand off. Milla stepped back and Tal saw the familiar spread of her fingers that meant she was about to reach for her sword.

"I'm tired!" he yelled. "I've just been almost drowned! All I want to do is sit down. Cut my throat if you like, but that'll make even more of a mess of your precious boat!"

He sat down. Milla clenched her teeth and drew her fist back as if she had taken Tal seriously and was going to hit him with that instead of a weapon, so as not to make him bleed. But Zicka plucked at her wrist.

"Do not fight!" the Kurshken asked. "Roquollol-lollahahinanahbek has had wet and muddy decks, even bloody ones, before — and will again. She is a working ship, not a relic of the past."

Milla scowled and turned away.

"Thanks," said Tal. "But if this is your boat, why is Milla so upset?"

"This ship," Zicka corrected, "once belonged to the most famous ancestress of Milla — Asteyr, who with Ramellan ended the war between the worlds."

"Who?" asked Tal. "What war?"

"Ask your Codex," replied Zicka. "Since you will doubt whatever I tell you."

"I will." Tal hesitated and then added, "Whose boat did you say this was?"

"Asteyr's," said Zicka.

"And what was the other name you mentioned? You said Asteyr and someone else ended some war?"

"Ramellan. Do you recognize the name?"

Once again, Tal didn't answer. He did recognize the name now. Ramellan was some sort of important Chosen from the dim past. He couldn't remember exactly why he was important. He was some sort of Emperor before the Chosen had Emperors, Tal thought. A name mentioned in passing in a history lesson, and nothing more.

Zicka stood by as if expecting Tal to ask more questions, but the Chosen boy was saved by a sudden shout from Milla.

"The Mountain! Dead ahead!"

Tal wearily stood up and looked ahead. Sure enough, there was a gray mountain rising out of the many channels and islands ahead of them. It was still some distance away, a few hours sailing at least.

"So, there it is," said Tal. "Do you know if the mountain is guarded?"

"No," replied Zicka. "I know only what the Codex has chosen to share with my forebrain."

"Your what?"

"Forebrain," said Zicka, tapping the lump between his rather poppy eyes. "We Kurshken have two brains. The forebrain is the animal mind, but we also have the 'rorquialosschurr,' or afterbrain. The Codex can project its thought into my forebrain and I can communicate with it from my afterbrain, or let the Codex use my forebrain to control my voice."

Tal tried to suppress a shudder. He didn't like the idea of having two brains. What if one of them didn't agree with the other one?

"So there could be guards," Tal said. "Though I suppose whoever put the Codex there wouldn't expect anyone to get the whistle from Hazror."

"Whether there are guards there now or not, all of Aenir will soon know if Cold Stone Mountain moves," said Zicka. "You must be prepared to flee as soon as you have the Codex."

"We'll take it back to the Castle," agreed Tal. "But I'll have to find somewhere I know to make the crossing safe. Where is the Chosen Enclave from here?"

"South," said Zicka. "A few days' travel, walking. Do you have to go there?"

Tal shook his head.

"No. But I have to be somewhere I know. If the Enclave is a few days south, does that mean the Sunken Stone Circle is somewhere near here?"

"Yes. Southeast. You could probably reach there by sundown, at a brisk pace. But that ring of stones is no place to be after dark."

"Yes," Tal agreed. "But I have been to the Sunken Stone Circle several times before, so I know it well enough to use it as a crossing point."

He looked up at the bow to where Milla was standing, shading her eyes to watch the river and the mountain ahead. Despite the sun, she cast no shadow.

"I'd better ... I'd better make my peace with Milla," Tal said, as he stared at the sunshine on the deck. He felt sick at what he'd done to her now, but he would never admit that.

He approached her slowly, all too aware of the Merwin-horn sword at her side and her acute reflexes. When he was four or five stretches away, and possibly out of reach of a sudden lunge, he stopped.

After a moment, Milla turned to face him. He saw hatred in her eyes, and flinched.

"Milla," he said, unconscious that he was holding his hands out to the Icecarl, as if he begged something from her. "I . . . wanted to say . . ."

"Your words are nothing," said Milla. "They are the mist that is parted by the ship, the ice chips under my skates, the blood that drips from day-old Selski meat."

Tal gulped. This was even harder than he thought. He couldn't believe he was trying to apologize to someone who was so alien to him. He felt strangely inferior standing here before her. She seemed taller somehow, the Sunstone ring on her finger flaming in the sunlight, the Merwin-horn sword bright, too. More like a Chosen of legend than anything else.

"I'm . . . I'm sorry," Tal said. He was shaking as he spoke, and there were tears glistening in his eyes, tears that were made as much of anger and guilt as they were of sorrow. "I didn't know . . . I just had to do it . . . My father told me I had to look after the family, that I had to do whatever it took to keep them safe. *Whatever* it took, and what it was was my shadow and your shadow, too, and I didn't even think what it would mean to you. And it was my fault that Gref climbed after me and got taken, and I *have* to find him and get him back. He's only nine and there's Kusi as well, and Mother . . . That's why I did it, that's why . . . Can you understand . . . can you . . ."

His voice trailed off.

Milla did not answer, but her eyes were no longer full of hate. Then she looked away, out over the water, and said, "Some of my people believe there is a great Reckoner of all Icecarl lives, a place where every hunt and battle is played out upon a vast board, where every birth and death, victory and defeat can be seen. There must have been a small carving there once, one of the smallest, of Selski bone or Merwin rib, that was Milla of the Far Raiders. But that piece has left the board now, and plays a different game of life. I do not know the hands that move me now. All I know is that I am not what I was."

There was another, longer silence, then Tal said, "Nor am I."

"Who knows what either of us will become," said Milla. She hesitated. "I understand why you sold my shadow, Tal of the Chosen. But I do not forget. And it is not the nature of an Icecarl to forgive."

Tal nodded slowly, though he wasn't sure what she meant.

"I cannot kill you," said Milla. "We have shared too much blood, and I understand too well why you have done what you did. One day you, too, may lose your future at the hands of someone you thought a friend."

·CHAPTER·
TWENTY–FOUR

They beached Asteyr's ship on a strip of black mud in the shadow of the mountain and walked up to the very edge of the stony monolith.

It wasn't a particularly big mountain, but it seemed larger than it really was to Tal when he considered that he was going to have to run underneath it. There was an awful lot of rock that would come crushing down if Adras couldn't keep blowing the whistle.

Adras had won the breath-blowing competition, though both Storm Shepherds had managed to blow their breath for hours. This was very encouraging to Tal. He'd thought they might only have minutes to get the Codex out.

"This is the place," announced Zicka, pointing up

to where a thick vein of black stone ran through the gray rock, rather like a dark lightning bolt. "The Codex is straight ahead, about five ship lengths in."

"A hundred and thirty stretches," said Milla. She took off her sword and laid it down, then shrugged off her Selski-hide breastplate and threw it down, too.

Tal looked up the mountain and then back toward the river and the ship. He felt certain that whoever had put the Codex here would have also left guards or wards, or some protective magic. But he could see nothing. There was no movement on the mountain, in the sky, or on the river.

That just made him more suspicious. There should have been birds or insects or something. But there was just a light breeze, whispering through the reeds behind them.

"I am ready," announced Milla. She stretched her arms above her head, and lifted her legs and shook them. Tal saw that they were marked with mottled bruises, but he knew enough about Milla now not to ask.

"There is only one thing I want to know before we run," said Milla.

"What?" asked Tal.

"Why is your hair green?"

"A creature vomited on it," said Tal wearily.

Milla smiled, but she did not laugh. Tal thought she would have laughed, before he'd given away her shadow.

In addition to the green hair, Tal's shoulders still hurt and he was damp. Fortunately his legs were in fine shape, apart from slightly burned feet.

There was no reason to delay. But he still hesitated, until Milla stopped her stretching and looked at him.

Tal knew that look. She was thinking he wasn't brave enough to go ahead.

"I'm ready, too," he said. "Adras? You know what to do?"

"Sure!" boomed the Storm Shepherd. "I just blow in the whistle. Like this."

He raised the whistle and started to blow before anyone could stop him.

A single pure note, almost too high to hear, came out of the whistle. It seemed to come from all directions, not just from the actual whistle. Echoes came back, multiplying the sound.

It grew louder and louder, and as the sound increased, the mountain moved.

It started with a rumbling deep in the earth, and a vibration that rattled every bone in Tal's legs before traveling up into his teeth. Pebbles and clumps of dirt fell from the mountain's sides, followed by shrubs and trees whose roots were shivered loose as the pockets of dirt they grew in were shrugged off the mountain's back.

Tal saw Adras look surprised. The Storm Shepherd hesitated a little and the note faltered.

"Keep blowing!" screamed Tal.

The Storm Shepherd nodded and kept blowing. The note steadied and grew even stronger.

There was a mighty crack, and a curtain of dust and earth exploded everywhere along the mountain's length. Tal and Milla shielded their eyes with their forearms and gingerly edged forward.

As the cloud of dust cleared they saw that the mountain was rising out of the earth. They could see daylight on the other, distant side, a gap only a stretch high. But the mountain continued to arch back, and the gap increased.

"Go!" shouted Zicka. "Go!"

Tal and Milla rushed forward, hunched over, running as fast as they could through the falling dust and over broken ground.

Milla counted steps as she ran, calling out every

ten. One of her paces was close enough to a stretch. At 120 or so, they should be able to see the Codex.

They ran on, into the deeper shadow directly under the mountain's belly. It was so close that Tal could have jumped up and touched rock. But he didn't care about that. All his attention was on finding the Codex.

"One hundred!" shouted Milla.

"There it is!" Relief filled Tal's voice.

He pointed up at a hole just ahead. There was a rectangle of silver light up there, bright here in the darkness.

They ran to it. Tal jumped up, but could not get a grip. He fell back. Before he could jump again, Milla used his back and shoulders as a vaulting board. She got up easily, and reached an arm back down to pull Tal up.

"Is that the Codex?" gasped Milla, pointing at the luminous slab.

The silver rectangle flashed, and letters appeared on it. Tal read the words without realizing it.

Yes, I am the Codex. Take me and run! Run! Run! Run!

Tal gripped one side of the Codex as Milla grabbed the other. Both of them looked down, and realized that the mountain was still rising. They would have to jump down at least six stretches now, or wait till the mountain started to lower itself again. But that would invite being crushed on the way back!

They lifted the Codex and jumped.

At that exact moment, the mountain lurched itself up even higher.

Tal and Milla landed hard, on their hands and knees, and dropped the Codex.

Pain blossomed in Tal's left shoulder and he cried out.

"Ahhh! My shoulder!"

"Swap sides!" Milla yelled, running around to get her hands under the Codex. "Use your right hand. It's not that heavy." She looked across and saw that Tal's left arm was hanging down much lower than it should. It was obviously dislocated, but she did not have time to push it back in place.

Tal bit back a sob and staggered around. He couldn't move his left arm at all, and he presumed it was broken in several places or something equally terrible. But it took only one glance at the vast expanse of rock above to make him get his right hand under the Codex and lift.

"Go! Go!" shouted Milla. They started running

again, a clumsy run with the door-sized Codex between them.

They were halfway back to sunshine and safety when the whistle stopped. At exactly the same time, the mountain stopped rising.

"Faster!" Milla shouted.

Tal screamed something, too, though he didn't know what it was. Every step was agony in his shoulder and he could barely keep a grip on the Codex with his good hand.

With a rumble that deafened them, the mountain started to settle back down. It lowered itself in sudden lurches and with frightening quickness. This was no slow and steady relaxation back into its own bed.

Tal saw Zicka in the narrowing band of sunlight ahead of them. The lizard was jumping up and down, screaming something, too. Adras and Odris were shouting. Milla was shouting. Everyone was shouting.

Then they heard the top of the Codex scrape on stone. A horrifying sound, even though it only lasted the second it took them to crouch even lower as they ran.

Thirty stretches . . . twenty stretches . . . the top

of the Codex scraped again and they were carrying it almost horizontally and neither could stand upright without hitting their heads . . . ten stretches and they were crawling and screaming with the stone pressing on their backs . . . five stretches . . . four stretches . . . their clothes were rubbing on stone . . . two stretches and then . . .

·CHAPTER·
TWENTY–FIVE

Their heads were suddenly in sunshine and the Storm Shepherds were dragging them out, with the Codex between them. For a terrible second it seemed that the mountain had closed on their feet. And then they were free.

"My shoulder, my shoulder!" Tal cried, half laughing with relief at having got out and half crying with pain from his arm.

Milla stepped up to him, placed one hand on his shoulder and gripped his arm with her other hand.

"Ow! No!" shrieked Tal. "I said I was sorry! Don't torture —"

Milla did something with both hands and there was a loud click as Tal's arm went back in his shoulder socket. Almost instantly the pain lessened to a dull ache.

"Oh!" said Tal, moving it experimentally. "Thanks."

"Dislocated," said Milla. She turned to Adras and grabbed a chunk of cloud roughly where his chest would be.

"What happened to you?" she asked fiercely, twisting the cloud-flesh. "Why did you stop blowing?"

"I didn't!" protested Adras. "I kept blowing, but no sound came out. It just stopped!"

"That's true," said Zicka.

Milla let go of the Storm Shepherd and quickly shrugged her armor back on. She didn't even seem to be out of breath, Tal noticed. But he felt a strange gladness in his heart. It was good to be back with Milla again, when it came to things like escaping from under a settling mountain.

"We have to get away from here," he said urgently as he bent down to pick up the Codex. Milla finished tying her sword scabbard back on her belt and bent to help him.

"I wonder how long it was under there," Milla said as she picked up her side of the Codex. It seemed a bit larger than it had been under the mountain. She was sure that it had been both thinner and less tall, though it was still about as wide as a door in the Castle.

As Milla spoke, letters formed on the surface of the Codex, black against the silver luminosity.

22 years, 23 days, 14 hours, 3 minutes, and 42 seconds.

"What does it say?" asked Milla. The letters were from the Chosen alphabet.

Even as Tal repeated the answer, the letters changed to Icecarl runes. Milla peered at them. She was not a great reader, but she had no trouble with numbers.

"Who put you there?" asked Tal.

Two Chosen carried me in. They were Julper Yen-Baren of the Fifth Indigo and Crislo Hane-Arrit of the Second Violet.

Tal was about to describe the Spiritshadow that took his brother Gref away and ask which Chosen commanded it, but Zicka got in before him.

"I greet you, Mighty Codex," he said. "If you were to give advice to us now, what would it be?"

Flee. Those who put me here watch carefully. We must return to the Castle. I must not be recaptured by the minions of Skerrako.

"Skerrako?" asked Tal. But he didn't get an answer. Milla was already lifting up her side, so he had to follow suit. Whatever words appeared on the surface of the Codex were seen only by the Storm

Shepherds, and neither of them could read Chosen script.

"Quickly!" Zicka ordered. "To the ship. I will put you ashore as close as I can to the Sunken Stones."

The Codex seemed a lot heavier than it had under the mountain, Tal thought as they lifted it over the side and onto the deck. Though possibly that was because he'd been scared to death.

They were back out in the middle of the stream when they heard the first awful screech from the mountain.

Everyone looked back. There was still a lot of dust around Cold Stone Mountain, but it was easy enough to see the thing that had made the awful, chilling call.

It was circling in the air above the mountain. A long and sinuous snake-thing with very long, thin wings that fluttered so quickly they were almost invisible. Its body was bright orange with black stripes, and it had a stinger on its end.

Tal stared at it and his mouth went dry. He knew what it was. He'd seen it in the Beastmaker game. It was part insect, part reptile and could be played for Temper, Speed, or Special. It was a Waspwyrm.

Tal had thought Waspwyrms were man-sized or smaller.

This one was bigger than the ship.

Somehow he knew that it had come to investigate the rising of Cold Stone Mountain.

It was looking for the Codex.

Tal hurled himself across the deck, throwing his coat over his head.

Milla had the same idea. A few seconds later, the Codex was covered by their coats. Tal was surprised to see just how smelly and dirty his coat was. He'd gotten so used to wearing it he'd forgotten how rank it was. He hoped the Codex wouldn't mind.

Tal looked back at the Waspwyrm. It was flying down to the point where they'd gone in to get the Codex. He wondered if it could scent them, or follow their tracks.

"We'd better hurry," said Milla grimly. "Whatever that is, it looks for us."

"It's a Waspwyrm," said Tal. He felt sick. "They're not very smart, but their sting is acid and they can squirt it. They also go crazy when they fight and they're very, very fast. That one is a giant. They're supposed to be small."

"How do they stand up to lightning?" asked Milla.

"Lightning?" repeated Tal. He felt a bit better. He'd forgotten about the Storm Shepherds. "I don't know. They're sort of half lizard, half insect. I suppose it would kill them."

"Good," said Milla and she went over to talk to Odris and Adras.

Tal kept looking back toward the mountain. He was relieved to see the Waspwyrm rise up and disappear back the way it had come, instead of following him.

But he knew that something would find them soon. They had to get to the Sunken Stone Circle and back to the Castle. The feeling of dread, the worry about Gref, was at its strongest now because they were so close. As soon as he could uncover the Codex he could ask it the questions that were burning in his head. As soon as it answered, he would know who was holding Gref . . . and perhaps what had happened to the rest of his family.

Half an hour later, they came to the farthest point south and east that the ship could go. After unloading the Codex, Zicka pointed out which direction the Sunken Stone Circle lay in and wished them farewell from the deck of the ship.

Milla clapped her fists together before the lizard, to give him honor, and Tal flashed his Sunstone, though guardedly in case anyone was watching from a distance.

"If ever you come to Aenir again," said Zicka, "you will find news of me, at least, at the place commonly called Kurshken Corner. It is where most of my people live. Roquollollollahahinanahbek and I wish you well, daughter of Danir, and son of Ramellan. I would like to talk to that Codex of yours, but I know now is not the time. Nor ever, I suppose, for we Kurshken are sworn never to cross to your world. Farewell!"

Without any sign or spoken word from the small green lizard, the ship turned back into the river and sped away. Tal and Milla waved once, then picked up the Codex and began to walk.

Adras and Odris, obeying Milla's previous instructions, flew above them at different heights, keeping watch.

599

Tal and Milla did not speak as they walked. It was an effort to carry the Codex, but that was not why they found it difficult to talk. Neither knew how to bridge the gap that had come between them. Both, in their own way, wanted to, but both were held back by what they were and how they had changed. Tal was not really a Chosen anymore and Milla was not really an Icecarl. But they did not know how to forge a new understanding or forgive each other for the things that had happened.

So on they trudged in silence, pushing themselves as fast as they could through the black mud, crushed reeds, and sudden pits of bubbling black metal that Milla called ghalt.

Finally Tal saw what he was looking for. They had come to the top of a hill, and there in the valley below was a circle of stones. A strange circle, for the stones were buried so that only the very tops showed, so they looked rather like large mushrooms from a distance.

"The Sunken Stones!" Tal cried out, though he barely had breath to do so. He'd been there several times and his family had once transferred back to the Dark World from here. Escape was in sight!

Before they could start down the hill, Odris called out from above them.

"Look out behind!"

Tal and Milla set the Codex down on its lower edge and turned to look.

First they saw the Waspwyrm. But it was not alone. Four other, smaller Waspwyrms flew with it. And on the ground there was almost an army of creatures, running, leaping, loping, and jumping down the previous hill. There were Vengenarls and Borzogs and Filjiks and all sorts of vicious things.

There was also a man running amidst the pack, a

man in the Violet Robes of a high Chosen, Sun-stones winking at his neck and on his hands.

"They'll catch us!" said Milla, rapidly calculating the relative distance between the Waspwyrms and themselves and to the stone circle.

"No," said Tal. "We'll fly. Odris! Adras!"

He held up one hand, keeping a tight grip on the Codex with the other.

Milla held up her hand, too, but she said, "I thought no Aeniran could touch the Codex?"

"They won't," said Tal. He was already clenching his teeth in expectation of his shoulder being wrenched out again. "We'll hold on to the Codex and the Storm Shepherds will hold on to... owww!"

601

The Storm Shepherds had swooped down and lifted them up. Tal's arm wasn't dislocated out of his shoulder, but it hurt almost as much.

"To the stone circle!" shouted Tal. "Right to the middle! Quickly!"

·CHAPTER· TWENTY-SIX

The Storm Shepherds dropped them into the middle of the stone circle, then both shot back up into the sky. They had to get above the approaching Waspwyrms to use their lightning.

Tal and Milla laid the Codex down. Milla was about to draw her sword and rush to the circle's edge, but Tal stopped her.

"No," he said. "Lie down next to the Codex and put your Sunstone on your chest! I'll speak the Way to the Castle. You need to repeat it in your head, and concentrate on the colors."

"No!" said Milla. "I won't leave . . . even you . . . here to fight alone."

"I'll leave, too!" said Tal. "But you *have* to go first. You don't know the Way."

Thunder boomed above them and lightning lit up

the sky. Tal and Milla looked across and saw the Waspwyrms break formation and momentarily circle back as Odris and Adras shot lightning bolts down at them.

"The Codex has to get back!" shouted Tal above the thunder. "It's the only way to find Gref. Ebbitt will know what to do with it."

"I cannot leave a comrade in battle," yelled Milla.

"It's not a battle!" shrieked Tal. He racked his brain, trying to think of something that would influence her, and babbled, "Please, Milla. You *have* to go first. Think of your clan. They need the Sunstone. Gref . . . Ebbitt . . . my people need the Codex. Whatever's going on, it'll be bad for the Icecarls, too. One of us has to get back."

Whatever Tal had said, it worked. Milla nodded decisively and lay down next to the Codex. She put her left hand flat upon it and held her Sunstone on her chest.

Tal took a swift look back at the approaching enemy, then bent down next to Milla. He raised his own Sunstone and began to speak the Way to the Castle.

Milla concentrated on his words, shutting out the crash of thunder and the distant roars and cries of their pursuers. She saw color spring out of her Sun-

603

stone and wash back over her face. As in her last crossing, the colors provoked different sensations on her skin.

Tal's face faded as the colors spread, and the sky changed color. But before the sky blurred away entirely, Milla heard Odris cry out, behind the words that Tal spoke. "Adras! I'm going!"

The Storm Shepherd dropped faster than a stone, reaching out one cloudy hand. Milla felt it touch her just as all the colors flashed brighter and became a rainbow.

Milla blinked, and was gone.

Tal stood up. Milla and the Codex had vanished, sent back to the Castle, back to the Dark World. Odris had gone with them.

Adras was still there, frantically flinging lightning bolts at the Waspwyrms. But while the Storm Shepherd was keeping the flying creatures back, the other creatures were already halfway down the other hill.

Tal felt an almost overwhelming desire to run. There were scores of terrible creatures charging at him. They would be all over the stone circle in a minute or even less. If he lay down and tried to transfer himself to the Dark World, they might get him before the spell was complete.

But they'd get him for sure if he ran.

"Adras!" Tal shouted even as he threw himself down. "Come as low as you can!"

He was shivering, Tal discovered, his hand unable to stay still on his chest. He stared at the Sunstone on his finger but didn't even try to take it off. He knew he'd drop it if he did.

He immediately started reciting the Way to the Castle. Red light spilled out of his Sunstone as he spoke the words, the light flowing like water across his chest and down toward his legs.

The thunder stopped and now Tal could hear howls and shrieks and screeches that made his heart pound faster than he thought humanly possible. All his aches and pains were forgotten. Every tiny part of his mind was focused on his Sunstone and on the Way.

Tal spoke even faster, adding the other colors. He'd never spoken the incantation so quickly. He was afraid that he'd garble the words and end up who knew where. But he was more afraid of the creatures that were probably almost upon his defenseless body.

The rainbow started to form. Through the fuzziness of it, Tal could see Adras diving down to him, one arm outstretched. They couldn't cross until the

Storm Shepherd touched him, as Adras had Tal's shadow. It was an anchor keeping him in Aenir.

As he saw the blurred shape of Adras swooping down, Tal saw a normal-sized Waspwyrm fly in. Storm Shepherd and monster met directly above his body. Adras reached down to touch Tal with one hand and bash the Waspwyrm with the other. At the same time the Waspwyrm jetted acid down from its sting.

Rainbow light flashed. Tal and Adras disappeared.

·CHAPTER·
TWENTY-SEVEN

Tal arrived in the Dark World screaming. Acid was burning through his leg. He jerked up to look at the damage and hit his head on the coffin lid. He'd forgotten that he'd left his body in the Chosen's Mausoleum. It had seemed the safest place at the time.

With an acid burn on his leg and his head cracked on the lid, choosing the coffin seemed very stupid. Tal reached up to try and shift the lid. As always when he returned from Aenir, his body felt very heavy and slow.

"This is very strange," said a voice that was somehow under him. Tal stiffened in shock, till he realized who it was.

It was Adras, who had become a shadow.

A puffy shadow-arm reached around Tal's body

and joined with him in opening the lid. But the shadow went straight through.

"You . . . you have to concentrate," said Tal. His voice sounded strange to his own ears. It, too, was different from in Aenir. He was also speaking through gritted teeth as he tried to cope with the pain in his leg. "To make your shadow-flesh strong enough to interact with stone or flesh."

"How?" asked Adras plaintively.

"I don't know," whispered Tal. "Think of it being . . . I don't know . . . tougher. Imagine."

Adras reached past him again, and this time the shadow-hand did not go through the stone. The lid began to slide open.

Tal dimmed the light of his Sunstone and Adras said, "What happened? I feel weak."

"Keep quiet," whispered Tal. He didn't want any Chosen who might be in the Mausoleum to hear them. "You're a Spiritshadow now. You need light to be strong."

"Oh," said Adras. Just as when he'd been a Storm Shepherd, he didn't know how to keep his voice down.

Tal closed his eyes and tried to breathe more slowly. Any minute now, he told himself, Ebbitt will be looking down and he'll use his Sunstone to stop the pain. Any minute now. All he had to do was concentrate on breathing.

"Tal! What happened?"

It was not Ebbitt. It was Milla.

Tal opened his eyes. Milla was looking at his leg, where tendrils of acid smoke were still rising. Odris loomed up behind her, a huge Spiritshadow. She still had the look of a Storm Shepherd, but was smaller than she'd usually been in Aenir. Interestingly, small sparks of darker shadow occasionally shot out of Odris. Tal had never seen that in a Spiritshadow before.

"Acid," whispered Tal. "Waspwyrm. Get Ebbitt."

"He's not here," said Milla. "He left me a note, but I can't read it. You've got one, too."

Tal lifted his head a little and groaned. There was a rolled-up scroll near his right hand. But he was too much in shock to pick it up or make any attempt to read it.

"Healing magic," he whispered again. "Use Sunstone."

"I don't know how," said Milla. She looked at his leg again. The acid had burned straight through Tal's fur leggings and eaten away the flesh underneath. She could see white bone. On the Ice, his leg would have to be cut off and the stump cauterized, unless there was a very skilled healer close by.

"Ask the Codex," Tal whispered.

Then he fainted.

Milla looked at the leg for a little longer, raising the fur. Then she went over to the coffin she'd just emerged from. The Codex was still in it. It had changed shape to fit, growing narrower and longer. But as she'd guessed, it still weighed as much as it ever had, and it took all her strength to lever it out and set it upright next to the coffin that held Tal.

It was also a noisy operation. When she had it set up, Milla looked around the Mausoleum to make sure the noise hadn't attracted any attention. But the vast hall was quiet. The tiny Sunstones overhead continued to flicker like the Aeniran stars they mimicked. There was no sudden flare of bright light. Nor was there any movement among the rows and rows of Spiritshadow statues that adorned the coffins.

"Odris," Milla said softly, "keep a watch on that door over there. Adras, you watch the main gate."

Odris turned to the door. Adras rose up to his full height, easily three times as tall as Milla, and said, "Why should I?"

"Because Milla said so," ordered Odris sharply. "So there."

Adras snorted. A small lightning bolt of dark shadow came out his nose, which made him giggle.

Milla ignored him and looked at the Codex. She looked at it for a long time. It seemed to her that if she asked it to teach her how to heal wounds with her Sunstone she was taking yet another step away from being a Shield Maiden. Or even an Icecarl.

Yet once again, there was the complex web of debts she owed Tal and those he owed her.

"I need to use my Sunstone to heal an acid burn," she said to the Codex. "Tell me how."

The silvery surface of the Codex rippled, but no letters appeared.

"Speak to me," said Milla. She rapped the surface of the Codex with her knuckle. It felt cold, like ice, but left no mark and had no effect.

"I order you to tell me!"

The Codex shimmered, but no words came.

·CHAPTER·
TWENTY-EIGHT

"Why don't you answer?" Milla said, her frustration making her voice harsh.

This time, Icecarl runes did appear, dark symbols rising to the silver surface as if from some great depth.

Because you did not ask a question. You must ask me questions.

"How do I use my Sunstone to heal an acid burn?" asked Milla.

Watch and learn.

The runes disappeared and a picture swam into focus. A picture so lifelike that for a moment Milla thought that it was real. It showed an Icecarl girl holding up a Sunstone ring. It took her another second to realize that the picture was of her.

More runes appeared under the picture. They told her what to do and then the picture of Milla did what the runes said. Then Milla copied the picture. When she got it wrong because she hadn't read the runes correctly, the picture repeated what it was doing until she got it right.

It took some time. Milla had to stop the Codex a few times to check on Tal. He was unconscious, but the wound was not bleeding. The acid seemed to have sealed off the blood vessels, which was some small mercy.

Finally, Milla was ready. She looked down on Tal and raised her Sunstone. Slowly, she called up a Blue Ray of Healing. It had to be exactly the right shade and density, but she had memorized that. It looked right.

As her forehead creased in the sharpest frown she'd ever had, Milla played the Blue Ray across the wound. Wherever the light touched, it soothed and healed. The flesh began to grow back.

Milla kept the Blue Ray going and started to build a second ray, the Yellow Ray of Replacement. This was the really hard one. It would put a layer of light over the blue, building up artificial bone, muscle, nerves, and blood vessels to act as temporary replacements until the real ones grew back.

The Yellow Ray wove back and forth, slowly replacing Tal's missing flesh, layer by layer.

Finally, it was done. Milla let the light sink back into the Sunstone and let out a deep sigh of relief. Only then did she notice that Tal was awake and watching her.

"Thank you," he said. "That was well done. You have a knack for healing."

"I am a warrior," Milla replied, and for an instant Tal thought she was offended. But she went on to say, "It is the mark of a true warrior to be a healer, too. Though that is more the way of a Sword-Thane than a Shield Maiden."

Tal sat up and gingerly felt his leg. It ached to the bone, rather like a nasty toothache, deep and constant. But he could use the leg, if he was careful.

Adras helped him climb out. It was strange to feel friendly shadow-flesh again, Tal thought. Somehow Adras did not feel unpleasant and clammy, as other Spiritshadows did.

"Didn't you say Ebbitt left a message?" Tal asked. Milla handed him the scroll that had been in her coffin, and got out the one that had been in his. Tal opened both. It took only a moment to see they were the same. He read it aloud so Milla and the Spiritshadows would know what it contained.

Dear Children,

Somebody thinks I have become dangerous, for certain Spiritshadows have tried to sniff me out. To draw them off your scent as well as mine, I have gone down, down, down, down, down, down, and then down once more, from my usual abode. Come join me there if you can. If you have the Codex, bring it with you. Trust no one, absolutely no one at all. Except me of course. I have found an Underfolk corridor from the Mausoleum that leads to one of their main stairs. If you take this way you should have few problems. Unless I have been caught using it, in which case you will have many problems. But then we all have problems.

615

Yours truly,

E.

"Typical Ebbitt!" groaned Tal.

"Where has he gone?" asked Milla. "I don't understand."

"The Seventh Underfolk Level," said Tal. "I think that's what he means."

He shook his head. "But I'm not going down

there. I have to rescue Gref. That's the main reason for getting the Codex in the first place!"

"I think we should take the Codex to Ebbitt," said Milla. "It cannot be lost to your . . . *our* enemies."

"No!" exclaimed Tal. "I *have* to rescue Gref!"

The effort of speaking made him even paler. Despite the Sunstone's healing magic he was still weak.

Milla did not answer, but her eyes narrowed as she looked at him.

"What do you mean when you say *our enemies,* anyway?" asked Tal.

"Now that I know much more, I think there are bad Chosen and . . . stupid Chosen. The stupid Chosen are not important. Your enemies are the bad Chosen and they are enemies of the Icecarl, too."

"Er, good," said Tal, but it was clear to Milla he didn't want to think about anything except finding Gref.

He looked at the Codex as he spoke. Milla caught the glance and said, "You must ask it questions. It will not speak otherwise."

Tal nodded and slowly made his way over to the strange silvery artifact. It looked a bit like a mirror, propped up against the coffin. But its silver surface did not reflect anything.

It took Tal a moment to phrase a question. It all seemed to have happened so long ago. Gref climbing up the Red Tower after him, the Spiritshadow that caught him and took him back inside . . .

"Which Chosen is the Master of a Spiritshadow in the shape of a Borzog?" asked Tal.

Words formed on the surface of the Codex. A great list of Chosen names moving across and up the Codex. Then they stopped and one name grew larger and larger.

Nilhir Jerel-Orim, of the Third Order of the Red.

"Where are the rooms of Nilhir Jerel-Orim of the Third Order of the Red?" asked Tal. He wasn't sure if the Codex could answer this sort of question, but it was worth a try.

The Codex answered immediately, with a clearly labeled map. As expected Nilhir had rooms in the Red Levels. But strangely enough, the Codex also showed him having a room in the abandoned White Levels — quite close to the Hall of Nightmares.

That was where they would be holding Gref, Tal thought. It had to be. He stared at the map, memorizing the location of the room.

·CHAPTER·
TWENTY–NINE

"It is not sensible to try and rescue your brother now," said Milla calmly. "We should take the Codex to Ebbitt. Then I will go on to the Ruin Ship."

She did not mention the Ice. That was left unsaid between them.

"No," said Tal stubbornly. "I have to rescue Gref! That's the whole point! I have to look after my family. It's what my father —"

"You have not asked about him," said Milla suddenly.

A movement caught her eye and she whirled, her hand on her sword. But it was only Adras and Odris, getting used to their new shadow-selves. They had already learned how to make themselves almost solid, and the reverse, to drift through stone. Now they were practicing shooting shadow-lightning.

Fortunately, unlike the real sort, it was not accompanied by thunder.

Milla waved at them crossly, pointing at the doors. They got the message and resumed their guard duty.

"No," said Tal quietly. "I haven't asked. I'm . . . I'm afraid of the answer."

Milla nodded, but she didn't really understand. Her parents were long dead.

"I suppose I should," he added. But he made no move to do so.

"I have made too many mistakes," said Milla. "My mistakes, since I do not believe everything is directed by some great Reckoner, and I just a piece upon the board. I should have returned to the Ruin Ship as soon as I had the Sunstone. I should not have crossed to Aenir —"

"I know, I know," interrupted Tal. "I *am* sorry —"

"You do not understand," Milla resumed. "I have decided that one more mistake will make no difference. I will help you rescue your brother. But we will have to hide the Codex here. And we cannot roam your Castle looking as we do now. And I need to eat and drink."

"We can get clothes and food and so on from an

619

Underfolk store," said Tal. "It's the middle of the night, so if we stick mainly to the colorless corridors in the midlevel we can get across to where I think they're holding Gref. It's . . . it's near the Hall of Nightmares. . . ."

Milla shrugged. Unlike Tal, the Hall of Nightmares held no particular terrors for her. She had proved immune to the Nightmare Machines, calling on the Crones to protect her.

"I hope we catch Fashnek by himself," she said, referring to the creepy keeper of the Hall of Nightmares.

"I don't," shuddered Tal. "We can't afford to start any sort of fight."

"Let's go, then," said Milla. "First we eat, and then we fight . . . or we sneak."

"We have to hide the Codex," said Tal. They walked over to it. Tal started to pick it up, but Milla didn't move.

"You must ask," she said. "The question will hunt you in your dreams if you do not."

Tal nodded. He desperately wanted to know that his father was alive, but he also desperately feared that the Codex would tell him he was dead.

"Ask!" urged Milla.

Tal put his hands together in an arch and scratched his nose. Then he cracked the knuckles on his left hand. Finally he asked the question, his voice gruff.

"Codex. Is Rerem Abitt-Erem still alive?"

Tal stopped breathing as letters swam to the surface. At first he didn't understand the answer. He had expected a simple yes or no.

What he got was *Not dead and not alive.*

"What do you mean?" Tal asked hotly.

Not dead and not alive.

Tal shook his head.

"What did it say?" asked Milla. Once again, before Tal could answer, the Codex supplied a translation in Icecarl runes.

"Codex. Where is Rerem Abitt-Erem?" Tal asked.

In the Orange Tower. Above the Veil.

Tal choked. His father couldn't be there! There was nothing up there but the Sunstone nets.

"How . . . how can he be not dead and not alive?"

He is the Guardian of the Orange Keystone. It has been unsealed and so he does not live. Until or unless the Orange Keystone is sealed again, he does not live. If it is sealed, he will live again.

"I don't understand," said Tal. What was the Orange Keystone?

He was about to ask another question when Odris suddenly came sliding back across the coffins, calling out in what she imagined was a whisper.

"People and shadows! Lots of them, coming here!"

Tal and Milla did not stop to talk. They picked up the Codex and slipped it into the coffin. It adjusted its shape as they pushed it down and slid the heavy stone lid across.

Then the Chosen and the Icecarl ran toward the Underfolk exit, where the servant sculptors worked. According to Ebbitt there was another way out there.

They had just left the Mausoleum when a great crowd of Chosen entered. Light filled the ancient hall, and many real Spiritshadows slipped in to mingle with the shadows cast by the statues on the Chosen tombs.

·CHAPTER·
THIRTY

Milla had to lead Tal away from the Codex. Not because of his wounded leg, which did slow him down. Because of the news about his father. How could he be in the Orange Tower? What did it mean that he was the "Guardian of the Orange Keystone"?

As explained by Ebbitt in his letter, Milla found the small door at the rear of the toolshed used by the Underfolk stonemasons. It led down a narrow corridor to a more usual Underfolk corridor. Like all such ways, it was only dimly lit by tiny Sunstones of inferior power.

Tal recovered himself enough at this point to take the lead. He was so rattled by the Codex's revelations that he didn't mind admitting to Milla that he didn't really know much about the Underfolk's corridors and storehouses.

However, he did manage to find his way to something he did know about: the laundry chute that he and his friends used as a shortcut between levels. And where there was a laundry chute, there was laundry. Dirty clothes, but what a Chosen called dirty now seemed clean to Tal, after the disgusting furs he'd been wearing.

Tal chose to throw all his Icecarl clothes into a basket and got dressed in a Chosen child's basic uniform of white trousers and shirt, though these ones had blue cuffs and collars that didn't match his rank.

Milla, however, put on a Chosen matron's dress over her armor and furs, a huge sack of a thing in solid yellow, with tiny Sunstone chips around the lower hem. She then ruined it by cutting a long slit at each side so she could run.

As instructed by Tal, Adras and Odris made an opaque wall between the two as they undressed. Not that Milla cared. But nudity was frowned on by the Chosen and Tal had not totally gone over to Icecarl ways.

Suitably disguised, they dashed across a colorless corridor and into more Underfolk passageways. Tal got lost for a while, and they had several close encounters with Underfolk, all of whom were pushing carts of food, or clothes or items made in their workshops far below. But every time the Underfolk drew near, Tal had Adras and Odris loom up, and the servants would avert their eyes and scuttle past in fright. The Storm Shepherds were easily the largest Spiritshadows Tal had ever seen, save for the Empress's Sharrakor. They also looked strange, if not particularly horrifying, unlike many spiky, fanged Spiritshadows. Adras and Odris looked like puffy giants, but their size alone was intimidating.

It was a bitter realization for Tal that he had found a powerful Spiritshadow after all, one that would have probably gained him automatic promotion to Yellow or even Blue. Only he had not bound Adras as a proper Chosen should. He had broken the law and gone to Aenir. He had given a Sunstone and a Spiritshadow to a non-Chosen.

Strangely, it didn't worry him. But he was growing more and more anxious about Gref. What had they been doing to him, off in some distant chamber where no Chosen or Underfolk would ever hear a cry for help . . . or a scream?

"Where now?" Milla asked, breaking into Tal's thoughts. They had arrived at an intersection. The Underfolk corridor branched left and right, but there was also an open doorway to an Orange level. Orange six, Tal saw, noting the arrangement of Sunstones in the ceiling.

Close to home. His mother was not far away, on her sickbed. Lost and dreaming. He wanted to see her, too.

"Which way?" Milla repeated.

Tal pointed down the left Underfolk corridor. His hand was shaking and he could not steady it.

They had to follow the Underfolk corridor and go down into the topmost Red level and then across into the White Rooms.

It took another few hours, because they had to cross almost from one side of the Castle to the other. As it got closer to morning, the Underfolk corridors got busier, too, and Tal was sure some of the Underfolk looked at them even as they bowed. But Tal wasn't worried about Underfolk. They never spoke to Chosen unless they were spoken to. They probably wouldn't remember the strange Chosen and the large Spiritshadows.

Milla didn't share this opinion. Some of the Underfolk looked very smart indeed, and Milla was certain they would gossip. She contented herself with glaring fiercely at any who dared to glance up at her. Hopefully this would make them think twice about talking about *her*.

The White Rooms were different from the rest of the Castle. Long abandoned, they were colder, darker, and much less clean. Dust rose as Tal led the way down one corridor, though there were halls and other corridors that seemed better traveled.

Finally, they came to a vast, cold hall where no Sunstones shone in the vaulted ceiling. The upper reaches were totally dark, and the only light spilled in from the three corridors that led there from south, east, and west.

Tal looked around suspiciously, but could see no reason for the lack of light, other than the usual failings of the White Rooms. Since no Chosen lived here, nobody bothered to replace the Sunstones or direct the Underfolk to clean.

"The room is on the far side of this hall," said Tal, pointing to the door on the northern side. He spoke softly but his voice echoed in the chamber. "A good place for a prison, I guess. No one would come here by chance."

"This could be a trap," Milla said suspiciously. She looked around the dark hall, noting the other two lit corridors and the footprints in the dust ahead of them. Unfortunately, she did not know enough about tracks in dust on stone. They were human footprints . . . but that was all she could tell.

"Maybe," said Tal. "But Gref's over there and I have to get him out."

"There must be guards somewhere." Milla drew her Merwin-horn sword. Tal noted that its glow was not what it had been. Merwin horns faded slowly but surely once they were cut from the heads of the beasts that grew them.

Tal made his Sunstone shed a low light and limped forward. "Adras. Go ahead of me."

Adras complied without asking questions, for which Tal was grateful. The Storm Shepherd still wasn't bound to obey, since he was a free-willed companion.

So Tal had broken yet another law of the Chosen, bringing Adras back to the Castle.

"Sometimes some laws have to be broken to save greater ones," Tal whispered. He'd heard that somewhere, though he had the sinking feeling it might have been his enemy Shadowmaster Sushin who had said it.

They were halfway across the hall now, and the light from the corridors was distant and weak. Milla kept looking up and around, expecting warriors to drop through a hidden trapdoor or come up from a secret way.

But no one did. They crossed the Hall and stood outside the door that the Codex had said was the entry to Gref's prison.

The door looked normal enough. Like most doors in the Castle it was made of thin metal leaves riveted to a frame in overlapping lines. It had a long handle of polished bronze.

"Adras," said Tal, "can you open this door?"

Adras shrugged. He leaned forward and turned the handle. The door did not budge.

"No," said the Spiritshadow.

"I mean break it down, or go through and open it from the other side."

"I'll do it," said Odris. She lay down and grew more translucent, and then slid under the door. A few seconds later, she slid back out.

"It's locked on both sides," she said. "I don't know how. There is no keyhole."

"Is Gref — a boy — in there?" Tal asked eagerly.

"There is something in the corner," said Odris. She sounded puzzled. "I'm not quite sure —"

Whatever she was going to say was cut off as Adras made himself as solid as possible and slammed into the door. It splintered into hundreds of individual metal leaves as the Spiritshadow slowly bulled his way through, dragging the broken frame, leaves, and hinges after him.

"That wasn't *that* loud," said Tal hopefully.

He'd hardly finished speaking when a deep horn blast sounded above their heads, the sound echoing throughout the hall. Startled, Tal and Milla looked up at a hidden recess above the door. It contained a pulsing Sunstone and a complex arrangement of pipes, leading to one huge pipe that opened out like a flower at the end.

"A wakener!" Tal cursed. "Just like in the Lectorium."

"I knew it was a trap!" Milla shouted.

Tal wasn't listening. He ran in after Adras, boots clinking on the broken metal leaves.

The room was not very big. There was no bed, no furniture at all. A single medium-sized Sunstone shone in the ceiling.

But Gref was there. The small boy hung suspended in a strange cocoon of shadow in the corner of the room. Tal could see his face, which was relaxed as if in sleep. But the rest of him was surrounded by a shape of darkness.

As Tal stepped forward to look, the shadow

moved. Gref slid down until he was sprawled on the floor. The shadow shook itself, and formed into a shape both Tal and Milla recognized.

It was a Hugthing. A Spiritshadow Hugthing. A free shadow, for there was no sign of its master.

Tal backed away, his Sunstone ring raised. He had to blast it before it wrapped itself around him, he knew. But Gref was right behind it.

Adras was not so careful. He roared and stepped forward, gripping the Hugthing by one shadowy corner. Instantly it wrapped around his powerful arm and started to squeeze.

"Odris!" yelped Adras.

Tal and Milla ducked to the sides as Odris charged into the room. The female Storm Shepherd grabbed another corner of the Hugthing.

Then they both pulled.

Tal dived under the tug-of-war and crawled over to Gref. His brother still hadn't woken up. Tal touched his face. It felt cold, far too cold to be normal.

He took Gref's hand.

It hung limp and lifeless.

Then he put his ear to the younger boy's mouth, hoping for the faint touch of breath.

There was none.

Tal slowly stood back up. He felt a million years old and tired, so tired that he wanted to go to sleep right there and then and not wake up until everything was right again.

But nothing ever could be right again.

Gref was dead.

·CHAPTER· THIRTY- O॒NE

The noise of the fighting Spiritshadows and the still-sounding wakener faded. The light dimmed. Tal stared down at the still form of his little brother from far away, his eyes fixed, unable to blink.

Behind him, the two Storm Shepherds roared as the Hugthing split in half with a horrible squeal. Then Adras and Odris stood on the halves and ripped them into quarters and then into smaller and smaller fragments of shadow. All these pieces flopped and rolled about the floor, unable to get a grip or do anything. A few tried to join together, only to be ripped even smaller by the furious Storm Shepherds and the tiny bits stuffed into cracks in the walls.

The wakener kept on blasting its single note every few seconds. In the silence between the blasts, shouts could be heard, close by. Orders being shouted. Not the surprised response of ordinary Chosen.

Milla knelt by Gref.

"He's dead, Milla," Tal said slowly. "He's dead."

Milla quickly touched Gref's throat, two fingers feeling under his jaw. She kept them there while she spoke urgently to Tal.

"There are Guards coming up the south and east corridors."

Tal didn't answer. He had totally and utterly failed. Gref's life was the price of his failure.

"We'll have to try the west corridor and fight our way out if we must," Milla declared. "Now, before they gather their full strength."

"I can't . . . I can't leave Gref here," said Tal dully. He couldn't think what he had to do, but he couldn't just run away. "You —"

Milla suddenly bent closer to Gref and pushed her fingers in harder.

"He's not dead!"

Tal couldn't believe what he was hearing.

"He's not dead," Milla repeated. "He's sick . . . or poisoned. Come on!"

Tal bent down and tried to pick Gref up, but his leg gave way. Milla had already turned to leave, but she looked back and shouted, "Get Adras to carry him, you idiot! Ready your Sunstone to fight!"

"Be careful with him," Tal instructed Adras. "Very careful."

Adras cradled the boy gently and ducked down to go through the door. As he bent down, light suddenly flared all around the doorway and on Gref's wrist. The Storm Shepherd staggered back and looked at Tal.

"I can't go through," the Storm Shepherd said. "Something is stopping me."

Tal saw what it was. There was a bracelet on Gref's wrist. A bracelet set with Sunstones. He looked at it carefully. The Sunstones were all quite small and they had been especially put together to create a particular effect.

Gref was obviously in a more secure prison than Tal had imagined. Unless he could get the bracelet off — and it was a single piece — or deactivate the spell, Gref was trapped there.

Milla looked back in to see what was holding them up.

"Come on!" she said. "There are Guards in the west corridor now! We have to attack and punch through!"

"I can't get Gref out," shouted Tal.

"Then leave him!"

Tal looked at the Sunstones set into the doorway. There were six of them, all welded deep into the stone. He'd have to pry all six out to annul the spell. It would take too long.

"Put him down," Tal said, though he choked saying it. He pointed. "Carefully."

Adras put Gref back down in the corner.

"Go!" said Tal.

But Tal lingered a moment. He raised his Sunstone ring and a hot blue ray sprang out. It cut into the stone and with a few decisive movements, Tal carved his name on the wall in letters a stretch high.

It was a message for Gref, in case he woke up. Tal was leaving him now.

But he would be back.

Out in the hall, Milla was already running for the western corridor entrance, with Odris close behind her.

Adras roared out a challenge to the Spiritshadows that were spilling out from the eastern and southern corridors, their Chosen masters close behind them.

"Die, little shadows!" roared Adras. Shadowlightning flickered from his hands, and he stretched himself to be more than fourteen stretches high. For a moment, even Tal was scared, and he understood why the Guards were approaching slowly. None of them — or their Spiritshadows — wanted to be the first to tangle with whatever Adras was.

To make them even less eager, Tal raised his Sunstone and concentrated on it. Red light flared in its depths and Tal coaxed it to the surface. Then he screamed a war cry and thrust out his hand.

Triple Red Rays of Destruction shot out from the stone, slicing across the darkness of the Hall, weaving together and then apart, striking stone, shadow and flesh. Sparks shot from stone, scraps of shadow flew, and Guards shouted in sudden pain.

Tal ran as answering rays shot out. He was already looking away when a shockingly brilliant white light flashed and he felt its heat on his face.

637

"Strong!" boomed Adras, who was running at his side. "Again! Give me light!"

Ahead, Milla's sword left a trail of luminescent afterimages as she cut at the two Guards who blocked her way. Odris grappled with their thin-waisted Spiritshadows, holding one off with a raised foot as she gripped the other and twisted and twisted, as if she were winding up a top.

Then all four of them were in the western corridor and there was no one ahead. Shouts and cries and the call of the wakener dimmed behind them as they ran and ran.

"Which way?" Milla shouted as they came to the first intersection. A Guard stepped out and was instantly bowled over by Adras, and her Spiritshadow flattened by a two-fisted punch from Odris.

"Not that way!" yelled Tal, as he saw more Guards coming up from the left. He turned and saw yet another squad coming from the right.

There was only straight ahead, and they were running again as Tal desperately tried to remember the Codex's map. He didn't know the White Rooms, and he was already a bit lost.

Besides, where could they run to?

"Guards ahead!" shouted Milla as they came to another intersection, a three-way fork in the corridor.

Tal stopped and stared. There were Guards ahead . . . but that was not the worst of it. Safely behind the first rank was the ponderous body of Shadowmaster Sushin, wrapped in the robes of the Deputy Lumenor of the Orange Order. He had his hideous, fanged monster of a new Spiritshadow at his side.

Sushin saw Tal at the same time. Despite his

638

fleshy arms, his reflexes were quicker than the boy's. His hand flashed up and a ball of orange light flashed out, screeching across the forty stretches between them.

Adras tried to bat it away but the ball went straight through his palm, without seeming to touch the shadow-flesh.

It struck Tal as he was raising his own Sunstone, desperately summoning a blue shield from its sparkling depths.

He was too late. The shield formed as the ball exploded around his head. Tal felt burning fire in his eyes. He screamed and fell back, twisting his hands into what he imagined were blackened sockets.

"Blind!" he screamed. "I'm blind!"

Sushin laughed, and the Guards and his own Spiritshadow charged forward.

The laughter stopped suddenly as Milla threw her Merwin-horn sword. It arced through the air like a golden lightning bolt and hit Sushin's left shoulder, the point sticking out his back. He stared open-mouthed at it.

The Guards and his Spiritshadow stopped and looked back.

Sushin closed his mouth. A smile started to spread across his bloated face.

Then he started to laugh again.

It was the laugh that made Milla decide to run. She knew she'd missed his heart, that it wasn't a killing blow. But no normal man could take such a wound and laugh.

Tal had described Sushin to her and she had heard his fear. Now she felt it, too.

This was no normal Chosen. His laugh made her feel cold inside — colder than the Ice.

·CHAPTER·
THIRTY-TWO☉

"Adras, get Tal!" shouted Milla. "Then run!"

"I can't see!" Tal cried out as he felt his ruined eyes.

Adras picked him up and shoved him under his arm and then they were running again, taking turns at random, always away from wherever they saw Guards.

Milla had the sense that soon every corridor would have Guards in it. They had to have a plan. She had to know where they were going.

The moment that no pursuers were in sight, she stopped. The others almost crashed into her.

"Blind!" screamed Tal. "He *blinded* me!"

Milla slapped him, hard. Then she held his hands and looked at his eyes.

"Your eyes are fine," she snapped. "It is like being snow-blind. You will recover."

"I will?" whispered Tal. He took a deep breath and then another. Blindness was the great fear of all Chosen. A blind Chosen was automatically relegated to the Underfolk, for they could not work with light.

"You will," confirmed Milla, though she wasn't really sure. His eyes did *look* normal. "If we get away. How do we get out of the White Rooms?"

"Where are we now?" asked Tal.

"I don't know! A tunnel!"

Tal thought for a moment, ignoring the pain in his eye sockets.

"The laundry chute," he said. "It'll be the only way between levels that won't be guarded. Find an Underfolk and make them show you the way."

"And how do I do that?" asked Milla.

"West. Keep going west."

Milla didn't answer. She just started running again.

Tal heard her footsteps, but he hadn't been picked up.

"Adras!" he shouted, panicked, sure that he had been left behind. "Adras!"

"Yes?" asked Adras.

"Carry me. And keep up with Milla and Odris!"

"Where did they go?" asked Adras, as he picked up the Chosen boy. "I wasn't looking."

Tal bent his head, exasperation fighting with fear inside him to see which would win. He was about to explode when Milla's voice came echoing back down the corridor.

"Adras! Come on!"

As Adras half slid and half ran with him, Tal cautiously felt his eyes again. Surely they had been burned? But he was calmer now, and his fingers assured him that his eyes were still there after all.

Then he found that Adras's shadow-flesh was quite cold, and he pressed his forehead against the Storm Shepherd's side so his eyes were cooled.

643

"What are you doing?" asked Adras, and he slowed down to look.

"Cooling my eyes," said Tal. A thought struck him and he asked, "Can you still make rain?"

Adras shrugged, a movement that made him nearly drop the boy. "I have to go puffy. If I go puffy I can't have legs. We could fly."

"No, no," said Tal. Having Adras fly in the narrow corridors of the White Rooms would be a disaster.

Then Tal heard two voices at the same time. One was obviously a Guard and the other Milla.

"There they are!" and "Hurry up! Hurry! I've found an Underfolk!"

Tal never heard what Milla said to the Underfolk because Adras didn't catch up before they were running again. He kept his eyes pressed against the cool shadow, blinking frequently.

Gradually, he became aware of light filtering into the corners of his eyes and he felt a great surge of relief.

Relief that was dampened by the shouts behind . . . and now ahead of them.

Tal risked taking a look. He could see, but only just. His vision was blurry and full of floating specks and dots.

They were in an Underfolk passage now, barging between rows of boxes and bags that could contain anything. Milla was screaming — at first Tal couldn't understand why and then he saw terrified Underfolk pressed up against the walls as they flung themselves out of the way. Then they had to do it again, seconds later, as the Guards came charging after, their swords out and Spiritshadows running with them.

There was no sign of Sushin, for which Tal was unbelievably grateful.

"Stop in the name of the Empress!" roared the lead Guard, and he paused to project a Violet beam of light at Tal. But he had not warned the Guards behind him that he was stopping, and they crashed into him just as he fired the beam. It hit a pile of cloth bags, exploding them into shredded pieces.

Fire caught and smoke billowed up, as Guards jumped over their fallen comrade and ran on. Spiritshadows spread to the outer walls and ceiling, where they could run more freely above and to the sides of their masters.

Underfolk tried to stay out of the way, in silent suffering.

"Chute!" said a voice Tal did not recognize. He hurled himself out of Adras's grasp and saw an old Underfolk man pointing at the swinging hatch that covered the laundry chute.

"You first!" said Milla. "You know the way!"

Tal hesitated, then dived in. He had his Sunstone lit up before the hatch even banged. It was dark in the chute, and he was afraid of what might be waiting in it for them. What if Sushin had guessed their plan?

Before he could think any more of that, Milla, Adras, and Odris came after him. Milla cannoned into his back and that was enough to push him off the lip, into the actual chute.

"Whoa!" yelled Tal as he shot down the greased stone chute. This was at least twice as fast as he usually went!

Before he knew it he was already whizzing past the next level, the brief outline of light around the hatch a momentary flash. Then the chute did a sharp switchback turn and Tal was tumbled on his side and the acid burn on his leg stabbed him with pain.

The next level seemed to pass in a second and they switchbacked again. This time Tal was almost upside down and Milla was pressed up against him, so they were like one big lump of laundry accelerating all the way down.

"Slow! We have to slow down!" screamed Tal as he pushed his feet against the sides of the chute. "Adras!"

"No!" shouted Milla. "Faster! We are pursued!"

Still Tal kept his feet against the sides, till his already worn soles were gone and his feet were burning worse than in the desert sands of Aenir.

Only then did he realize that Milla was laughing. She laughed all the way down, and was still laughing when all four shot out at the very end of the line, bouncing and crashing through stacked bag after bag of dirty Chosen washing.

As soon as they stopped, she was up and had the hatch closed and its lock turned.

"Now where are we?" she asked.

"Underfolk Seven," said Tal, looking around. "The Main Laundry."

"That was fun," said Adras. Odris nodded her agreement.

"No it wasn't," said Tal sternly. He turned to Milla and said, "And why were *you* laughing?"

Milla looked at him.

"My sword," she said. "It is up there, in the monster . . . the one that looks like a Chosen. Shadowmaster Sushin."

"So?" asked Tal wearily. Milla was still blurry and he couldn't make out the expression on her face. What was funny about that?

"I threw it to save you," said Milla. "That means you have to go and get it back for me."

Tal's jaw dropped. He couldn't believe what she was saying. It was bad enough that Gref was still a prisoner and sick as well. And the Codex was up in the Mausoleum, where it was no use to anyone.

Now she wanted him to get her sword back?

From Sushin?

"Ha ha!" Milla laughed. She clapped her knuckles together. "Your face!"

"You —" Tal began. Then he stopped. A slow, hesitant smile began to spread across his face.

"We got away," he said. "But you want me to think that I have to go —"

"Yes, yes," laughed Milla as they kept moving.

"It is an Icecarl joke!" Tal wanted to laugh along... but then he thought of Gref, and the laughter stuck in his throat till it came out as a single sob.

There was a tremendous crash and a ringing sound as the hatch of the chute bent out and then snapped back.

Instantly, Milla's laughter stopped.

"Quick!" she said. "Which way?"

Tal squinted, his heart pounding. He still couldn't see properly. Was it the third door that led out to the Lower Underfolk Cavern? Or the second?

"That way!" he said, and then he was stumbling around the laundry bags with the others close at his heels.

They were only just through the door when a Guard's Spiritshadow gingerly slid under the hatch and reared up to look around. Satisfied that it seemed safe, it unlocked the hatch.

Moments later, more Guards and Spiritshadows spilled out of the chute — stretching, grumbling, and cursing. The chute was not suited to full-grown Chosen. More and more came out, and then the last two had to reach back in and help out a particularly round and heavy Chosen.

It was Sushin. He held the Merwin-horn sword in his hand, and there was a great hole in his orange robes at the shoulder.

But there was no blood.

ABOUT THE AUTHOR

Garth Nix was born in 1963 and grew up in Canberra, Australia. His book *Sabriel* won Best Fantasy Novel in the Aurealis Awards for Excellence in Australian Science Fiction and was named an ALA Notable Book and a Best Book for Young Adults. His novel *Shade's Children* was named an ALA Best Book for Young Adults and an ABA Pick of the Lists. He is also the author of *The Ragwitch* and *Lirael: Daughter of the Clayr* as well as the forthcoming series The Keys to the Kingdom. He currently lives in Sydney, Australia.

www.theseventhtower.com